FALL FROM GRACE

FALL
FROM GRACE

A NOIR THRILLER

CLYDE PHILLIPS

WILLIAM MORROW AND COMPANY, INC.
NEW YORK

It is the policy of William Morrow and Company, Inc., and its imprints
and affiliates, recognizing the importance of preserving what has been written,
to print the books we publish on acid-free paper,
and we exert our best efforts to that end.

Library of Congress Cataloging-in-Publication Data
Phillips, Clyde.
Fall from grace / by Clyde Phillips.
        p.   cm.
        ISBN 0-688-15744-0
        I. Title.
    PS3566.H476F3   1998
    813'.54—dc21   97-36057
                               CIP

Printed in the United States of America

First Edition

2 3 4 5 6 7 8 9 10

BOOK DESIGN BY OKSANA KUSHNIR

www.williammorrow.com

FOR MY WIFE, JANE.
Thank you for your faith, inspiration, and patience.
Without you there would be no book,
only the intention of writing one someday.

AND FOR MY BABY DAUGHTER, CLAIRE.
Your sweet sunrise face completes the circle.

ACKNOWLEDGMENTS

I want to thank my agent, Helen Breitwieser, for her wisdom, advice, and enthusiasm. She believed in this book and helped discover the author within the writer.

I'm grateful to my editor, Claire Wachtel, for seeing right away that this book had potential, and for helping me turn that potential into reality.

Stan Berkowitz was invaluable in getting me out of corners into which I had painted myself.

Robert Lewis read this book more times than any friend should have to read a book, and his notes were always insightful and occasionally diplomatic.

Heidi Wenzel, my researcher, was always reliable and always right.

FALL FROM GRACE

1

The dozen or so commuters squinted against the setting sun as they crossed the Monterey Airport tarmac. American Eagle Flight 6, a twin-prop twenty-seater, sat waiting for them, its baggage bay open.

Graham Maxwell paused to let a young couple hand their suitcases off to the baggage handler and hurry up the steps. He had noticed in the terminal that the woman was newly pregnant, just beginning to show, and he remembered back years ago to when he too was an expectant father.

Life was full of promise then, the wonder of the unknown casting an intoxicating spell on him and his wife, Dorothy. A decade had passed since Dorothy died, and now that she was gone, Graham Maxwell was no longer a man in a hurry. He turned his wedding ring unconsciously with his thumb, worrying it like a rosary.

Passing his overnighter to the baggage worker, Graham started up the steps of the little plane. Glancing back, he saw the airline employee roughly toss his expensive leather suitcase into the belly of the aircraft and look at him defiantly.

Breaking off the silent confrontation, Graham's eyes moved to the man's feet, where he saw that the sole of the baggage handler's right work boot was five inches thick, his balance dependent upon a wide black band of wood and rubber.

Maybe, Graham thought, that is why he's so angry.

Ducking his head to enter the plane, Graham Maxwell paused to study his fellow passengers. The pregnant couple was seated in the rear left, the woman's head resting against her husband's shoulder, both already dozing. A young Hispanic woman traveling with an old man listened intently as he spoke softly into her ear.

"*Sí, abuelo. Sí,*" she said, and Graham knew that this man was her

1

grandfather. His thoughts went to his granddaughter, Lily, teetering on the balance beam between serious little girl and uncertain teenager.

Moving forward, crouching a bit under the low ceiling, he passed a family of four. The children, miniature versions of their parents from coloring to clothing, sat across the aisle from each other, the younger boy stubbornly refusing to fasten his seat belt.

Near the front right, Graham found a vacant aisle seat and, with a nod to the young grad student at the window, sat down. Through the open cockpit door, he watched the pilots work through their preflight checklist, pushing buttons and toggling switches with practiced precision. After a short while, one of them clicked the door closed and the plane began to taxi forward.

The pilot's voice scratched over the intercom. "Good news, folks. We're number one for takeoff and we should be in the city a couple of minutes early this evening. So sit back and enjoy the flight. We'll have you home in no time."

With a potent surge, the plane leaped forward, took the wind, and banked gracefully past the ebbing sun. Its right side dipping into the northward turn toward home, American Eagle Flight 6, a lone bird with sixteen souls under her wings, carried her precious cargo past the last sunset of their lives.

— —

All along the left side of the aircraft, passengers slid the plastic shades down for relief from the still-penetrating sun. Graham Maxwell pushed back in his seat and crossed his legs, inadvertently brushing the calf of his seatmate.

"Sorry," he apologized. "Not much legroom on these things."

The young man looked over and smiled.

Graham extended his hand. "I'm Graham Maxwell."

"The lawyer?"

Graham nodded.

"The Graham Maxwell who brought the Subway Commission to its knees for negligence on the environmental impact survey?"

A flicker of pleasure crinkled Graham's eyes. That had been a huge and satisfying victory for him. "Well, we had a powerful ally on that one."

"Which was?"

"The law. We happened to be right."

The young man chewed on this for a reflective beat, then reached over and shook Graham's hand. "Zach. Zach Saltzman. Third year at Bolt."

Graham smiled to himself. A law student. Of course.

"Who knows?" Zach shrugged, "I may be calling you someday for a job."

"Who knows?" Graham agreed. He made up his mind that if this fellow could muster the confidence to ask for an interview, he would grant him one.

The plane droned on, the passengers settling in.

After a while, Zach turned to Graham. "Excuse me, Mr. Maxwell. I don't mean to intrude. And I don't want you to feel ambushed here, but I would really appreciate it if . . ."

The plane suddenly and violently stuttered, as if its engines, for the briefest of moments, had lost their breath. The passengers looked around nervously, fear setting in. The pregnant woman startled awake; the young Latina took her grandfather's hand.

But the plane regained its momentum, slipping along once again on its soft cushion of air.

"I hate these things," Zach said, a frown creasing his lips.

Graham nodded his assurance. "We'll be all right."

The plane lurched again, impossibly stopping in midair. Then, as screams of terror filled the cabin like a flame, the tiny craft rolled to the right and began to drop like an injured bird. Magazines and briefcases and the little boy who wouldn't fasten his seatbelt were all sent pummeling forward.

The sharply sloping perspective out the cockpit windshield revealed the severity of the pitch as the pilots struggled to control their wounded aircraft.

"This is American Eagle Six. We're having a problem here," the pilot called into his headset.

"Engine one is flamed! Two's failing!" the copilot yelled.

And then, with one last sickening jolt, the plane surrendered its tentative hold on any hope of survival and yawed forward into an irreversible nosedive. "This is American Eagle Six. We're going in," the pilot said.

The copilot crossed himself. "Shit."

Graham Maxwell, his face tight with fear and resignation, looked over to Zach Saltzman just as the young man was vaulted from his seat and

3

thrown into the bulkhead. Graham brought his left hand to his mouth and kissed his wedding ring, thinking not of himself or his daughter or his granddaughter; willing himself to have the last image in his mind be only of his wife.

"Soon now, Dorothy," he whispered. "Soon."

2

It rained that day because it always seemed to rain on such days, the persistent showers turning the ginger-hued cement of Grace Cathedral a deep cinnamon brown. Presiding over her city from atop Nob Hill, this bold and handsome Gothic church was a house of many memories. Christenings and confessions, marriages and communions. All of the chapters in the book of life, including, on this day, the last.

Hundreds of Graham Maxwell's family, friends, and colleagues were pressed into this holy place to hear the eulogies and the tributes as his time among them was honored. Within the cathedral's great hall, beneath the glorious stained glass, the mourners sat upon blue velvet pew pads listening to Patrick Colomby send his oldest friend on his last journey.

In the first row facing Patrick, Graham Maxwell's daughter, Jenna Perry, a beautiful and resilient woman on the eve of her thirty-fourth birthday, nodded in affirmation as her father's law partner recalled his old friend's idiosyncrasies. A former collegiate swimmer, she still possessed the grace of her athletic past. She reached over and put her hand in her own daughter's lap, hoping that Lily could emerge from the hurt and confusion of this awful day and respond to her.

Patrick Colomby, standing among the wisping candles, concluded his homage with, ". . . and so, as we take you to be at the side of your beloved Dorothy, I say good-bye for now, Graham. You were my partner, my conscience, my friend . . ." Lily unconsciously leaned away from her mother and into the sturdy reassurance of her father. Tilting his head back to hold in his tears, David Perry pulled his daughter close. Lily snuffled her face into his jacket and sobbed as if all the troubles of the world lived in her young body. Jenna, her heart breaking, stroked

Lily's hair only to have her daughter push even deeper into her father's arms.

Daddy's girl.

——

Outside Grace Cathedral, curious passersby and photographers from the *San Francisco Chronicle* and *USA Today* watched from across the street. David, just under six feet tall and handsome in a disarming way that made women comfortable, carried Lily down the rain-washed steps to their limousine, his wife holding on to his elbow. Once Lily and Jenna were in the long black car, David turned, his intense brown eyes searching the crowd until he found Patrick Colomby just reaching the sidewalk. Working his way through the throng of mourners, pausing here and there to receive a condolence or a hug, David caught up with Patrick.

"Beautiful speech, Patrick."

"Wise and kind Graham," Patrick mused. "We lost the best of us. How's Jenna?"

"Not so good. It's bad enough losing a parent; but not this way." Looking back to the limo, he went on, "But Lily's the one I'm worried about. She was devoted to her grandpa."

Patrick put his hand on David's shoulder. "We all were." He leaned forward and spoke softly. "Listen, David. I was more than Graham's friend and partner, you know. I'm the executor of his will—as he was of mine. I went over his papers last night, and there's quite a bit of money coming to your family."

David tried to stop him. "Patrick, I—"

"All I can say," Patrick persisted, "is . . . use it. Take the girls on a long lavish vacation. Someplace quiet. We'll hold down the fort at the firm for as long as it takes until you get back."

David glanced over to the limousine and saw the deep grey of his daughter's woolen dress. "Thank you, Patrick. You've been a great friend to us all."

He started to go when Patrick said, "One other thing, David."

David turned back.

"I'm on the cusp of becoming an old man, and I've been through two too many marriages . . ."

"And one great one," David reminded him.

"Yes," Patrick agreed, "one great one. All I'm trying to say is, don't let the money change you and Jenna, and what you have in Lily." He grasped David's hand and shook it firmly, emphasizing his point. "Come to me whenever you need to talk. I'll always be there for you and the girls. It's the least I can do for Graham."

Patrick released David's hand and crossed through the crowd to his own limousine. David watched him for a long moment, reflecting on his words, before rejoining his family for the short drive back to Pacific Heights.

3

Clarissa Gethers kissed her mother and father good-bye as the housekeeper loaded her suitcases into the trunk of her Mercedes convertible. Lost in thought, she crossed to the car. She had called him as soon as she had gotten to her parents' house two nights ago. Then again yesterday and once more last night. And he had never called back.

"You going straight down?" her father asked.

"I think I'm gonna get some exercise first," Clarissa said. "Let the traffic die down a little."

"Phone us when you get home, honey," her mother called as Clarissa climbed into the car. "Let us know you're okay."

"I will." Clarissa backed out of the cobbled drive of her parents' mansion, nestled on an oak-lined hilltop in Pacific Heights.

Blessed with her mother's slim frame and her father's chestnut hair and shocking blue eyes, Clarissa seemed to float easily through her privileged life.

But that was far from the truth.

Home this weekend from Stanford, she had gotten up early to have breakfast with her father. Later, while her mother packed her bag for her, Clarissa had stolen away to the guesthouse bathroom and thrown up her meal into the toilet, a torrent of water from the faucet muffling the sounds of her retching.

She drove slowly along the dew-moistened street, her parents' house receding in the rearview mirror until she took the gentle curve to the right and it disappeared. Clarissa stopped the car for a moment and absorbed the view of the bay, the early-morning fishing boats puttering beneath the broad expanse of the Golden Gate Bridge. She had planned to go to her gym near Union Square to sort out her worries and maybe try calling him one more time, but as soon as she saw the bridge, she knew she would be down there in a matter of minutes.

Just then she noticed the sprinklers come on at the Perry house, the fine spray misting the elegant lawns. Her thoughts went to Lily Perry's grandfather who had died in that plane crash. It was hard for her to believe that it had been almost a year since that tragedy had struck their neighborhood.

Clarissa had been baby-sitting for Lily when it happened, and it was she who had gone down to pick her up at the Peabody Middle School. She had taken her back up to this house and waited with her until David and Jenna came home.

Just last night her mother had mentioned that she'd heard the Perrys were having problems.

"Trouble in paradise" was how she had phrased it.

Clarissa had nodded, thinking to herself that she knew all about paradise and its troubles.

Rolling down her window to get a clearer look at the bridge, she wondered if Graham Maxwell, wherever he was right now, was at peace.

— —

The Golden Gate Bridge was out of focus this morning. Lily delicately turned the knobs of her grandfather's telescope between her thumb and forefinger, just as he had shown her. In the past year she had grown from being an awkward preteen to closing in on the beauty she would inherit from her mother. Loosening the neck stay, she pivoted the telescope on its fulcrum until the center of the great bridge's span came home to her like a favorite painting.

"Sorry about the focus, Lilliput. I was looking at the stars last night. Couldn't sleep."

Lily turned to see her father at the bottom of the stairs, standing next to her mother's trophy case filled with the ribbons and plaques from her swimming days. David Perry put down his garment bag and double-width lawyer's briefcase and crossed to his daughter.

"Me neither," Lily said, looking up to him. It was then that he noticed she'd been crying.

Before David could respond, their housekeeper, Pilar, came into the room with a glass of grapefruit juice. "Oh, Mr. David. It is too sad," she said as he took the glass.

"I know, Pilar."

Shaking her head and muttering under her breath, Pilar returned to the kitchen as David tried to lure his daughter into a less upsetting conversation.

"How's traffic on the bridge?"

"Usual. Bumper-to-bumper." But that was all she offered.

Carrying Lily's Speedo gym bag and book satchel, Pilar whammed through the swinging kitchen door. She dropped Lily's things at her feet and retreated to her haven, where she made an audible show of displeasure, clanging pots and pans as she slung them onto their overhead hooks.

David looked to the door and smiled at the racket. Then he turned back to Lily and gestured toward her gym bag.

"You gonna be late for practice?"

"They're chlorinating the pool," Lily answered. "We can't use it till after school."

David sniffed a little laugh. "Don't want your hair getting any greener than it—"

"How long will you be gone, Daddy?" Lily interrupted, her eyes brimming.

"Until your mom says it's okay to come back."

Stepping closer to Lily, David reached across and started to put his hands on her shoulders. But before he could, she collapsed into his chest. "I was always the special one in school," Lily cried. "The one with two actual parents in the same house. And now I'm just another kid whose mom and dad broke up. Where's the fairness in that?"

David leaned over and kissed her on the top of the head. "It's just for a little while, sweetie. Just so Mom and I can work some stuff out."

The shadow of the little girl she was trying to leave behind got the better of her and Lily stomped her foot on the floor. "But why can't you work it out while you live with us?"

"We tried. We really did," David explained softly. "And we both decided it would be better for all of us if I took the condo."

"Better for you guys, maybe," Lily said, pulling away. "Can't I go with you?"

"Not yet, honey." David looked up to see Pilar standing in the kitchen doorway, listening quietly. Knowing that David regarded her as part of the family, she didn't bother to turn away as he continued talking with Lily.

"We'll figure this out, Lilliput. I promise. Besides, my new place has a satellite dish. Twenty-four-hour MTV."

"MTV already is twenty-four hours."

"Oh." David started to go on, then saw Pilar look past him to the stairs. Glancing over his shoulder, he saw exactly what he expected to see, if only because she had promised not to come down here while he talked with their daughter.

Jenna Perry stood leaning against the newel post, her arms crossed tightly over her chest, her right cheek pulled in as her jaw pulsed defiantly. David drew Lily into one last hug, gathered up his stuff, and, with a final shrug to his wife, walked out of his dream house.

Lily glared at her mother and ran to the window. She pulled back the curtain and peered through the glass. Clarissa's Mercedes was just passing by, heading down the hill.

— —

David strode across the driveway, the windblown moisture of the sprinklers brushing his face. He whipped open the back door of his black BMW 740 and threw his suit bag and briefcase onto the seat. As he pushed the door closed, he spotted the thin white exhaust of Clarissa's Mercedes dipping below the incline of his street.

He glanced toward the house, toward the window where he knew Lily would be standing, and gave her a little wave. Then he climbed into his car and turned the key. The engine hesitated slightly before catching. David slipped the car into gear and pulled away, all the while fighting the impulse to look back again.

4

J enna stood watching her daughter. She knew that Lily loved David more than she loved her, and she'd long ago accepted it. But it still unsettled her.

David had always tried to compensate for working so hard, often too hard, especially after Graham's death. He would come home late at night, and it was as if only he and Lily lived in this big house. He would kiss Jenna hello and go upstairs to Lily's room, sometimes waking her, and the two of them would talk the evening away. By the time he finally came to bed, Jenna would already be asleep. Or pretending to be.

And so she had taken a lover.

Elliot Sanders was an old friend in an equally unhappy marriage, and she had found comfort with him. It was dangerous and invigorating. But she had been careless and David eventually found out. His sharp lawyer's mind had disassembled her stories, and he had confronted her.

David pursued it, and soon Jenna confessed to other indiscretions earlier in their marriage. David's temper flared, and he said he couldn't live in a marriage without trust. Jenna, equally incensed, suggested that he move out. David, rashly, had bought the new condo in less than a week.

Jenna shook her head at the memory of a dream gone sour and crossed to Lily.

"Hey . . ." she whispered as she looped a stray strand of hair behind her daughter's ear. "You okay?"

She expected Lily to flinch and move away. But, to Jenna's surprise, Lily looked up, her eyes pink and wet. "I'm so sad, Mom, my stomach hurts."

"I know, honey," Jenna said and wrapped her arms around her little girl. "Know what?"

"What?"

"Pilar told me that Clarissa's up from Stanford," Jenna began. "Maybe after school we can all go over to Sausalito and have a girls' day out. We can take the ferry and go by the bridge."

"Too late, Mom," Lily said as she untangled herself from her mother. "Clarissa already left."

"Oh," Jenna said as Lily headed back toward the telescope. "Then when she comes up for her birthday, I'll invite her over and you guys can do something together. Would you like that?"

"Whatever," Lily murmured as she sat on the stool and released the stay on the telescope.

Jenna stood there watching her daughter's back for a long, silent moment. Then she glanced at Pilar in the kitchen doorway and went upstairs.

—–

Clarissa zipped her windbreaker tight to her neck, checked the clasps on her Rollerblades, and set out for a vigorous—and needless—calorie-burn across and back over the Golden Gate Bridge.

Gliding smoothly through the tourists, joggers, and cyclists, squinting against the morning glare in spite of her expensive Oakley sunglasses, Clarissa passed under the first great orange tower and redoubled her effort toward the next, almost a mile away. She felt the coolness of her own sweat beneath her nylon jacket, and she was pleased that a few more unwelcome ounces were evaporating from what she considered to be an imperfect body.

With each thrust of her legs, the memory of her unreturned phone calls faded farther away, until, at last, she was churning along effortlessly, her disappointment over him virtually gone.

As she neared the bridge's midpoint, she stopped. And when she did, when her breathing slowed again, thoughts of him pushed their way back into her mind. Drawn to the railing, she looked down to the bright churning water more than two hundred feet below.

And she felt that urge again. The magnetic allure of going over the side and floating to her own oblivion.

She knew that, although the water looked so inviting, in reality it was as unyielding as the sidewalk she was standing on.

But still, she mused, it would all be over so quickly. A gasping moment of pain and then . . . an eternity of peace.

That would show him.

Pressing down on the railing with her palms, Clarissa raised herself onto the toes of her Rollerblades and leaned forward. Each time she was here she felt this same ease with which her balance, her hold on life, could be tipped. Coaxed upward and over with a mere shifting of her weight.

It would be so easy. So perfect. So . . .

"No!" Clarissa shouted, startling the young couple next to her, who had paused to look back at the abandoned monument of Alcatraz.

Ripping herself from the rail, she whirled around and raced back to Vista Point. When she got to her Mercedes, she stripped off her Rollerblades. Without bothering to pull on her tennis shoes, she started the car and sped south through the Presidio, heading as fast as she could toward Palo Alto.

— —

"Come, *chica,*" Pilar said softly. "I will take you to school now."

"One more minute," Lily said peering through the telescope. She had watched, fascinated, as Clarissa tore along the walkway of the Golden Gate Bridge, her long legs stroking so gracefully. Then Clarissa had gotten into her completely cool Mercedes and fishtailed out of the parking lot.

Locking off the telescope, she grabbed up her gym bag and her books and, without calling up to her mother, followed Pilar out the front door.

5

As usual, there was no heat in the trailer.

After pouring himself another glass of vodka, the man rummaged through his stack of dirty clothes until he found an old army jacket. Pulling it on over his tattered sweater, he switched on his TV to the midnight movie and tore open his bag of Kentucky Fried Chicken.

The stray cat that had adopted him a month ago jumped from the sink to the small dinette table. His third glass of vodka only now warming its way to his brain, the man pulled some skin off a chicken wing and tossed it to the cat. Snatching up the morsel, the cat leaped to the top of the refrigerator and ate hungrily.

Hazily amused, the man bit into a chicken leg and finished off the bottle of vodka, clanking it into a box with the other empties.

What the hell, he thought to himself, I got the late shift tomorrow. I can sleep until—

The front door exploded inward, its hinges almost ripping from the frame, and someone burst into the tiny space.

Startled out of his near stupor, the man began to stand up. But the intruder, switching on a blinding halogen headlamp, rushed forward and slammed him backward, the trailer's thin wall buckling under his weight.

"Hey, what the fuck?" the man yelled.

In a swift slashing stroke, the intruder smashed the television screen with a short hardwood club. Then he quickly scanned the small space, his headlamp cutting smoky laser arcs, making sure they were alone.

When the beam swept across a window, the man briefly saw the reflection of the intruder's face. And, as he recognized him, he realized that he was already dead.

"I won't call you anymore," he whimpered, struggling to rise. "I'll leave you alone. I promise!"

The intruder lashed out with his club and brought it crashing down on the back of the man's head, cracking his skull like glass. The man fell over, sending the box of vodka bottles clattering across the floor.

Stepping over the bottles, the intruder grabbed the man's army jacket and dragged him across the grimy floor and out of the trailer, his limp body scudding across the rough dirt.

Only dimly aware of the life ebbing out of him, the man surrendered any hope of survival and allowed himself to be pulled along as if in the fatal grasp of a lion.

There was the sliding sound of a van door opening. Then he was lifted off the ground and heaved inside, landing in a heap against the hard steel of the wheel well.

The intruder slid the door shut, climbed in, and started the engine. Quickly surveying the clearing to make sure no one had seen him, he gunned the motor and disappeared into the night. It all had taken less than a minute.

Just as he had planned.

6

—•—

Tucked under Broadway, in a forever decaying North Beach neighborhood, a low unraveling building creaked awake to receive its first round of visitors for the morning. Headlights swathing through the ground fog, an ancient white school bus pulled into the alley next to the Chez Vous ice rink. Twenty-five girls and two teachers climbed down from the bus and hurried inside.

In the chill hollows of the ice barn, the girls laced up their borrowed skates and ventured unsteadily onto the cloudy ice. Not yet able to see beyond a couple of feet in the curious indoor fog that clung to the surface, the girls tentatively explored the rink, their little bodies cutting ghostly paths in the mist.

A few of the more patient skaters extended themselves into a routine of stretches. Using the dasher boards as a barre, they hooked their skate heels onto them and reached forward until their fingers touched their toes. After a while, some of the older girls glided to center ice and began to try out the moves they had seen on television the night before.

As the rink warmed, the ice became less and less opaque, a skeleton of pipes becoming visible beneath its frozen shell. One of the children braved a move she had seen last night and stumbled as she caught her skate tip on something. Ignoring it, she skated off to be with her friends, just barely getting out of the way as an older girl, the best skater among them, back-skated into the same corner and flung herself into a graceful spin.

Feeling the others watching her, she tightened her body, causing it to whirl even faster, until, her momentum spent, she spiked her toe into the ice as she had so many times before. But this time her blade hooked onto something protruding through the surface and she fell awkwardly on her behind.

Indignant, and a little embarrassed, the girl looked into the ice, search-

17

ing for whatever it was that had caused her to fall in front of her class-mates. Her eyes finally settled on an unexpected shape just beneath the surface. Gradually, as the ice continued to clear, it yielded its secret to the girl, and she shrieked in terror. The others raced toward her. Following her violently waggling finger, they too dissolved into a horrified wailing as they scrambled to get off the ice, to get away from the strange man's body trapped in this frozen tomb.

There was something unusual about this man, something more than his being frozen in their ice with the collar of his army jacket poking through. The sole of his right work boot was much thicker than the other. Fully five inches thick.

7

In a narrow beige-and-white house in the Marina District, Jack Snyder finished the knot in the same tie he'd worn yesterday. On the dresser before him lay a wallet, a ring of keys, handcuffs, SFPD Badge #3358, and a holstered service revolver with a speed loader in a worn leather sleeve.

The bedside telephone rang, startling Jack out of his morning routine. Before he could answer it, a woman, her short dark hair still damp from the shower, stepped out of the bathroom and picked up the receiver. Jack cinched his tie into place and pulled on his sport coat as Jane Candiotti, nearing forty and hating every passing minute of it, hurried across the room and scooped the gun, the handcuffs, the badge, and the keys into her purse. She was tall and slender, like most of the women in her large Italian family, and her lively brown eyes set above high cheekbones made her pretty face seem almost beautiful.

"Gotta go," she said, kissing Jack on the lips. "Buncha kids found a body stuck in the ice at a rink in North Beach. Can you imagine? Those poor babies."

"I'm outta town till a week from Saturday," Jack said as she scurried for the door.

Jane stopped and turned around, trying not to show her disappointment. "But it's my dad's barbecue this weekend. We talked about this."

"I'll try to get back, but I don't know." Jack shrugged. "I'll call."

Jane stood at the door, wanting desperately to leave and desperately to stay and finish this. "So basically, you're never going to meet my family."

"I said I'll call." Then, trying to lighten the mood, he went on, "Thanks for last night. It was really special." Closing the gap between them, he snaked his arms around her waist and tried to pull her into him. But she resisted.

"What?" Jack asked, already knowing the answer.

Jane drew away. "I've got a bunch of traumatized children to deal with," she said, her hand on the knob. "Plus I'm feeling a little shitty myself." She yanked the door open.

"I'll . . ." Jack began.

"I know," Jane stopped him. "You'll call. Put the key back under the geranium when you leave."

She stepped out into the bracing coolness, reminding herself of the job she had to do and willing herself not to start another day by crying over a man.

— —

"A piece of his jacket was sticking through and Julie tripped on it and started screaming like crazy, so we went over to help her up . . . and then we saw him. . . ." The image of the frozen man pushed its way back into her memory and little Megan Chen couldn't continue.

Some of the girls sat shivering in their dilapidated school bus. Others, like Megan, stood around outside in clutches of two or three, waiting for their parents. A jumble of cop cars, an ambulance, and a Mobile Command Trailer clogged the street. Two young uniformed policemen unspooled yellow crime scene tape from lamppost to lamppost until the entire block around the Chez Vous ice rink was cordoned off.

Jane's breath clouded into thin wisps of vapor as she sat with Megan and two other girls on a low concrete wall, their legs dangling. Jane one of them. "Did you guys know this man? Did he work inside or hang around here?"

"Nah," Megan offered. "He's like a total stranger."

"Kinda looks like a homeless guy," Julie Thomas added, looking for her mom's van through the gathering crowd.

" 'Scuse me, ladies." Kenny Marks, Jane's partner, stepped in. A couple of years younger than Jane and born into a family of cops, Kenny had never really had a choice about what his career would be. Which was fine with him; he loved being on the force.

Boyishly handsome and just over six feet tall, he'd had his share of women when he was younger. Then he had worked his way up to Homicide and met Jane. Before long, they'd had something between an affair and a relationship. Now, partners for the past year and a half, they had settled into a comfortable and loving friendship. "Lieutenant wants us," he said to Jane.

Hopping down, Jane turned to the girls and gave each of them one of her cards. "Any of you guys think of something else, or if you just need to talk, call me, 'kay?"

The girls nodded quietly, each in her own far-off place, as Jane and Kenny walked away.

"Jesus, what a morning," Jane said as she took the carton of yogurt Kenny offered for her.

"Could be worse."

"Oh?"

"Yeah." Kenny smiled. "You could be lying dead in the middle of six tons of rock-solid ice."

Jane looked back to the girls on the wall. Sally Banks, a policewoman from their precinct, was just now bringing them hot cocoa. "Yeah," she said bitterly, "and feeling no pain."

"Uh-oh. Jack?"

Jane nodded tightly, not wanting to pursue it. A Dodge minivan screeched up and a woman, a nurse obviously called away from work, flew out the door, under the tape, and across the street. Before she could get halfway, Julie ran into her arms and broke into long racking sobs. Her mother clutched her close and rocked her from side to side until the panic subsided and she knew she was safe again.

Kenny turned to Jane. "Son of a bitch. I'm sorry, Janie. I thought Jack was the one."

"So did I."

Sergeant Oswaldo Castillo raised the crime scene tape for them as they approached the Mobile Command Trailer.

"Thanks, Ozzie," Kenny said as they scooched under.

"You bet, Inspector." Ozzie, in his early fifties, had a full head of thick grey hair and the ready smile of a beat cop. "Thought I'd seen everything," he said, gesturing toward the rink.

"Yeah," Jane agreed. "Me too."

The lead forensics officer, Aaron Clark-Weber, stood next to the trailer, holding a cup of coffee in both hands. Thin to the point of being too skinny, Aaron smiled at Jane and Kenny through the steam rising from his coffee.

"Hey, Aaron," Jane greeted him. "What d'ya know?"

"I know this cold is hell on my arthritis," Aaron answered, flexing his bad knee.

"I meant about the deceased."

"Only that he's still dead and that the ice hasn't even begun to thaw." Aaron was about to continue when the door of the Mobile Command Trailer flew open and Lieutenant Benjamin Spielman stuck his head out. He hated one thing above all others: waiting.

"How long's it take to defrost a fuckin' ice rink anyway?" he bellowed.

Jane glanced over to Kenny. "A reasonable question," she said, spooning the last of the yogurt into her mouth.

8

——

David Perry felt the warm wind rush up to meet him as he took the stairs down into the Montgomery Street BART station. Dressed in a well-tailored business suit and carrying his laptop computer in a black leather case, he was an elegant anomaly among the usual patrons of San Francisco's subway system.

He purchased a ticket from an automated machine, inserted it into the turnstile, and rode the escalator down to the train platform.

Once there, David noticed that although BART seemed modern and bright with its sleek slant-nosed trains and smooth granite walkways, it was starting to look a little tired after years of constant traffic. A tiny filigree of cracks webbed the ceiling, evidence of a water leak somewhere in the strata above.

He leaned forward to listen for the squeal and to feel for the wind of an oncoming train. But the percussive throbbing of a boom box drew him back around until he saw a young black man in a Chicago Bulls sweatshirt sitting on one of the flat round benches that looked like waterless fountains. His arm was possessively looped around the neck of his young girlfriend. She looked at David and used the stub of her cigarette to light another, blowing a flume of smoke his way. Next to her was one of the thousands of No Smoking signs that papered all of the BART stations.

In the two weeks since he had moved out of the house and into his condo, his already fragile relationship with Jenna had soured considerably. Rambling late-night telephone harangues, missed appointments, promises unkept time and again; these and more were the clouds of his wife's gathering storm. Lily, caught in the middle, was beginning to show signs of how hurt her little soul really was.

The southbound Daly City train slid into the station, and the doors whooshed open. Before any of the passengers could exit, the boom-box couple wedged their way onto the car. Stepping aside to let others get off before he got on, David could feel the coiled kinetic power of the train. When the doorway cleared, he entered and found a seat next to a middle-aged woman of mixed descent, her head bowed intently as she read the latest Amy Tan. With a bonging warning signal, the doors merged closed, and the train lurched forward.

The train quickly gathered momentum, tobogganing through the dark tunnels. Without warning, it burst into harsh, brilliant sunlight and rapidly slowed until it squealed to a stop at the Powell Street station. Dozens of schoolkids piled in, all backpacks, bookbags, baggy pants, and energy. With another bong, the doors closed, and the train sped toward the next terminal down the line.

David stood and two yabbering girls jammed into his seat. He wove his way among the strap-hangers toward the next car and passed through the between-cars door.

Picking his way carefully down the fast-moving car, David came to an empty aisle seat and sat down wearily. The man who was staring out the window next to him glanced over for a moment, then returned his gaze to the row houses whipping by. David craned back to see the BART map near the doorway in the middle of the coach, but couldn't quite read it from where he was sitting.

"Excuse me," he said to his seatmate. "How many more stops to Daly City?"

Barton Hubble turned to David and replied, "Five, maybe six." He was a stocky man, a couple of inches taller than David, with close-cropped hair and the torso, hands, and arms of someone who worked hard for a living. His torn and greasy jeans and washed-out flannel shirt were in vivid contrast to David's beautiful suit.

"Thanks," David said. He opened his laptop and began tapping out notes on the case he was working on.

Barton Hubble eyed David's tasseled loafers and obviously expensive computer. "You a famous writer or something?"

"Hardly," David laughed. "I'm an attorney."

The train whined to a stop at the Sixteenth Street Station in the Mission District and most of the schoolkids got off. As the bong sounded and the train moved out, Barton Hubble watched David work, all the while forming a question in his mind. "Can I ask you something? Sort of a legal thing."

"Sure."

Hubble thought for a moment, putting the sentence in order as he rehearsed it in his head. "I live in this shit-hole apartment in not exactly the best part of town? And we haven't had hot water in almost a month."

"That's awful."

"Fuckin' A it's awful." Hubble sat up straighter, filling with purpose. "There's babies and old people livin' there."

David reached inside his jacket and came up with his silver card case, a gift from Jenna. He pulled out a card and handed it to Hubble. "Call my office. I'll have one of my paralegals hook you up with the Renters' Rights Bureau. They're pretty good at this stuff."

"Won't cost me nothing, will it?"

"Your tax dollars at work."

Hubble nodded his thanks, then returned to staring out the window. The train came to an unexpected stop between stations, and David looked around curiously.

"This your first time on BART?" Hubble asked as he watched David fidget.

" 'Fraid so. My wife, uh . . . asked me to move out."

"Been there. Done that."

"It gets worse. My damn car wouldn't start this morning."

Hubble, his interest piqued, turned to face David. "What kind of car?"

"BMW."

"No shit?"

"Absolutely none." David smiled. "Why?"

"You happen to be sitting next to the finest German car mechanic in the Bay Area."

"No shit?" David laughed.

"Absolutely none," Hubble answered. "And sir, I'd consider it a privilege you let me come by and fix your car for ya."

"That's very generous," David responded. "But I can't let you do that."

"Why not?" Hubble persisted. "You just gave me free legal advice. Wasn't nothing to ya, right?"

David shrugged as the train started up again and made its way toward Glen Park Station. "Well no, but . . ."

"And makin' a Beemer that don't start into a Beemer that does ain't nothin' to me. Do it all day long."

25

"I really appreciate it, but . . ."

"Tell you what," Hubble continued as he rose and took up his brown paper lunch bag. "I use any parts you can pay for 'em."

David relented. "You have a deal, Mr. . . ."

"Hubble. Barton Hubble." He offered his hand.

"David Perry," David said as he shook hands.

"This is me," Barton said as he headed for the door. "You got two more till Daly City." When he reached the door, he turned back and called, "I'll be in touch, Mr. Perry."

David watched him go as the doors slid closed and the train rolled forward.

9

━━

David checked his reflection in the smoke-dark glass of La Folie's front door. He straightened his tie and entered the elegant French restaurant. It was here that he and Jenna had celebrated their anniversaries earlier in their marriage.

"Ah, Mr. Perry, welcome back," the maître d' said as he shook David's hand. "It's been a long time."

"Good to see you, Henri."

"Are you meeting your wife?" Henri asked as he led David to a corner table. "Or are you here on business?"

"A little bit of both, I guess," David said as he took his seat. He was having drinks with Jenna to respond to her opening volley in their divorce proceedings. His meeting in Daly City had finished a little later than he had planned and he had been concerned that he was going to be late.

The front door opened, spilling sunlight into the entry. And there was Jenna.

As she strode toward David's table, heads turning as she passed, he couldn't help but appreciate that his wife had always known how to make an entrance.

She sat down without a greeting or a smile. "Chardonnay," she said to Henri.

"Iced tea, please, Henri," David said.

There were big issues to address, and David knew that he had to begin slowly. "The painters ever show up to do the front bathroom?"

"They left yesterday," Jenna said coolly. "You all settled in?"

"I haven't exactly finished unpacking," David answered with a lightness he didn't feel. "In fact, I haven't exactly started unpacking either."

Henri brought their drinks and set menus before them. Jenna sipped her wine, leaving a textured kiss of lipstick on the rim of her glass. "Did you get Theo's letter?"

Theo was Theodore Kaplan, an old sailing crony of her father's and one of the most ruthless—and expensive—divorce attorneys in Northern California.

David flushed. "Yes, I got it." He squeezed lemon into his iced tea. "I've gotta say that the language in that letter was unnecessary, provocative, and . . . hurtful."

"What's the matter? The big-shot lawyer's afraid of a little hardball?"

"Jen, if we go through with the divorce, we both know the money will work itself out. There are formulas for this sort of stuff, and we'll come within a certain percentage of what's fair." He pushed his drink aside and leaned forward. "But trying to deny me visitation of my own daughter? What the hell are you thinking?"

For the first time in one of their arguments, Jenna did not back away. "I'm thinking of what's best for Lily," she said. "Her schoolwork's going into the toilet, she's stopped taking her swimming seriously, and she's depressed and noncommunicative all the time. The counselor said this would be best."

"Counselor? For God's sake, Jenna, she's depressed because her mother's sleeping with Elliot Fucking Sanders instead of her father."

Jenna sat back in her chair, feeling people nearby glancing toward their table. "Do you really want to go into the reasons for my having an affair? Do you really want to open that can of worms again?"

"Our marriage was wounded, Jenna," David said, his voice rising. "You could have worked with me to try to save it or . . ."

"Way I look at it," Jenna interrupted, "I put it out of its misery."

A busboy ventured forward and put a basket of warm sourdough rolls on the table. They both ignored it, sitting there in silence until Jenna spoke again. "I don't know what happened to you," she said, shaking her head sadly. "You're not the man I married."

"The man you married lived in fear and subservience to you and your father's money." David nodded solemnly. "Those days are over, Jenna."

With that, Jenna rose, David standing with her. "I've got to go meet Lily's schoolbus," she said as she dug in her purse for the valet parking ticket. "In the interest of not disrupting her life too much too soon, I'm still going to let you have her this weekend, as you planned." She started away, then turned back. "But after that, it'll be entirely up to me when and if I allow you to see her."

"Jen . . ." David started to say, but she was already at the door.

Feeling the eyes of the other diners boring into him, he sat back down and reached across the table for Jenna's wineglass. He took a long swallow and closed his eyes. Then he pulled out his wallet and placed a credit card on the table.

Henri approached. "On the house today, Mr. Perry," he said.

— —

Barton Hubble hated grease.

He stood at the bathroom sink in his tiny Chinatown apartment and meticulously scrubbed his hands.

Ming Wei Wu sat on Barton Hubble's bed, sipping orange juice. Waiting. Not yet sixteen and slender with breasts like soft doorbells, she and Hubble had found each other one night as each of them prowled the back streets like cats. She looking for someplace to sleep, he looking for someone to sleep with.

The bathroom door opened and Ming rose up onto her knees as Hubble emerged, shirt off, his powerful torso glistening.

"I swear to fucking God I gotta get out of that goddam garage before it kills me," he said as he crossed to the bed. "Fuckin' rich bitches are driving me out of my mind."

Ming lifted herself up and, smiling, kissed him on the chest. Ignoring her, Hubble finished off her orange juice. "Yesterday it was that old cunt told Otto I didn't finish her car on time 'cause I was too slow."

Nodding, Ming unbuckled his pants and slipped them down his legs.

"Today," Hubble continued, his anger rising even as Ming pulled off his underpants and kissed his penis, "this rich babe in Daddy's Mercedes accuses me of stealing a necklace from her glove compartment. Crock of shit." He looked down as Ming took him in her mouth. "Oh God, baby," he moaned.

Grabbing her roughly by the hips, Hubble deftly turned her around until she was lying facedown over the side of the bed. Knowing what was coming, Ming spread her legs and winced only a little as Hubble entered her from behind.

"I hate them all," he said as he thrust his penis deep within her, his loins slapping against her buttocks.

Ming turned to look back at him and grinned, the corner of her mouth curling upward as he intensified his pumping. Hubble held his closed fist next to her face. "Accusing me of stealing," he grunted, his orgasm building. He opened his hand and a necklace with a speck of a diamond at its center slipped from his fingers and cascaded onto the sheet by her hair.

Ming looked at the diamond, glinting like the light in a doll's eye, and looked back at Hubble, silently asking the question.

"Yes, baby," Hubble said as he started to come, his breath a rapid shallow gasp. "It's for you."

Ming Wei Wu neither spoke nor understood a word of English. Her eyes pooled with grateful tears at the kindness of this man.

10

Jane finished with the little makeup she wore and stepped from her bathroom into the bedroom, its far wall already dappled with a cottony white light.

She took a leftover scrap of garlic toast from the lowered ironing board she used as a dining table. Covered with a crisp linen tablecloth and adorned with her grandmother's silver candlesticks, this was where Jane had had dinner last night. Sitting alone in front of the television, she'd had an evening of puttanesca, Barbara Walters, and SportsCenter. Munching on the bread, too late now to clean up, Jane dropped her gun, badge, and cuffs into her bag and headed into the hallway.

The rows of framed pictures arrayed on the Parsons table were like an open family photo album. Four generations of Jane's large and robust Italian family smiled back at her as she passed, heading for the front door. She stopped to adjust the frame of her father's photo—Poppy beaming into the lens with the joy of a patriarch surrounded by his progeny—and noticed her answering machine's message light blinking. She rewound the tape and pressed play.

It was Jack.

"Hi, Janie. You there? Maybe you're in the shower. Anyway, sorry I missed you. . . . Look, I'm not going to be able to get back to town in time for your dad's barbecue."

Having already given up the ghost of whatever remained of this relationship, Jane exhaled a long sigh of resignation as Jack continued, "I know you're disappointed. Maybe another time, huh? I'll call."

Shaking her head and smiling in spite of herself, Jane reached out and pressed the erase button, the last vestige of an unfulfilling romance gibbering backward until it no longer existed.

31

"Fuck you too, Jack," Jane said beneath her breath and turned to the sound of Kenny's car honking at the curb.

— —

Jane had always hated the way Kenny drove, weaving his Explorer in and out of traffic, dipping into the parking lane to whip past slower cars. It was as if the teenage boy in him refused to acknowledge that he was now a thirty-five-year-old man.

Kenny dropped the Explorer into gear and darted away from the sidewalk before Jane could click her seat belt into place. Reaching behind her seat, he came up with a small white paper bag. "Mixed berry," he said, handing it to her. "They were out of blueberry."

Jane pulled the carton out of the bag and peeled back the lid. "Just as good," she said softly as she dipped the plastic spoon into her yogurt.

Her sober tone caught Kenny's attention. "Hear from Jack?"

"He left a message."

"And?"

"And . . . it's over."

Kenny put a hand on Jane's arm. "Look on the bright side."

"And that would be?"

"Now you can take me to Poppy's barbecue."

"You had your chance."

In a flash of anger, Kenny tore to the right, passing a cable car, and pulled back into the center lane. "That wasn't a chance. That was an audition."

Jane shook her head. "Kenny . . ."

"Just because way back when," he kept on, insistent, "I made the fatal mistake of saying I wasn't sure if I wanted kids—and boom, I'm an asshole?"

Closing her eyes to maintain her composure, Jane opened them and turned to Kenny. "Think. Do I really want to have this conversation right now? Especially right now?"

Coming to a reluctant stop at a red light, Kenny looked over to see the pleading in Jane's eyes. Such was his abiding affection for her that he immediately relented. "You're right. I'm an asshole. Sorry."

Jane nodded her acceptance of his apology. They'd been through too much together to let something like this occasionally recurring flare-up linger for long. The instant the light turned green, Kenny gunned the Explorer into the intersection. A pickup truck with an aggressive driver not unlike Kenny had been trying to make a late left turn and was forced to slam on its brakes, just missing Kenny's car.

"Hey lady," the driver yelled to Jane, "your husband can't drive for shit!"

Jane rolled her eyes to the driver, mimicking her agreement.

"Let me shoot him," Kenny said through clenched teeth.

"But that would be wrong."

"You're right. Think of the paperwork," Kenny said as he swung his car around the pickup and careened into a banking right turn toward North Beach.

— —

The detritus of the crime scene investigation littered the perimeter of the Chez Vous ice rink. The Styrofoam coffee cups, cigarette butts, and black plastic film canisters would all be there until the wind took them. Snippets of yellow police tape flapped against lampposts like tiny flags telling the world that this neighborhood had been visited by death.

Kenny pulled the Explorer halfway into the alley next to the rink in that defiant way cops have of parking wherever they want. Jane sat there for a minute, taking in the magnified warmth of the sun through the passenger window, before joining her partner in front of the car.

Across the street, a young dark-skinned man, maybe twenty years old, leaned against a fire hydrant. He had a paper bag which barely concealed a tall can of malt liquor in one hand and a joint in the other. He took an exaggerated hit on the weed and held it in longer than necessary. Then he let the thin blue smoke stream out his nostrils, his red and glassy eyes never once blinking as he stared a malevolent challenge at Jane and Kenny.

"How about him?" Kenny asked. "Can't I shoot him?"

Jane glanced over as the punk finished his malt liquor in a protracted, dripping guzzle and tossed the can into the puddled gutter. "Fine by me. But I don't think he'd feel it."

"Good point," Kenny said as he followed Jane into the mouth of the alley.

"Jeez." Jane recoiled. "Smells like a toilet in here."

"That's 'cause it is." Kenny pointed to an abandoned cardboard hovel strewn with soiled blankets, fast-food wrappers, and empty Thunderbird bottles. "I don't think we're in the Marina anymore, Toto."

Halfway down the graffiti-covered wall was a rusted metal door. Padlocked. Kenny, ever inquisitive, gave the chain a perfunctory tug. It held fast. Jane, continuing ahead, her hand over her nose against the vile odor, came to a barred window about five feet off the ground. Its screen was half torn away and someone had left a sturdy plastic milk case just below.

"Think our iceman was skinny enough to get through these bars?" Jane asked as Kenny came up.

"If it's three A.M. and you need to be warm, you get as skinny as you need to get."

A slight breeze roiled the air just enough to intensify the lingering stench. "Let's get out of here," Jane gasped, hurrying toward the street.

When she reached the Explorer, she leaned back against the hood and watched Kenny as he poked at the cardboard shanty. Jane let her gaze drift from Kenny and took in the whole alley, trying to absorb whatever information it might hold.

She understood that murders, all crimes for that matter, were links in a chain of events. If she could uncover the previous link—an argument, a threat, a motive—she would have a leg up on the next link—fencing stolen property, revenge, a possible serial killing.

She shook her head and muttered under her breath, "If this even was a murder."

Kenny came up, unlocked the door, and he and Jane climbed in.

"Kinda funny, you know," Jane mused as Kenny started the car.

"What is?"

"You break into a building to get out of the cold . . . and you end up freezing to death."

"It's not without its irony," Kenny said as he gunned the engine and skittered through a huge puddle, sending a rush of slimy water onto the loitering pot smoker. "Oops."

11

A white Range Rover sat next to David's black BMW in the brick-ribboned driveway of his condo in Presidio Heights.

An elderly woman, slowly walking by with her Filipino nurse, paused as the sounds of an argument emanated from inside. The woman looked indifferently to her nurse and shuffled farther down the sidewalk, at her age no longer having the capacity or the curiosity to worry about the travails of others.

The door whipped open, loudly banging into a stucco-covered wall. David, incensed, stormed out into the cool morning air. In an instant, Jenna, her face flaring with rage, appeared in the doorway.

"Don't you walk away from me!" she yelled.

David wheeled to confront her. "I will not have this conversation in front of Lily!"

Jenna shook her head with disdain. "Problem is you don't want to have this conversation at all."

"No!" David shouted. "The problem is you get unhappy, you have an affair, you decide to leave me . . . and I have to move out!" He stopped, trying to collect his thoughts. "And now you're going to completely deny me visiting rights to my own daughter?"

"Every time she sees you, she comes back to me all surly and uncontrollable," Jenna said, fighting to stay calm now that their argument had found its way outdoors. "It's too confusing for her."

"I know what you're doing, Jenna. You're holding her for ransom to get me to settle. And it's not going to work!"

Before Jenna could respond, Lily poked her head into the doorway. Her parents' fury immediately abated. "Get in the car, sweetie," Jenna said gently.

Lily looked to David, as if for permission, and he crossed over to her and knelt down to talk to her. "It's okay, Lilliput," he said, brushing

35

her hair back off her forehead. "I'm sorry you had to see us fighting like this. Sometimes we get too angry."

David rose and put his arm over her shoulder to coax her to the Range Rover. "You're lucky. You've got your swimming to take your mind off things."

Lily looked up to him, too tired of it all to even cry anymore. "It'll take like two million laps to take my mind off this stuff, Dad."

"Good thing you're getting an early start," David laughed weakly as he pulled Lily into a hungry hug and helped her into her mother's car.

Jenna got into the Range Rover, slammed the door in one last show of anger, and roared away.

David stood on the sidewalk, his eyes following the car until it fell from sight below the steep hill. Turning, he heard the throaty rumble of a powerful engine and looked to his right to see an enormous tow truck pulling up, a heavy-duty winch perched like a figurehead on its front bumper.

Barton Hubble yanked back hard on the emergency brake and climbed down. "The wife?" he asked, gesturing with his head in the direction Jenna had taken.

"Yeah. The wife."

"Couldn't help but notice you guys ain't exactly on the road to reconciliation."

"Far from it," David said. "This a coincidence or . . ." He nodded to his BMW. ". . . a house call?"

"House call. A very nice young man at your office helped me out with my little landlord problem and I'm here to pay you back." He reached into the cab of the truck and came up with a battered red toolbox.

"But that's really not . . ."

"Don't even start. I drove all this way. I'm here. And I'm going to fix your car. Okay?"

"Okay," David shrugged. "That's some truck you have there."

"She's ugly. But she works."

— —

In less than five minutes, Barton Hubble stood back from the engine and called, "Try it now!"

David turned the key in the ignition and the BMW purred to life.

"When was the last time you took her in for a service?" Hubble asked as he slid the hood closed and wiped the grease from his hands with a faded orange rag.

"Long time," David admitted, getting out of the car.

"Watch your step there. Wouldn't want to get grease on those nice loafers."

"Thanks," David said as he avoided the oily smear in the driveway. "I've been a little out of it lately."

"Tell me about it."

"How long were you married?" David asked.

Hubble snorted. "Five years longer'n I shoulda been."

David reached into his pocket and brought out his wallet. "So, what do I owe you?"

"Like I said, Mr. Perry, we're even." Barton Hubble threw his tool-box behind the seat of his truck.

David spotted a San Francisco 49ers bumper sticker next to the truck's right taillight. "You a Niners fan?"

"Big time."

"You gonna watch the Dallas game?"

"Are you kidding me?" Hubble said as he hoisted himself into his seat and closed the door. "I guess you're going to the game, huh?"

David smiled. "This one's in Dallas. Kinda far to go on a Monday night." Hubble laughed as David went on, "Sometimes, if I can get out early enough, I go to this sports bar near the office. Can't watch the Forty-Niners and Cowboys without a little noise, y'know?"

Hubble cranked the engine. "Ain't that the truth," he said, popping the truck into gear and holding in the clutch. "See you around." Releasing the clutch, he drove off slowly, David watching him go, until he slipped over the same hill Jenna and Lily had gone down.

12

— • —

CLARISSA ROSE GETHERS

PI BETA PHI

STANFORD UNIVERSITY

PALO ALTO, CALIFORNIA

Dearest one,

I know you told me that it's over between us and that you don't want me to call anymore. But it's just too hard. I'm sorry.

The last time we talked—too long ago!—you said that you'd always been upfront with me and that you never made any promises. That's true. But there was one thing neither of us ever counted on.

I fell in love with you.

Contrary to what you might think, I didn't plan to or really even want to. But it happened.

My birthday is coming up soon and I'm going up to the city for that weekend. (Remember my birthday last year? That was so fun!)

My parents are throwing me a party. Believe me, I don't want them to, but you know how they are. I'd love for you to stop by. Honest, just stop by. You don't even have to stay. Just come by for a little while.

I promise I won't make it awkward for you.

I just want to see you again.

Okay? Please call.

My love,

Clarissa

Clarissa

— —

Patrol Officer Sally Banks ran her fingers through her close-cropped hair as she stood over the console of the Nineteenth Precinct's dispatcher, Cheryl Lomax. Cheryl, a middle-aged black woman, had a row of family photographs lined up like little soldiers in front of her dispatch radio. "I can't break away right now," she said to Sally, her long lavender fingernails cutting the air. "I already took my break."

"Okay," Sally nodded as she tapped a Marlboro Light out of its package. "Guess I'll just have to smoke one for you." As she opened the stairwell door to go have a cigarette on the landing, Kenny entered. He had a bag of microwave popcorn under his arm and a Coke in either hand.

"Good timing. Thanks, Sal," Kenny said as he crossed the bullpen.

"Anytime, Inspector," Sally smiled. She stole a glance at his butt and, trading appreciative looks with Cheryl, stepped into the stairwell.

Kenny, his arms full of food, passed by the glass wall of interrogation room one. He tapped his forehead on the glass until Jane tore herself away from staring at the blackboard on the far wall. She rose, scraping back her chair, and opened the door for him.

"Anything on the iceman?" Kenny asked, putting the cups of soda on the table.

Jane took a Coke and crossed to the blackboard. Exasperated, she ticked off the meager data they had been able to compile so far.

"Race: Caucasian. Gender: male. Age: forty to fifty. Address: unknown. Tattoos: U.S. Navy. Distinguishing characteristics: disfigured right foot. Autopsy report: pending. Name: unknown." She sat down heavily and held the frosting drink cup against her wrist. "So, it's a dark and stormy night. Our friend breaks into an empty ice rink and lies down for a little nap. Then the maintenance man or somebody turns on the ice-making thingie and what do we get? Cryogenics."

"Could happen," Kenny said, munching on the popcorn. " 'Cryogenics.' Good word."

"Thought you might like it." Jane got up and touched the blackboard as if urging it to give up a secret. "I don't buy it. Of all the places a bum could flop for the night, the cold hard concrete floor of an ice rink has to be about last on the list."

"Given that we basically have nothing on this guy, it's a stretch to think it was anything but an accident," Kenny countered, automatically taking the devil's-advocate position. It was how they worked best: seeking the opposite of any theory in order to explore all the options. "What? You think some crippled guy randomly gets whacked and—"

"That's just it," Jane interrupted. " 'Random' implies without reason. My instincts are screaming at me that the victim was killed for a reason."

"Like what?"

Jane gave a half-smile. "Somebody wanted him dead?"

"Ooh," Kenny teased. "You're good."

The door opened and a uniformed officer entered. Mike Finney was in his mid-twenties, but, because he was some thirty pounds north of healthy, Lieutenant Spielman had recently restricted him to desk duty as communications liaison. His moist, pasty complexion, his exaggerated size, and his basic policy of inertia had brought the other cops in the building to nickname him Moby. ‒ A P ‒

"You wanted to see me, Inspector?" Finney asked, already homing in on the popcorn.

"I called you two hours ago, Moby," Kenny said. "Where've you been?"

"Lunch," Finney answered as he emptied the popcorn bag into his mouth.

Knowing how much Finney got under her partner's skin, Jane stepped in. "Do you have the autopsy report on the ice rink John Doe?"

Finney pulled an envelope from his back pocket. "Right here."

Jane grabbed it from him and tore it open. As she devoured the information, Kenny glared at Finney. "And when were you going to give this to us?"

"Soon as you asked."

Kenny looked to Jane for some sympathy, but she was engrossed in what she was reading. Turning back to Finney, Kenny waved his hand dismissively. "See ya, Moby. You've been a great help."

"Anytime, Inspector," Finney said, eyeing the sandwich girl pushing her cart along the bullpen.

After he left, Kenny leaned in to read over Jane's shoulder. "What do we got?"

"First of all, we got fingerprints," Jane said, still reading the report. "Which means we got a name. Warren Fincher. Forty-seven. Lived in a trailer out in the boonies. He was a flight mechanic on an aircraft carrier 1970 and 1971. Medical discharge after injuring his right leg in a forklift accident in June of '71."

Kenny took the last page from her and read aloud. "Autopsy shows his liver was shot. Probable assumption is he was an alcoholic. Primary cause of death: trauma to the back of the head. Either from blunt force . . . or a fall."

Putting down her pages, Jane turned to Kenny. "What's it say about family?"

Kenny quickly scanned the rest of the report. "Only that there isn't any."

Jane sat on the edge of the table and sipped her Coke. "Pretty shitty, dying alone."

"Dying alone is one thing," Kenny responded. "Dying unsolved is another."

"Then it's up to us, Inspector," Jane said, "to make sure that doesn't happen."

13

— —

Sitting in the glow of his computer, David Perry noticed the clanging halyards on the flagpoles atop the Comstock Building across the way. He found himself drawn to his office window on the fifty-fourth floor of the Bank of America Building.

"Knock-knock?" Patrick Colomby said as he tapped the doorjamb with his wedding ring.

David turned from the window. "Patrick, come in."

Closing the door behind him, Patrick entered and dropped into a club chair across from David's desk. "Blowing like a motherfucker tonight," he said, making small talk. "Aren't you going to watch the game?"

"Maybe the second half," David responded, wondering where this was going. He tilted his head toward his computer screen. "I want to catch up on some stuff."

Patrick narrowed his eyes, studying David. "How are you feeling, David?"

David chose his words carefully. "I'd be less than candid with you if I were to say my separation from Jenna didn't have some effect on me."

"Can't go through something like that without getting a little dented," Patrick agreed.

In court, this sort of preliminary chatter was called throat-clearing, a smoothing of the way before the business at hand was put on the table. David decided to seize the reins from Patrick.

"Look, Patrick, first my father-in-law dies, now his daughter leaves me. My nepotism coupon running out?"

Patrick poured himself some water from the pewter pitcher on David's side table. "Anything but. I came to see if, with all your . . . distractions, you might have time to take point on Shepherd-Ramsey."

Shepherd-Ramsey was the largest schoolbus manufacturer in the country. Just over a year ago, one of its buses had crashed and a number of young students had been killed and injured. The company was denying any negligence in the lawsuit brought against it. This was the sort of case that combined the nobility of being on the right side with the opportunity, in victory, for a prodigious fee well into seven figures.

David was stunned. "Are you serious?"

"Absolutely," Patrick said, enjoying this. "You've already got a rapport with that little girl down in Daly City. I'm afraid she's going to be a very reluctant witness. You're a gifted trial lawyer, and you've got a wonderful relationship with your own teenage daughter."

They both looked to a snapshot of Lily, Scotch-taped to David's monitor.

"How's she doing with all this?" Patrick asked.

"Back and forth," David began, rocking his head, still surprised. "Moody one day, off the wall the next." He let out a tiny laugh. "Come to think of it, she's always been like that."

Sharing the laugh, Patrick rose and offered David his hand. "So, is it a yes? Will you help us out?"

David grasped Patrick's hand. "It's an enthusiastic—and grateful—yes, Patrick."

"Fine then." Patrick crossed to the door and stepped aside to let Myra, the cleaning lady, enter. "See you first thing for a strategy briefing."

Myra hadn't realized the office was still occupied and hesitated in the doorway as Patrick left. "Sorry, Mr. Dave. Want me to come back later?"

"That's okay, Myra," David said as he pulled his laptop from its docking station and slipped it into its carrying case. "I was just leaving."

But Myra stood rooted in place in the doorway, something clearly playing on her mind.

"What?" David asked, intrigued.

In spite of herself, Myra started to cry as she came into the office and handed David an envelope. David took out the official-looking piece of paper and scanned down the page. When he got to the bottom, he looked up to Myra. "You got your papers!" He beamed. "Congratulations!"

Myra nodded, tears streaming, and threw herself into a quick awkward hug with David. "Thanks to the letter you wrote, Mr. Dave. God bless you."

"Myra," David said as they separated, "you got your papers because you're a wonderful, hardworking woman. I was proud to help you."

He snapped his briefcase shut and headed for the door. "When's the ceremony?"

"In only two days."

David stopped in the doorway. "Can I come?"

Her tears came again. "I would be so happy."

"Me too," David said as he made his way toward the elevators.

Myra rushed into the hallway. "Mr. Dave," she called.

David turned to her, holding the elevator door open with his arm. "Yes?"

"Be careful tonight. It is too windy outside."

"I'll be careful," David said, entering the elevator. "I promise."

Myra watched as the elevator doors slid together, then, dabbing at her eyes, pushed her cleaning cart into David Perry's office.

— —

The night wind flung the dirt against the side of the trailer like a rain of hail. Jane and Kenny climbed out of the Explorer and hunched across the clearing to the shattered front door.

Unbuttoning his coat and unsnapping his shoulder holster, Kenny nodded to Jane to switch on her flashlight. She trained the powerful beam inside the trailer as Kenny yanked the door completely away from the frame.

Without warning, something erupted from deep within the trailer and burst by Jane and Kenny. In an instant, Kenny had his pistol out and cocked as Jane spun the light around and caught a glimpse of the cat just as it hurtled across the clearing and into the woods.

"Scared the shit out of me," Kenny said as he entered the trailer.

"Poor thing," Jane responded as she joined him in the narrow room. Her beam penetrated the darkness, landing first on the scattering of vodka bottles. "There's a surprise," she said wryly.

When the light fell on the caved-in television, Kenny asked, "You gonna watch the game?"

"Probably . . ." Jane answered, her attention drawn to the countertop.

There, next to a mound of gnawed chicken bones, was a crumpled wad of money. "There's more than a hundred dollars here," she said.

"Rules out robbery," Kenny offered.

"Our Mr. Fincher was having himself a nice quiet chicken dinner and a little something to drink . . ."

"A little?"

"Okay, a lot. Maybe he was watching TV with his kitty on his lap," Jane continued. "Next thing he knows . . ." She cast the light on the linoleum floor; a trail of scratches led out the door. "Dinner's suddenly over."

"Chickenus interruptus," Kenny joked.

"And we go from suspicious circumstances to homicide," Jane said as they stepped outside and started toward the Explorer.

"I'll get some uniforms down here to cordon off the area."

"And let's have Aaron's team do their forensics thing. Something could turn up."

"Will do." Kenny opened the door for Jane. "Something bugs me about all this."

"What's that?"

"If you're gonna kill this guy, why take him all the way to some piece-of-shit ice rink in North Beach? Why not dump him in a ditch or an alley or something like any self-respecting killer of our drunken citizens?"

"That's just it," Jane said softly.

"That's just what?"

"It's the big fuck-you," she answered as she stepped outside.

"To whom?"

"To the police," Jane said as Kenny joined her. "Whoever killed Warren Fincher is one mean and arrogant son of a bitch."

— —

The girls of Stanford's Pi Beta Phi sorority house had a long-standing tradition of inviting boys from nearby fraternities over to watch *Monday Night Football* in the basement's chapter room. With the San Francisco 49ers playing the Dallas Cowboys, the biggest regular-season game of the year, the room was a joyous racket of youthful enthusiasm and sexual tension.

Clarissa Gethers had taken dinner with her sorority sisters at the usual time. But, wanting to check her machine to see if he had called after her latest letter, she had declined the entreaties of her roommates to join them for the football party. Besides, she had another meal to purge.

Climbing the elegant center stairway, she noticed the bay windows at the landing rattling violently against their hinges. She hadn't realized how windy it was tonight.

She wedged a folded magazine insert between the windows to keep them still and looked outside. Palm fronds from the sorority next door were torn away and sent floating across the connecting yards. Water in the birdbath flew sideways out of its bowl, and the porch swing beneath the rear overhang banged repeatedly into the wall of the clubhouse.

Clarissa rounded the corner and headed up the next flight of stairs. When she was halfway to the second floor, the power went out with a low buzzing hum, plunging the house into an eerie darkness.

She had a choice: up or down. She chose to continue up the stairs to her room, and just as she reached her doorway, the lights came back on. Howls of mock disappointment filtered up from the chapter room. Someone made a joke, too far away for Clarissa to hear, and the kids laughed nervously.

Breathing a quick prayer—"Please let there be a message"—she pushed open her door. She looked to the right, toward her desk. The tiny red light on the answering machine shone steadily, unblinking. He hadn't called.

The feeling, when it came, always caught her by surprise. The utter despairing emptiness that clutched her heart with dread.

Unable to fight off the sadness anymore, she made up her mind that tonight would be the night. She would drive back to the city and go to the bridge.

Her heart pounding, she raced down the stairs.

Tearing across the parquet floor of the foyer, Clarissa yanked open the front door and ran headlong into one of her sorority sisters. Startled out of her own swirling confusion, Clarissa gave out a tiny involuntary shriek.

"Jesus, Clarissa," her sorority sister exclaimed. "Where the hell are you going?"

Clarissa immediately threw on a smile. "Nowhere special. Just getting some air."

"Well, forget it, girlfriend," her sorority sister said as she took her arm and kicked the door closed. " 'Cause it's blowing like a bitch tonight and we got a chapter room full of eligibles."

Clarissa reluctantly allowed herself to be pulled back into the house and down the stairs to the party.

14

— ı —

D avid Perry hurried across the lobby of his office building, nodding to the maintenance worker who guided the high-speed
polisher over the Italian marble floor. It always seemed futile to
try to make contact with this man, his head perpetually framed in the
halo of Walkman headphones. At the security desk, David stopped
to talk with Frank, the elderly black security guard who had been at
his post every weeknight since the building had opened almost thirty
years ago.

"How's your boy doing, Frank?" he asked as he pulled on his overcoat. Through the tall lobby windows, he could see the wind-whipped
debris lashing about in tight violent circles.

Frank looked up from the tiny TV he brought from home on Monday nights during football season. "He's back from the hospital, Mr.
Perry. Doctor wants to try some new stuff on him. Calls it a cocktail . . .
but he says it might could make him sick." Frank drifted off, thinking
of his son lying alone in the living room of their house, probably too
weak to watch the game he loved. "I don't know . . ."

"You tell him, when he's up to it, I have two seats on the fifty-yard-
line with his name on them," David said, pulling up his collar and pushing against the revolving door.

"Ain't you takin' your car?" Frank asked, gesturing in the other direction toward the parking garage.

"I'll come back for it. I'm gonna go to Terry's and watch some of
the game. I could use a drink." David leaned into the door until it took
him outside.

"Tell me about it," Frank muttered as he went back to watching
the game.

— ı —

Terry's SportsWall boasted a vast bank of televisions, all tuned in, on this night, to the 49ers game. Jerry Rice extended himself in a kaleidoscope of sixty-four images as Steve Young's pass slipped just beyond his fingertips and a collective groan filled the room.

David entered, slung his overcoat on a hook by the hostess station, and waded into the crowd. As a waitress, her tray laden with drinks and pretzels, moved from in front of him, he noticed someone and stopped.

Barton Hubble, his small table filled with dead beer bottles, sat watching the game. His plaid shirt was relatively clean, but he still wore the same grimy work boots. David figured that he had changed his shirt before leaving work to make himself more presentable.

He approached Hubble's table. "Who's winning?"

Hubble looked up. "Fuckin' Cowboys. Up by four." He regarded David's briefcase and laptop. "You leavin'?"

"Just got here."

"Then take a load off," Hubble said, taking his heavy green greatcoat off the other chair. "Want a beer or something?"

"Beer sounds great," David said as Hubble flagged down the waitress.

"Coupla Buds." He turned back to David and gestured to the TV screens. "You were right. This is a great place to watch a football game."

— —

Kenny's Explorer pulled up outside Jane's house in the Marina. "Wind got your trash cans. Want me to get them?"

"I can do it, thanks."

They sat there for a while, an awkward silence filling the car, until Kenny said, "So, whattaya doin' later?"

"A little bill-paying, a little pasta." Jane shrugged. "A little *Monday Night Football*."

Jane knew that Kenny was waiting to be asked inside. Waiting, but too proud to pursue it himself. She gave him a little apologetic raised-eyebrow look that told him it was not going to happen.

"O-kay." Kenny blew a long sigh. "You need your butt kicked in Jeopardy! or your furniture rearranged, you know who to call."

"Who?"

"Jeopardy!, me. Furniture, Moby."

Jane reached across the seat and kissed him on the cheek. "I know it's a complete waste of breath, but . . . drive safely."

She climbed down from the Explorer, righted her toppled trash cans, and went up the walkway to her house. Looking back, she knew Kenny would still be there, waiting to make sure she got inside safely. Jane unlocked her door, switched on the hall light, and turned to wave good-bye. Kenny nodded to her, gunned the engine, and screeched away from the curb. Jane watched as he raced around the corner, his petulance pushing him to drive even more recklessly than usual.

Not feeling like saving the world tonight, Jane entered the sanctuary of her home and closed the door.

— —

Well into his third beer, compared to Barton Hubble's fifth, David spoke loosely and freely, as if he were talking to an old friend.

". . . and then her lawyer sends me this letter? About how I shouldn't see my daughter for a while? It's like we never said 'I love you' to each other, never shared the unbelievable miracle of Lily's birth . . . never had any hope." David trailed off as Steve Young aired one out for a streaking wide receiver. Intercepted. "I mean, I'm a lawyer and I know how to play hardball. But I'd never send a letter as cold and hurtful as that."

"And she's the one fucked around on you?"

Biting his lower lip, all David could manage was a nod. Barton Hubble saw that he was on the verge of tears. The waitress came by and plunked two more beers on the table. "Don't worry, honey," she said to David, sticking her fingers into the empties and lifting them onto her tray. "It's just a little interception. We'll get it back."

As she walked away, David looked to Hubble and let out a laugh. "Is there no life in this town other than football?"

"Guess not," Hubble answered, tipping back his beer.

— —

The faint grey flicker of the television screen was the only source of light in her bedroom. Jane, seated on the edge of the bed in front of the lowered ironing board, poured herself a glass of Chianti and began to eat her dinner. Drawn to look back at the empty pillows stacked against the headboard, she reflected on what had brought her to this stage of her life, a life passing her by. The decisions and indecisions that, when reckoned with, added up to yet another moment of searing loneliness like this.

Trying to chase those thoughts from her head, Jane picked up the remote and zapped the TV louder.

——

The 49ers lost in the last minute as Dallas kicked a field goal with less than ten seconds remaining in the game. Disgusted patrons settled their bar tabs and made for the front door, another night of guilty pleasure at Terry's SportsWall already behind them.

But David, nursing beer number four, still had plenty on his mind as he rambled on to Barton Hubble with surprising facility. ". . . It's not even the money . . . though there is a shitload of it. It's Lily. I mean, it's confusing enough to be a thirteen-year-old these days without getting into the every-other-weekend routine with your father . . . if your mother regains her sanity and lets you see him."

The waitress, clearly wanting to go home, put the bill between them. Each man grabbed for it, and a miniature tug-of-war ensued. Barton Hubble was stronger and more determined. "It's the least I can do," he said, pulling out a small wad of singles and fives.

"Thanks," David said as he hailed the waitress. "Can I have some water, please?"

"You have room for more liquid?" Hubble asked.

"Not really. I just feel like I need to dilute the beer if I'm going to drive home." The waitress brought the water and Hubble's change. David loosened his tie and touched the water glass to his forehead. "Y'know, I've never told anyone the stuff I told you. It's the fascinating thing about strangers hooking up."

"Especially over drinks," Hubble agreed. "Look, about your wife and kid—it's a motherfucker. I know you've heard it all before, but it just takes time."

"What does?"

"Getting whole again."

"I know I'll be all right eventually," David said after a long searching pause. "But what about Lily? She wakes up one day, and bam! She's the child of a broken home." He reached over to pick up his briefcase and laptop. "My wife's so goddam selfish, I swear I'd give anything if . . . ah, fuck it." He rubbed his eyes and stood up. "I gotta get going."

Shooting back his shirt cuff to check the time, he looked at his wrist and rolled his eyes. "Shit. I lost my watch. I gotta get it together."

Barton Hubble dropped a five-dollar bill on the table, pushed his chair back, and stood up. "You sure you're okay to drive?"

"I'm fine. My office is just around the corner. The walk'll clear my head." He offered his hand. "Didn't mean to talk your ear off."

Hubble took David's hand and gave it a solid shake. "Game of life is much more interesting than the game of football. Glad I bumped into you." He pulled on his greatcoat as they walked to the front door. "Until the next time." While David took his overcoat from the hook, Hubble peered out the window. "Looks like the wind finally died down."

"Had to some time."

"See you around," Hubble said. He walked out the door, turned left, and hustled across the street to the mouth of the BART station. David watched as the escalator carried him from sight, down to a train that would glide into the station and take him home.

15

The windstorm the night before had blown away the haze that usually clung to the bay in the early morning. Lily, her Speedo gym bag and her book satchel at her feet, swiveled her grandfather's telescope slightly to the left, to below the Golden Gate Bridge's Vista Point parking lot, and, killing time, watched as a row of tour buses chugged up the hill to the gift shop. Swinging farther left, she caught sight of something going on through the rows of eucalyptus trees that served as the windbreak for the Presidio Veterans' Cemetery. But there was a copse of trees between her and whatever was happening there this morning, and, frustrated at not getting a good angle, she shifted the scope back to the bridge.

In the sharp unsullied air, the bridge, its flawless International Orange span spreading over the bay's open gate, seemed so naturally nestled between the shores of her end points that surely God must have put it there a million years ago. Lily tilted the telescope up and down the South Tower, trying to absorb the sheer immensity of the structure. She panned the arching roadway, just now filling with traffic, until she reached the far North Tower, the suspension cables dropping from its shoulders like the wings of an angel.

She heard someone call her name.

"Lily."

And she wheeled around.

"Lily," Pilar said again, standing in the foyer by the front door. "Come, *chica*. Your mama's still in bed, so I will take you to school."

Lily pulled the focus of the telescope back to the South Tower and locked it off. Then, grabbing up her bags, she crossed to Pilar. "Seems like Mom's always in bed these days," she mumbled as they went out the door.

——

The softest hint of a breeze rustled the leaves high up in the stand of eucalyptus trees. That and the luffing of the huge American flag were the only sounds this morning in the Presidio Veterans' Cemetery. The only sound until a military chaplain took his place at the head of the flag-draped casket suspended on broad cloth straps over an open grave. His thinning blond hair couldn't disguise the fact that he was a young man, only recently elevated to chaplain of this nearly full graveyard.

With a solemn nod to the honor guard of four uniformed soldiers and a glance to the eight empty folding chairs next to the mound of dirt, the chaplain opened his missal and began a eulogy for a man he had never met.

"Petty Officer Second Class Warren A. Fincher is today laid to rest among his comrades-in-arms. The soil of his country, which he fought so bravely to defend, welcomes him home. And a grateful nation, forever indebted, gives her young warrior his final resting place. May God cradle him in his arms. Amen."

The honor guard stepped smartly forward and folded the flag into the traditional triangular wedge. The sergeant of the guard, having been through this many times before, turned his back on the empty chairs and handed the flag to the chaplain. The soldiers dispersed quietly, leaving the casket to the graves detail, who expertly lowered it into the ground and, starting up a loud sputtering backhoe, quickly filled the hole.

On a gentle rise overlooking the grave, the sounds of the backhoe just now reaching them, Jane and Kenny turned away and started down the hill.

"Nobody came," Jane said, shaking her head.

At the bottom of the hill, Aaron Clark-Weber was just getting out of his car. "Dispatch said you guys might be out here."

Jane nodded. "Can't hide from the all-knowing Cheryl Lomax."

"Anyone interesting show up?"

"If they did," Kenny offered, "they came disguised as empty chairs."

Jane smiled at her partner and turned to Aaron. "Your team find anything of use out at the late Mr. Fincher's trailer?"

"Shoe prints, tire prints," Aaron said. "Everything but fingerprints."

"And that tells us . . . ?" Jane prompted.

"That unless a late-model Chrysler-product minivan turns in its owner," Aaron laughed, "we don't have diddly."

Jane pulled open the door of the Explorer. "Great. Fuckin' great." And she slammed the door closed.

Aaron looked to Kenny. "She have a personal interest in this one?"

"She's a homicide cop," Kenny said as he walked around to the driver's side. "We take them all personally." He climbed in, started the engine, and drove away.

Aaron watched as the Explorer followed the curve of the cemetery's lane until it was out of sight. "Yeah, and I'm just a putz in forensics," he muttered. Slightly favoring his bad knee, he slipped into his car and headed back to the station.

— —

Maiden Lane was where they went. A two-block-long alley just off Union Square, Maiden Lane was a narrow canyon of elegant cafés, pricey beauty shops, and discreet pharmacies. For the idle ladies of the hills—Nob Hill, Pacific Heights—with a day to spend pampering themselves, Maiden Lane was the only place in town.

Jenna Perry had been there all day. Once Pilar had driven off with Lily, she had dozed for another hour before showering and dressing. After picking up her girlfriend Maggie Donnelly, another San Francisco socialite with time and money on her hands, Jenna gave her Range Rover to the valet and set about to do Maiden Lane from top to bottom.

At two in the afternoon, Jenna met up with Maggie again at the Akimbo Café for a quick coffee. Maggie held a window table for them while Jenna went to the counter to order their drinks. "One decaf cappuccino, one decaf latte . . . and two sugarless biscotti."

The young countergirl took her money and gave her a plastic tag with a number on it. Jenna dropped a dollar into the tip jar and, turning to join Maggie, walked right into the man behind her.

"Sorry," Jenna said. "I didn't know you were there."

Barton Hubble smiled, carefully avoiding her eyes. "S'okay," he said softly.

Jenna passed by him and crossed to her table as Hubble stepped up to the counter. "Coffee," he ordered, as he turned back to appreciate Jenna's slender, athletic body, thinking she was smaller than he remembered.

16

From the air, the city of San Leandro, just across the bay from San Francisco, looked like any other working-class suburb. Small, well-kept houses stood row after row along both sides of its narrow tree-lined streets. The school system was decent enough, the churches and markets each wished they had a few more patrons, and the population of young people was steadily dwindling. Moving on to greener, or at least different, pastures.

Jane Candiotti was born into this town, into a neighborhood near its center. And it was here that she had learned to walk on her family's front porch, had learned to ride a bike in the driveway, Poppy running next to her with a steady hand on her shoulder. She had learned about boys from her older cousins, and she had learned a generous lesson from her mother. She had learned that it was all right to want a life that was different from her parents' life. That it was permissible, even encouraged, to leave San Leandro. As long as you returned when your family called.

The backyard of 314 Oak Street was, on this Saturday, brimming with Jane's family. Aunts and uncles and cousins and their kids had come back home from all over Northern California—one married cousin had flown in from Seattle—for Poppy's family-reunion barbecue.

Just past his seventy-third birthday, and only now allowing himself to enjoy his retirement from the small corner grocery store he had owned for almost forty years, Paolo Candiotti had planned this party for months. The phone calls, the travel plans, the discreet loans. Poppy always said he was doing it for the children, some of whom were now in their fifties, to give them a sense of who they were and where they came from. But whenever any of them saw the joy in his still-boyish eyes, they knew the simplest of truths: Poppy missed them, missed his family, missed his wife.

A long table in the middle of the yard groaned under an avalanche of stuffed peppers and hunks of Parmesan, calamari and clams, pasta and prosciutto, olives, onions, and breads. Poppy spritzed the grill with water, sending up puffs of aromatic steam. "Round them up, Timmy!" he called to his son. "These babies are done." Expertly using a set of tongs, he began to load stacks of sausages, chicken, and corn onto the platters his nieces and nephews presented.

Jane's brother Timmy, in his late twenties and still more boy than man, started to herd the children into some sort of manageable collection of over-amped and hungry kids. Coming down the steps of the back porch, her arms wrapped around four two-liter bottles of soda, Jane caught her brother's eye.

"Tell him to slow down, will ya?" he implored. "He thinks he's forty or something."

Jane followed Timmy's gaze over to Poppy. Her father's eyes were filled with happiness as his youngest sister, Lucy, helped him slap even more food onto the grill. "That's not entirely a bad thing, Timothy," she said as she crossed to bring her father a cool drink.

— —

Later in the afternoon, as the sun fell behind the California oaks, they all lay about the backyard like seals on a beach. Even the kids seemed a little stunned by all they had eaten.

Jane sat on the rail of the back porch watching her father swaying peacefully in his favorite hammock, an infant great-nephew lying on his chest. The screen door creaked behind her and Jane turned to see her Aunt Lucy coming out of the house with two cups of coffee. She handed one to Jane and leaned against a post, cooling her coffee with quick, short breaths. "How you doin', honey?"

"Pretty good," Jane answered. "We've got this case? That guy they found in the ice . . ."

Aunt Lucy touched her arm. "Janie, I ask how you doin', and you talk about work. Honey, there's more to life than work, isn't there?"

Fighting to suppress a flash of irritation, Jane said simply, "No, actually . . . not right now, Auntie."

Aunt Lucy was about to respond when Timmy came bounding out of the house with his camera. "Wake up, you guys! It's photo-op time! Somebody help Poppy out of the hammock!"

Amid halfhearted protests, the family stirred itself awake and began to assemble for the traditional portrait. Poppy swung his legs over the side of the hammock, handed the baby off to its mother, and walked on his weary legs to the tiny lopsided gazebo he had built for his wife so many years before. Lucy put down her coffee and, grabbing up the twins, joined her brother. In that moment of confusion, Jane took the opportunity to retreat inside the house, knowing that Aunt Lucy saw her—and knowing too that Aunt Lucy knew why.

Once in the house, Jane turned to her right and pulled back the soft white curtain to watch through the screen as her family, laughing and teasing, gathered around Poppy and Aunt Lucy for the group photograph. Couples coupled up, pulling their children onto their laps. Some of the teenagers climbed up on the side of the gazebo, and, as always, one or two of the smaller kids were off on adventures of their own and would have to wait for next year's picture.

As Timmy set the timer and ran to flop down in front of his family, and as everyone watched the tiny red light blink its countdown, and as her entire family yelled out a lusty "Spaghetti!" Jane quietly slipped out the front door and, achingly alone, went home to her house in the Marina.

— —

Barton Hubble was pretty sure he had the timing right as he took the elevator to the top of the Fremont Building. After everyone else had gotten out, he punched the button for the fortieth floor and flexed his knees as the car descended.

Two older businessmen and a bicycle messenger got on at the fortieth floor and pressed the parking-level button. When the elevator slowed at thirty-seven and stopped at thirty-six, Hubble, pleased with himself, stepped to the back wall as the doors opened.

Jenna Perry entered, oblivious to him as Hubble had figured she would be, and pushed the lobby button.

As the elevator stopped at subsequent floors and as the car grew increasingly more crowded, Jenna was forced, unknowingly, back into Barton Hubble, her hair brushing against his face. Seemingly uninterested, but a familiar visceral surge rising in his throat, Hubble calmly watched as the floor indicator lights ticked off one by one until the car reached the lobby.

The doors slid open and most of the people in the front piled out, clearing a path for Jenna. Just as she started to exit, Barton Hubble leaned forward slightly and inhaled the sweet fragrance of her hair. And then she was gone and the doors were closing.

The bicycle messenger looked over to Barton Hubble. Just making contact. Hubble seized his glance with his own eyes, held it, and forced the bicycle messenger to break off and stare at the floor until they reached the parking level.

17

A nyone looking at the sky in San Francisco that night would have
remarked on the moon.

David Perry stood at his office window, distracted by the intensity of the moon's white-yellow light. He stood there for a while,
looking both through the glass and into it. When his eyes came upon
his own mirrored face, he turned away and went back to his desk to
finish the rough draft of his cross-examination for the Shepherd-Ramsey
trial. Picking up his microcassette recorder, he riffled through his notes
and began to prep his questions.

"How many students were on the bus at the time of the accident? . . .
How many students were wearing seat belts?" He clicked off the recorder and walked back to the window, his face bathed in the moonlight, and thought for a moment. Then, switching on the recorder once
again, he held it up to his mouth and said, "How many students even
had access to seat belts?"

Pilar came out of the kitchen and noticed the moonlight beaming in
through the glass of the Perrys' front door. She wanted to go out to her
apartment over the poolhouse to watch the late news on the Spanish-
language station, but she felt the need to check on Lily one last time.

Her bedroom illuminated as if by sunshine, Lily slept the deep innocent slumber of a young teenager. Today's swim practice had been par-
ticularly strenuous, working on her relay touches for hours after the
regular session, and she was exhausted. Pilar quietly opened the door,
made sure Lily was covered, and padded across the room to pull the
drapes closed. With one last look to the little girl she had known almost
since her birth, Pilar clicked the door closed, went outside to her apartment, and turned on her TV.

She didn't notice the passing sweep of the Range Rover's headlights as Jenna Perry pulled into the crescent driveway out front.

Jenna had known when she had left the house earlier that evening that she would be cold when she got home. But she liked the way the light cotton sundress hung on her body and thought that a sweater would detract from its appeal. She also knew that she shouldn't have had that third margarita, but what the hell. It wasn't that long a drive from Maggie's party to her house. A little bit buzzed, she hadn't felt this good in a long time.

Hurrying across the brick driveway, her shoulders hunched against the cooling night air, Jenna noticed that the entryway light wasn't on. Probably that damn timer again. No matter, though; the moon was uncommonly bright tonight. Pulling her housekeys from her oversized shoulder bag, she bent forward to examine her reflection in the front-door glass. Not bad, she thought to herself.

Something moved. Something, or someone, behind her. Startled, she whirled around, and there was Barton Hubble.

A tiny cry of fear rose in Jenna's throat, but she managed to push it back. Better to act calm, in spite of the terror exploding in her chest, and talk to this man, whoever he was. "Uh, can I help . . . ?"

Barton Hubble attacked swiftly, silently. Grabbing her throat in both his gloved hands, he flung Jenna's head backward into the front door with such force the glass shattered. Uncomprehending, she struggled desperately, kicking out again and again. Feeling him increase the pressure on her neck, Jenna strained to scratch his face, but Hubble pressed his thumbs across her windpipe and shook her violently, slamming her body into a potted plant and sending it crashing to the ground. Jenna's hands fell away from his face, and as she flailed about wildly, she felt something strange even in this frenzied moment.

Her hand brushed against Barton Hubble's exposed erect penis, and she realized that except for his work boots, he was naked from the waist down. For a fleeting, bargaining instant, she was relieved, thinking that this madman only wanted to rape her.

But Barton Hubble heaved her off the ground by her neck and hurled her once again into the wall. Summoning the last of her strength, Jenna let out a muted squeak of a scream, knowing even as she began to lose consciousness that Lily was too deep a sleeper and Pilar was too far away to hear.

—–—

David Perry was pleased with his night's work and eager to put Shepherd-Ramsey before a jury as he stood waiting for the elevator to come. When the doors slid open, David, lost in thought, didn't notice Myra just emerging with her cart.

"Hello, Mr. Dave," she said brightly. "You're working too much these days."

"Got an important case, Myra," he said, pushing the button for the lobby.

Myra nudged her cart into the hallway. "See you tomorrow."

"*Hasta mañana,*" David smiled as the doors closed.

— —

As Jenna crumpled to the ground, one of her white espadrilles falling into the debris of broken pottery and glass, Barton Hubble pulled a rag from his shirt pocket and stuffed it into her mouth. He deftly wound duct tape around her head, then stooped low and looped his forearm across her neck. Like a lifeguard rescuing a helpless swimmer, he dragged her, barely conscious and still whimpering, toward his truck.

— —

David emerged from the elevator and crossed the lobby. Frank, as always, was at the security desk. "G'night, Frank. Got an update for me?"

"Well, Mr. Perry," Frank said, looking up from that morning's *Chronicle* the early shift had left for him. "He had a pretty good day today. He's even making noises 'bout sittin' in the yard tomorrow."

"That's great. Tell him I said hi," David said as he turned left and headed for the parking garage.

"I always do, Mr. Perry," Frank called after him.

— —

Barton Hubble released the handbrake, and his huge truck, headlights dark, slipped forward, gaining momentum as it descended the steep incline. He popped the clutch and the engine rumbled to life.

Jenna, lying slumped on the floor, her mouth, arms, and legs bound tightly with duct tape, was only vaguely aware of the engine vibrating. She thought she was moving, but couldn't be sure.

She thought she was alive, but couldn't be sure.

18

Lily didn't remember closing her drapes the night before. Wondering at the darkness in her room when she first woke up, she rolled over to look at her clock radio. Six-fifteen. Lying back, she listened to hear if anyone else was awake. But the big house seemed to be filled with a blooming cushion of silence. An eerie emptiness. It was still fifteen minutes before Pilar was due to come in from her apartment, so Lily had a choice: stay in bed and snooze a little longer, or go down and start her own breakfast so that she could have exactly what she wanted and not all that starchy stuff Pilar always made her eat.

As she lifted herself out of bed, she realized she had forgotten how sore she was. Maybe she would ask her mother to talk to Coach Tanney about giving her some time off.

Lily opened the door to her bedroom, sunlight streaming in from the skylight over the foyer, and immediately sensed that something was out of order. She could feel the cool morning air, hear the mockingbirds quizzing each other from outside, clearly, as if a door or window were open. Head cocked as she listened, she went downstairs.

"Pilar?" she called, but not too loudly because she didn't want to bother her mother. No answer. Lily walked past the telescope and checked all the back patio doors. Locked. Looking out across the pool, she could see Pilar's steamy bathroom window and knew she was still in the shower.

An oversized Jeep drove by, its knobby tires treading loudly on the pavement, its sound distinct and close. Curious, Lily followed the sound to the front door. She heard the crackle of glass first as she stepped on it with her tennis shoe; then she noticed the splintered window in the door. "Mom!" she yelled upstairs, her alarm growing. "Someone tried to break in last night!"

Tugging the door open, she saw the broken flower pot, its dirt strewn about, and still more glass in the entryway. To her it looked more like vandalism, a teenage prank of toppling planters, than an attempted burglary. Her first thought was that she hoped it wasn't one of the boys from her school. She would really hate it if . . . and then she saw it.

There, on its side, in the dirt between the walkway and the flowerbed, was her mother's white espadrille.

——

The Filipino nurse effortlessly pushed her mistress in her wheelchair. It wasn't unusual that, this early in the morning, the older woman didn't have the strength to manage her walker. But she still wanted to be outside, regardless of the hour or the weather, and the nurse had long ago given up trying to dissuade her.

As they approached the condo with the black BMW in front, they heard a phone ring inside, and they looked at each other. Someone had something to say to someone else this early in the morning?

A moment later the front door of the condo flew open and David Perry, his shirt unbuttoned, a belt and jacket in his hand, bolted down the walkway and jumped into his car. He turned the engine over, pulled it into gear, and screeched away, the back end shimmying on the dewy blacktop.

"That poor man just got some bad news," the old lady said, shielding her eyes from the sharp angle of the sun.

"Think I should go and close his door?" the nurse asked.

They stayed there a while longer, musing on this vexing dilemma.

"I just don't know," the old lady finally said.

——

It had been another sleepless night for Jane, and the last thing she needed was a phone call this early in the morning.

"Hello?" she said groggily, not yet opening her eyes. Somewhere in the sleepy recesses of her mind she was already hoping that this call wasn't about Poppy. No matter what time at night the phone rang— and, given that she was a cop, late-night phone calls were hardly rare— her first half-waking thought always went to the phone call she knew would someday come. The phone call about Poppy.

Slowly sitting up in bed, gathering her bearings, Jane listened to the vaguely familiar voice of someone just finishing the number three shift down at the precinct. As the dispatcher on the other end went on about some problem in Pacific Heights, something about a missing woman, Jane observed the wreckage of last night's dinner on the ironing board and realized that she had fallen asleep with the television on again.

"Okay. I'm on my way." She hung up and swung her legs over the side of the bed, willing the sleep from her head.

The phone rang again.

"Hello," she answered, this time with a bit more authority. "Yeah, they already called." She stood up and carried the phone toward the bathroom. "I hate this shit. . . . Uh-huh . . . Okay, Kenny, I'm ready in five minutes."

Jane hung up the phone and placed it on the dresser. Pausing only to turn off the droning TV, she foraged through the stack of clothes she had been meaning to take to the cleaners.

19

Racing each other on their bicycles, their legs pumping furiously as they stood into their pedals, the two brothers couldn't remember a more exciting day in Pacific Heights. They skidded up next to the television news trucks in front of Lily Perry's house and, straddling their bikes, watched in boyish fascination as crime scene photographers flashed their way up and down the front path.

Ozzie Castillo strolled up to them. "You guys live around here?"

"Yeah," said the older brother. "What happened?"

"Not sure yet," Ozzie answered. "You notice anything unusual last night?"

The older boy shook his head and Ozzie started away. Then the younger brother said, "I did."

"What was that?" Ozzie asked, taking out his notebook.

"The moon," the kid replied. "It was like totally bright."

Slipping his notebook back into his pocket, Ozzie resumed his post by the driveway entrance next to the Explorer parked on the sidewalk. What the hell; it had been worth a try.

A young black policewoman unspooled crime scene tape—virtually unheard-of up here—around the vast rolling crescent of the Perry front yard. The two boys continued to watch as Aaron Clark-Weber's forensics investigators tagged minute pieces of what they thought might be evidence and called to the photographer to come over to shoot it.

There hadn't been this much activity on the hill since Lily's grandfather had died in that plane crash.

Inside the Perry house, another forensics team was hard at work, picking at the foyer's oriental rug with tweezers, videotaping the shatter pattern of the window glass, checking the telephones for the last number dialed.

Amid this commotion, David and Lily sat in the breakfast nook. They

65

were being interviewed by Jane and Kenny while a Spanish-speaking officer questioned Pilar in the doorway.

Jane's eyes wandered to the photos on the refrigerator: snapshots of Lily with her swim team, or getting on the school bus on a rainy day. There was one of her and her mother dressed in matching overalls and striped T-shirts . . . but none of David.

". . . and when I heard the birds like there was a window open or something, I came downstairs," Lily said slowly, her father absently rubbing a soothing hand up and down her back. "That's when I saw the door. I looked outside and then I called my dad."

"Which phone did you use?" Jane asked.

"That one," Lily said, indicating the portable phone in the kitchen.

Kenny made a note. "And where were you last night, Mr. Perry?"

David pulled Lily in close. "Working till about midnight. Then home."

Jane and Kenny exchanged looks. Then Kenny turned back to David. "Sir?"

Looking from one to the other, David explained, "My wife and I had recently separated. I have a condo a couple of miles from here in Presidio Heights."

Lily started to shake, her little body shivering uncontrollably. Pilar scurried in from the kitchen doorway, took off her own sweater, and wrapped Lily in it.

David, his eyes pleading with Jane, asked, "Can she go upstairs for a while?"

"Sure," Jane said, her lips pursing in sympathy. Now she understood why there were no pictures of him on the refrigerator.

David handed Lily over to Pilar and watched as his daughter crossed the living room. A fingerprint tech stepped aside from dusting the banister as Pilar led Lily up the stairs. Once he heard her door close, David turned to Jane and Kenny.

"Do you have any idea what may have happened?"

Kenny rose and washed his hands in the kitchen sink. "It's way too soon, Mr. Perry. We would just be speculating if we . . ."

"Then I'll do the speculating," David interrupted, searching Jane's face for a crack in the police facade. "Can we just say the word here? My wife's been kidnapped, hasn't she?"

Jane looked straight back at David. "It appears that way, sir."

As if physically pushed away by her words, David recoiled, his back touching the wall. He took a long time formulating his next question.

"So what do we do now, Inspector?"

Jane leaned forward, trying to reinforce the connection between them as someone he could trust.

"Everything we can, Mr. Perry," she said. "Everything we can."

— —

An hour later, Jane went out the back door of the Perry house and walked past the pool to where David sat talking with Patrick Colomby.

"We're ready, Mr. Perry."

"Want me with you?" Patrick offered.

"Yes. Please, Patrick. I do," David said as he rose.

Jane leaned in. "This way, sir." She led them back around the pool and stopped to hold the door open. "Wonderful view," she said, taking in the glistening bay, framed on the left by the Golden Gate Bridge.

"Yes," David agreed. "We had some happy times out here."

Patrick put a gentle, guiding hand on David's shoulder as they entered the house. Crossing the living room, David saw Lily on the second-floor landing. Pulling away from Pilar, she ran down the stairs. "Can't I go too?" she pleaded.

Holding Lily's hand against his side, David turned to Jane. "Any reason why not?"

"None whatsoever," Jane said. "It might even help."

— —

The local news crews had done this before. Usually it was some single mother in some tumbledown East Bay neighborhood tearfully begging for the safe return of her lost child snatched on its way to school. More than likely by the ex-husband.

But this was different. As different as it gets. A Pacific Heights socialite from one of San Francisco's oldest families violently taken from her own front door in the middle of the night by an unknown assailant. A couple of the older news technicians mentioned Patty Hearst under their breaths, but the reference was lost on the youthful reporters.

The front door of the Perry house opened and the jumble of correspondents pressed forward, the extended towers of their satellite trucks poised to beam this story back to their stations.

Jane and Patrick stepped out first and moved deferentially to the side as David and Lily emerged, surprised at the confusion of cameras and microphones. David took a long moment to compose himself. As if he were in court about to speak to a jury, he familiarized himself with the mosaic of faces before him.

Then, raising up a photograph of Jenna sitting beneath a *palapa* on a beach on St. Bart's, her sunglasses on top of her head—a picture David had taken just a year ago on their family getaway after Graham Maxwell's death—David put his arm around Lily and spoke.

"This is my wife, Jenna Perry. Somebody took her from us last night, and right now she must be very frightened. So please, whoever has her, please just call us. We'll do whatever is necessary to get her home safely."

From her vantage point on the second step, Jane scanned the crowd of neighbors and onlookers in the street behind the press. She caught Kenny's eye as he casually strolled through the throng, glancing into faces, searching for a hint, a clue, anything. He stopped and stood on his toes, just another curious bystander, as David went on.

"If anyone has seen Jenna, either last night or this morning, please call the San Francisco Police Department or your local sheriff's station. We are . . ." He glanced at Patrick. ". . . in the process of working out the details of a reward for information leading to the safe return of my wife . . . my little girl's mother."

Suddenly tearing up, David hesitated. Lily looked up to her father, not sure if he could finish. Just as Patrick was about to step in and help him, David found the control to continue.

"When Jenna left the house last night, she was wearing a yellow sundress and gold earrings. She had a large black shoulder bag and a vintage Rolex watch. And . . ." David took Jenna's soiled shoe from Aaron Clark-Weber. "She had on a white espadrille like this." His hand trembled as he held his wife's shoe up for the cameras.

"Poor fucker," the CNN reporter whispered to his cameraman.

Unable to go on, David squeezed Lily into him and retreated into the house. As Patrick turned to follow, Jane scanned the crowd, looking for Kenny. She saw him standing amid some of the neighbors. "Anything?" she asked with her eyes.

"Nothing," his eyes answered back.

20

The young couple had been hiking the main trail up Mount Tamalpais every Saturday since the baby was two months old. With the infant tucked into a Snugli on his wife's tummy, the new father unleashed their golden retriever and laughed as she bounded up the hill.

Running headlong over the trail, the dog suddenly ground to a halt and barked back to her master.

"Oh, God," the husband said. "It better not be another skunk."

"Luna!" the wife called. "Come here, girl!"

But Luna, usually obedient, leaped off the trail and scampered into the underbrush, disappearing from sight.

"Luna! Come!" the husband yelled in the no-nonsense voice that always brought her running back from the most tempting adventures.

From somewhere deep in the woods Luna let out a pitiful yelp. Then, her voice contorted in a pleading whine, she began to bark in a pitch much higher than ever before.

"She's hurt!" the wife shouted, alarmed.

The husband raced up the hill and dashed off the trail. Bursting through the tangle of shrubs, he followed the beacon of his dog's urgent barking until he found himself in a clearing.

"Luna," he said softly. "Come, girl."

But Luna was frantically scratching at the ground with her front paws, sending roostertails of dust and pebbles scattering about as she continued to whine.

"What d'ya got there, girl? A gopher?" the husband said as he approached. Bending down to snap on her leash, he caught sight of a fragment of yellow cloth peeking through the dirt. Intrigued, he began to scrape away some of the loose gravel. When he finally understood what lay just beneath the surface, he jumped back in horror.

"What? What'd you find?" he heard his wife ask as she pushed her way through the bushes.

"Stay there!" he shouted, his voice rising in panic.

— —

The park rangers brought the police up the trail in their four-wheel-drives.

It took only a few minutes of careful digging to reveal the body of Jenna Perry lying twisted in a shallow grave, her blue bulging neck clearly broken. A dirty white espadrille still on her left foot.

As the SFPD helicopter droned overhead, the lieutenant in charge took out his cellular phone and punched in a set of numbers. "Patch me through to crime scene Alpha," he commanded.

— —

Lily sat on the top step of the staircase watching all these people in her house. Jane and Kenny were standing in the front doorway chatting with Lieutenant Spielman and Aaron Clark-Weber. Her father was on the phone across the room, near the telescope, talking to his mother in Florida in a low hushed voice.

Through the upstairs window, Lily spotted something moving very fast. It was Ozzie Castillo running across the lawn with a portable phone in his hand. Peering between the rails of the banister, Lily saw him race up and hand the phone to the lieutenant. Taking the phone, he spoke in a whisper, then listened. "Shit," she thought she heard him say. The lieutenant turned to huddle with Jane and Kenny, gesturing toward David.

Reading Jane's lips, Lily saw her say, "I'll go."

Standing up to get a better view, Lily watched as Jane crossed the room and said something to her father. He hung up the phone and Jane said something else. Then her father sagged and Jane reached out to steady him.

Her heart fluttering like a tiny trapped bird, Lily saw her father search the room with his eyes, until he looked up and found her. Then, with everyone stepping aside, Lily watched her father slowly walk through the room and, his eyes never leaving hers, climb the stairs. When he got to the top, he took her face in his hands, and she could see in his eyes what she had secretly known all along.

Her mother was dead.

"Oh, Lilliput," her father said.

21

It occurred to David that in buildings like these, the fluorescent lights were on all the time, day and night. Certainly down in the basement of this building where there were no windows, the humming greenish-white lights were never turned off.

He sat on an unforgiving black Formica chair, alone in a long corridor. Far off in some distant hallway a stairwell door opened and a couple of workers, unseen by David, joked their way up the stairs, their laughter curling through the silent vacuum of a government building at midnight.

Patrick Colomby had offered to come down here with him, but David had declined, not really thinking it through. He heard an elevator ping around the corner and listened as its doors slid apart and the soft fall of footsteps came his way. He wasn't expecting anyone and didn't bother to turn to see who it was. When he caught a glimpse of someone heading toward him, he looked up.

"Thought you might not want to go through this alone," Jane said as she approached.

"Thanks . . . I don't."

An interior door opened and a heavyset Asian woman motioned for them to come inside. David rose and smiled emptily at Jane. "Whew," he said, his nervous breath rushing out of him.

"You don't have to do this," Jane suggested.

David nodded. "Yes, I do."

He lowered his eyes and followed Jane into the main viewing room of the San Francisco City Morgue.

22

━ ─ ━

TO: Dr. Anthony Tedesco
   Chief Medical Examiner
   City of San Francisco

FROM: Dr. Tina Wong
   Asst. M.E.

DATE: September 8, 1997

RE: Jenna Maxwell Perry, deceased

Positive identification was made of Jenna Maxwell Perry, female Caucasian, age 35 yrs., 7 months, DOB 3/15/61, DOD 9/7–8?/97, by David Stephen Perry, age 39, husband of the deceased. This affirmation occurred at 11:55 P.M. on this day and was attested to in writing by Mr. Perry. Also present were myself and inspector Jane Marie Candiotti of the San Francisco Police Department.

Remains have been transferred to the County Coroner's Office.

cc: file

─ ─

Jane leaned against the far corner of the oversized elevator and thought about what had just happened. David stood at the wall by the button panel, looking at the lights as they flicked on and off during their ascent. It seemed like a hundred yards from where Jane stood to where David was. Although Jane had been on this elevator dozens of times, it just now dawned on her why it needed to be so cavernous: most of its passengers were on unpadded stainless-steel gurneys, riding down to their last encounter with a system that had watched over their lives from birth.

In the viewing room, when the assistant medical examiner had asked David if he wouldn't rather look at a Polaroid to identify his wife, David had looked at Jane, his eyes begging for a way to make this move faster. "Tina, Mr. Perry would like to see his wife personally," she had said, infusing her voice with just the right amount of official police authority.

"You got it, Inspector," Tina had said as she lifted the faded yellow sheet and revealed Jenna Perry's body, exposed from the shoulders up.

A tiny choked sob had caught in David's throat as he reached out to touch his wife's damaged neck with the back of his fingers. "Poor baby," he had said, bending down to kiss her, first on the forehead, then on the lips, and finally on the tip of her nose—as if he were merely saying good night as she fell asleep.

And then, in the comedy of errors that seems to occur in peak moments of crisis, nobody had had a pen. David could not sign the affidavit of identification. Unnerved, Tina had pulled the sheet back up to cover Jenna and scurried from the room, leaving Jane and David alone with the body for the eternity of half a minute until, breathless, she returned with a blue ballpoint and David signed the document.

Yes, it was his wife. Yes, the body, the person, beneath that yellow sheet, on that cold steel bed, was Jenna Susan Maxwell Perry.

The elevator slid to a stop at the parking level and the doors parted. But David Perry just stood there, as if anchored in place by the weight of his grief. Jane stepped forward and gently put a hand on his shoulder.

"How you doing, Mr. Perry?"

"I'm . . . I'm not sure."

Ushered by her, he passed through the cement-grey corridor to the parking garage. "Nobody should have to go through what you just did," Jane said, rummaging in her bag for her car keys.

"Y'know," David began, "in the deepest, darkest, most secret corners of a marriage, in the place you never want to go in your head, you think about stuff like this. What will it be like when . . . someday . . . my wife dies? Someday years from now." He shook his head. "And the thought is so awful that you push it from your brain."

They arrived at David's BMW. "Look, Mr. Perry . . ." Jane started to say.

"David."

"David. The best thing to do is exactly what you're doing."

"Which is?"

"Talking about it," Jane said. "The stuff you keep inside turns into pain, and the pain turns into poison."

David unlocked his car with his remote. "And what makes you so smart about this stuff?"

"I'm a cop. I've seen a shitload of pain out there," Jane said quietly. Holding her key ring in her teeth, she fished in her bag until she found a card and handed it to David. "You ever need to unload, give me a call. I'm a good listener."

David took the card. "Thanks, Inspector." Slipping it into his pocket, he let out a little laugh. "It's kind of ironic . . ." he began.

"What is?"

"I'm heading home now to spend the night with my daughter in the house my wife threw me out of. Life's a bitch, huh?"

"Life's a motherfucker," Jane agreed. "See you downtown tomorrow. Want me to send someone to pick you up?"

"Nah, I can handle it." He pulled open the car door and started to get in. "Inspector Candiotti . . ." David said.

"Yes?"

"Thank you so much for coming down here tonight. It . . . it made a difference. I won't forget your generosity."

Jane wanted to say something like "It's my job." But she just smiled and said, "You're welcome, David," and trudged up the incline toward her car.

23

CLARISSA ROSE GETHERS

PI BETA PHI

STANFORD UNIVERSITY

PALO ALTO, CALIFORNIA

Dear Lily,

It's almost midnite and my Mom and Dad just called to tell me about what happened to your mother and I hope it's not too late to send this fax.

I'm *so* sorry.

I know this must really be hard on you. I can't imagine what it would be like if one of my parents died.

Lily, I've known you since you were a little kid, and you've always been so special. Bright and funny. Kind and generous. But now it's time for you to take. Accept the love and strength offered to you by your father, your friends, your aunts and uncles . . . and me.

I'll be up next month for my birthday and I'll call you. If you want, we can get together. Maybe we can even go for a ride over the bridge and have lunch in Sausalito. But basically, we can just be together.

Take care, Lily . . . and know that you are loved.

Clarissa

P.S.: See you soon.

— —

Jane stood outside the interrogation room watching through the one-way glass as David rose to shake hands with Kenny and Lieutenant Spiel-

75

man. "That the husband?" Finney asked as he came up behind her, finishing off a bag of Famous Amos.

"Yeah, Moby. That's the husband," Jane replied to his reflection without turning. Finney shrugged and moved on.

Lieutenant Spielman switched on the reel-to-reel tape recorder. "Nine September 'ninety-seven," he said into the microphone. "Present are myself, Lieutenant Benjamin Spielman, Inspector First Class Kenneth Marks of this precinct, and David Perry, the husband of the deceased, Jenna Maxwell Perry." Then, pushing the microphone to the center of the table, Lieutenant Spielman addressed David. "Mr. Perry. There's every indication that this was a follow-home assault perpetrated upon your wife, but we still need to ask you a few questions."

David surveyed the room, its institutional blandness. "I understand."

Kenny took off his jacket and draped it over the back of a chair. "Sir, did your wife have any enemies that you know of? Anyone who would want to cause her harm?"

"No," David said. Being an attorney, he knew enough to just play it straight without embellishing matters. The cops had a sense of where they were going with this line of questioning, and David was perfectly content to let them get there.

"No one?" Kenny continued. "No crank phone calls? No Peeping Toms? Nothing unusual at all?"

David tilted his head back and stared at the ceiling as he tried to recall. "Not that I know of, Inspector."

Kenny nodded, rocking his head back and forth, pretending to formulate the next question. But everyone in the room knew it was all part of the act. Kenny had known what the next question would be when he and Jane had prepared for this session hours before. "Mr. Perry, you say you were separated from your wife. Had she been unfaithful to you?"

Narrowing his eyes, David held Kenny's unwavering stare. Then he broke it off and looked directly into the mirror. Directly at Jane. Although she, better than anyone, knew he couldn't see her, she found herself looking away, avoiding David's eyes.

As she did, she noticed the smell of cigarettes. Sally Banks had just stepped up beside her and was looking in at David. "Cheryl said he was cute, but—" Jane cut her off with a glare and turned back to the glass, waiting for David's answer.

"Yes, she had been unfaithful to the marriage," David finally answered.

"Is it possible she had more than one lover?" Kenny pressed.

"It's possible, but I think there was only one."

"Do you know his name?"

David looked to Lieutenant Spielman, imploring him for an explanation.

"I know this is indelicate, Mr. Perry," Lieutenant Spielman said. "But we all want the same thing here: to find whoever killed your wife."

David poured himself a cup of water. "Yes. His name is Elliot Sanders." He laughed weakly. "An old friend of the family."

"Thank you," Kenny said, moving on. He glanced at Lieutenant Spielman, then back to David. "And where were you the evening of your wife's abduction?"

"Working at my office until around midnight. Then home in my condo."

"Any witnesses to that fact?"

"Yes, of course." The irritation crept into David's voice. "What is this?"

Lieutenant Spielman crossed the room and stood next to Kenny, as if to show solidarity in this unsavory procedure. "You stand to inherit a considerable amount of money from your wife's estate, Mr. Perry. I'm sure you can understand that a good cop would find that provocative. Well, Inspector Marks is that good cop."

Kenny glanced through the one-way to where Jane always stood during interrogations, then he turned back to David. "Mr. Perry. We think you should call your lawyer."

David half rose from his chair. "Why?"

"We want you to take a lie detector test."

24

— —

FD-498 (Rev. 6-24-87)

POLYGRAPH REPORT

DATE OF REPORT: 9.10.97
DATE OF EXAMINATION: 9.10.97
BUREAU FILE NUMBER: 41K-SF-742263
FIELD FILE NUMBER: 41K-SF-742263
FIELD OFFICE: San Francisco, California
EXAMINEE NAME: Perry, David Stephen
CASE SYNOPSIS: Examinee's wife, Jenna Maxwell Perry, was kidnapped and murdered 9.7/8.97. It is at the request of Lieutenant Benjamin Spielman (SFPD, Homicide) that this polygraph test be administered.

On 9.10.97, Examinee arrived at the Nineteenth Precinct Station House of the SFPD. Purpose of the examination is to determine if Examinee was or was not involved in the kidnap and/or murder of the above-named deceased.

QUESTIONS

1. **Q:** Are you sometimes known as David?
   A: Yes.

2. **Q:** Regarding the kidnapping and murder of your wife, do you intend to be completely truthful with me about that?
   A: Yes.

3. **Q:** Are you convinced that I won't ask you any surprise questions on this test?
   A: Yes.

4. **Q:** Did you kidnap your wife?
   A: No.

5. **Q:** Did you murder your wife?
   A: No.

6. **Q:** Have you ever broken the law?
   A: Yes.

7. **Q:** Did you kidnap your wife?
   A: No.

8. **Q:** Did you hire anyone to murder your wife?
   A: No.

9. **Q:** Do you have a valid California driver's license?
   A: Yes.

CONCLUSION

It is the conclusion of this examiner that the recorded responses are indicative of truthfulness on the part of the examinee.

Signed: Alejandro Rivera, examiner.

25

Lieutenant Spielman came up to David after the session and offered his hand. "Thank you for your cooperation, Mr. Perry. This isn't easy for any of us." He indicated Jane and Kenny standing at a respectful distance against the far wall.

"I know that, Lieutenant," David acknowledged, as he rolled down his sleeves.

"Anything else?" Patrick Colomby asked.

Kenny glanced at Jane and stepped forward. "Yes, Mr. Colomby. Please make sure your client informs us of any travel plans that would take him out of the city for the next little while."

Patrick, some four inches taller than Kenny, leaned in close. "My client will travel wherever and whenever he chooses, Inspector. If that poses a problem for you, I suggest you speak with your superiors." Taking David's elbow, he turned and started to walk away.

"I only asked you to inform us," Kenny began, his face flushing. "Nobody said anything about preventing Mr. Perry from going . . ." He paused to find just the right inflection. ". . . 'wherever and whenever he chooses.' "

Jane found herself inching forward as Patrick stopped and turned back to Kenny. "What is it about you people," he asked disdainfully, "that always has to have the last word?"

From his desk across the room, Ozzie Castillo looked up from the burglary report he was filing. He surveyed the bullpen. Everyone was watching.

Kenny was starting to close the space between them when Lieutenant Spielman put a hand on his shoulder. "Be assured, Mr. Colomby," he said, "that we people will do everything we can to find Mrs. Perry's killer. Thanks again for all your help."

With a curt nod to the polygraph technician and to Jane, Patrick led

80

David out of the room. Jane watched as David, his head bowed, almost walked into the ladder of a heating repairman. At the last instant, Patrick gave him a little tug and David avoided a collision.

"I want you two to keep loose tabs on Mr. Perry," Lieutenant Spielman instructed as he scanned the polygraph readout. "Check in every once in a while on his financial transactions, his comings and goings, the whole bit."

"It would be a pleasure," Kenny said, still agitated over his encounter with Patrick Colomby.

"Jesus, you guys!" Jane said, her face reddening. "What would you do if he'd failed the polygraph?"

"Arrest his ass," Lieutenant Spielman answered quickly. Then, his voice softening, he went on, "Take it easy Jane. It's just procedure. You know that."

"Yeah, you're right," she sighed, glancing at Kenny. "Sorry. It's just that . . . I'm the one who had to tell him that his wife was dead."

Lieutenant Spielman nodded. "Not exactly in the job description, huh?"

"Not exactly."

With a sympathetic nod, Lieutenant Spielman turned and left the room. Jane gathered up her notes and looked to Kenny. "I gotta learn to not get so involved in these things."

"Then what were you doing down at the M.E.'s last night?"

"Huh?"

"Report has you in the room for the IDing of the body."

"Not that it's any of your business," Jane began, not sure where this was going, "but I overheard David . . . Mr. Perry tell his lawyer back at the house that he wanted to do it alone." She crossed to the door. "I thought it might be a mistake for him to be by himself. So I went down there. Simple as that."

"Sort of the Mother Teresa of the SFPD?"

"Knock it off, Kenny," Jane said forcefully. "Go use your considerable detecting gifts where they're needed. Like, I don't know . . ." She smiled to signal the cessation of potential hostilities. ". . . solving a crime or something. Okay?"

They stepped out into the bullpen.

"Only if I get to shoot someone."

"Maybe if you're good. So, we out of here?" Jane asked as she headed toward her desk.

"Gimme a minute," Kenny said, turning in the other direction. "I'll catch up to you."

— —

Officer Finney tipped the jumbo Coke back and drained the cup. Putting it down, he picked up another cup of similar capacity and set to emptying it of its contents as he sat in his tiny cubicle, engrossed in a manila folder. Kenny's face appeared over the top edge of the cubicle and startled him.

"Watcha up to, Moby?"

"Oh, hey, Inspector," Finney said, holding up the *Car & Driver* he had hidden in the folder. "Checkin' out a new van for the wife."

"She's a lucky woman," Kenny said as he came around to Finney's chair.

This, as did all jokes about Finney's weight, appetite, or laziness, failed to do any damage as it sailed unnoticed over his head. "Thanks," he said.

Kenny dropped a file on top of the magazine. "If you can find the time in your capacity as communications liaison, I need you to do a little background on our Mr. Perry." He spoke slowly, as if to a child. "Check out his law school, past employment, social clubs . . . the whole deal." Then, lowering his voice and stealing a look over his shoulder, he added, "And while you're at it, take a peek into the life and times of Patrick Colomby, too."

"And you would want this when?" Finney asked, his face screwing up at the prospect of having to do two things in the same day.

"The word 'soon' comes to mind," Kenny said as he backed out of the cubicle and crossed toward Jane's desk. He dug out his car keys and held them up to her. "Still waiting for you, Inspector," he teased, heading for the stairway.

Jane raced to catch up with him as he opened the fire door at the top of the stairwell. "Weren't you just the least bit rough on Mr. Perry today?"

"Actually," Kenny said as they started down the steps to the garage, "I thought I was kinda great. You were a bit easy on him, though."

Stopping on the landing, where Sally Banks was finishing a cigarette, Jane turned to Kenny. "The man's wife was murdered!"

Hastily stomping on her cigarette, Sally scooted up the stairs. Kenny gave her enough time to make her getaway before saying, "Estranged wife. And, any way you slice it, your Mr. Perry is in for a ton of money thanks to the late Mrs. Perry."

Jane leaned on the handrail. "I don't know. There's something about this case."

A soft laugh escaped from Kenny. "Don't you mean this guy? C'mon, he's good-looking, he's rich, and . . . now he's single."

It was all Jane could do to keep from hitting Kenny. "Tell me you're kidding."

"Only mostly."

"You are really an asshole," Jane seethed as she stormed back up the stairs.

Kenny, instantly regretting how far he had pushed her, called out, "Jane! Come back! I really was kidding, okay?"

Ripping open the fire door, Jane spit back, "I'm taking a cab." She whammed the door closed with a resounding thud.

26

J ane caught a ride to Mount Tamalpais the next morning with Sally Banks. Not really feeling like talking, she rocked silently with the car's gentle motion as it climbed the mountain trail.

"Thanks for the lift, Sal," she said as they pulled up near the site of Jenna Perry's shallow grave.

"Want me to hang?"

"Nah," Jane said as she got out. "I'll bum a ride."

As Sally backed her squad car down the dirt path, Jane pushed through the scrub growth and came upon a crime scene in the midst of a full-scale forensics investigation. Fingerprint techs, tire and footprint specialists, even a K-9 patrol had all converged on the clearing.

Aaron Clark-Weber was down on one knee, magnifying specs over his regular glasses. He carefully whisked at a small object with a thin artist's paintbrush and, determining that it was just a pebble, tossed it into a pile and picked up another.

"Hey, Aaron," Jane said as she came up behind him.

Turning to see Jane approach, Aaron smiled. He pushed his magnifying specs on top of his head and rose. "Hey, Inspector," he said as he shook the numbness out of his bad knee.

Jane looked down to the slight depression in the ground. "This it?"

"Yeah," Aaron nodded. "Not much of a final resting place, is it?"

"Not hardly," Jane said as she squatted down. She sat on her haunches for a moment, then placed the palm of her hand on the dirt in the middle of what had been Jenna Perry's grave. Closing her eyes, she tried to feel for the intangible, for whatever secrets this dreadful place might yield. Then, dusting off her hands, she stood up. "What do you have so far?"

"Coupla things," Aaron said as he pulled his notes from his coat pocket.

Jane nodded, prompting him to continue.

"Okay. One: Medical says she wasn't raped. Two: She was abducted, but the family was never contacted, so it wasn't for ransom." He looked up, and Jane motioned for him to go on. "Three: She was found still wearing an expensive pearl necklace, gold earrings, and her Rolex, so it wasn't even a robbery gone bad."

"What's it all tell us?"

"Basically," Aaron said, "this woman was assassinated."

Jane crossed to a folding table where plaster-of-Paris molds sat drying in the sun. "But why?"

"When we know the why," Aaron said as he joined her, "we'll be that much closer to knowing the who."

Jane indicated the various casts on the table. "Anything here?"

"From the boot prints we got," Aaron said as he carefully picked up a cast of a shoe impression, "we can establish that the killer was a big man. Over six feet and around two hundred pounds. The victim was five-three and weighed about half what her killer weighed." He put the mold back on the table. "She never had a chance."

"Anything special about the boot? Is it exotic or . . ."

"Nothing there," Aaron said. "It's from Sears. Probably the most common type of work boot out there."

Jane gestured to the other molds. "What about the tire stuff?"

"All different kinds up here," Aaron answered. "Mostly trucks, which isn't too surprising." He looked around at the rough terrain. "This isn't exactly the place you wanna take your Lexus."

Shaking her head, Jane sat on the back bumper of the forensics wagon. "You think it was just one killer?"

"Too soon to be positive," Aaron said. "But it looks that way."

Jane stayed there for a while, unable to chase away the image of Jenna Perry dying alone out here in the woods.

Suddenly cold in spite of the coming sun, Jane clutched her jacket close to her neck. "This is a shitty one, Aaron."

"As shitty as it gets," Aaron agreed.

"When can you release the site to my department?" Jane asked. "We need to do a grid-pattern search before any rain comes and washes away my precious little clues."

Aaron looked at his watch, then at his forensics team. "Can't say exactly. Definitely by morning, though. I'll post some patrol units over-night to make sure nothing is disturbed."

Jane nodded and started to say something else about how awful it must have been for Jenna, when she noticed Kenny headed her way. In spite of herself, she was glad to see him.

"Heard you were out here," he said as he came up. He nodded to Aaron, then turned to Jane and smiled a contrite smile. "Need a ride?"

Jane leaned into the familiar security of her partner. "Desperately."

"Sorry about yesterday," Kenny said as they crossed the clearing toward his Explorer. "I was completely out of line. Forgive me?"

Jane looked up to him, grateful beyond words that he had shown up when he had. Realizing that the trust they had built up, stone by stone, over the years was more important to her than anything else, she grinned and said, "You gonna quit driving like a teenager and start driving like a grown-up?"

"Promise."

"Then . . . I forgive you."

They arrived at the car. "Where to?" Kenny asked.

Jane opened her notebook. "Let's go talk to some of Jenna Perry's friends."

"Ooh, rich people. I love interviewing rich people," Kenny joked as they climbed in. "They're so . . . sincere when they talk to us poor old civil servants."

He dropped the car into gear and was about to blast out of there when he remembered his promise to Jane. Lightly touching the gas, he glided the Explorer down the dusty path to the main road.

"That's a good boy," Jane said.

27

*J*ane had felt pretty good when she left the house that morning. Seven hours sleep, her new gabardine suit, plus she was having a good hair day. Even Kenny, who was annoyingly blind to such things, commented as he dropped her at Maggie Donnelly's house before going off to interview another of Jenna Perry's friends.

"You losin' weight?" he asked, which was as close to a compliment as he could get.

"Maybe," Jane smiled as she took in the vastness of the Donnelly mansion. It was here that Jenna had partied the evening away the night she was murdered. "Some house, huh?"

"This is a house? I thought it was the Pentagon," Kenny said as he yanked on the gearshift. "See you in like half an hour."

Jane watched him drive down the street to another of Jenna's girl-friends who lived in a house only slightly less intimidating than this one. Brushing lint off the back of her arm, she rang the doorbell. Strains of a popular song chimed from deep within the house. Jane recognized it, but couldn't remember the name.

The heavy door was pulled open and an Asian houseboy greeted her. "Inspector Candiotti?"

"Yes. Miss Donnelly is expecting me."

He stepped aside for her to enter. "Please to come."

Jane passed through the massive doorway into the mahogany-trimmed entry hall. A chandelier the size of a fireworks explosion dominated the room. The houseboy saw Jane looking up. "It's Venetian," he offered. "Nineteenth-century."

"I was going to say Venetian."

"Yes. Miss Donnelly is by the pools." He led Jane through the reading parlor, the smoking parlor, and the sun parlor to the rear of the house. As they emerged into the sun-drenched gardens, Jane noticed two full-sized swimming pools on either side of a white cabana. She glanced at the houseboy.

"Freshwater and—" he began.

"—and saltwater?" Jane asked, half joking.

"And saltwater." He nodded to the cabana. "Miss Donnelly."

As Jane crossed the terrazzo tiles, shielding her eyes from the glare of the morning sun, she regretted having worn such a heavy suit. She felt the first cool tingle of sweat at the bottom of her neck and silently cursed herself for yet again failing to check the weather in the *Chronicle* before leaving the house.

Maggie Donnelly leaned against the far corner of the cabana, sunglasses on top of her head. Her silk suit, the color of mocha, hugged her exquisitely sculpted body like a caress. "Iced tea?" she asked as Jane came in from the light. "Or something with a little more personality?"

"Tea's good," Jane said as she took in the scene. The couches out here were more expensive than the one in her living room. When Maggie bent over slightly to pour the tea, Jane glanced down the open front of her blouse. Boob job, she found herself thinking.

"Sugar or Sweet 'n Low?" Maggie offered as she handed Jane her drink.

"Neither," Jane said. "I'll rough it."

Maggie smiled and sat on the arm of the couch. As she did, Jane saw that her lips were a little red and puffy. Collagen injections, Jane mused. Shaking her head, she knew she had to chase these distractions out of her mind or she'd be completely useless.

But she couldn't help it. How did a woman get to be this beautiful and this rich? Jane could see that she had had help with the beautiful part, but a little pre-interview digging had shown her that Maggie Donnelly had amassed her own considerable fortune in real estate and the stock market. Rich, beautiful, and smart.

Jane hated her.

"How can I help you, Lieutenant?" Maggie asked, crossing her legs, letting a sandal dangle.

"It's Inspector, Miss Donnelly," Jane said as she took out her notebook. Flipping it open, she pretended to find her place, using the pause to equal the playing field a bit.

"First of all," she began, "I know that Jenna Perry was a good friend of yours and I'm sorry for your loss."

"She was my best friend," Maggie said.

"I'll just ask you a few brief questions, then I'll let you get back to . . ." Jane looked around. ". . . whatever I interrupted you from."

"Take your time, Inspector."

"Mrs. Perry was at a party here the night she was murdered." Jane saw Maggie's lips crinkle into a frown. "Did she arrive or leave with anyone?"

"No. She came alone, stayed a couple of hours, and left by herself." Jane made a note. "And you're certain?"

"Yes." Maggie sipped iced tea that Jane suspected probably wasn't all ice and all tea. "I greeted her at the door when she got here and saw her off myself later that night." She took off her jacket and draped it over the back of one of the couches.

"Uh-huh," Jane said as she scribbled something down. "Was there anyone at your party who might have bothered Jenna? Maybe followed her home?"

Maggie shook her head. "No. It was just a friendly dinner party." She stood up and unbuttoned her blouse, revealing a deeply tanned body beneath her white bikini bra. Stepping out of her sandals, she lowered her silk pants and let them fall into a puddle of pool water, where they turned from mocha to a darker shade of coffee. Jane waited to see if she was going to let these very expensive pants just lie in the water. She was.

Maggie stepped out of the cabana and into the sun. Squinting, Jane followed. "Just a few more questions, then you can take your swim."

"Take your time, Inspector," Maggie said as she sat on an upholstered chaise. She had situated herself in such a position that Jane had to look into the sun as they talked.

Jane walked around the chaise, putting the sun on her already sweaty back. "We're all aware that the Perrys were having marital problems. Did Jenna have a lover that you know of?"

Jane had maneuvered herself so Maggie would have to turn and look directly into the sun when she answered. But she responded without looking at Jane.

"Yes."

"Do you know who that lover is?"

"Yes."

"Can you tell me his name?"

Maggie pulled her sunglasses down onto her eyes and looked at Jane. "But you already know his name, don't you?"

The doorbell chimed its familiar tune again, and Jane could see the houseboy passing by the sun parlor windows.

Jane shrugged. "I'm just looking for corroboration."

"Fine then. It was Elliot Sanders," Maggie said. "A nice guy. A great fuck. But he didn't kill Jenna."

"How do you know?"

"Because, Inspector," Maggie said, "he loved her too much."

Jane saw the houseboy pull open the tall glass doors. "And how do you know he's such a great fuck?"

"Maybe Jenna told me." Maggie smiled cryptically.

The houseboy stepped onto the verandah and announced, "An Inspector Marks for Inspector Candiotti."

"My ride," Jane said, closing her notebook.

"Fine then." Maggie stood up. "I'll see you out."

"That's very gracious, but it won't be necessary," Jane said. "Thank you for your time."

"Not at all," Maggie said as she watched Jane cross the verandah and follow the houseboy inside. Then she fortified her iced tea and sat wearily on the couch, knowing that this would be yet another day in which she would get nothing done.

Kenny stood in the entry hall, his neck craning as he looked up at the chandelier. He lowered his gaze as Jane and the houseboy came in.

"Nice light," he said.

"It's Venetian," Jane said as the houseboy opened the door for them. They were just about to step outside when Jane stopped and asked, "The song the doorbell plays, it's driving me crazy. What is it?"

" 'The Way We Were,' " the houseboy said as he closed the door.

— —

"Your Miss Donnelly is sure a fine-looking specimen," Kenny said as they climbed into the Explorer.

"She's the poster child for silicone and collagen," Jane said. "You like that stuff?"

"All I said was she's good-looking," Kenny protested. "It's not like I want to take her home to Mommy." He started the car. "Other than the chemistry lesson, you learn anything in there?"

Jane checked her notebook. "I think it's time to visit Jenna Perry's boyfriend."

Kenny pulled onto the street. "A Mr. Elliot Sanders, as I recall."

"The same." Jane turned a page. "His office is in the city. Corner of Clay and Montgomery. Why does that sound so familiar?"

"It's the Transamerica Building," Kenny answered, nodding to the skyline before them.

Jane spotted the trademark pyramid of the Transamerica Building in the financial district. "I've hated that building since the day it was built."

"Yeah," Kenny agreed. "It's sort of the Fuck You school of architecture."

"Think we should call ahead to Mr. Sanders?"

"He's got the bad taste to work in that building," Kenny smiled, "we can have the bad taste to walk in on him without an appointment."

"Good point," Jane said as Kenny gunned the engine and they sped off down the hill.

28

There was no secretary to greet them when Jane and Kenny arrived at the offices of Elliot Sanders & Associates, Investment Counseling, on the thirty-ninth floor of the Transamerica Building. No secretary, no water cooler, no plants, no pictures on the walls.

"Must be one of those Art of the Deal minimalist guys," Kenny said.

The door to the inner office opened and Elliot Sanders stepped out. "Can I help you?"

He was a small man, compact, with thick red hair. Jane found herself thinking about what Maggie Donnelly had said about his performance in bed.

"I'm Inspector Candiotti, and this is Inspector Marks," Jane said after the slightest pause. "We're from the Homicide Division of SFPD. Mind if we ask you a few questions?"

Elliot's shoulders sagged slightly. "About Jenna?"

Jane took out her notebook. "Yes, sir. About Mrs. Perry."

Stepping aside, Elliot motioned for them to enter his office. "Come in."

The office was small, but the view of the bay and the Golden Gate Bridge was unobstructed.

"Great view," Kenny observed as he sat on the couch.

"Never a bad day up here," Elliot offered. "No matter what the weather."

"You just moving in?" Jane asked as she sat on the arm of the couch, next to Kenny.

"Moving out," Elliot answered. "I've had a rough go lately."

Kenny put his foot on the edge of the glass coffee table. "What about your 'associates'?"

"You're looking at them. I'm Elliot Sanders and I'm the associates."

Jane leaned forward. "Mr. Sanders, we have corroborated testimony that you and Jenna Perry were . . . involved romantically."

Elliot sat heavily in his desk chair. "It was the worst-kept secret in town."

"How long had you been seeing each other?" Kenny asked.

"Almost a year." Elliot's eyes grew moist. "We started up a couple of months after her father died. He was killed in that plane crash in Monterey."

"We know," Kenny said.

"Anyway," Elliot continued, "her marriage was in trouble and mine was falling apart. We had known each other for years. I guess she was needy and I was lonely and we just . . . got together."

"Sir," Jane began softly, "did you love her?"

"Very much," Elliot said, his gaze drifting out the window. "I'm really going to miss this view."

"It is beautiful," Jane agreed. "Did Mrs. Perry love you?"

Elliot Sanders brought his attention back to Jane. "She did at the beginning. But when her husband found out about us and then my wife got wind of it, Jenna just stopped seeing me." He snapped his fingers. "Like that."

Kenny rose and stood against the window, trying to keep Elliot focused. "And were you angry at her for breaking off with you so suddenly?"

"I was more hurt than angry," Elliot began. And then it dawned on him. "Wait a minute. You're not accusing me of killing her, are you?"

"We're just asking questions here, Mr. Sanders," Jane said.

"But as long as we are," Kenny said, "where were you on the night she was murdered?"

Elliot Sanders pursed his lips and shook his head. "I was at a Boy Scout Jamboree with my sons. My wife threw me out after she learned about Jenna. I missed my boys terribly. No way I was going to miss that Jamboree."

"Any witnesses that can place you there?" Jane asked.

"Yeah. My two sons and about fifteen hundred other people."

Jane looked to Kenny. "Anything else?"

Kenny shook his head and turned to Elliot. "Thank you for your cooperation, Mr. Sanders."

He and Jane started to leave, then Jane turned back to Elliot. "Please indulge me a little speculation. It's my job," she said with a disarming shrug. "But is it possible, sir, that you were hurt and angry enough to hire someone to maybe frighten Mrs. Perry and, through no fault of your own, it got out of hand?"

Jane and Kenny studied Elliot's face as he answered. "I'm not offended by the question, Inspector. I hope you're this thorough with everyone you talk to and that you find Jenna's killer." He opened the outer door. "But, no. It's not possible."

Kenny stepped into the hallway. "Why not?"

"First of all, because I'm not that kind of guy. And secondly, I'm broke. I can't afford this office—I can't even afford the newspaper anymore." He looked at his name on the door. "Heh, a bankrupt investment counselor. Some fuckin' mess I've made, huh?"

"Thanks again for your time, Mr. Sanders," Jane said as she joined Kenny in the hall.

They walked down the plushly carpeted corridor to the elevator bank.

"Y'know," Kenny said, "I almost feel sorry for the guy."

The elevator arrived with a muffled ping and they got on.

"Almost, but not quite," Jane agreed as she pushed the button for the lobby.

29

David Perry quietly pushed open the door to Lily's room. It was eight in the morning and she'd had a terrible night.

Patrick Colomby and the others from the office had stayed until after midnight. Then David had talked with his mother in Florida until the sun came up on her and, worn out, she had gone to bed.

David, finding himself a stranger in his own house, had wandered the rooms for hours, first upstairs, then downstairs, through the small dark hours of the night.

Lying on the couch, a glass of tequila and ice on the coffee table beside him, he had stared at the ceiling, and his mind had filled with the photographs of his life. His childhood in San Francisco, undergrad and law school at UCLA. His time as an arrogant, headstrong young prosecutor.

He remembered meeting Jenna one Thanksgiving at his old college roommate's house up in Tiburon. Their courtship, their wedding at Grace Cathedral, their honeymoon. An entire month alone in a villa on the west coast of Italy, thanks to Graham Maxwell.

He lay there on the couch the rest of the night, watching the inky blackness of the ceiling turn to grey. He had heard the first tentative chirps of the birds awakening in the elm tree out front. The thud of the newspapers landing on his doorstep. The cars starting down the street.

He had showered and made a few calls to the East. And after breakfast, he had checked on Lily. She was still mercifully asleep.

— —

Jane sat on the open tailgate of the Explorer watching Kenny address the Police Academy volunteers. She smiled to herself as she remembered how much Kenny had been looking forward to this morning. It was a chance for him to be in charge of a major crime scene and fifty subordinates, and he had been excited at the prospect.

She took a swig from her water bottle and grinned. Must be a guy thing, she mused.

"Okay, most of you know the drill," Kenny shouted as the police cadets, in blue jumpsuits, and the Explorer Scouts, in beige jumpsuits, pulled on their rubber gloves and huddled in the cool morning mist. "The body of the female Caucasian was found right there." He indicated with the toe of his hiking boot. "We've kept this area under surveillance in the hope the killer might return to the scene. He didn't. And that's why you're here graciously donating your Saturday morning to the city of San Francisco—whose citizens, as soon as they wake up, will be most grateful to you, I'm sure. So, it's up to us to do a grid-pattern sweep of this entire area, looking for clues, looking for anything."

The searchers, most in their teens or twenties, were eager to get started, each hopeful that he or she would be the one to unearth something that would crack the case. "Your group leaders will assign grid zones to you, and you will then fan out at double arm's length and walk in step while scanning the ground, the brush, and the trees. If you find something, there are a number of things to remember."

Kenny ticked them off on his fingertips. "One, first and foremost: Don't touch it! Let me say that again: Don't touch it!" He glanced over to Jane. She smiled her approval, and he went on, "Two: I don't care if it's a broken beer bottle or a pile of raccoon shit—use your whistle and call for your team leader to look at it and, if necessary, to photograph it, tag it, and bag it."

Kenny crossed to a contour map of the area and used his pen as a pointer. "This is the site of the shallow grave where our victim was found. She died of asphyxiation brought on by strangulation. She also had a broken neck. Her mouth, hands, and legs were bound with duct tape. But we have, as yet, been unable to lift any fingerprints of the assailant, so we figure he was probably wearing gloves. Therefore, we would really love to find some gloves out here. Or duct tape. Or anything else not usually found in nature."

A small commotion drew everyone's attention to the underbrush near the hiking trail. Four mounted police officers, their horses snorting clouds of steam, emerged and clopped over to the command center. "Sorry we're late," the lead sergeant apologized to Kenny. "Van wouldn't start."

"Welcome to the San Francisco Police Department," Kenny said. "I'll brief you guys in a minute." He turned back to the other searchers. "Okay, team leaders! Make sure everybody has a whistle, rubber gloves, and a full canteen! Fan your squads into their grids and get them started!"

As the recruits and Scouts formed up and began their search, Kenny tilted his head back to address the cops on horseback. "This is the Jenna Perry discovery site. You guys all have grid search experience, so I don't need to drag you through it. Why don't you each take a quadrant and oversee our police babies? Y'know, kinda keep them from contaminating the stuff they find, keep 'em moving, the whole bit."

"You got it, Inspector," the sergeant said. He led the two other male riders and one female rider into the search area.

Kenny joined Jane at the Explorer and caught her looking at him with smiling eyes. "What?" he asked as he took a pull from her water bottle.

"Nothing," Jane said. "It's just that you look like you're enjoying yourself out here. That's all."

"You know what?" Kenny said. "I guess I am."

The shrill summons of a whistle cut the air. Kenny motioned for the photographer to follow him as he and Jane ran to where a young Hispanic Explorer Scout was standing, her finger pointing to a torn strip of yellow police tape. Glancing at Jane for sympathy, Kenny said to the Scout, "Good work. We'll take care of this. You guys keep going."

As the others spread out, Jane laughed. "You said it yourself: not found in nature." She picked up the tape and put it in her pocket.

"Yeah, I'm the schmuck," Kenny admitted.

After a few hours, the sun working its way through the clinging morning mist and warming the meadow, the searchers had covered almost the entire primary target area. At first the whistle calls had come every few minutes. A Colorado license plate, a guitar pick, a crushed Dixie cup, an unused condom, a cigarette butt discarded by the police photographer, a torn paper plate, even a hoofprint from one of the police horses had all been either dismissed or placed into evidence bags.

"What d'ya think?" Kenny asked as he drained the last of the water from the bottle. "Time to send the puppies back to the kennel?"

Jane looked at her watch and shook her head in dismay. She had hoped that Jenna's killer had made a mistake, left something behind that could lead her back to him. "How 'bout another half hour?"

"Okay," Kenny agreed, although Jane could tell he thought it was useless. "If you think we . . ."

He was interrupted by the crackle of his police radio. "3H66, this is dispatch."

Kenny grabbed the microphone. "Dispatch, this is 3H66. Go ahead, Cheryl."

"Jane with you?"

"Yeah," Kenny said and handed her the mike.

Jane pressed the transmission button. "What's up, Cheryl?"

"I'm patching Ozzie through," Cheryl said. "Something big's going on around here."

There was a buzz of static, then Ozzie came on. "3P21 to 3H58. Jane?" The excitement in his voice was unmistakable.

"Here I am, Ozzie," Jane said as Kenny leaned in to listen.

"Jane, some lady in Chinatown called in a tip on the Jenna Perry murder. The lieutenant's rolling three units as we speak," Ozzie said. "He wanted me to let you know."

"We're on our way!" She turned to Kenny, but he was already racing to the driver's side of the Explorer. As Ozzie filled her in, Jane slammed the tailgate closed and Kenny backed up to let her in the passenger side.

"Hey, Nat!" Kenny shouted to the mounted police sergeant. "We got a tip we're gonna check out. Keep at it another half hour and fax your report to me!"

"You got it, Inspector!" Nat called from his horse. "Drive carefully!"

"You bet," Kenny said as he stomped on the gas and fishtailed across the dirt path to the main road.

30

Kenny squeezed the Explorer through the midmorning traffic on Bush Street and, two wheels up on the curb, cranked a hard right onto Waverly Place. Three squad cars fell in behind him and they caravaned through the narrow streets of Chinatown.

Jane pounded the dashboard with her fist. "C'mon. C'mon!" she implored. "I don't want to lose this guy!"

Kenny floored it and his car leaped forward, sending a delivery boy scurrying into a doorway. "How's my driving?" he asked, excitement shining in his eyes.

"Don't start with me," Jane cautioned as she scanned the addresses racing by. "There!" she yelled. "On the right!"

Kenny pulled the Explorer halfway onto the sidewalk, and, weapons drawn, he and Jane ran into Ang Zhu's Grocery Store. The other cop cars slid to screeching stops and a half-dozen officers piled out, Ozzie in the lead.

"The back room," Jane whispered as she and Kenny scurried past rows of flattened brown ducks and shark fins. They came to a corrugated metal door and stopped, one on either side, their pistols next to their faces. Kenny glanced down to a basket of snakes, gutted on pink ice.

"People eat this stuff?" he asked.

Shooting him a look, Jane said, "Okay, on my three. One, two . . ."

Before she could get to three, Kenny wheeled and kicked the door in. "SFPD!" he shouted as he stormed in.

Jane poured in after him just as Ozzie and his partner hustled up.

The room was dark, illuminated only by a small television playing cartoons.

A young Chinese woman jumped to her feet, her lip bleeding and her eye swollen. "Finally you here!"

"Where is he?" Jane hissed at her.

The woman pointed to a corner where a man was lying on a filthy mattress. Jane and Kenny, their bodies crouched in anticipation, inched forward. They advanced step by cautious step until they were next to him and could see that he was sleeping.

On a nod from Jane, Kenny reached down and ripped the blanket off the bed. Startled, the man bolted upright and blinked into the muzzles of the pistols pointed at his face.

"Aw, fuck," he said and started to lie back down.

Kenny grabbed him by the hair and threw him against the wall.

"That him! He kill rich lady!" the woman shrilled.

Jane and Kenny exchanged a look. This man was barely five feet tall. "What you want?" he demanded.

Jane leaned in. "Where were you the night of September seventh?"

"In jail," the man spit. "I get out this morning." He leveled a stare into Jane's eyes. "Check it out, bitch."

Kenny whammed him into the wall. "Show the lady some respect, son."

The Chinese woman pushed past Jane and started scratching at the man's back. "He no respect ladies! He no respect no one! He hit me all the time! You take him now!"

Jane gently guided the woman off to the side. "Did you tell me he killed the rich lady so we would take him away and he wouldn't hit you anymore?"

The woman sniffed back a sob.

Jane put her hand on the woman's shoulder. "I promise you we'll take him away if you tell me the truth. Did he kill the rich lady?"

"No, Miss." The woman bowed her head. "He in jail, like he say."

Jane drew in a deep breath and turned to Ozzie. "Oz, take him in. Battery, assault, anything else you can think of that'll stick."

As Ozzie stepped in, Jane motioned for Kenny to follow her out of there. As she did, she noticed that there was dirt under her fingernails.

Dirt from Jenna Perry's grave.

A crowd had gathered behind the squad car perimeter outside Ang Zhu's Grocery Store. Jane came out into the sunshine first, wiping her dirty hand on her handkerchief. Kenny caught up to her and, seeing that she was upset, opened the door to the Explorer for her.

Having raced around to the driver's side, he climbed in and started to nudge the car through the throng of people. They parted reluctantly, irritated at this intrusion into their world. Just as it seemed the way was clear, one man stood in front of the Explorer, his back to Kenny.

"C'mon, move it, buddy!" Kenny called out the window. But the man, his arm draped around the neck of a skinny Chinese girl, remained in place. Kenny tapped the horn, not wanting to get out to deal with this guy. Finally, the man stepped aside.

Free from the hold of the crowd, the Explorer tore away, brushing by the stubborn man.

Barton Hubble looked up and followed Kenny's car with angry eyes. Blinking through the blue exhaust, he wondered what all the commotion had been about.

31

It was the night Clarissa Gethers had been dreading: her twenty-first birthday.

As she drove her Mercedes up from Palo Alto, she hoped that, just this once, her parents would listen to her and allow this birthday to pass with relatively little fanfare. The one saving grace would be if he had gotten her letter and showed up. Even if it was only for a little while, she bargained, that would be enough.

She thought about how she measured her life by the number of lies she told each day. "I feel fine." "School's great." "I met this guy."

Just that morning, she had been in the second-floor bathroom with one of her roommates pretending she was having her period. She had put in a tampon and complained about cramps—even borrowing a couple of Advils.

But it had all been a charade. Another facet of the mask she wore.

The truth was, she had stopped menstruating almost four years ago. Not long after she had surrendered to the ritual of purging her meals.

When she got near the house, she stopped, her heart sinking. Even from the street Clarissa could see the enormous white tent rising like a hot-air balloon in the backyard. Four catering vans were in the driveway and a platoon of valet parking attendants waited at the curb. A reggae band was playing, its steel drums sending echoes of another world bouncing off the night sky.

As Clarissa pulled up to her house, a Land Cruiser arrived and two of her girlfriends emerged with their dates. Behind them, she could make out an old beau of hers handing his Porsche over to a parking attendant. Her parents would have been perfectly happy if she had married him when he had asked during her sophomore year. "God," she muttered, as she watched him tuck a gift under his arm and go in the front door. "Thanks for keeping it small like I asked."

Closing her eyes and trying to control her increasingly rapid breathing, Clarissa willed herself to pull up to the valet and make the best of the evening. "Easy now, girl," she whispered. "Last thing you need is an anxiety attack," she reminded herself, remembering what her psychiatrist had been saying to her all year. "It's only one night, just a couple of hours. And then it's over and you're out of here."

The parking attendant pulled her door open and handed her a pink claim check. "Welcome to Clarissa's big night," he said breezily.

"Thank you," she responded blankly as he jumped into her car and tore off down the hill.

Letting out every last ounce of breath in her body, daring to hope one last time that he'd be there, Clarissa Gethers walked up the driveway past the catering vans, through the front door, and into her big night.

— —

Lily lay in bed watching *Saturday Night Live,* the sounds of the party down the street pushing their way into her room. Clicking off the television, she fell back on her pillow. She was excited about spending the day with Clarissa tomorrow.

If her Dad said it was okay.

Clarissa's parents had invited David to the celebration, but, to Lily's disappointment, he had declined. It wouldn't be such a bad idea for him to go out at least once, she thought. And this was only a party down the street.

Lily looked over at her mother's swimming trophies that her father had moved into her room for her. After her mother's funeral, it had been pretty hard on both of them, Lily remembered, when she and her Dad had packed up all the clothes and shoes and stuff and given them to Pilar for her church. Some of her Mom's friends came by, and her Dad asked them to take whatever they wanted. But they didn't come around that much anymore. Just a phone call once in a while to see how they were doing.

Even at school it was pretty weird, Lily thought. Sometimes she would catch a couple of kids looking at her. Kids she didn't know. Or maybe she would hear a giggle as she walked by between classes. But Lily imagined that if some other girl's mother had been killed like hers, she'd probably steal a look or make a stupid joke too. It was just kids being kids.

Thank God for swimming. Those long hours of practice were her meditation, her time to think. She felt her body changing, lengthening. And her Dad said she looked more and more like her mother every day.

Outside, the music abruptly stopped, and Lily heard a couple of hundred voices sing an off-key chorus of "Happy Birthday." Then what seemed like dozens of cars all started up at the same time and the swinging arcs of a parade of headlights played across her ceiling in a procession of people departing.

Her mind and body now completely awake, Lily got out of bed and went down the hall to her father's bedroom. She peeked in through the slightly opened door and saw that he was asleep, the reading light still on, his glasses and laptop on the bed next to him.

Aware of a creeping loneliness rising in her chest, Lily thought about waking him. But he had been working so hard lately on that trial, and he really had been so great with her—taking her to school whenever he could, showing up for her swim meets. She decided to let him sleep.

Going downstairs, Lily took a Snapple from the refrigerator and padded over to her grandfather's telescope. She put her drink on the coffee table and pulled her stool in close. Reaching around to pop off the lens cover, Lily closed one eye and peered through the aperture. She fiddled with the focus and swiveled the scope's body around until she found what she was looking for.

The bridge.

— —

He never came.

It had been a party to make her parents proud, and Clarissa had done her best to enjoy it. But now that it was over and she had the back gardens all to herself, she finally understood how unhappy she really was.

Tonight, she vowed, there would be no more lies.

The low soothing call of a foghorn was carried up to her by the night wind off the bay. Looking out through a veil of tears, Clarissa saw the bridge, the Golden Gate Bridge, its arms open like an angel's wings.

— —

Finally tired enough to go to sleep, Lily finished off her Snapple and, after one more glimpse of the bridge through the telescope—very light traffic this late at night, she noted—she crossed the living room toward the stairs. Stopping to double-check that the front door was locked and the alarm was on, she was surprised to see, through the little inset window, Clarissa Gethers blasting down the hill in her Mercedes convertible.

Climbing the steps to her bedroom, Lily tried to imagine where in the world Clarissa was speeding off to so late and in such a hurry on her birthday.

32

Clarissa Rose Gethers
Pi Beta Phi
Stanford University
Palo Alto, California

Dear Mom and Dad,

It's not your fault.

The pain I'm in sometimes gets too big and I don't know any other way to make it go away.

I get so tired.

Please tell Grandma that I'm sorry.

My stuff should go to Cindy and Jennifer. And my car to cousin Jeff.

I have a safe deposit box in Palo Alto. It's at the Wells Fargo on McNamara Street and the number is G40104317. The key is Scotch-taped under the middle drawer of my desk at Pi Phi House.

It's just a bunch of photos and papers and things. Also Grandma's necklace is in there.

I try so hard to please you. But lately I feel so empty. So unimportant. I owe the framing place $104.00.

You're going to want to bury me with Grandpa and the others. I wish you would cremate me and scatter my ashes over the hills behind our Colorado place. But I know how much I've hurt you with this, so whatever you decide to do is fine.

106

I'm sorry for what you're going through right now.

Please remember me,

Clarissa—

Clarissa pulled her Mercedes into the mist-shrouded parking lot of Vista Point just below the Golden Gate Bridge's South Tower. Shivering in the cold, she turned to look at the car next to her. Two young lovers sat on the hood huddled beneath a blanket, their backs against the windshield as if at a drive-in theater. But all there was to see this night was a shaggy wall of fog.

Clarissa put the envelope in the glove compartment and got out of the car.

A freighter churned by, unseen in the vapor, its foghorn inquiring of the night. Clarissa closed her eyes, squeezing them tight as if to expel any equivocation, and, after a moment, started up the winding path toward the roadway.

The couple watched as she passed into the mist.

"That girl's not wearing a jacket," the boy said.

"Not my problem," answered the girl.

On the concourse above, Clarissa approached the South Tower, struggling to stay in the moment as car after car whapped by, tires shishing over the glistening pavement. After a few yards, she arrived at a gate, locked at night. Given the bridge's infamous history, it seemed sensible. A quick step onto the roadway—the horn of a speeding FedEx truck dopplering by—a little jump back onto the sidewalk, and she had defeated this meager attempt at security.

Pausing to peer up at the tower, rising seven hundred feet above the black ruffling waters of San Francisco Bay, she could barely make out the crimson pulse of the airway beacon.

Interesting, she mused. I always thought I'd be afraid when I finally came here.

Her resolve deepening with each step, she quickened her pace.

And then she was running, tears of gratitude and relief pooling in her eyes. Passing under the tower, she looked only ahead, drawn to the promise of peace.

She stopped at the bridge's center, her lungs aching, her breath coming in fragile gasps.

Clarissa leaned her forehead against the coolness of the bridge railing and caught her breath. Then she climbed onto the waist-high railing and lowered herself to the steel beam on the other side. Clutching the uprights behind her, she looked to the ocean below.

But there was only fog and the faint whisper of the freighter far off in the darkness.

A final serene smile curving her lips, Clarissa Gethers at last did what she had prayed for years she might one day have the strength to do.

She let go.

As she opened her arms, the wind caught her. Like a falling angel, she vanished into the silent cloud of fog.

33

D avid Perry, coming down the stairs in a T-shirt and sweatpants, stopped to watch as Lily scanned the bay with her telescope. "You're up early for a Sunday," he said as he came into the living room and, turning off the alarm, opened the front door.

"Couldn't sleep," Lily called over her shoulder.

Scooping up the *Chronicle* and *The New York Times,* David closed the door with his hip. "Man, I sure could. I think I fell asleep with the light on again."

"You did."

Pouring some coffee from the automatic maker, David crossed past the breakfast nook to gaze out at the bay. A delta of brown pelicans, their prehistoric profiles graceful in flight, rode the updrafts as they chased a small flotilla of fishing boats under the bridge. "Should I be concerned about you not sleeping, Lilliput?"

"Nah. It was just one of those nights. You know, with the party and everything." The truth was, she had gotten up early to wait for Clarissa's call.

David moved to her and kissed the back of her sweet-smelling hair. he leaned into him to acknowledge his affection, but stayed glued to the view through her telescope.

"How's traffic on the bridge?" David asked, slipping into their familiar routine.

"That's the thing. It's like totally screwed, Dad. There must be a major accident or something, 'cause the cars aren't moving at all."

"Lemme see," David said, changing places with her.

Before he could peer into the eyepiece, he was distracted by someone running through the back gardens. As if being chased by some invisible predator, Pilar raced around the pool and through the back door into the house. At first, Lily thought Pilar was in such a hurry because it was so cold outside. Then she saw that Pilar was crying.

David stood up. "Pilar, what is it?"

Fighting to catch her breath between sobs, Pilar managed to say, "Oh, Mr. Dave. It's too terrible. Carmen just called. It's on the TV!"

Carmen was the Gethers housekeeper, a woman from Mexico City with whom Pilar had spent many hours on their days off. David grabbed up the remote and clicked on the small white television in the breakfast nook.

As the picture resolved into clarity, the three of them immediately recognized an image that was as much a part of their lives as their own reflections: the Golden Gate Bridge. A handsome young reporter from KGO—the word "Live" floating in the bottom right corner of the screen—spoke excitedly into his remote camera from the bridge's roadway.

". . . all night to recover the body. Clarissa Gethers of the prominent Gethers sugar family had turned twenty-one only yesterday . . ."

"Pobrecita," Pilar whispered, crossing herself.

David looked over to Lily, but she was already back at the telescope, pivoting it on its fulcrum until she found what she was looking for. Because her back was to her father, he couldn't see the tears slipping down her face.

The television correspondent continued his report. ". . . It's often easy to call stories like these 'senseless tragedies,' but this death, an apparent suicide, surely made sense to Ms. Gethers. And she carried that secret with her, as have so many others before her, to the icy waters below the Golden Gate Bridge. This is Nicholas Fleming reporting live."

Zapping off the TV, David started for the telescope, his curiosity pulling him along. The phone rang. A quick glance at the still-distraught Pilar confirmed to David that he should answer it himself. He got to the kitchen phone by the second ring. "Hello?"

Although the sun had been warming the homes on the hills of Pacific Heights for hours, it had yet to have much effect on the warren of cheap, noisy apartments in the backstreets of Chinatown. Barton Hubble sat in the grimy window of his one-room flat, in the thin shaft of sunlight only now slicing through the alley.

"Dave?" he said, his voice somehow shifting the word sideways.

David started, not at the vaguely familiar voice, but at its unconcealed drip of menace. "Who is this?"

"An old friend."

Sitting on the banquette, David looked over to Lily. She was still occupied with the tragedy on the bridge. Then to Pilar. Pulling on her sweater, she was just going out the front door, probably to be with Carmen. "Is this . . . Barton?" David asked, already knowing the answer.

Barton Hubble strained to open his window a crack, and the clattering sounds of an awakening Chinatown came rushing in. He ran his hand forward over his closely cropped hair. "Excellent . . . Dave." He turned to catch a glimpse of Ming warming herself in a hot bath.

Switching the phone to his other ear and turning away from Lily, David said, "Look, Barton, whatever you're calling about, this isn't a good time. There's been a death in the family."

Barton Hubble's face twisted into what was, for him, a smile. "That's what I want to see you about. Sausalito Ferry. Tomorrow morning, ten-fifteen. Main deck. Be alone." Enjoying the starring role in his own little drama, he pressed his thumb down on the phone's cradle and released it, listening for the dial tone.

David hung up, his mind racing. Then he noticed Lily's shoulders heave in a silent sob and he realized his daughter was weeping.

He crossed to her and knelt down next to the stool. "Lily, sweetie," he said softly. "Tell me."

Lily swiveled to face him, her face streaked with tears. "Oh, Daddy," she cried. Too distraught to continue, she fell into her father's arms.

David held his little girl tight to his chest and gently rocked her back and forth. "It's okay," he cooed. "It's okay, baby."

34

Looking out the window of her house, Jane could tell something was wrong. Kenny, who had been on his best behavior for weeks now, careened around the corner and skidded to a stop only inches from her trash cans. Curious, Jane came down her walkway and climbed into the Explorer just as Kenny dropped it into gear and whipped into a screeching U-turn.

"What?" she asked, watching his jaw flex.

"It's Monday and I stopped to get your yogurt like always," Kenny explained, handing her a small white bag. "And it's crowded in there. So I pick up a *Chronicle* to kill time . . ."

"And?"

"And this." Kenny tossed her the paper. "Bottom right."

Jane let the paper drop open in her lap and read the headline out loud. " 'Pacific Heights Hit by Second Tragedy.' " She looked over to Kenny. "Uh oh."

"It gets better," Kenny said, cranking into a hard left turn.

" 'This elegant community of some of San Francisco's most prominent families has been shaken to its core by the apparent suicide of Clarissa Gethers, twenty-one, the daughter of Noble and Patricia Gethers of the Gethers sugar fortune. The tragedy follows by only weeks the as yet unsolved kidnapping and murder . . .' "

" 'As yet unsolved,' " Kenny spit.

" '. . . of socialite Jenna Maxwell Perry, thirty-five, the daughter of the late Graham and Dorothy Maxwell. Mrs. Perry was abducted from her home on September seventh and her body was found the next day in a shallow grave on Mount Tamalpais. Police have no leads and few, if any, clues in the brutal slaying of the daughter of one of our city's most venerated families. San Francisco Police Chief Lucien Biggs could not be reached for comment . . .'"

"Because he's in fucking Vegas," Kenny yelled, whacking the steering wheel with the heel of his hand. "Playing golf!"

"Y'know," Jane said, "There are two really crummy things about this."

"What's that?"

"One, David Perry and his daughter have to be reminded about Jenna's death from the morning paper. And two, the *Chronicle*'s right. We don't have shit."

Kenny shot her a look. "Not for lack of trying. We've been working like dogs on this case."

"No. Not for lack of trying. But an A for effort doesn't mean fuck-all if we don't find the bad guy."

Kenny let his breath slip between a small crease in his lips until he felt himself calming down. "Yeah," he conceded. "You're right."

"Great," Jane said. "Now slow down or I'll have you arrested for reckless endangerment of a police officer."

"Go ahead. It'll be your first collar in months."

— —

At the station, Jane left Kenny to deal with the morning briefing while she went upstairs to make a phone call. Because of her recent skirmish with Kenny over the David Perry issue, she had been reluctant—unnecessarily, she concluded—to have any informal communication with him. But, she now realized, that wasn't prudent either. In other cases she and Kenny had investigated together, it often happened that casual contact with a principal—be it a survivor, a suspect, or a friend—could lead to information useful to solving the crime. It could be something as simple as a name suddenly remembered or a conscience suddenly guilty.

In any event, it had been too long since Jane, or Kenny for that matter, had spoken to David Perry. Maybe he had learned something new about his wife from one of her friends and didn't realize the significance. She and Kenny had interviewed them all, but most of them had been anything but forthcoming to the police. "Rich people circling the wagons," Kenny had commented at the time.

Or maybe Lily had remembered something neither of them thought was significant, but could somehow be a lead to a crack in the case.

Maybe, Jane thought, I just feel guilty because, thanks to the *Chronicle*, it now seems like we dropped the ball.

Picking up her phone, Jane dialed David Perry at work. His secretary answered on the first ring. "Mr. Perry's office."

"This is Inspector Jane Candiotti. Is Mr. Perry in?"

"Good morning, Inspector. No, he left a message on voice mail last night that he had a meeting out of the office this morning and wouldn't be in until after lunch. May I leave word?"

"Yes, thank you," Jane said, aware of, and curious about, the tiniest hint of disappointment she was feeling. "He has my numbers."

Hanging up, she sifted through the papers on her desk. She came upon a copy of the faxed report from the grid-pattern search of the gravesite. Quickly scanning to the bottom of the last page, Jane came to the filing officer's conclusion.

NO EVIDENCE OF CONSEQUENCE RECOVERED.
(signed) Nathaniel Fuller, SFPD, Mounted.

35

D avid was cold standing at the starboard rail on the main deck of the Sausalito Ferry. He chided himself for being fooled by the sunny mirror of reflection he had seen when he checked the bay from the telescope. As the mammoth boat chuffed over the blue-white foam, David wished he had brought an overcoat.

It had been a long time since David had taken the ferry. Lily had loved it when she was younger, always falling silent when they passed by the Golden Gate Bridge. Seen from a boat, the bridge loomed as large and immovable as a mountain range. David recalled how Lily's first serious drawings as a child were of the bridge, bright orange crayon sketches set against blue sky and green ocean. The primary colors of her childhood.

"Coffee, Dave?" Barton Hubble asked, jarring David out of his introspection.

David spun around to discover Hubble holding two cups of steaming coffee. Warmly dressed in his heavy wool greatcoat, he stood between David and the sun, a pulsing aura of hazy sunlight defining the outer edges of his hulking body. Instinctively maneuvering to his left in order to bring him into better focus, David said, "Look, Hubble. If you know anything about my wife's murder, we have to . . ."

"I do know something," Barton Hubble interrupted as he poured four sugars into one of the coffees and let the wind take the empty packets. "I know who did it."

David grabbed the rail as if to keep from falling over. "What are you talking about? Who?"

Barton Hubble squinted his eyes into narrow slits and smiled. "Me."

David took a step back and stammered, "What the fuck are you talking about?"

Without actually moving, Barton Hubble was somehow closer to

David. "You said you'd give anything, remember Dave? But I'm a reasonable man. I only want, say . . . five million."

"You sick son of a bitch," David shouted, his face flushing with rage as he lashed out and slapped the coffee cup out of Hubble's hand.

Feeling the inquisitive stares of nearby passengers, Barton Hubble assumed the role of a boisterous buddy. He reached out and clamped a powerful hand on David's shoulder. "Oh, Dave. I had that coffee just the way I like it. Right temperature, right sweetness. I wish you hadn't done that." His voice was a perfect modulation of serenity.

An overweight woman in a Miami Dolphins jacket ventured forward and looked closely at David, as if trying to remember the name of a long-lost schoolmate. "Ain't you that poor fella from the TV had his wife killed? I said a prayer for ya."

David turned away from the woman. "No . . . uh . . . you . . ."

As Hubble took her elbow to send her back to her friends near the bow, his face brightened into a broad grin. "My friend gets asked that all the time. Some resemblance, huh?"

"Spittin' image," the woman said, rather enjoying the winning smile of this nice man as she walked away.

When David was sure she was too far away to hear them, he pushed his body into Hubble, forcing him back against the rail. "Listen to me," he said through clenched teeth. "I am not your friend!" Barton Hubble stood there without expression. "And I'll tell you something else," David continued. "I'm going to the police."

Before David could react, Hubble ground the sharp heel of his heavy work boot into the top of David's foot. "I really hate those shoes, Dave."

Leaping back as if his foot had been shot, David staggered to an empty row of deck chairs and grabbed the arm of one of them, grimacing in pain. Barton Hubble was on him in an instant, speaking in carefully measured, even rehearsed, words. "Do not threaten me, Dave! You go to the police and it's only a matter of time before someone discovers your pricey little Rolex in the immediate vicinity of where they found . . ." He leaned in with a conspiratorial whisper. ". . . Jenna."

David looked at his wrist. "So that's what happened to my watch. You took it!"

"When I fixed your car. Kinda smart for a dumb ol' grease monkey, huh?"

"What's to keep me from going up there and scouring the area until I find it myself?"

Hubble lifted his hands, palms up in a conciliatory shrug. "Nothing," he said. " 'Cept it ain't there yet."

The ferry was nearing Sausalito and the other passengers converged on the main deck. David let a young couple pass, then looked at Hubble. "What if I decide to take my chances with the Rolex?"

"Let's say you do and the police pick me up," Hubble said. "Then I just tell them what you told me."

"What? What did I tell you?"

Hubble smiled broadly. "It was that night at the sports bar and I believe it went something like this." He held his hands out in mock exasperation, mimicking David. "My wife's so goddam selfish . . . I swear I'd give anything if . . ."

David sniffed derisively. "And you think that'll stand up in court?"

"Maybe. Maybe not," Hubble said. "But think about it. Do you really want to take it that far? To let it get that public?" He locked his eyes on to David's with laserlike intensity. " 'Cause if you go to the police, that's only the beginning of how ugly it'll get for you . . . and what's left of your family."

David averted his eyes. Sensing a win, Barton Hubble moved in for the kill. "Let's make this completely clear, Dave, so there's no misunderstanding," he said as the ferry slowed and reversed its engines in preparation for docking. "You don't come up with the money, my money . . . it's the end of life as you know it."

The ferry gently bumped into the dock, David found himself swirling in a crowd of people, their collective urgency to get off the boat pressing him inexorably closer to Barton Hubble. Carried along on the same human wave, Hubble jostled repeatedly into David. They were like two pieces of jetsam caught in an endless eddy.

"You know what's so wonderful about strangling a woman, Dave?" Barton Hubble rasped into David's ear as he clasped his upper arm in a painful vise of a grip. "All the while you're doing it, you know she knows she's dying. It truly is the ultimate power."

He released his arm, and David felt himself yielding to the tide of passengers, allowing himself to be swept into the crowd surging from the boat. Straining to turn around, he looked back to see Barton Hubble, his face contorted in a ghastly grin, his head tilting back in a soundless mocking laugh.

Struggling to maintain his balance in the swarm of people, David fought his way to the railing. Having regained his footing, he turned back for a final glimpse of his tormentor.

Barton Hubble was gone.

36

Patrick Colomby sat at his desk, his tie loosened, as the liveried waiter served him his lunch. He was just about to take his first taste of soft-shell crab when David knocked politely and entered the enormous corner office. His hair was still windblown from the return trip on the ferry, and Patrick noted that he seemed distracted.

"Sorry to interrupt, Patrick," David said as he crossed the room.

"Come in, come in," Patrick gestured. "I could use the company."

David sat in a deep brown leather club chair at the side of the desk. "I won't take much of your time."

"Would you like some lunch? We have soft-shell crab and . . ."

The waiter stepped in to freshen his wineglass with a Chardonnay from a winery in which Patrick was part owner. "And baby loin lamb chops," he said, standing by to see if David would like to choose.

"Nothing, thanks," David said holding up his hand. "I've got lunch with the Shepherd Ramsey people."

The waiter nodded and exited through a paneled mahogany door as Patrick took an appreciative sip of his wine. "I read your brief. You're making me look like a genius for putting you on that one."

"My mission in life," David smiled. "Patrick, can I ask you something? Off the record?"

"Of course you can." Patrick put down his wineglass and dabbed at his lips with a linen napkin.

"This is all a little awkward, but . . ." David seemed to run out of steam as he hesitated.

"The money?" Patrick asked. "Is it about the money?"

Swallowing hard, David nodded. "Well, yes."

Patrick wheeled his chair around toward David to take the barrier of his desk, and its implied power, out of the conversation. "I can tell you two things about the money: how much and when," he began.

"Depending on how well we can shelter you, the two of you should realize between . . ." He paused, not for effect, but because this was so important. ". . . sixty and seventy-five million."

David leaned back into his chair and broke eye contact with Patrick, his gaze drifting out the window.

"I know," Patrick went on. "It's a lot of money. As to the when . . . it's hard to say. Given the intricacies of the estate and California's inheritance statutes, it could be up to a year."

A trace of disappointment shadowed David's face. "Thanks, Patrick, for not making this any more difficult than it already is . . . for Lily and me."

"Are you in some sort of trouble, David?"

"Why? What do you mean?"

"Financial trouble," Patrick answered. "I know you borrowed pretty heavily for the remodel on the big house, and it could take forever to sell your condo." He reached across the space between them and put a paternal hand on David's knee. "All I'm saying is, if you need something to get you through the next little while, we'll be happy to help."

David rose and shook Patrick's hand. "Thank you. For your understanding . . . and for your friendship."

"You're a good man who's had a lousy run, David. Things'll get better. And when they do, I want you to still be here with us."

"I'll let you get back to your lunch," David said as he headed for the door. "Thanks again."

"David," Patrick called.

David turned back. "Yes?"

"How's Lily? She was pretty close to the Gethers girl, wasn't she?"

"She had a hard night last night," David said. "But I just called and she's doing better now."

"It's such a shame. Young girl like that taking her own life."

"It's as bad as it gets," David responded as he went out the door.

— —

David sat at his desk, the telephone cradled against his ear. While he waited, he tapped his pencil against a paperweight of the Golden Gate Bridge. A gift from Lily one Father's Day, it had become a fixture on his desk. His secretary came in and handed him the morning's messages. David had begun to leaf through them when someone came on the line.

"Hello, Roberta, No, I didn't mind holding. Thanks for taking the call." David listened for a beat, his eyebrows rising in curiosity as he came across Jane's message. "Yes, we did; and thank you for your note. It meant a lot to us." He slipped the message into his coat pocket. "Listen, the reason I called is I think we should lower the price on the condo. Let's just unload it, take the cash out of it, and walk away. I really don't want to have to think about it anymore."

He nodded as his broker rattled off a set of options. "Uh-huh. If you think that'll work, it's okay with me. Thanks, Roberta."

Hanging up the phone, David grabbed his sports coat from the back of his chair and hurried out of the office.

37

The flattening light of the late-afternoon sun had everyone in the police station looking at their watches. It seemed as if it had been getting dark at an impossibly early hour lately, and they still weren't accustomed to the sun being so low at only a few minutes after four o'clock.

Kenny came in from chasing down yet another empty lead on Warren Fincher and crossed the bullpen. Jane was plodding through an interview with a reluctant witness to a shooting in Little Italy. Not wanting to get pulled into the paperwork that came with such questioning, Kenny found himself talking to the top of Finney's head poking up over the low wall of his cubicle.

"Hey, Moby. Where you been the last couple of days?"

Dropping a greasy bag of deep-fried nacho chips into his drawer and kneeing it closed, Finney swiveled his chair around to face Kenny. "Hospital," he answered, wiping his hands on his pants leg.

"With what?"

"Stomach stuff."

"Sorry to hear it," Kenny said with as much sincerity as he could feign.

"Good news, Inspector," Finney said, trying to keep the conversation alive. "Cousin of mine can get a new minivan for the wife at ten percent over cost."

Kenny was about to tell Finney that any dealer in San Francisco could get him a new car for 5 percent over cost, when he remembered something that had been lurking somewhere in the haze of forgotten things.

"Whatever happened to those background checks I asked you to run on David Perry and his boss?"

"Oh . . . uh, nothin' yet. I been kinda indisposed."

"I know that you take your duties as communications liaison very

121

seriously, Officer Finney," Kenny began. "And I assume that this is you telling me you're going to get on it right away, right?"

"You bet, Inspector. Right away!" Finney agreed.

"I'd really appreciate that, Moby."

Kenny noticed that Jane had finished with her interview and, pulling an envelope from his pocket, walked across the bullpen to her desk.

Jane looked up as he approached. "We're an inch away on the Little Italy shooting."

"And that's why I left you alone on that Q & A. Didn't want to muck up whatever rapport you had going." He pulled a coupon out of the envelope and wagged it at her. "You wanna maybe go to the Oyster House for happy hour? They got two for one, today only."

It took Kenny a moment to realize that Jane was no longer looking at him. He followed her eyes to the corridor by the elevator, where David Perry was asking something of one of the police volunteers who worked reception. The elderly woman pointed toward Jane's desk, and David started across the room.

Kenny watched as Jane stood up quickly; too quickly, he thought. "Mr. Perry," she greeted him. "What brings you up here?"

"I got your message . . ." he began, catching Kenny toss Jane a quizzical look. "Thought I'd come by to . . . I don't know . . . talk."

"That's great, Mr. Perry," Kenny said, stepping in. " 'Cause we're here to listen. Pull up a chair."

"If it's all the same to you, I kind of wanted to talk with Inspector Candiotti."

Jane, fighting the urge to smile, felt a tickle of pleasure as David went on, "If that's all right, Inspector Marks?"

"Of course it's all right." Kenny shuffled his feet. "Why wouldn't it be all right?"

Before this could get any more painful for Kenny, Jane stepped in and snatched the coupon from his hand. "You hungry, Mr. Perry?"

"I could eat," David said.

As the two of them headed for the elevator, Sally Banks emerged from the evidence room, a box of car radios in her hands. She noticed Jane leaving with David and stole a glance toward Kenny. Then she looked to Cheryl at the dispatch desk and the two of them exchanged a quick smile before going on about their business.

38

— • —

From their waterside table at the Oyster House, Jane and David, inhaling fresh oysters and beer as fast as they were brought to them, paused to watch as the sun finally set beyond the curve of the sea.

"How beautiful," Jane said, her face bathed in the waning half-light.

"I never get tired of watching a sunset," David said. "Especially in this city."

"It's one of our many splendors," Jane agreed.

"Anyway, where was I?" David asked.

"You started to feel that your marriage was too damaged to last in any real way, and . . . ?"

". . . and it just deteriorated into one of those things where you stay together for the child. I'd do anything for my daughter. Even stay in an unhappy marriage," David admitted, taking a contemplative pull on his beer.

"She's a great kid. You're very lucky."

"Heh, luck isn't exactly what comes to mind when you play word association with David Perry. It's been a rough go lately."

"I know," Jane said as she prepared two more oysters with horseradish and Tabasco sauce. "We're doing everything we can to find whoever . . ." She didn't want to say the word, but now it just hung there, waiting for a voice. ". . . killed your wife. And we will. We're good at what we do."

"You always get your man?" David joked.

"Professionally anyway," Jane replied, instantly regretting it. "But don't worry. Your misery streak is over. It's time to get on with your life."

"I sure hope so. The next time I settle down, whenever that day comes, I'm going to be absolutely sure it's with the right person."

"No such thing."

"As the right person?"

"As being absolutely sure," Jane said as she slid one of the oysters over to David.

"Maybe not," David said, picking up the icy half shell. "Do I sound awful talking about Jenna like that?"

"You had a shitty marriage. At least you had the courage to do something about it."

"Not really. She threw me out."

"Then she was a fool," she said impulsively. "Now it's me who sounds awful."

They tipped their heads back and slipped the oysters into their mouths. Jane took a sip of her light beer and immediately set about to prep two more.

"How is it," David asked as he watched her, "how is it no one was ever lucky enough to persuade you to marry him?"

Jane felt herself blush. "To tell you the truth, that's a question I and about twenty-nine thousand of my relatives have been known to ask."

"It's no good being alone, Jane."

Jane felt a warm glow beneath her cheeks. David had finally called her by her first name. "Have you ever really been alone in your life?" she asked, handing him another oyster.

"Good question," David acknowledged. "Not exactly, I guess. I got married to Jenna a couple of years out of law school. We had Lily five years later." He knocked back another oyster and chased it with his beer. "But that time I spent alone during my separation . . . it was unbearable. Life just seemed empty. . . ." He felt Jane sit back in her chair, pulling away. "What?" he asked.

"Nothing." Jane shook her head. "It's not my favorite subject, is all."

David reached across the table and lightly touched Jane's hand. "I'm sorry." His hand rested there a moment, then he brought it back. "I've been a little self-indulgent lately."

"Forget it," Jane said, appreciating the contact that David felt secure enough to offer. "So, subject change coming," she laughed. "What brought you to the station today? I mean, why didn't you just call?"

David smiled. "In the interest of not being so self-indulgent, how about if I tell you some other time?"

Jane's first impulse was to decline the offer. To play it safe. But she was tired of playing it safe. "Like when?" she asked.

"Like Saturday night?" David asked, and then quickly added, "Or is this all too weird?"

"It's a little weird," Jane admitted. "But Saturday night would be great."

— —

The two of them were quiet as David drove Jane back to her house in the Marina. Jane slid the seat back and tried to think when she had last had this electrifying buzz tingling her face. It had been a long time.

"Turn right here. Fourth on the right," she said, wishing this ride would never end. She wasn't sure if she was imagining it, but, from how deliberately David was driving, she thought he might be feeling the same way as well. Or was that too much to expect? Her life had been so full of unmet expectations that she couldn't really identify what she was feeling until the sensation finally came forth and took a name for itself.

Hope.

"Nice," David said, pulling her out of her reverie.

"What?"

"Your house. I love these places down here." He reached over and squeezed her hand. "Until Saturday then."

"Until Saturday," Jane said and got out of the car, the bracing night air clearing her head just enough for her to know that what she was feeling was real.

— —

David could see from the sliver of blue light spilling out from under her door that Lily was still awake. She was working at her computer, busily tapping away, when he opened the door. Taking care not to frighten her, he spoke softly as he crossed the room. "Hey, Lilliput."

"Hey," she said, the keyboard clicking under her fingers.

David kissed the top of her head and dropped his arms over her shoulders. Resting her left cheek on her father's hand, Lily asked, "Where were you, Daddy?" She had gone back to calling him Daddy recently.

"I had a meeting," David said. "How you doin', honey?"

"Sometimes good. Sometimes not so good. Tonight's okay, though."

David pressed in to look at her monitor. "What d'ya got there?"

"Just writing in my diary."

"Since when do you keep a diary?"

She stopped typing and looked up at her father. "Since Mom."

"I see." David sat on her bed and leaned back against her poster of the U.S. Women's Swim Team winning the gold in Atlanta. He looked around the room. Her mother's trophies, the *Party of Five* poster, sketches of the bridge. "What kind of stuff do you write?"

"I dunno. Thoughts. And feelings." Lily turned back to her computer. "Sometimes I write her a letter."

"Does it help?"

"Yeah, a lot." She pushed her chair back and stretched. "Maybe you should try it."

"Maybe I should," David said. "You going to sleep sometime tonight?"

"Soon, Dad."

David decided not to make an issue out of how late it was. If anyone knew the resiliency and needs of her own body, it was Lily. Rising, he kissed her on the tip of her nose. "Goodnight, sweetie."

Before he could start out of the room, Lily stood up and wrapped her arms around her father. "Goodnight, Daddy."

David picked her up and gave her a squeeze. Then he let her slide back down and crossed the room.

"Daddy?" Lily called just as he got to the door.

"Yum?"

Lily sat back at her desk, the glow of the monitor surrounding her head in a halo of blue-green light. "Who's Barton Hubble?"

"Uh, why?"

"He called tonight," she said. "Twice. Said he was a friend of yours."

"He's some guy I met when I was living in the condo," David said. He stepped into the hall. "Did he leave a number?"

"Uh-uh. He said he'd call back."

39

It had been a frustrating week for Jane.

Two more tips on Jenna Perry's murder had proved to be dead ends. The witness to the Little Italy shooting had second thoughts about stepping forward and recanted her testimony. And since she and David had gone to the Oyster House, Kenny had been just a little cool toward her. Nothing overt. But it was as if there were a pane of glass between them whenever they talked.

Jane had tried to get Kenny to warm up to her again. But he kept insisting that nothing was wrong. She decided to sit back and let it play itself out, and, in fact, when she said good-bye to him that Friday night, Kenny had said, "Maybe I'll talk to you over the weekend."

It was an innocent enough statement, but Jane preferred to think of it as a sign. "I'll be around," she had said.

— —

Jane woke early the next morning and took her cup of tea to the window seat. The *Chronicle* unread on her lap, she watched the freighters push their way across the bay, a few sailboats dotting the windblown surface near Alcatraz.

She considered opening the newspaper, but she knew she wouldn't be able to concentrate. The prospect of spending the evening with David so distracted her that she put on her sweats and went out for a run around the Palace of Fine Arts.

Later, when she returned from the market, there was a message on her answering machine. Jane pressed the button. "Hi, it's David Perry. Just double-checking that tonight's still okay. If I don't hear from you, I'll see you at seven. Hope I don't hear from you. Bye."

Jane smiled. At the first sound of David's voice, she had been sure that he was calling to cancel. She shook her head and vowed to try to stop thinking that way.

Jane spent an unusually long time bathing and getting dressed that afternoon. She finally settled on the fourth outfit she tried on, a navy-blue pantsuit, and went into the kitchen to pour herself a glass of Chianti. She wasn't sure what she was feeling, but she knew that whatever it was, she liked it.

The phone rang.

She picked it up on the second ring. "Hello."

"Hey," Kenny said. "It's your partner in crime-fighting."

"Hey," Jane said, looking at her watch. Five minutes to seven.

"I was thinking," Kenny went on, "since we have so much fun rubbing elbows with the upper classes, why don't we drop in on Patrick Colomby? Says in the paper he's speaking to the Bar Association at the Fremont."

"Kenny, why do you have such a hard-on for this guy?"

"He's arrogant as hell. He gave me shit in front of my fellow officers." Kenny paused. "And since his partner and his partner's daughter died, he has total control of the law firm and he's now officially richer than God. C'mon, it'll be fun."

An arc of headlights brushed past the window as David pulled up outside. "Uh, sure. When is it?"

"Tonight at eight-thirty," Kenny said. "I'll pick you up. Dress nice."

"Oh," Jane said quickly. "I can't tonight." She heard David's door slam and the chirp of his alarm.

"Why not?" Kenny asked, and Jane could feel the disappointment in his voice.

"I've got plans."

The doorbell rang.

Jane knew that Kenny could hear it over the phone. "But maybe we can harass Mr. Colomby another time, okay?"

"Sure, Jane," Kenny said evenly. "See ya Monday."

"Have a good night." She rang off, took a quick look at herself in the mirror over the Parsons table, and crossed to the front door.

Taking a deep breath, she pulled it open. David, dressed in jeans, a white shirt, and a black leather jacket, stood in a pool of yellow porch light. "Hi," he said, breaking into a smile as he offered his hand.

"Hi yourself," Jane said, taking his hand. "Come in." She stepped aside as David entered. "This would be the living room," she gestured.

"Nice."

"And over here we have the kitchen."

David poked his head in. "Good place for the stove and refrigerator," he joked.

Jane stopped at the photo gallery on the Parsons table. "Your typical Italian family."

"Wow," David whistled. "There's a million of you guys."

"You know," Jane shrugged, "Catholics."

David laughed. "Any more to see?"

To her surprise, Jane felt a flush of shyness about showing him her bedroom. "Couple of bathrooms and my bedroom."

"Lead the way."

Jane headed down the hall and nodded to a door on the left. "Guest bath," she said. At the end of the hall, she turned right into the bedroom and to her horror saw that the ironing board was still in front of the bed where she had used it as a dining table. "Uh, the bedroom . . . such as it is."

Not quite entering the room, David looked around and said, "Very nice." They started back down the hall. "You have a beautiful home."

"Thanks," Jane said as she picked up her coat and purse. "Where are we going?"

"I was thinking Lobster Alley up in Tiburon."

"Fantastic," Jane said as she pulled the door closed.

— —

Outside the restaurant after dinner, Jane pulled her jacket tight against the evening chill as David handed the ticket to the valet. He walked back to her, smiling. "I've never seen anyone eat a lobster so . . . thoroughly before."

"In a big family," Jane laughed, "you get a lot of practice finding the good stuff in a lot of weird lobster extremities."

A voice came from behind them.

"David? David Perry?"

David turned to see a couple coming out of Lobster Alley. The man was David's age, but balding and much heavier. The woman, also overweight, was a year or two younger. They were both smoking cigarettes.

"It's me! Tommy, Tommy Boyle!"

"Tommy," David said, and Jane could tell he was forcing an enthusiasm into his voice as he offered his hand.

Tommy Boyle bulled past David's hand and pulled him into a vigorous hug. "Goddam!" he exclaimed as he released David. "You look fuckin' great. Life must be treatin' you pretty good, huh?"

David nodded demurely. "You still living in the city?"

"Yeah. I'm still in the old neighborhood—the old house, even," Tommy said. "My dad retired and I took over the store." He looked to Jane. "Shit! Where's my fuckin' head?" He tugged his wife forward. "Say hello to Donna. Donna, this is David Perry. Remember I told you about him and me running together in the old days? Doin' all kinds of bad shit? This is him!"

Donna Boyle put her cigarette in her mouth and held out her hand. "A pleasure," she said, squinting against the smoke.

David turned and brought Jane into the circle. "Jane, this is Tommy and Donna Boyle."

Jane, aware of David's hand on her back, smiled. "Hi, everyone."

David raised his hand and rested it on Jane's shoulder. "So, Tommy, good to see you."

"Gimme a call sometime," Tommy said. "I still got the same number since high school." He turned to Jane. "Jean," he said, and no one bothered to correct him, "have David tell you about me and him and the shit we used to do."

Two pairs of headlights swept across them as their cars were brought up. Tommy appraised David's BMW, gleaming black and elegant, as the valet opened the door for Jane. "Fuck, David, you're doin' great!" He pulled him into another exuberant hug. "I'm happy for you, man."

David tipped the valet, shook Tommy's and Donna's hands, and got into his car. He buckled his seat belt and, with a wave, drove off.

Tommy watched him leave as he handed the valet two quarters and climbed into his battered ten-year-old Chevrolet station wagon. He lit another cigarette as Donna got in. "Fuckin' David Perry," he muttered. "Doin' all right." He slipped the car into gear and drove out of the parking lot.

——

As David guided the car south onto Highway 101, Jane looked over to him. "Y'know, I had you pegged for private school. Or at least San Francisco's equivalent of Beverly Hills 90210."

David let out a little laugh. "Far from it."

The highway curved down the low hills of southern Marin County and fed them onto the Golden Gate Bridge. Jane craned her neck to look up at the North Tower. "Y'know," she began, "growing up in San Leandro, we were always jealous of this bridge. We had the good old dependable and interminably grey Bay Bridge, and the rest of the city had this glamour baby."

"So, basically," David said, "you were suffering from bridge envy."

"I got over it," Jane laughed. "But I gotta admit, this is one beautiful bridge."

They passed beneath the South Tower and followed the road's arc beyond Vista Point.

"Lily's always been fascinated by this bridge. She spends hours at her telescope just watching the traffic." David grinned. "Better than watching TV, I guess."

Jane nodded and sat back in the seat, enjoying the comfort of the moment. After a short while, she turned to David. "So," she began, "what kind of shit, as Mr. Tommy Boyle so gracefully put it, did you guys do?"

David turned toward the Marina. "Do I need my lawyer present?"

"Probably not. Statute of limitations should smile kindly on you."

David chuckled. "It wasn't much, really. Stealing bicycles, drinking, stupid stuff like that." He shook his head. "I guess it was more important to Tommy than it was to me."

"The guy still lives in the same house, has the same phone number, and works in his father's store." Jane twisted in her seat. "I can understand how the past might be more interesting to him than the present."

They stopped at a red light, and David turned to her. "You really get it, don't you?"

"Get what?"

"People. You understand them," David said. "I admire that in you."

"Thanks," she said softly and realized that she wasn't used to being complimented.

The light turned green, and David slipped the car forward. "Tommy used to be this good-looking guy. Great body, big hair—he always had his pick of the girls."

"And you?"

"I was kind of awkward around girls. Sort of a self-esteem thing. I just had trouble connecting."

"So, no girlfriends?" Jane asked, loving this private tour into David's past.

"There was this one girl, Stephie Miller. She was a beautiful redhead, and I was crazy about her. But I could never get up the nerve to actually ask her out. So Tommy did it for me."

"Tommy?"

"He asked Stephie Miller if she would go out with me, and she said yes, and . . ."

"And the rest is history?"

Falling quiet, chewing on the inside of his lower lip, David lowered his window about an inch and leaned into the cool air.

"What?" Jane asked.

David's head bobbed as if he were rehearsing what he was about to say. Glancing over his right shoulder, he pulled up at a white curb in front of a row of mailboxes and put the car in park.

"Stephie's mother dropped her off at my parents' house. Tommy and his girlfriend were already there." David spoke quickly, pushing the words out. "I had this Mustang convertible back then. I'd worked all these shit jobs after school and every summer to buy it, giving my father twenty bucks a week. We were all going to go to the beach."

"Ever the romantic, huh?"

"Ever hopeful," David said soberly. "Anyway, we were getting ready to leave when Tommy looks out the window and yells, 'Somebody's stealing your car!' He and I blast out of there and catch the guy, and Tommy's ready to beat him up when the guy says he's a repo man."

Outside, a college girl put her book bag on top of one of the mailboxes, dropped a letter into the middle one, and pulled the handle back again to make sure it had disappeared. She retrieved her book bag and, leaning into the wind, went off down the street.

David watched her go, then looked back at Jane. "I tell this guy he's full of shit. I'd been making payments on my car, twenty bucks a week." He sighed. "By then my father had caught up to us, and the repo man asks me, 'Where do you send the money?' I told him that I give it to my dad and he sends it on to you guys. The repo guy looks me straight in the eye, and then he looks over to my father . . ." David broke off the story for a moment, letting Jane catch up to it.

"Oh God," Jane whispered.

"Right. We all figured it out at the same time. Even Tommy Boyle couldn't say anything, we were so shocked." David's eyes moistened. "There I was with Stephie Miller—a girl I hadn't dared even dream about—and my father slaps me across the face and yells at me to get in the house. I was so humiliated, all I could do was run inside, leaving everyone standing there while the repo man drove my car away."

David took in a long breath and held it. Then he blew it out, his cheeks puffing. "Some great parenting, huh?"

"You poor thing," Jane said. "What happened to Stephie?"

"She was sweet enough to call the next day. But I never called her back. From that time on I just kind of kept to myself. Sort of a self-imposed exile." He looked to Jane. "So, yes I do know about loneliness. I've been there . . . and I never want to go back."

He put the car into gear, his hand brushing Jane's left leg, and nudged the BMW into traffic.

Jane turned to look at him. They had found a bond in a place so intimate it almost took her breath away. Loneliness. "Fasten your seat belt," she said quietly. "It's the law."

David clicked his seat belt into place and smiled. "When I finally moved out of the house and worked my way through college I promised myself two things. One: to never be that poor again. And two: if I ever had a kid, to be the best father in the world."

"Are you?"

"I'm trying like hell," David said.

"What about your father?"

"What about him?"

"Is he still alive?"

David followed the curve of the road toward the Marina. "I don't know."

Glancing to his right, he saw the college girl from the mailbox climbing the steps of a dreary Victorian house. She reached the front porch, the windows dark, and went inside.

— —

David pulled up outside Jane's house. After he had told his story, he'd turned on the CD player and they had ridden the rest of the way listening to Miles Davis. Switching off the engine, David got out and opened Jane's door.

They walked up the path to the porch, David close by her side, but not touching her. Jane resisted the urge to lean into him, to provoke him to put his arm around her. She unlocked the door and turned to him.

"Want to come in?"

"I should get home."

"I had a wonderful time," Jane said as she looped her bag over the doorknob in case David was going to kiss her goodnight.

"Me too." He offered his hand. "Any chance you're free tomorrow night?"

"But it's a school night. What about Lily?" Jane asked, delighted he'd invited her out again.

"She has her Monday-morning workout," David said. "She'll go to bed early and I'll leave her with Pilar. Then you and I can spend some time together. I have a surprise for you."

Jane stood back a step, still holding David's hand, and examined his face. "What are you trying to do here?" she asked with a smile.

David broke eye contact and looked at his feet for a second. "I'm just trying to . . . connect."

Squeezing his hand with both of hers, Jane said, "I'd love to see you tomorrow night."

"Great," David said, sounding relieved. He turned to go and was halfway down the path when he looked back and smiled. "Really great."

"Don't forget my surprise!" Jane called after him.

"Wouldn't think of it." He got to his car and waved back to Jane.

Her face warming, she took her bag from the doorknob and waved back. Then she closed the door and switched off the light, her front porch falling into darkness.

40

As they drove through the Presidio the next night, Jane wondered if David were going to take her over the Golden Gate Bridge to another one of the seaside restaurants in Sausalito or Tiburon. The view back to the city from their harbor windows would be spectacular on a night like this.

They were crossing the Vista Point parking lot when David paused to let the evening's last tourist bus back out before coasting into its parking place. He pulled on the emergency brake and switched off the engine.

"C'mon," he said, opening his door. "I want to show you something."

"The Golden Gate Bridge on a crystal-clear night?" Jane said as she got out of the car. "You are ever the romantic."

"Like I said," David smiled, "I am ever hopeful."

He put his hand on her back and guided her up the winding path toward the bridge concourse. Jane leaned into his hand, absorbing the pressure of his touch.

An oil tanker, its long flat deck illuminated by a series of lights so that it looked like a moving runway, churned under the bridge.

Jane stopped at the midpoint of the path and watched as the huge ship plowed through the harbor water. "My dad used to take me down to the docks when I was a kid. He'd tell me about coming over from Italy. Again and again. Same story every time. He would get so melancholy, tears in his eyes—it was like a new story each time he told it."

"You're lucky you guys have such a good relationship," David said as he followed the tanker's progress.

Jane turned her back on the bay and looked up at him. "David, can I tell you something? Something personal?"

"You have carte blanche to reveal any secret you want about yourself."

"It's not about me," Jane said. "It's about you."

David straightened. "What is it?"

"I did some checking," Jane began, feeling her way along. "And your father died three years ago."

David looked away, his gaze moving up to the bridge. "Well . . ." he said, but didn't finish the thought.

Jane stepped in, feeling the need to be closer to him. "Are you okay? How do you feel?"

"About my father dying? 'Relieved' I guess is the first thing that comes to mind. He wasn't a good man." He shuffled his feet. "Maybe I'm a little sad at the finality of it all. And a little sad for myself." He started up the path again. Jane was about to follow when he stopped and turned around. "I gotta say, in the interest of honesty between you and me, I'm not sure how I feel about your checking me out like that."

"It's my nature," Jane replied. "And my job."

"What else did you learn?"

"That your alibi is solid," Jane said, in too deep to back out now. "The security guard in your building, I think his name is Frank, vouched for you completely."

"What is this?" David's face reddened slightly. "Have you been going around trying to prove that I had something to do with Jenna's death?"

"No," Jane said, holding her ground. "I've been trying to prove that you didn't. I also talked to Myra, and she corroborated your story."

"Of course she did. It's true."

"She also told me about how you helped her with her citizenship papers. How kind and generous you are." Jane's eyes pleaded for David to understand. "I talked to a lot of people about you, David. I think it makes sense for me to want to know about you if . . . if I'm going to go out with you."

"You're right. I'm sorry," David said. "It's all a little confusing, y'know?"

"Believe me, I know," Jane said as she took his hand. "C'mon. You said you had something to show me."

— —

Jane couldn't tell which was more profound, the noise or the smell, as she stood in the tiny elevator. David stood so close to her she could feel

136

the warmth of his breath on her cheek. He had told her to close her eyes in anticipation of a spectacular and unforgettable surprise. As the elevator vibrated and clattered along, the musty smell of old steel and grease permeating the car, Jane felt as if she were floating, disconnected from the pull of gravity.

"Okay, I can't stand it," Jane shouted over the rattle of metal on metal, her eyes squeezed shut. "How much longer?"

David laughed. "Where's your spirit of adventure?"

"My day job's for adventure. My evenings are for fun."

The elevator ground to a stop. "Then get ready for both," David said as he slid the grate open and leaned into the door with his shoulder.

"Now?" Jane asked.

"Now!"

As David guided her through the narrow door, Jane opened her eyes and gasped. "Oh my God!" she exclaimed as they stepped onto the catwalk on top of the South Tower of the Golden Gate Bridge. Accidentally disturbing a nesting pair of seagulls who went fluttering and squawking aloft, David undid the safety chain and pulled an awestruck Jane onto the deck. "Sorry about that," he said, gesturing to the soaring birds. "They don't get too many visitors at night."

Jane couldn't stop looking around. Every sensation at that very moment was new, foreign in an almost unimaginable way. Exploding with excitement, she ran to the chest-high bulkhead wall and peered down to the roadway. Her hair blown back, her eyes stinging deliciously, she saw twin rivers of red and white lights as the night's traffic coursed over the bridge.

Looking across the bay at San Francisco's unique skyline, the city's buildings standing like luminous dominoes, Jane shouted over the coming wind, "Are you kidding me? How did you do this?"

David joined her at the wall. "Friends in high places."

"No, really. Tell me."

Leaning in to be heard over the wind, David said, "I've been coming up here since I was a kid. Father of a friend of mine worked maintenance for the Bridge Commission. For some reason, they never changed the locks."

Jane lifted herself up onto her toes and looked straight down over the rail to the foaming sea as it crashed into the tower's cement pier. "Whoa, this is high!" she said as she recoiled from the dizzying height.

"Imagine standing on top of a seventy-five-story building and looking over the edge," David said as he joined her. "That's how high up we are." They stood there for a moment listening to the wind humming through the cables. David thrust his hands into his jacket pockets and scrunched against the cold. "What do you think about when you look over?"

Jane shrugged. "What everybody else does, I guess."

"You mean, what would happen 'if'?"

"I have to admit there is a certain morbid attraction, something magnetic, about it. Just to experience that free fall." She looked to him, her eyes shining. "Wouldn't you want that rush, just once in your life, if you knew you could survive it unharmed?"

"You're the cop," David laughed. "I'm just a lawyer. This is about all the excitement I can stomach."

"You hear about the Gethers girl?"

David bit his lip. "She was a neighbor."

"Of course she was. I didn't think," Jane said. "Jesus, and she only jumped from the roadway. Poor thing."

She found herself beginning to fall into a reflective mood, her loneliness, her depressions, whittling away at her spirits. David felt her darken and stepped back with his arms outstretched. "What's wrong with us? It's a fantastic night, we're the only two people in the world, and we're talking about suicide?"

Pulling two quarters from his pocket, he handed one to Jane. "Make a wish," he said as he tossed his over the side. "Your turn."

"Look out below!" Jane yelled as she flipped the quarter over the rail. They heard an immediate plink as it hit some unseen something. Rising on their toes, they leaned over and saw that her coin had landed on a painter's scaffold lashed to the other side of the low wall. "I'm such a girl."

Happier than she had been in too long a time, she rotated in a full circle, drinking in the panorama. "God, I have got to get a camera."

"What's a grown woman doing without a camera?"

Jane hesitated, pursing her lips. "You left out 'single.' As in grown 'single' woman." She wrapped her arms around herself. "I don't know. . . . When you're in a relationship, there always seems to be a hundred cameras around. Your life becomes a series of snapshots coming home from Foto-Mat. But . . . ." She broke off, not wanting to continue.

David, careful until now not to make any precipitate, or unwelcome, contact with her, took her into his arms. Raising her head to look at him, her lips only inches from his, Jane smiled her gratitude and her permission.

"Can I tell you something?" David asked softly.

"Anything."

"I'm holding you, and I'm feeling you against me . . . and we're up here all alone . . . and I really need to kiss you right now."

"Good thing," Jane said, her eyes glistening. " 'Cause I really need to be kissed right now."

Tipping her head back and parting her lips for him, Jane received David in a deep needy kiss. Their tongues, at first tentative and unsure, found each other and in their own way made their connection that much more vital. Pressing into him, pulling him into her, Jane could feel him respond as their embrace intensified.

Still in the kiss, David parted her coat and put his hands on her waist. Jane thrust forward, her pelvis arching against his. Just as David was about to slide his hands up to her breasts, they were interrupted by the insistent beeping of her pager.

"Shit," Jane cursed as they came up for air, their kiss still very much alive on her lips. "See what happens when you make out with a cop?"

"It is a learning experience," David joked as he lifted the safety chain. "C'mon, you can call from the car."

— —

David leaned against the side of his BMW watching a lone fishing trawler, its nets suspended from her booms like diaphanous wings, putter its way back to port. Glancing through the windshield, he could see Jane, lit by the interior reading light, finish her phone call and hurry from the car.

"Duty calls?" David asked as he came up to her.

"It's my father," Jane said, choking back her fear. "They think it's his heart."

"Where?"

"Kaiser in Oakland."

"Let's go!" David called as he ran around to the driver's door.

— —

It had been another sleepless night for Lily. Hours had passed since Pilar had gone out to her apartment in back, and Lily had thought about calling her best friend, Jobie Zeman, but then remembered she was in

139

Hawaii with her parents. She had thought about watching TV, or banging around the Internet, or maybe even reading. But even as these options played through her mind, she had already known what she would do.

She had been looking through the telescope for almost an hour, watching the traffic, trying to pick out words on the sides of trucks as they whipped along the bridge's roadway. She thought she saw two seagulls fly off the top of the South Tower, but they were too small and too far away for her to be sure. Besides, that would be too weird. Seagulls flying at night.

Later, she had noticed the running lights of a trawler—a fifty-footer, she had guessed—as it came in under the bridge and slipped across the bay. She followed it for a while, until it disappeared behind some buildings.

The headlights of a car racing through the parking lot caught her attention, but she never got a good look at it. Putting the lens covers back on the telescope, she padded upstairs to bed.

41

The hospital loomed broad and dark, a few lights still on here and there. The parking lot nearly empty, the hallway lighting dimmed, it was as if this cold grey beast of eleven stories had drifted off to sleep.

The night nurse at the sixth-floor ICU brought David some coffee and, thinking he was part of the family, gave his arm a consoling squeeze. David stood in the doorway looking at Poppy Candiotti as he slept peacefully amid the monitors and IVs. Jane's brother Tim shuffled nervously back and forth across the room, seemingly the only one in the entire hospital with any energy. Occasionally he would catch David's eye, but he always averted his gaze and retraced his steps like a convict pacing his cell, a prisoner of his own inadequacy.

Jane came down the quiet corridor toward her father's room. Her heart lifted when she saw David, his back to her, still at the door, right where she had left him. For once in her life, when there was a crisis, she had someone with her. Lightly touching David on the shoulder, she entered the room.

Tim saw his sister and stopped, frightened. "What'd they say?"

"Daddy's blood gases indicate a mild heart attack," Jane said, her voice calm and soothing.

"Oh God," Tim murmured.

"They're sure he'll be okay," Jane went on. "They'll know tomorrow if he'll need a bypass or not."

Sitting heavily in the Naugahyde chair, Tim, his face drained of color, his mouth partly open, stared at his father. Jane crossed to him, squatted down, and spoke softly. "Timmy, you handled this perfectly. All the stuff they put into Poppy, he's not waking up for hours. Maybe you should go home and get some sleep."

"I want to stay," he protested, his eyes red with weariness.

Jane leaned in and kissed her father lightly on the lips. "Then I'm gonna go. You'll be okay?"

"Yeah," Tim said absently as he shook David's hand good-bye. At the door, Jane turned back to see her brother sit down again and lay his head on the side of Poppy's bed. Resisting the impulse to go back in and comfort him, she took David's arm and walked away.

— —

"Thanks for being there. I can't tell you what it meant to me," Jane said as she lit the candles on the ironing board. "Maybe I should get a dining room table before I worry about a camera, huh?"

"It's been a hell of a night," David said as he sat on the edge of the bed. "How about if you don't worry about anything right now?"

Jane smiled. "It's a deal." She peeled back the Saran Wrap from a dish. "Cold pizza?"

David helped himself and took a hungry bite. "Mmm. Eggplant and prosciutto?"

"Made it myself."

"Amazing," David laughed. "You can do everything."

Suddenly solemn, Jane put down her pizza and sipped at her Chianti.

"What?" David asked, putting his hand on her arm.

"That's the problem: I can do everything," Jane sighed. "Because I have to do everything. Story of my life." She felt tears coming and struggled to hold them back. "My mom died when I was twelve, so I had to raise Timmy . . . and my father."

She rose and went to her nightstand for a tissue. "Need a diaper changed? A splinter removed? Your dogs walked when you go to Mexico? Help with the rent?" She blew her nose. "Need the doctor talked to when your father has a heart attack and you don't have the skills to face reality?" Spent, she fell back on the bed. "I'm so tired of it all, I could just cry." Then, feeling the tears slide down her face toward her ear, she laughed. "Heh, I am crying. Oh, shit . . ."

David reached across to the Kleenex box and gave her a handful of tissues. Then, lying next to her, his head on his arm, he said, "You're not the only competent one here, you know. Let me help you."

Jane dabbed at the corners of her eyes and looked at him, searching his face as if to find the truth behind the words. "I can't tell you how many times I've looked over to where you are right now and imagined a moment like this." She poked his shoulder. "Are you for real?"

David nodded. "Yes, Inspector. I'm for real."

"Really for real? 'Cause if you're not, you better get out of my bed, Mister." Folding himself into the contours of her body, David pulled her into a lingering kiss. Jane gasped in a tiny shiver of ecstasy and lifted her thigh between his legs. Pressing hungrily into her, his passion intensifying, David maneuvered himself on top of her and began to unbutton her blouse. Her heart fluttering, Jane willed herself to relax, to be entirely present in this wonderful moment. And then David stopped, pulling away.

"I'm sorry," he said. "I've got to go."

"It's too soon after, isn't it?"

"It's not that," David said, understanding that she was talking about Jenna. "Lily's home with Pilar, and I need to be there when she wakes up." He swung his legs over the side of the bed and put his hand on her belly. "Come with me."

Jane put her hand on his. "You sure about this? You can still . . ."

Grabbing her hand in his, David pulled her into his arms. "First of all, shut up. Second of all, get your stuff." He stood up, bringing her with him. "This is the night someone takes care of you."

42

———

There were five stools, none of them matching, at the Wang Lu Grill. Built into the maw of an abandoned garage in a bleak Chinatown alley, its menu consisted of suspicious-looking scraps of meat mixed with vegetables rejected by the other restaurants.

Barton Hubble had left Ming back at the apartment to read her comic books while he cruised the dripping Blade Runner alleys behind Chinatown. He came to the Wang Lu Grill, parked his tow truck in front of a fire hydrant, and stepped out. The clamor of the mainstream restaurants drifted toward him from beyond the dark buildings. He took the end stool next to a young Chinese couple dressed in tight motorcycle leathers. Barton Hubble glanced around. No motorcycle.

Sipping on the beer Wang Lu had plunked down in front of him, Hubble looked directly into the girl's almond eyes. Still stoned from whatever she and her boyfriend had been smoking for the past couple of years, the girl did not shrink from his stare. Holding his eyes with hers, she sucked her bottom lip in her teeth and put her hand, her nails painted a deep blue, on the man's thigh. Sliding her hand to his crotch and cupping it in her palm, the girl bit into her own lip until a tiny teardrop of blood appeared at the corner of her mouth.

The boy tipped his head back and moaned as the girl applied more pressure between his legs. Then, seeing that she was looking past him, he turned to see if Barton Hubble was watching.

He was.

A crooked grin creasing his face, Hubble finished his beer, tossed a couple of bucks onto the counter, and returned to his truck. Turning the engine over, he released the clutch and slowly drove away.

———

From the street, the Perry house looked tranquil in repose. The soft yellow hue of the entryway light bloomed in the coming mist, the tiny red lights of the security alarm pad standing sentry by the front door.

Barton Hubble sat in his truck, engine idling, headlights off, and watched the house. He imagined himself inside. Not as an intruder, but living there. He thought about coming home to this place at night and waking up there in the mornings.

Of taking women there.

Releasing the emergency brake, he let the huge truck slip forward, gaining speed as it slid down the hill. The Perry house passed from sight, receding in the distance behind him, and he wondered which was the little girl's room.

Turning a corner at the bottom, he switched on his lights, threw it into gear, and roared into the night, just missing David's BMW as he came to his street from the other side and started to climb the hill, Jane's head on his shoulder.

43

Opening the door only slightly, not wanting to let in too much light, David slipped into Lily's bedroom and saw his daughter sleeping the sleep of a teenager. Conked out sideways across her bed, one sock on, one sock probably downstairs, she shifted in her slumber to an even more improbable angle. Turning back to share a smile with Jane, David took a spare blanket—a beige and maroon monstrosity that her Grandma Dorothy had crocheted for her when she was a baby—and covered his little girl. Then he leaned over and kissed her on the tip of the nose.

Softly pulling the door shut, David took Jane's hand and led her down the hall. "God, I wish I could sleep like that."

"The sleep of the innocent," Jane replied, her mind racing with anticipation as they came to David's bedroom.

David stepped aside to let Jane enter first, then he came up behind her and, nuzzling her hair, snaked his arms around her waist. Jane leaned into him, responding, but not with the abandon of earlier in the evening. "You okay?" David asked, turning her to him.

"I guess. It's just that . . . I mean . . ." She looked to the bed.

Putting his hand on the back of her head, David pulled her forward and kissed her on the forehead. "For the last year or so, Jenna and I had separate bedrooms. I was in here, and Jenna slept in the guest room at the end of the hall. She said she liked it because it was small and cozy. I think she liked it because it was far away from me."

Jane put her purse on the night table. "This is all a little weird, y'know."

"For me too," David admitted as he brushed her hair out of her eyes. "If you want, I can take you home. Or we can just sit downstairs and have a fire. Or . . . whatever you want."

"What I want," Jane said, putting her arms around him, "is to take you up on your promise."

"Which was?"

"To let this be the night someone takes care of me."

"Good answer," David smiled as he eased her onto the bed.

"What about Lily?" Jane asked.

"You saw the way she sleeps. I'll take you home before she wakes up." He kissed her on the lips, and the two of them fell back on the bed.

Jane, her passion finally conquering her fears, groped at David's belt. Unfastening it and pulling down his zipper, she slipped her hand inside and took him between her fingers. He felt strong, she thought, strong and hot.

Rolling on top of her, David flicked his tongue in her ear, and as she moaned her encouragement, he unbuttoned her blouse. Sliding down her body, he kissed her breasts, and as her legs fell open to welcome him, he pulled her blouse off her shoulders. To get her blouse completely off, she would have to let go of him, and neither of them wanted that just yet.

Reaching around to unhook her bra, David whispered into her ear, "Uh, it's kinda been a while. Do you have any protection?"

Jane nodded toward her purse. "Yeah, a snubnose thirty-eight. So you better be good, buddy."

Their laughter evaporated the last of their tension, and they enjoyed the magic of taking off each other's clothes for the first time. As they melted together, Jane's desire and need and pain blended into David until, for the briefest of moments, she was lost, no longer of this world.

No longer wounded.

44

J ane dreamed of water. Of standing on the sandy beach, crowded with
working-class families, that her father used to take her to when she
was a child. The Bay Bridge glistened in the sunlight in her dream, for
this moment at least no longer the poorer sister to the Golden Gate Bridge.

Someone called for Jane in her dream, someone in the water. Jane
ran to the edge of the sea, the water lapping at her ankles like a kitten,
and peered into the glinting waves. There was no one there. She heard
the call again, louder now. Leaping forward, she plunged into the water,
the warm water, and found, to her delight, that she was soaring over the
wavetops, dipping and floating like a seabird.

The water rushing by beneath her, Jane swooped on swirling breaths
of misty air. The wind whooshed by, whispering in her ear. She heard
her name again. Someone calling. Someone in trouble. Frantic now,
she scanned the roiling sea from above until she saw a man just ahead,
flailing his arms in desperation. Tilting forward, she coaxed her body
into a dive and burst into the water next to him. From below, as she
struggled upward, she saw that the man was her father.

Kicking, straining against the now-freezing water, she pushed herself
toward the light and finally broke the surface with a gasping breath.
Reaching out, she grabbed onto Poppy and held him against her chest
until he was calm.

"I've got you, Poppy," she sighed. "I've got you."

Jane opened her eyes and thought, in that fragile instant between
sleeping and waking, that she was still in the water. David's bedroom
was just now filling with the beginnings of morning light. Stretching
luxuriously, savoring the feel of the musky cotton duvet on her skin,
she turned to check the time on the clock radio. Five-thirty. The sound
of David peeing drifted in from the bathroom, and Jane smiled. There
was an unspoken intimacy, a sort of safety, in it.

The bathroom door opened and David, buttoning up a light blue dress shirt, emerged. "You awake?"

"Every part of me," Jane said as he sat on the edge of the bed and kissed her on the lips in that comforting way that said last night was for real. Jane fluffed the pillows behind her and, pulling her knees up, leaned back against the headboard. "Thank you for last night, David."

Turning to her, his face suddenly earnest, David took her hand. "Can I ask you something? About . . . the case?"

Stroking his hand, her fingers grazing the downy hairs of his forearm, Jane nodded. "Of course. Anything."

"Well, that article in the *Chronicle* intimated that you weren't really any closer to catching . . . uh, whoever did it. And . . ."

"Look," Jane said, taking his lead. "The newspaper was only partly right. We don't have everything, but we do have something."

David raised his eyebrows. "Like what?"

"We ran a hair-and-fibers. At the site of the shallow grave and . . . here. We've got a blood type from scrapings from under Jenna's finger-nails. B negative—very rare. We have shoeprints, or rather boot prints, matching at both scenes, and we have fibers from a woolen work-type shirt." She paused. "Two things we don't have, though."

"Can you tell me?" David asked. "Or is this too complicated now that we're . . . together?"

Jane smiled. "It's not the most ethically pristine situation possible. But I'm not about to trade last night for a life sentence of living by the rules." She kissed his hand, loving the mere fact of being able to do it, just like that, and went on. "One of the things we don't have is a fiber sample from a pair of pants. There was quite a struggle, and it's unusual, given that we got scrapings, shirt fibers, hair, and boot prints, that we wouldn't get any traces off the assailant's pants."

"What does that tell you?"

Jane squeezed his hand as if to prepare him. "That maybe he wasn't wearing any."

"Christ," David said, shaking his head. "What's the other thing you don't have?"

"The guy," Jane said, her face setting with purpose. "But we will. I promise you . . . and I promise Lily."

"Speaking of Lily, we should get it together so I can take you home," David said as he pulled on his shoes. "What's next in the case?"

She leaned over the edge of the bed and searched for her blouse.

149

"The FBI should be getting back to us this week on the tire molds we sent them. Something like thirty of them from the parking lot at the base of the hiking trail. Plus, we're just completing a scan on all the murders committed on the entire West Coast the last ten years that have any similarities to this one." Pulling on her blouse and gathering up her bra and panties, she started to get out of bed. "Murders like this do not usually go unsolved. The assailant may strike again, or . . ." She let the unfinished sentence float in the air between them.

"Or what?" David asked.

"Or he might try to contact you."

David stood up, his back to her, and tucked his shirt into his pants. "Me? But why?"

"Hard to say why these lunatics do the things they do. Sometimes it's just for the perverse thrill of it," Jane said as she swung her legs over the bed. "But chances are, sometime, he's going to strike again. And it's my job to get the fucker before he does."

She rose up on her toes and kissed David on the cheek. "So, Mr. Perry," she teased, "is that why you called? To grill me for information I probably would have told you anyway?"

"Hey," David smiled. "You called me!"

"Right. But is that why you returned my call in person?"

"Half the reason."

"What's the other half?"

David pulled her into a long arousing kiss. "You're the detective," he said. "You figure it out."

They looked at each other, the memory of the night before still warming their skin. Jane glanced at the clock, "Look, I . . ."

She was interrupted by the sudden ringing of the phone, its bell sounding harsher, more strident, this early in the morning.

"Jesus," David said, tensing. "It's not even six yet."

As abruptly as it began, the ringing stopped, a faint residue of reverberation hanging in the room, like the fading echo of a far-off church bell.

"I hate it when the phone rings at weird times," David said. "It's never good news."

Jane's thoughts went to Poppy, lying with his damaged heart plugged into a series of machines in a hospital across the bay. "I know."

Realizing that Jane was thinking of her father, David took her in his arms and kissed the top of her head. Just then the bedroom door opened and Lily appeared, wiping the sleep from her eyes. "Daddy, the phone woke . . ."

David and Jane quickly separated, like teenagers caught in an embrace by disapproving parents. Lily stood there in shocked disbelief. "Fuck!" she shouted and ran out, slamming the door.

Furious with himself, David punched his leg in frustration. "Shit!" he said. "I've got to go to her."

"Of course," Jane urged, trapped in precisely the situation she had wanted to avoid. "I'll be okay. Just take care of your daughter."

As David hurried from the room, calling after Lily, Jane shook her head and sat on the bed to pull on her slacks and shoes. Then she looked at the telephone and the callback to reality it represented. She lifted the receiver to dial her own number. Checking her machine.

There were three messages. All from Kenny. The last one a curious mixture of apology and concern. "Jane, I know I'm a pest and I'm sorry for calling so many times. First I was calling to tell you we have a meeting with the lieutenant tomorrow just before roll call. Then I got worried 'cause it's after midnight and you're still not home. Or are you monitoring your calls? Hello? Janie?"

——

David stopped at the bottom of the stairs. Lily was where he knew she would be—at the telescope. "How's traffic on the bridge?"

"Pretty sucky," Lily answered without looking at him.

David moved toward her. "And how're you feeling about me right now?"

Lily turned to face her father, tears in her eyes. "Also pretty sucky."

Halting in the middle of the room, David held out his hands in apology. "I'm sorry, honey. I should have handled this better. I . . . just didn't know how." An agonizing silence hung between them, David not sure of how much to say, Lily not wanting to talk.

Finally she looked up to him and wiped away a tear. "Is what it is, Dad."

David started forward again. "I really struggled with all this, Lilliput. How not to cause you any . . ."

"Did you guys do it?" Lily demanded, her face flushing.

"That's not necessary, honey."

Lily stood up abruptly, her hands flailing at her thighs as if she were trying to fly away. "How could you bring her home with you? How could you do that?" she cried. "How could you do that to me?"

David took a few steps closer. "It was stupid and selfish, and I wish I had handled everything differently. You know I would never do anything to hurt you."

"Too late," Lily said. Her feet started to move, as if they had an independent need to be somewhere else. Then she stopped, frustrated at not knowing what to do.

"Lily, listen to me," David said. "You know your mother and I were having problems. Big problems. I've been alone a long time now . . . and I needed to be with someone. I made a mistake, a big mistake, the way I did it. And I apologize." He inched toward her. "Can you even begin to understand?"

Wiping her nose on the sleeve of her T-shirt, Lily looked at her father. "My brain can understand it, Dad. Doesn't mean it doesn't hurt, though."

"I know. You're right," David said. "Look, sweetie. I'm going to come over to you now. And when I get there, I'm going to hug you . . . if you let me."

Gingerly, as if approaching an injured puppy, David began to close the distance between himself and his daughter. But before he could take two steps, Lily burst away from the love seat and raced forward, throwing herself into his arms. David swept her up off the floor. "I'm so sorry," he said over and over into her hair. Then, their emotions spent, he let her slide back down and, his arm over her shoulder, led her to the kitchen.

David grabbed two grapefruits from the bowl on the cooking island, cut them in half, and pressed each half into the electric juicer while Lily washed her face at the sink. "Since when do you know so much about 'doing it'?" he asked as the machine whirred out a translucent pink stream of juice.

"God, Dad, I'm thirteen!" Lily answered, taking two glasses down from the cupboard. "Besides, we get cable."

David poured her a glass of juice and looked up to see Jane standing at the swinging door. "Can I come in?" she asked, testing the water.

Lily turned and studied her, assessing her silently, not yet willing to let go of the hurt.

"Want some juice?" David offered, trying to preserve the semblance of normalcy. "It's fresh."

Jane waved her hand in thanks. "I'm late for a meeting. I called a cab." As she stepped into the room, she noticed that someone had changed the photos on the refrigerator. There were now shots of David and Lily in the pool, on the Golden Gate Bridge, at a soccer game. She looked to Lily. "Good morning, Lily. I'm sorry about all this. It was dumb—the dumbest thing I've ever done in my life."

"Yeah," Lily said, looking away. She drained her juice, put the glass on the counter, and went back to the telescope.

"Well," Jane shifted nervously, "that went well."

The doorbell chimed and a male voice called, "Taxi!"

Jane leaped toward the front door, grateful for the reprieve.

"Wait up," David said. He glanced at Lily. She was watching the two of them while pretending not to. "You free tonight?"

"That depends," Jane answered as she pulled on her coat.

"On what?"

Cocking her head and taking just enough of a beat to lure Lily's attention her way, Jane said, "On whether Lily will join us."

The two of them turned to Lily, cognizant of the power they were giving her. Lily looked to her father, pointedly not addressing Jane, and said, "Maybe . . ."

"Great!" Jane said as she opened the front door.

"Thank you, Inspector," David said as he held the door for her, each of them longing to kiss the other.

"No. Thank you," Jane said, lightly touching his chest, letting her hand linger, unseen by Lily, before dashing down the walkway to the waiting cab.

David stood there, watching her go, the taxi trailing a grey-white flume of exhaust. Then, biting back a smile, he went inside to his daughter.

—

Lowering the cab's dusty window, trying to dilute the stale smell of a thousand cigarettes with a rush of cold air, Jane caught a glimpse of the Golden Gate Bridge between two houses at the beginning of the downslope of David's street. The bridge quickly disappeared, a brief strip of orange spanning a watery vista. And as the taxi dipped down the hill, its heater clattering uselessly, she wondered which of these homes belonged to the Gethers family.

Collecting her thoughts, Jane reflected on the past twelve hours and the extraordinary events that, when remembered as a string of interconnected occurrences, made her heart race with the sheer intensity of it all. The last few evenings with David had been wonderful, everything she had hoped they would be. Conquering the summit of the South Tower of the Golden Gate Bridge, something she had never imagined was even remotely possible, was a memory she would cherish forever. Their kiss in the wind, with the seagulls hovering over them, their perfect white breasts against the perfect black sky, was as if she had finally had her turn in the romantic dreams of all the little girls in the world.

She remembered the phone call about Poppy and the drive to Oakland.

There was David's back as she came down the hospital corridor toward Poppy's room. How instantly familiar and safe it had felt. She thought of crying in her bed. More to the point, crying in her bed in the arms of a man she wanted to care about. Being comforted. Being touched. The magic of making love in a way that had no top or bottom, no boundaries. And, after a while, no fear. The sweet sleep. The dream. The water in the dream. And Poppy, so helpless.

And Lily.

Jane blushed at the memory of being discovered by her lover's daughter. She completely understood, even empathized with, how Lily felt and why she had reacted the way she had. Jane knew she had been careless and selfish. Something she rarely was; and, when she plumbed the innermost reaches of wherever such decisions to act irrationally come from, she smiled.

Because, given the opportunity, she knew she'd do it again. At last, she was immersed in life rather than floating on the surface. She leaned forward to look at the clouds coming in over the bay and she knew that today it would rain.

But she didn't care. She was happy.

45

As she climbed the stairs at the police station, Jane knew that Kenny's cop instinct would lead him to realize that last night wasn't just another Sunday evening spent alone watching *60 Minutes* with a bowl of pasta in her lap.

"What the hell," she muttered as she leaned into the door and entered the bullpen. Even as she smiled an awkward hello to Cheryl Lomax, a sense of dread rose in her throat, not because of Kenny, but because she was late. She hated being late.

Kenny and Ozzie came out of Lieutenant Spielman's office. "*Buenos días,*" Ozzie said as he took a shotgun from the weapons locker and headed for the parking garage. Kenny glanced into Finney's empty cubicle and crossed to Jane at the coffee setup.

"When's the meeting?" she asked, pushing her voice out, hoping it sounded normal.

"Half an hour ago," Kenny responded without emotion. It was as if they were two strangers talking about business for the first time on the telephone.

"Shit. Sorry," Jane said.

Usually, when Kenny poured himself a cup of coffee, he would pour Jane a cup of decaf as well. It was one of the many routines they had developed as partners. But this time he took his mug off the shelf and poured only one cup. "I told the lieutenant you had a doctor's appointment," he said, stirring in a Sweet 'n Low. "Woman's stuff. Scares 'em off every time." He turned his back on her and headed for his desk.

"Thanks," Jane called after him.

Kenny sat on the edge of his desk, sipped his coffee, and looked through the steam at Jane. "Were you monitoring your calls last night or were you out?"

Not wanting to have this conversation be any more public than it already was, Jane crossed toward him, gesturing with her palms up. "C'mon, Kenny."

Kenny held firm. "Well?"

"Out," Jane said.

"All night?"

"What if I were?" Jane asked, exasperated. "My private life's my private life."

"You want a private life separate and apart from your partner?" Kenny spit. "You make your own excuses to your lieutenant. You want me to cover your ass, you tell me what's going on!"

Cheryl looked up from the dispatch desk. From the way Kenny spoke through his tightly clenched teeth, his jaw bouncing, Jane saw that he was even more upset than she had imagined. She closed her eyes, trying to decide whether or not to tell him where she had been. Then, remembering how wonderful she had felt in the taxi, and knowing she couldn't spend her life sparing Kenny's feelings at the expense of her own, she said simply, "I spent the night with David Perry." Watching Kenny's body tense, Jane went on, "I wanted to find a better way to tell you."

Kenny stood up and moved a couple of steps away. "Why? Why should it matter?"

"I thought it did."

"No," Kenny said as he headed for the stairs. "It only used to."

Hurrying to catch up, Jane put her hand on Kenny's shoulder and was surprised at how violently he spun around. "Kenny, listen to me," she pleaded, hating the fact that their drama was playing center stage in the bullpen. "My father had a heart attack last night, and . . ."

Kenny's eyes flickered with worry. "Poppy? Is he all right?"

"Yeah, I think so," Jane said. Relief welling inside her, she hoped for a respite in their running battle.

But Kenny wasn't prepared to make peace. "Remember when I suggested, way back when, that maybe your Mr. Perry might be of such interest to you because he was good-looking and available and et cetera? And you called me an asshole?" His eyes danced with fury as he flung the words at her. "And I, once again, thought, Okay, I'm an asshole. I'm wrong again, just like I was wrong when I committed the mortal sin of not being sure about having kids when I was thirty.

"And I go home thinking I'm the idiot, and I spend the last couple of weeks kissing your ass so that maybe you'll forgive me!" Closing the space between them in one stride, Kenny grabbed Jane's arm and pulled her to him, speaking directly into her ear. "You're fucking a man who's a principal in an ongoing murder investigation. Just how desperate are you?"

Releasing her, he wheeled around and crossed to the stairs. Throwing the stairwell door open, he elbowed past Finney just as he was about to enter and tore down the stairs.

Finney watched Kenny fly down the steps, shrugged, and approached Jane, eight survivors from a box of a dozen doughnuts in his hand. "Jelly?" he offered.

Jane, her eyes filling with tears, shook her head and sat heavily in her chair, only then noticing the small white bag in the middle of her blotter. Without opening it, she knew that Kenny, optimistic and hopeful and dependable, had brought her a yogurt this morning.

46

––

A yellow schoolbus sat in the slums of the SFPD Vehicle Impound Yard. It lay in the mud on its ruptured belly, its roof crushed down through its windows, both its axles broken.

David slowly circled the ravaged bus, shaking his head as he read the empty promise of the peeling letters on its side: "Shepherd-Ramsey, the One to Trust." He had seen the police photographs, taken both at the scene of the tragedy and in this yard. But nothing could come close to the naked impact of standing next to it and imagining the terror those children must have gone through when it toppled off the roadway and rolled over and over, trapping some of them for up to four hours of life-changing agony.

David nodded to himself as he decided to bring the jury down here to see this skeleton of tortured steel firsthand. " 'The one to trust,' " he said in disgust as he got back into his car. The first drops of rain were speckling his windshield as he turned out of the yard and headed for the Bayshore Freeway back to the city.

––

Through a scheduling quirk, Kenny had to be in court the rest of the day, testifying on an old robbery case of his from the days before he had moved up to homicide.

Sitting on the radiator, Jane, her feet on the windowsill, her elbows on her knees, sat watching the rain. It was falling heavily now, curving down the window and washing the grime away in tiny vertical rivers.

The confrontation with Kenny had happened over two hours ago and she knew that this feeling of anxiety was going to be with her for the rest of the day. How could she have handled it differently? she wondered. She supposed she could have taken it more slowly with David;

she could have laid some groundwork with Kenny; she could have waited until the investigation into Jenna Perry's murder was closed.

But, for the first time she could remember, she had decided not to wait, not to be so cautious. And now Kenny was hurt and angry, Lily was confused, and she was even more resolute that she had to begin living her life—not for Poppy or for Timmy or for Kenny, but for herself.

Dropping her feet to the floor and rolling up the top of her turtleneck against the chill of a rainy autumn day, Jane turned to see Lieutenant Spielman coming her way. "How's your father?" he asked. They had worked together for years and been through the divorces and births and, sometimes, deaths that anybody endures.

"I just talked to Timmy. They think they can avoid a bypass with an angioplasty," Jane said.

"That balloon thing?"

"Yeah."

"That's terrific. Tell him I asked after him," Lieutenant Spielman said. He turned to go. "I've got a meeting at the Hall of Justice. What can I tell them about the Jenna Perry case?"

Jane started toward her desk. "Tell them it's in good hands."

"I know that," Lieutenant Spielman said as he crossed the bullpen.

"And Ben?" Jane called.

He turned around. "Yeah?"

"Tell them I'm going to solve this fucker."

Lieutenant Spielman smiled. "I know that too, Jane."

—　—

The waiter placed a plate of Dover sole, asparagus, and pearl onions before Patrick Colomby. He was sitting at his desk, coat off, scanning a few of the six newspapers he read every day.

He was about to begin his meal when his secretary, Mrs. Roman, appeared in the doorway. She had been with Patrick for fifteen years and rarely lost her composure. But now she was flustered.

"What is it, Estelle?"

Mrs. Roman stepped partway into the spacious office. "There's an Inspector Marks in reception."

"Tell him that David's out of the office," Patrick said, "researching a case." He picked up his fork and began to eat.

"I did," Mrs. Roman responded. "He's here to see you."

Patrick put down his fork and chewed thoughtfully. "Well," he said after a moment, "ask him to please come in."

As Mrs. Roman left the room, Patrick turned to the waiter. "The sole is excellent today, Martin."

"Glad you like it, sir," the waiter said. There was movement at the door, and he and Patrick turned as Kenny strode in.

His pace slowed as he absorbed the enormity of Patrick's office. "Thank you for seeing me without an appointment, Mr. Colomby," he said as he neared the desk. "I'm testifying downtown and I kind of have a time thing."

Patrick rose and shook Kenny's hand. Then he gestured to one of the leather club chairs. "Please, Inspector, have a seat."

"I won't take much of your time," Kenny began. "It's my lunch hour."

"Mine too," Patrick smiled. "Would you like anything? Dover sole, maybe a seafood salad?"

"I had a sandwich on the way."

Patrick nodded, and the waiter quietly took his leave through the hidden door. "So, what can I do for you, Inspector?"

Kenny disliked this man intensely. But he realized that Patrick was a formidable adversary—powerful and well connected—and he knew that his usual confrontational method of investigation would do him no good in this situation. He forced a smile. "Just a couple of questions and I'll let you get back to your lunch."

"Fine then," Patrick said. Looking pointedly at Kenny, he continued to eat.

"Mr. Perry has stated that he worked . . ." Kenny flipped open his notebook. ". . . until just about midnight the evening of Mrs. Perry's murder."

Patrick sipped his wine. "David's billing log for Shepherd–Ramsey attests to that."

"Shepherd–Ramsey? The school bus company?"

"Yes."

"You guys are handling them?"

"No," Patrick said evenly, "we're representing the children."

"Oh," Kenny said. He leaned forward slightly in the chair. "And, sir, where exactly were you the night Mrs. Perry was killed?" He studied Patrick's face for a reaction. He got none.

Patrick put down his wineglass and continued eating. "At home," he said after a moment.

Kenny made a note. "Any witnesses?"

"My wife and grandson." Patrick dabbed at his lips. "And my house staff."

"I see," Kenny said. He paused to look around the office. The elegant furniture, the artwork, the photographs of safaris and ski vacations. Patrick Colomby with various dignitaries. Kenny recognized Chief of Police Lucien Biggs standing with Patrick at a charity golf event. "Is it true that Jenna Perry inherited a substantial amount of money following the death of her father?"

"Yes, it is."

"Is it also true that, since her murder, you have access to and control over a substantial portion of that money?"

"Most of the money is tied up in . . ." A hint of irritation betrayed Patrick's face. "What exactly are you implying?"

"I'm not implying anything, Mr. Colomby," Kenny said. "I'm just asking questions here."

Patrick wiped his hands on the linen napkin and dropped it onto his food, the meal and this interview now over. "Jenna Perry was my goddaughter, and Graham Maxwell was my partner and my best friend," he began, his anger building. "There is a line, Inspector Marks, among civilized people, and you've just crossed it, thereby overtaxing my hospitality and overstaying your welcome."

He rose, indicating that it was time for Kenny to leave.

Kenny started to protest, then noticed two extremely large security guards at the office doorway. Patrick, he realized, must have summoned them with a button under the desk.

"Nice talking to you," he said. Then he locked his eyes into Patrick's. "I'll see you around."

47

David slushed to a stop at the bottom of the off-ramp. The cross street was a thoroughfare of heavy traffic racing to beat the afternoon rush, thereby creating its own afternoon rush. The rain fell in dense blurry sheets, tattooing his car like a drum. His windshield was fogging, and as he waited for the light to turn green, David switched on the defroster. Suddenly his car was bumped from behind. David glanced in his mirror, but the back window was fogged up as well. Flicking on the rear window defroster, thin horizontal lines of clarity immediately appearing, he turned around to see who had hit him.

Without warning, the BMW lurched forward as the rear bumper was rammed again. To his horror, David realized his car was being pushed through the crosswalk and into the near traffic lane. A huge semitrailer, its horns blaring angrily, just missed his front end as it roared by.

Virtually standing on the brake pedal, David whipped around and saw Barton Hubble's face, his eyes like windows into hell. With a malevolent grin, he pressed his huge tow truck into the back of David's car, propelling the BMW into the snarl of speeding cross traffic.

Frantically searching for a break in the river of cars, David cranked the steering wheel hard to the right and stomped the gas pedal to the floor, sending his car clambering onto the sidewalk. Once there, he was able to find an opening and slip safely into the traffic.

Looking in his mirror, David saw Hubble, his truck windows rolled down in spite of the rain. Slowly raising his hand, Hubble let something shiny and silver dangle from his fingers. David's watch. From the peculiar bobbing motion of his head, David could tell, even as he pulled away, that Barton Hubble was laughing at him.

The school buses sat idling in the rain, queued up like circus elephants as they received their passengers in front of the Peabody Middle School. David, the image of the battered Shepherd-Ramsey bus still in his head, squinted through the whapping windshield wipers until he saw Lily. Her head uncovered in adolescent carelessness, she was darting across the lawn toward her bus. He felt proud as he admired the agile lope of her athletic body. Lowering the passenger window, David honked his horn and called, "Lilliput!"

Spotting her father, Lily changed course without breaking stride and heaved herself inside the BMW. "Daddy, this is a bus day, not a carpool day!" she exclaimed as she squiggled out of her parka and fussed to arrange herself on the seat.

David watched as the first bus pulled away from the curb, forty-five trusting kids on their way home. "I kinda finished early today," he said as he slid into traffic, a quick uneasy glance behind him to make sure he was alone. "And I wanted to see my girl."

"What happened to the car?" Lily asked. "The back's all scraped up."

David flushed. "I think the parking guy backed into one of those cement things. They're gonna fix it next week."

"Oh," Lily said, the excitement of unexpectedly seeing her father already melting away.

Feeling her mood shift, David touched her cheek with the back of his fingers. "Can we talk a little about what happened this morning?"

"I guess," she said, looking out the rain-dotted window.

"I want to say again that I'm sorry, honey, and I've felt bad about it all day long."

"Me too."

"You know, don't you, sweetie," David continued, "that whatever you feel, I feel too. That there's a corner of my heart, a big corner, that you live in . . . and always will. No matter who comes into my life."

Lily turned her face to him, her little flower of a face, as he went on. "Maybe someday I'll meet someone new, or maybe it'll be Jane, but whatever happens, that part of me that's you will always be safe inside me. And there is nothing that has happened or could ever happen that will change that."

Sucking on her bottom lip, Lily sat there nodding as she played with the drawstrings of her swim team parka. Then she lifted her head and said, "I want you to be happy, Daddy."

Throwing an armlock around her neck and pulling her over to kiss the top of her head, David said, "God, I love you."

"Me too, Daddy. Can we open a window?"

Smiling, David pressed a button, and the passenger window lowered a few inches. Then the memory of Barton Hubble broke through the surface of his awareness and a flash of dread pulsed through him. Lily closed her eyes into the thin spray of rain that brushed her face through the open window. "Daddy?" she said after a while.

"Hmm?"

"Sometime in the next couple of weeks, can you take me down to the bridge?" Lily asked, her eyes still closed against the mist.

"Sure, sweetie," David answered, reaching out to touch her hair.

48

The clouds had moved on that night, taking their burden of rain to the southeast. Despite the cold, David had insisted on barbecuing the swordfish on the outside grill.

Jane searched the kitchen, looking for a corkscrew to open the bottle of Pinot Grigio she had brought, the portable phone cradled on her shoulder. "I'll be there first thing in the morning. Get some sleep, Timmy. Poppy's gonna need you."

Lily covered a bowl of Brussels sprouts with a taut sheet of Saran Wrap. She watched Jane rummage for the corkscrew, trying to make up her mind whether or not to help. It was an odd scene to her, this woman in the kitchen waving to her father through the patio window while she talked on their phone and looked through their drawers.

Lily yanked open the junk drawer, pulled out the corkscrew from beneath the jumble of tools and batteries, and plunked it down on the counter. Jane nodded her thanks as she finished her phone call. "Don't forget, Aunt Lucy wants to be there too, and she needs a ride. Uh-huh. See you tomorrow." She clicked off the telephone and returned it to its place on the windowsill as Lily popped the microwave door and inserted the bowl of Brussels sprouts.

"You think maybe," Jane began, knowing she was venturing into potentially dangerous territory, "you should poke a few holes in the plastic?"

Lily's instinctive teenage defiance got the better of her. "I know what I'm doing," she said in a tone that was harsher than she had intended.

"Okay, okay," Jane said, not wanting to engage. "What're you drinking?"

"Water," Lily responded as she punched the buttons on the microwave and pressed the start button.

"Sounds exciting."

"I'm in training," Lily said, rolling her eyes.

Jane could only shrug a little laugh as she vowed to pull back a bit and approach Lily only if and when she was invited. "Sorry. Lost my head."

Lily was turning to Jane, about to respond, when the microwave gave forth an unnatural smoky belch. Quickly opening the door, Lily pulled out the bowl of ruined vegetables. She looked to Jane with an expression somewhere between embarrassment and irritation just as David entered puffing with pride.

"Swordfish doesn't get any better than this." He put the tray of grilled swordfish steaks on the cooking island and crossed to the cupboard to get the dinner plates.

"Problem?"

Lily held up the spoiled Brussels sprouts and was about to speak when Jane said, "I screwed up the veggies. Sorry." She turned to Lily. "How 'bout we make a salad?"

Sensing that there was a little drama being played out in the middle of his kitchen, David grabbed the plates and headed for the dining room. "I'll set the table."

"I know what you're up to," Lily said as she opened the refrigerator to dig out the salad ingredients.

Jane pulled the cork from the wine bottle. "Will it work?"

Lily rinsed off the lettuce and broke it apart before answering. "There's a lot going on right now."

"I know," Jane acknowledged. "And I only want to be part of the good stuff. I'm trying as hard as I can," she said, fighting back the urge to approach her. "I understand that it's hard for you, my being here, and I'll try not to rush anything. I only hope that you'll be as patient with me."

Lily was turning to Jane, ready to answer, when the phone rang. She rose up on her toes to retrieve it from the windowsill and clicked it on. "Hello," she said, and as she listened, her face lit up. "Jobie! Oh my God, when did you get back? Oh my God, was it like the best ever? Oh my God! Hang on." Flushed with happiness, she called out to David just as he returned from the dining room, "Dad! Jobie just got back from Hawaii. Can I please eat in my room? I really need to talk to her! Please?"

David stole a quick glance at Jane. "You bet," he said.

"Jobie, I'm gonna make a plate and call you back in like two minutes!" She hung up, took a piece of swordfish and some salad, pulled an Evian from the refrigerator, and raced up the stairs.

David took Jane in his arms. "Thanks for covering for Lily with the microwave adventure. She always does that."

" 'Oh my God!' " Jane laughed, as she burrowed into the warmth of his sweater. "She's such a teenager."

—–

The Nineteenth Precinct had already rotated over to the night shift by the time Kenny stopped in on the way home.

After his visit to Patrick Colomby, he had spent the entire day waiting to testify in the robbery case and had never been called. If the next day proved to be as fruitless as today was, Kenny figured, at least he could get some paperwork done.

Nodding to the third-shift dispatcher, Kenny crossed to his desk and started to go through his files. The door to the locker room opened and Lieutenant Spielman came out. He was dressed in a new suit and was just finishing knotting his tie.

"Hey, Ken," he said. "How's the trial going?"

"Bigger waste of tax money than usual," Kenny said. "Going to a prom?"

"I wish," Lieutenant Spielman laughed. "Mary's dragging me to the opera."

"Jesus."

"Trade-off is she has to go to a Raiders game." Lieutenant Spielman turned to go, then stopped. "Ken . . ."

Kenny looked up from his desk.

"Rumor has it you and Patrick Colomby had an unscheduled interview earlier today."

Sitting on the edge of his desk, Kenny said, "How'd you hear?"

"Little birdie in the mayor's office called a little birdie in the deputy chief's office."

Kenny felt himself tensing. "And that little birdie . . . ?"

Lieutenant Spielman shrugged. ". . . called me."

"And this is you telling me to lay off?"

Taking a step forward, Lieutenant Spielman put his hand on Kenny's shoulder. "This is me telling you not to do anything stupid." He looked around the room, then continued, "This is me telling you to keep on being a good cop. Play by the book as much as you can. Throw the book away when you have to." Lieutenant Spielman buttoned his suit jacket. "But do whatever you have to do to solve Jenna Perry's murder. Okay with you, Inspector?"

"Okay with me, Lieutenant," Kenny said. He watched Lieutenant Spielman cross the bullpen, smile to the dispatcher, and step onto the elevator.

— —

The piñon wood surrendered its sweet fragrance as it crackled in the fireplace. Sitting on the banquette in the bay window, their backs propped against overstuffed pillows and their feet under each other's butts, David and Jane sipped brandies and looked out across the gardens to the Golden Gate Bridge. Its strands of lights twinkled back at them through the clarity of an after-rain evening.

They sat there for a while, each lost in introspection. Then David leaned forward and kissed her, his lips lingering on hers, their foreheads touching, trading warmth. "When can I see you again?"

Jane pulled back and studied him. "You sure you're not another one of those guys who are bad for me?" she asked. " 'Cause that's what I attract—men who are genetically predetermined to break my heart."

"Like Kenny?"

Jane took his hand in hers. "How'd you know?"

"It's all over his face."

Jane sat there for a moment, trying to determine just how much to reveal this soon in their relationship. "Actually, I broke his heart," she began. "He was just a little too young and I was just a little too impatient. Next thing you know I'm back in the lonely club seeing the department shrink twice a month for depression and . . ." She trailed off, looking out the window as if searching for an answer to an unasked question.

David reached over and pulled her to him. "Worried about your father?"

"Only in the sense that his mortality is now closer than it was before," Jane admitted. "I mean, I'm sure tomorrow will go okay. But it somehow feels like this is the beginning, the beginning of . . ." She couldn't bring herself to say the words.

"I know," David said, nuzzling his nose in her hair and stroking her back, his hands ironing the worry away. "Can I tell you something about what happened to me today?"

She kissed his hands. "Of course you can."

"I went to the junkyard today and saw the wreckage of that schoolbus I told you about. Those kids never had a chance." He shook his head at the memory, and Jane put her arms around him. "I was so upset I went and picked Lily up at school. I don't know how I'm ever going to let her get back on a bus after that."

Jane smiled at him. "It just breaks my heart how much you love her."

"Mine too," David said. He separated from her and stood up, crossing to the coffee table. "Got something for you." He pulled open the drawer and took out a small gift-wrapped present.

Jane swung her legs down to the floor as David put the box in her hands. She looked up to him, her eyes flashing with gratitude even before she opened it.

"Go ahead," David prompted.

Tearing off the wrapping paper, Jane immediately saw what it was from the logo on the box. "A camera!" she said as she jumped up and hugged him. "Someone actually gave me something I wanted. Someone actually paid attention." She kissed him on the lips and then, to her surprise, clung to him as if her life depended on it.

"What?" David asked, leaning back to look at her.

"Oh, David . . . I'm just so scared."

"About what? That things won't work out between us?"

"No," Jane said, sitting back on the banquette, turning the camera over in her hand. "That they will. . . . It's what I've wanted for so long. But, I mean, I don't know if I'm ready. If I have the skills to actually do this."

David took her face in his hands and kissed her. "There's only one way to find out," he said and pulled her head to his chest.

49

This was the church where Jane had been christened. This was the church where she had taken for her confirmation name Lucia, the name of her godmother, Aunt Lucy. She had learned her catechism and had celebrated her First Communion here. This was the church where, not long after, she had grieved at her mother's funeral and where, until a few years ago, she had hoped to be married.

And then, around the time she turned thirty-five, she had stopped coming to Mass, no longer sitting with her father and Timmy and Aunt Lucy and all the many others who shared her face and her name.

But, having just left Timmy and Aunt Lucy at the hospital, relieved beyond all imagining that the procedure had gone flawlessly and that her father was already awake and complaining, Jane felt the need to give something back.

She lit a candle in the vestibule of this tiny neighborhood church, its school bell ringing across the yard in the rooms where she had gone to elementary school. Then she went up to the priest, just now entering from the sacristy, and, with a small nod, put an envelope in his coat pocket.

This was the same priest who had presided over her First Communion and her mother's funeral, but in this light, and in this context, he didn't recognize her.

"Bless you," he said.

"Thank you, Father," Jane replied as she turned to leave, knowing that the next time she returned to this church, so much smaller than she had remembered, it would probably be for Poppy.

50

Lily's breath came in deep rasping gulps, a grimace of terror defining her face as she ripped through the thick growth of trees. Running as fast as her legs could carry her, twigs and leaves raking her body, she crashed deeper into the brush. A quick glance behind confirmed that he was getting closer. No matter how fast she ran, he always got closer. As she tore past a stand of eucalyptus, her mind racing through the alternatives of which way to go, someone leaped out from behind one of the larger trees and grabbed her. The man from behind closed the distance in a flash and the three of them fell to the ground as Lily screamed and screamed.

In delight.

There was something about playing hide-and-seek that touched a primitive nerve in Lily, and she exulted in the utter joy of, just this once, being a child again. As David and Jane tickled her into giggling submission, her feet thrashing like delirious puppets, she felt, for an instant, transported. "Stop, you guys!" she yelled between gasps of laughter, and all three of them knew she didn't mean it.

Rising to his feet, David hefted his daughter over his shoulder like a bag of flour. Loving every second of it, Lily kicked in mock protest as Jane stood up and followed them back to their picnic blanket. Golden Gate Park was relatively empty on this cool Saturday morning—a few Rollerbladers, a couple of joggers, a man silently practicing the stork-like contortions of Tai Chi.

Running ahead, Jane grabbed her new camera out of her bag and turned around to snap David and Lily just as they emerged from the trees. Lowering himself to his knees and releasing Lily, David flopped back onto the blanket and covered his eyes with his forearm. Lily immediately jumped up. "Again!" she cried, and blasted back into the trees.

Jane fell to her knees as David called out, "We're too old!"

"You win, Lily!" Jane yelled. "We surrender!"

Lily crashed headlong through the woods, ignoring their calls, until she found herself in a new, unfamiliar clearing. Bending over, her hands on her knees, she tried to catch her breath. She heard David shout again, and, still caught up in the game, edged backward against a thick tangle of undergrowth, a mischievous smile pulling at her lips, until she was only a few inches away from Barton Hubble.

He stood there, patient as a spider, still and silent as death. When David's voice again carried through the thicket, she leaned back even farther, pressing deeper into the springy snarl of bushes, so close to Barton Hubble that he was able to sniff her hair, drinking in the innocent shampoo aroma of this child.

"Lilliput!" David's voice pleaded, clearer now, as he had come a few feet into the woods and was yelling through the megaphone of his cupped hands. "No way we're coming after you again. C'mon, sweetie!"

Barton Hubble's fingers twitched reflexively as he thought of this girl's mother and how sweet she had smelled to him that day in the elevator. He had known then that he could take her whenever he wanted, that it was only a matter of time; and that, the knowing, was the extreme rush for him. The chest-tightening, mind-burning anticipation. The power of someone so strong over someone so helpless. So unaware.

Tensing, he began to lean forward just as Lily pulled away from the hedge. "You guys are no fun!" she called out as she trudged back toward her father.

Barton Hubble felt the constricting fullness evaporate from his disciplined predator's heart. He pulled back from the clearing and, as quietly as he had appeared, was absorbed into the underbrush.

— —

All the way home, Lily jabbered on David's car phone while Jane leaned her forehead into the coolness of the passenger window. When she had pulled up at David's house earlier that morning, she had had no idea what to expect from their first outing as a sort of experimental threesome. The day had gone, she thought, exceedingly well, and she was fighting the urge to further cement the connection between herself and Lily, and, consequently, between herself and David.

More than that, she was beginning to realize that she needed to examine her growing affection for David and her responsibility to Lily. Certainly David seemed a kind and generous father, much as he was a kind and generous lover. Lily was a normal young teenager forced to adjust to a completely abnormal situation—her mother's death, her father's new romance—and she was, it appeared, doing so admirably.

But when Jane dug deeper, a gnawing concern seeped to the surface. Was it her own neediness that drew her into this family? Could she, if she decided to, have a frank discussion with David—so busy, so distracted—about where they were and where they were going?

As David pulled into the crescent of his driveway and they all climbed out of the car, Jane resolved to look for the appropriate opening so that she could get a sounding from David on how he felt.

David, his hand resting lightly on the center of Jane's back—they had decided not to show too much physical affection in front of Lily for the time being—turned the key in the front door just as the phone began to ring. Lily burst by her father, already running for the stairs. "I've gotta e-mail Jobie!"

Jane watched her go, marveling at her energy, then turned to David. "And I'm going to pee," she said as she headed for the front powder room.

"Well then," David joked, "I guess I'll just take this call." He snatched up the foyer phone. "Hello."

As soon as he heard the hesitation on the other end he knew who it was. He stood there and listened to the riot of sounds from Chinatown. "Is it you?" he asked of the noise.

Barton Hubble was at his perch on the windowsill in his wretched little apartment. "It's me and I need to see you, Dave," he said in his disquieting voice. Ming looked up from the bed at the strange way he sounded.

David glanced toward the powder-room door. "After that stunt you pulled at the off-ramp? I don't think so."

"Don't fuck with me," Barton Hubble warned. "If I had wanted to push you into that intersection, I could have. But I have no interest in your dying, Dave. Only your living. So I look forward to seeing you tomorrow at noon at the big clock on Fisherman's Wharf. Or . . ."

"Or what, you son of a bitch?" David demanded.

Barton Hubble let the question dangle between them, fluttering like a moth caught in his web, until he finally answered, "Or . . . Lilliput." Hearing David take a sharp breath on the line, Hubble smiled to himself and said, "Bring a jacket, Dave. It gets chilly this time of year." Satisfied with his performance, be hung up and sat on the edge of the bed. Ming put her hand on his back, and he turned to her.

David heard Jane washing her hands in the powder room and returned the phone to its cradle just as she emerged. "God, you're beautiful," he said as the light from the front door fell across her face.

With a quick look up toward Lily's room, Jane, her doubts melting away, gave him a peck on the lips. "You're not too hard to look at yourself." To her surprise, David pulled her into a deep longing hug. "I know," she whispered into his ear, thinking the embrace was coming from a place within him similar to the place she had just touched within herself. "Me too."

— —

Dear Clarissa-

It's a little after three in the morning and I was lying in bed thinking about you.

After my Mom died I started writing to her on my computer—my thoughts, my dreams, what I did today; that kind of stuff. Then tonight I figured why not write to you?

I saw your mother today from my school bus. She was backing her car out of your driveway and Mr. Imhoff, our bus driver, had to stop for her because she wasn't looking where she was going. I hope she doesn't have an accident.

My Dad's been working like crazy lately. Mr. Colomby put him in charge of a really big case, and I know he'll win it. Pilar says he works so hard so he won't have to think about my Mom so much. But I don't know.

He's been seeing this lady. She's a cop he met when my Mom got killed. It's kind of weird having her around all the time, but she tries to be nice to me—and she is. I know my parents had a lot of problems and that my Dad was really lonely for a long time. And now he seems so happy that I'm happy for him.

Clarissa, I think about you all the time. I wish I could have seen you just once more. Maybe I could have helped you even though you were going to come over to try and help me. It would have been nice to get together.

The night of your birthday party I sat in my room and thought

174

about how lucky you are. So beautiful and popular. And how much I wanted to be like you.

And now you're gone and I'm totally confused.

I'll be your friend forever.

Love,

Lily

51

———

D avid was late.

It had been years since he had come to Fisherman's Wharf and he hadn't counted on the ubiquitous post-earthquake construction. Rather than spiral through one of the cavernous commercial parking structures and risk not finding a space, he pulled up to a seafood restaurant near the cable car turnaround and gave his car to the valet.

The first thing he noticed as he hurried past the outdoor fish markets was the sound. The annoying diesel clatter of idling tourist buses mingled with the staccato of jackhammers. A panhandling saxophone player stumbled through the scales, searching for a riff he could then repeat in the hope of coming up with something that sounded vaguely like music.

Seagulls sat atop the dock pilings, squatting into themselves against the chill. Oily brown sea lions lifted their heads and filled the air with a chorus of barks, delighting the tourists who lined the rails and snapped their photos with disposable cameras.

Bombarded by the steamy smells of boiling lobster, crab, and shrimp, David quickened his pace as he cut between a T-shirt stand and a postcard rack to cross the street toward the big clock on the corner, its Roman numeral dial reading four minutes after twelve. Skirting a mounted policeman who was patiently allowing a young father to hoist his toddler son up to stroke the horse's rubbery nose, David stepped up onto the sidewalk. He scanned the crowd that had gathered to listen to another starving, though talented, saxophone player render a passably decent "Take Five."

No Barton Hubble.

Yet.

Then, remembering his encounter on the Sausalito Ferry, David realized that whichever direction he looked, Barton Hubble was probably going to appear in the other. Wheeling around, he saw Hubble, in his dark green greatcoat and heavy black work boots, emerge from the exact spot in the crowd David had been watching only moments before.

Hubble peeled off a few ones and dropped them into the saxophone player's instrument case before closing the distance between himself and David in what seemed to David not enough steps. Standing this close to him again, and recoiling from the implied threat of his proximity, David felt that Barton Hubble had somehow grown.

Hubble smiled and nodded back to the street musician. "I've always considered myself a patron of the arts, Dave."

Grabbing the fleshy skin behind David's biceps, making it clear that there was the potential of real harm in his grip, Barton Hubble led David away from the crowd. "Glad to see you dressed warm. See? It's good when you listen to me."

David stopped walking and yanked his arm out of Hubble's grasp, his eyes sideslipping furtively to see if the mounted policeman had noticed the sudden movement. But the young father and his little boy still had his attention.

"No more quick little arm motions like that, Dave," Hubble said, his eyes narrowing into malicious slits. "Too many cops around. Got it?"

David averted his eyes and nodded.

"Good boy," Hubble said, pleased with himself. "Did you think I was just going to disappear on you, Dave?"

"I had my hopes."

"That isn't going to happen. We have so much unfinished business, you and I." He gestured with his chin for the two of them to begin walking again.

"Look," David began as they walked even farther away from the mounted policeman. "I tried to get you some money. But it's all tied up in probate."

Hubble's face flushed a deep red. "I don't care," he seethed. "You're the big-shot lawyer with the fancy shoes. You figure it out." He leaned forward. "I took the chance. I did you the favor."

"Killing my wife was no favor to me!" David responded, his spit flying through his clenched teeth. "You're insane!"

Hubble pressed into David, forcing him against the chain-link fence of an abandoned construction site. He thrust his face in so close that David could smell the faint odor of stale coffee on his breath and said, "That's a distinct possibility. But you still owe me."

"Bullshit," David said as he started to sidle away. But Hubble blocked him by putting his heavy work boot just against the side of David's dress shoe, the inference of a crushed foot very much alive in both their minds.

"But it's not bullshit, Dave," Hubble said, his voice rising. "It's a stone fact. And if you don't give me my money . . ." He paused, his eyes boring into David. ". . . my five million dollars, Dave, I'm going to become even more unpleasant than I already am."

"Like what?" David asked.

"Like making sure a certain Rolex shows up at the site of a certain shallow grave."

Bristling, David pushed Hubble away. "Do what you need to do, Hubble," David said, careful to keep his distance. "I've got two unimpeachable witnesses who will testify that I was working late that night. If this has to go public, I'll survive. I'm going to the police. And you can go fuck yourself!"

David stormed away, his shoulders tensing against a blow that never came. Hubble blew his nose into his hand, and wiping it off in a pocket of his greatcoat, called out, "Hell, maybe I'll just turn myself in!"

David stopped and turned around. "What?"

"Maybe I'll just go to the police and tell them I did it," Hubble sneered as David took a few steps back toward him. "Of course they'll ask me why. And that's where the problems really begin for you."

"What the hell are you talking about?"

"You see, Dave, I had no reason to kill your wife. I didn't rape her. Hell, I didn't even steal her jewelry. Basically, I had no motive." He paused to let the import of what he was saying sink in. "But you did. You said it yourself: 'There's a shitload of money.' " Hubble leaned forward. "So I'll just go to the police and tell them you hired me to do it . . . for the money."

"You're sick."

"You say you have witnesses?" Hubble went on, ignoring him. "Well, so do I. I mean, come on, what's a fancy guy like you doing having drinks with a grease monkey like me at a big-deal place like Terry's SportsWall? Musta been, what, couple hundred people there that night who saw us?" Hubble smiled evilly. "Shit, you even gave me your fucking business card."

"You pull that, you're going to jail for sure. Probably the gas chamber."

"My life already stinks," Hubble said. "Way I look at it, it's a gamble.

178

I'm gambling you don't want to get your dick caught up in this and you'll pay me my money. Do you think it's a good gamble, Dave?"

David looked away.

"Here's the deal," Barton Hubble continued, twisting the knife. "You don't give me my money and it's me who goes to the police. And then, Dave, you are totally fucked."

He wheeled around, his greatcoat flaring as it caught the wind, and strode away.

52

D avid pulled into his parking space beneath his office building, took the stairs up to the lobby, and crossed to see Frank at the security desk. "How's it goin', Frank?"

"Jus' fine, Mr. Perry," Frank answered as he plugged in his portable television. "Big game tonight. Cowboys comin' to our house," he said, his rheumy eyes sparkling in anticipation.

"Yeah," David agreed. "We owe them one. How's the boy these days? You think maybe he's up to going to a game?"

"He's slippin' away from me, Mr. Perry." He made a sucking noise, pulling his cheek between his teeth. "Won't be long now."

Putting his hand on Frank's arm, David said, "You need anything, you just . . ."

"I know that," Frank said, cutting off the difficult conversation. "You been very kind. Thank you, sir."

— —

Through mutual, and unspoken, consent, Jane and Kenny had stopped carpooling to and from the station. Still occupied with the testimony in his old robbery case, Kenny had spent most of the past week stuck in the witness holding room of the Alameda County Criminal Courts Building. Easy duty for most cops, but Jane knew he must be climbing the walls with boredom. A tiny, affectionate smile played at the corners of her mouth as she thought of her partner—difficult, naive, loyal Kenny—enduring the torture of waiting to be called day in and day out while the world continued on its path without him.

Jane sat at her desk reviewing the FBI report on the boot prints and tire prints from David's house and Mount Tamalpais. As she digested the results, she contemplated putting some kind of conciliatory message on Kenny's answering machine. Her phone rang. She picked it up on the second ring. "Homicide. Inspector Candiotti."

"Hello, Inspector," David greeted her, nodding his thanks as his secretary brought him a plate of cold cuts from the dining room.

"Hey!" Jane smiled. "Hello yourself."

"I'm underwater here on Shepherd-Ramsey, but I wanted to know if you can break away tomorrow for lunch."

Enjoying this unusual midday contact, Jane said brightly, "Will you take yes for an answer?"

"You bet I will. One o'clock at Camille's?"

"Until then," Jane said as she rang off.

"Until then," David replied, although he knew she had already hung up.

53

Still smiling at the drubbing his 49ers had given the Cowboys, Frank drove his old Ford station wagon down the last incline to his little house in Richmond.

Squeaking to a stop, Frank lifted the handle of the portable TV in one hand and grabbed up a bag of barbecued chicken wings in the other. His son barely slept these days and had called his father at work for this, tonight's craving.

Nudging the car door open with his shoulder, Frank stepped into the street. He was about to use his hip to close the door when, from out of nowhere, silent and lethal as an owl, a huge tow truck came hurtling down the hill, gathering deadly speed as it descended, and slammed into him.

The bag of chicken wings exploded into the air and the television shattered along with Frank's bones as the breath and the life were extinguished from his body.

Continuing on without slowing, the friction of its tires on the wet asphalt its only sound, the tow truck came to the bottom of the hill. Then, with a great throaty roar, like a lion after a kill, its engine ignited and it disappeared into the darkness, leaving Frank's body, crumpled and broken, lying in a puddle of blood and muddy rainwater near the driveway of his house.

— —

Myra loved the sunrise. For her, the coming dawn meant she would soon be home with her family.

As she passed the security desk in the empty lobby, she made a mental note to make some tamales for Frank's son. He loved her tamales. Pulling her coat collar tight to her chin, she entered the parking garage and started toward her car.

The smell of exhaust caught her attention, and she turned to see a large tow truck against the near wall, its engine idling and its lights off. Myra smiled at the truck's driver and got into her car.

She started her engine and waited for the heater to come to life. Then she pulled out of her space, tires squealing on the slick cement, and curved down the ramp toward the exit. Just as she came around the last bend, she noticed the tow truck, its headlights and dome lights ablaze, closing in behind her.

At street level, Myra turned right and headed south across town. She glanced in her mirror and was relieved to see that she was alone. Descending the long slope of Church Street, she stopped at a red light and looked down to adjust the heater. When she looked up again she was startled to see the harsh beams of the tow truck hurtling toward her.

Terrified, she floored the accelerator and tore through the intersection. Hubble revved his powerful engine and brought his beast of a truck to within inches of Myra's little car. Blinded by the explosion of light in her mirrors, Myra urged her car forward, racing for home and the safety of her brothers.

Hubble tapped the back of her car with the oversized winch on his front bumper. Shaken, Myra squinted into her mirror. She couldn't be sure, but she thought she saw the truck's driver laughing.

Stepping harder on the gas pedal, Hubble pressed the truck into Myra's car. Myra took her foot off her accelerator and still her car sped along the empty morning street, propelled by the enormous engine of the heavy truck.

Insane with panic, Myra glanced up and saw that she was only two blocks from home. She pulled down on the steering wheel, throwing her car into a hard left turn. The truck smashed into her left rear fender and sent the car screeching sideways into a row of newspaper vending machines.

Myra scrambled out of her car and was about to run screaming toward her house when Barton Hubble grabbed her arm and spun her around. She hadn't even seen him get out of the truck.

Trembling, Myra looked into his face, and when she saw his eyes, her blood ran cold. "Please, Mister, what do you want from me?"

Barton Hubble took a step forward and put his hand on her shoulder, next to her neck, and smiled.

54

The sun burned like a white-hot hole in the sky. It was the brightest day Lily could remember, maybe even the brightest day she had ever seen.

The bridge seemed more silver than orange in the shimmering light off the mirror-smooth waters of the bay. As soon as her father stopped the car at the Vista Point parking lot, she was off and running up the long winding sidewalk, streaking past the cyclists and joggers and tourists.

Her father called after her, "Lily! Wait up!"

Running faster now, Lily felt as if she were floating over the roadway; cars and trucks, their windshields like brilliant mirages, speeding by. Glancing back as she ran, she saw her father just now cresting the rise from the parking lot, his hands cupped to his mouth. Calling. But Lily heard nothing.

She raced beneath the South Tower, its cables spreading like wings, and found this part of the bridge more crowded. Pushing and humping her way along, both driven and pulled, all she could hear was the sound of her own breath rushing in and out, mingling with her sobs. As her tears cooled her face, she forced her way through the mob, her father receding in the far distance. She stopped, heaving for air, at the midpoint between the two towers.

Moving her head from side to side, trying to glimpse her father through the throng, Lily grabbed onto the railing and boosted herself up, unnoticing passersby milling along. Once on the rail, she lowered herself to the steel beam on the other side and, reaching behind to grab one of the supports, she looked down. Water was her friend, the place where she had always gone to find peace. She peered into the gently lapping waves until she could see herself in the vast reflective surface, an imperfect, fluttering other self who opened her arms to summon her.

Lily smiled.

She knew it was time.

She turned to see her father desperately pushing against the tide of people. "Lily!" he screamed. "Please!"

Lily smiled to her father and then with one last deep breath, as at the start of a swimming race, she let go. As her body dropped into space, a pillow of wind came up to catch her and she floated like a little angel toward the beckoning waters of San Francisco Bay.

"Mommy," she said.

— —

"Lily?"

Pilar stood over Lily's bed and gently shook her shoulder. "Come, *chica*. Time to get up."

Startling awake, Lily noticed that the morning sun was beaming into the room, brighter than she ever remembered.

— —

David stood at the kitchen counter, sipping grapefruit juice and catching up on the previous Sunday's *Chronicle*. Lily came down the stairs and padded across to her father. "Sleep okay?" he asked as he poured her some juice.

"Yeah," Lily answered.

Finishing off his glass, David squeezed his daughter into a loving hug. "Pilar's taking you to school today. I've got an early meeting. See you tonight, sweetie." He took up his briefcase and headed for the front door. "Please make sure she eats something," he said to Pilar as she came down from Lily's room.

"Bye, Daddy," Lily said absentmindedly as she gathered up his newspaper and shuffled over to the breakfast nook.

"Pancakes or French toast?" Pilar called out from the stove.

But Lily didn't respond. She had pulled out the magazine section of the paper, and the cover photo had captured her. The Golden Gate Bridge, rendered by a photo artist, loomed like a death skull. Superimposed over it was a ghostly transparent picture of Clarissa Gethers. The caption read: "The Golden Girl and the Golden Gate."

"I said, pancakes or French toast?" Pilar repeated.

"Uh, French toast is good," Lily replied, unable to take her eyes off the magazine.

55

Long shadows played across the gleaming marble floors of the lobby of David Perry's building as he entered from the parking garage. Quickening his pace to catch the express elevator, he noticed a middle-aged woman with short salt-and-pepper hair sitting behind the security desk, giving directions to a young couple.

Curious, David let the elevator go and approached her. When the young couple left, David leaned in. The woman looked up. "Can I help you?"

"I work on fifty-four. Uh, where's Frank today?"

"Oh, you didn't hear?" the security guard said. "He was killed last night. Hit-and-run right in front of his house. They say it was like a Mack truck hit him."

David looked on the floor behind the security desk and saw the newspaper the early shift always left for Frank. Then he stared out the window at the traffic passing silently by.

"Did you know him very well?" the security guard asked.

"Yeah. We were friends," David said as he turned away and headed back to the parking garage.

— —

The house Myra shared with her two sisters and two brothers was directly behind her landlord's house. David, his BMW parked incongruously among older, humbler cars, had been knocking on the door for almost a minute, lime-green flecks of paint flaking off onto his knuckles.

"There's no one there, *señor*," said a woman's voice as he heard a screen door creak behind him.

Turning around, David smiled at the beautiful young woman with an infant girl on her hip. "When will they be back?"

"They won't," the woman said matter-of-factly.

"You mean not today?" David asked as the baby reached for his keys.

"I mean not ever."

David handed his keys to the little girl, who, making soft wet cooing sounds, put them in her mouth. "She's teething, no?"

The woman relaxed a bit and smiled. "She's teething, yes."

"I'm an old friend of Myra's. We work in the same building in the city," David explained. "I was the one who wrote that letter for her to help her get her citizenship papers."

"Ah yes. I remember you from the ceremony." She nodded. "I'm Maricela, You're Mr. Perry, right?"

"Yes. David Perry." David shook her hand.

"I am very sorry, sir, about your wife," Maricela offered. "Myra was very upset for you."

"Thank you," David said. "Where is Myra? Where is her family?"

Maricela shook her head. "She and her brothers left maybe seven o'clock this morning. With everything. The plane, I think, stops in Texas, then it goes to El Salvador."

"Do you know why?"

"All I know, Mr. Perry, is Myra was very nervous like I've never seen. She didn't even ask for her security deposit back. Just gone like this: pffft." The baby gave a little laugh at the strange sound her mother made.

Gently taking his keys back from Maricela's daughter, David said, "Thank you very much for your time."

"De nada, señor," Maricela said. She opened the screen door and went back into her house.

—–

David had gotten to Camille's twenty minutes early and, uncharacteristically for him in the middle of a weekday, had ordered a tequila and soda. Feeling the grip of a complicated morning loosen from around his chest, he sat staring pensively out the window at the patio tables, empty but for a couple of busboys smoking cigarettes. He thought about Myra and wondered why Barton Hubble hadn't just killed her too.

Before he could react to the shadow he felt fall across his back, a cloth napkin was pulled over his eyes. Ripping it away, he bolted to his feet.

Jane took a step back, her face blushing with embarrassment. "I'm so sorry. I didn't mean to startle you like that."

David struggled with whether or not this was the time to tell Jane about Frank's death and about the hold Hubble had on him. Stepping into the space between them, he kissed her on the lips. "I was just . . . uh, absorbed in Shepherd-Ramsey," he said wearily. "I've got that little girl on the stand soon. She falls apart, the whole thing goes to hell."

"I know you'll be great," Jane said as they sat down. She reached into her purse and brought out a Fotomat envelope. "Speaking of little girls . . ." She passed the photos to David. "That's one hell of a photogenic daughter you've got there."

Flipping through the pictures, David came to the one of him carrying Lily over his shoulder in Golden Gate Park. "Yikes! I look a hundred years old."

"You do not." Jane took his hand and kissed it. "I love that picture. And I love my camera. Thank you for being so generous . . . and so considerate."

The waiter came by, and they ordered iced teas and antipasto salads, David gesturing for him to take away his unfinished drink. "So, how's your day treating you so far?" he asked.

"Is it okay if we talk about the case?" Jane searched his eyes to see whether or not this was a bad time.

"You mean, my case?"

"Well, yeah," Jane said.

"Sure. Got anything new?"

Excited, Jane put her palms on the table and leaned closer to David. "We got the FBI stuff back yesterday, and we learned a lot."

"Like what?"

"There were identical tire imprints from the clearing in the woods and from the parking lane in front of your house. Large tires, like from a truck," Jane added. "We're cross-hitting this data and some boot-print stuff with the National Investigation Resources computer bank in Atlanta. We should know something in a day or two."

"Like who did it?"

"Not likely, but possibly," Jane said. "But we hope to start narrowing in on him. It's a process. Sometimes a long one. And I feel good that we're this much closer." She sat back as the waiter arrived with their iced teas.

"Being a homicide cop makes me nuts sometimes." She squeezed the lemon into her glass. "Because it basically means moving from the front lines where you fight crime, maybe even prevent it . . ." She sipped her tea. ". . . to the rear echelon, where all you can do is react to crime. Sometimes it's frustrating. But, believe me, something will turn up . . . or someone will fuck up. It happens all the time."

The sounds of someone singing "Happy Birthday" drifted toward them, and they turned to see the waiters and waitresses gathering around a corner booth. The women in the booth were all in their thirties and, from the look of them, fairly well off. A waitress placed a piece of fudge cake, a single candle flickering, on the table. As the restaurant staff dispersed, the celebrant blew out the candle, and her friends, chattering giddily, all reached over to hug her.

The other patrons clapped lightly and returned to their meals, but Jane saw that David had noticed something she had also seen. The birthday girl resembled Jenna Perry. Her hair was a similar length and color, and her figure was almost identical. Jane suspected the exuberance in the way she laughed as she and her friends dug into their dessert was probably reminiscent of David's wife too.

The waiter delivered their salads and twisted black pepper onto them. Distracted, David only toyed with his, rearranging it more than eating it. "Pilar told me something disturbing this morning," David said without looking up.

"What?" Jane asked as she put her hand on his.

"Carmen, the Gethers housekeeper, told Pilar that . . ." He put down his fork and took her hand. ". . . after Clarissa killed herself, Noble and Patricia—they're her parents—went through her diary and safe deposit box."

"Understandable, considering the circumstances," Jane offered. "What'd they find?"

David brought his eyes up to meet hers. "Seems Clarissa was obsessed with some guy. They couldn't tell if it was someone from school, a teacher maybe, or just someone she met. But it was a pretty heavy-duty crush."

"That poor girl."

David nodded. "Her poor parents." He looked away again.

"David, you've got too much on your mind," Jane said as she squeezed his arm. "When your case is over—after you win Shepherd-Ramsey—how about a little trip to the wine country? Just the two of us?"

David smiled. "It's a date."

"We can eat, drink, and be very merry," she said, her eyes

189

shining as she wondered if all the loneliness she had been through in her life had somehow brought her to this place with this man at this moment.

David kissed her hand. "All I'll bring is my toothbrush."

"And all I'll bring is my camera," Jane laughed as they began to eat.

56

Jane leaned across David's car and kissed him on the ear as he pulled up to the police station. "Talk to you later," she said as she tugged on the passenger door handle.

Before she could go, David reached over and took her into a long embrace, kissing her deeply on the lips. "See you soon," he said as they separated.

She got out of the car and lingered on the sidewalk, watching him slip the BMW into traffic and, with a wave, drive away. Then, deciding to take a short cut, she headed into the parking garage and crossed between the cars to the stairway.

Kenny stepped out from behind his Explorer, its engine still crackling as it cooled. Jane, surprised, but not up for a confrontation, greeted him, "So the expert witness returns. How'd it go?"

"The fucker walked," Kenny said without a trace of warmth.

The case had been routine, and Jane knew that Kenny didn't have any real investment in its outcome other than simple justice. But his foul mood revealed a deeper affront, and she immediately understood two things: Kenny was far from over their battle of the other day; and worse, he had seen David drop her off.

Which meant he had seen them kiss.

Caught unprepared, Jane decided to defer another showdown until she could figure out how to have a real conversation with Kenny. Besides, his anger and hurt were still so evident that she knew any attempt at explanation would just deteriorate into warfare between them.

"I've got a ton of shit on my desk. You coming up?" She started to go around him toward the stairway, but Kenny wouldn't budge, and there wasn't enough room to pass comfortably.

"We need to talk, Jane," he said flatly.

From the tension in his voice, Jane could tell he had probably been

191

preparing for this moment all those days in the witness waiting room. "All right," she sighed, surrendering to the inevitability of it all. "But not here."

As they passed through the fire door into the relative privacy of the stairwell, the thought crossed Jane's mind that this man with whom she had shared so much, with whom she had made love, was now as cold and remote as a stranger.

As soon as the door was closed, Kenny turned to her and asked, "So, is it love?"

Jane took a moment. "Not yet."

"But it could be," Kenny stated, not as a question, but as a fact.

Not willing to submit to an interrogation, especially in these circumstances, Jane looked Kenny in the eye and said with finality, "God, I hope so." Brushing past him, she started up the stairs.

"What's the big attraction?" Kenny called after her. "Big house? Big car? Big money?"

Sagging, Jane stopped on the landing and turned back to him. "Kenny . . ."

"His daughter?" Kenny sneered.

Feeling herself about to lose her temper, Jane seethed, "That is so unfair!"

But Kenny was not to be deterred as he ascended the stairs and joined her on the landing. "Or is it that he's a widower?" he pressed. "Does that make him more vulnerable to you? Someone else for you to take care of while you completely compromise this investigation?"

All hope of civility evaporated as Jane exploded, her fury resounding in the cramped stairwell. "What's the big fucking crime here?" she demanded. "That I may have found someone I can really love? Finally?" Furious, she whacked the wall next to the standpipe with her open palm. "That I may have found someone secure enough and . . ." She locked in on Kenny, making sure he heard and understood her every word. ". . . mature enough to be able to make a commitment without asking for a three-year grace period?"

Kenny, caught off-guard by Jane's wrath, raised his voice beyond all civility. "That is not what I said! If you'll fucking bother to remember . . ."

The upstairs door whamming open caught them both by surprise, and they turned toward Lieutenant Spielman, who stood fuming in the doorway. "Let's take a walk, children," he said, then wheeled around and headed through the bullpen for his office.

Passing through the gauntlet of Cheryl Lomax, Sally Banks, Ozzie Castillo, and the others in the squad room, Jane and Kenny followed Lieutenant Spielman into his office. Only Finney, a takeout menu from a new submarine sandwich place on his lap and a telephone at his ear, failed to look up.

Lieutenant Spielman closed the door and sat on the edge of his desk. Jane took a seat on the couch. Kenny elected to remain standing, leaning against the bookcase, his arms folded defiantly across his chest. Sitting there, Jane thought about all the times the three of them had worked long into the night in this same office trying to solve, usually successfully, one case or another.

"Let's make this real quick and real plain," Lieutenant Spielman began. "I think I know what this is about, and I'm not even going to go there. All's I care about is, can you do your jobs?" He looked to Jane.

"Uh, sure, Ben," she said, meeting his gaze, then quickly glancing to Kenny. "Of course we can."

"Fine, then," Lieutenant Spielman said as he turned to Kenny. "And you?"

Kenny chewed on his inner cheek, his jaw bouncing in that way that Jane had seen so many times before when he was troubled. He looked first at Jane, giving nothing away, then at Lieutenant Spielman. "I want to be reassigned."

Jane half rose off the couch. "C'mon, Kenny," she pleaded, abashed that she had let this situation get so out of hand.

Pushing away from the bookcase, Kenny put his hand on the doorknob and looked at Lieutenant Spielman. "We done?"

"Consider yourself temporarily reassigned, Ken," Lieutenant Spielman said. "Accent on 'temporary.'" Kenny gave a tight nod and left the room, pulling the door closed behind him. "Happens every time," Lieutenant Spielman sighed. "Fuckin' office romances."

A tiny laugh slipped out of Jane's mouth. "You knew?"

"This is a police station filled with people who figure stuff out for a living. Everyone knew."

"Sorry, Ben." Jane stood up and started to go.

"One other thing, Jane," Lieutenant Spielman said, stopping her. "Rumor around here has you, how do you say, converting a professional relationship to a more casual liaison with a certain survivor of a certain murder victim."

Jane blushed with a flood of anger. "If you're talking about me and

David Perry, it's true, Ben. I've been seeing him. And it's nobody's business. Not Kenny's and, with all due respect, not yours."

"You're right. What you do with your personal life is your business," Lieutenant Spielman said coolly. "But what you do with your professional life is my business. And, toward that end, I'm taking you off the Perry murder investigation until I can figure out what to do with you."

Stunned, Jane stepped toward him. "Ben," she said quietly, "you can't do that."

"I can, and I have," Lieutenant Spielman said. "Turn your files over to Kenny. He'll be lead investigator until further notice."

"Please, Ben."

"There's nothing further to discuss. I'd suggest you take a couple of days off and give this whole thing a lot of thought." He crossed in front of her and held the door open. "Good-bye, Jane."

Jane stormed through the bullpen, whipped open her file drawer, and pulled out the folder on Jenna Perry. Without a word, she reached across and flung it at Kenny's chest, sending papers fluttering to the floor. Then she took her handbag from under her desk, strode past the other cops, and burst through the stairwell door.

As if at a tennis match, the heads of his colleagues turned in unison to see Kenny's reaction. But he had none for them. Instead, he put the file back together and crossed to Finney's cubicle.

Finney was just finishing ordering on the phone. "You know what? Better make that two of 'em." Feeling Kenny's presence, he began to speak more hurriedly "Yes, that's right. Officer Finney. Nineteenth Precinct. Second floor. Oh, uh—these coupons still good? Great!" He hung up and swiveled his chair to face Kenny.

"As you may or may not have noticed, Moby," Kenny said, "I've been away. I had a really bad time and I'm in a really bad mood. So, tell me something good."

Finney screwed his face in concentration. Then, his eyes brightening, he said, "Credit union came through. The wife picks up her van tonight." He started to turn back to his desk. "Thanks for asking, Inspector."

Kenny stopped Finney's chair from turning with his knee. "Could it really be that you don't know what I'm talking about?"

Puckering his lips and moving them from side to side across his face, the faint glimmer of a distant memory fought its way back into Finney's head. "Oh! I was supposed to do something for you, wasn't I? Don't tell me." He stared at his desktop for a long moment, forcing some thought about something other than food and cars to present itself. Finally, it came to him.

"The fax!"

Kenny sighed, resisting with every fiber in his body the urge to strangle this man. "Right. You were doing backgrounds on David Perry and Patrick Colomby, remember?"

" 'Course I do," Finney said.

"And . . . ?"

"Machine's broke," Finney announced with finality.

Grabbing Finney's necktie, Kenny yanked him to his feet. "Then go to fuckin' Kinko's and use theirs," he hissed. "Because, Moby, if you don't, I swear to God I will shoot you dead!"

Spinning on his heel, he grabbed his jacket from the back of his chair and stomped to the elevators. Finney, not entirely sure what had hit him, sat back down at his desk. "I'll go after my sandwiches," he muttered. "What's everyone so impatient about?"

57

It was a painfully familiar feeling, Jane thought, as she sat on her bed watching TV with the sound off, the rest of her house hushed in darkness. She would get angry, she would get hurt, and her first impulse would be to be alone. Sipping her second glass of Chianti, her legs vibrating in agitation, she got up to run a hot bubble bath, then remembered that she hadn't yet checked her answering machine.

As she walked down the hallway toward the living room, she paused to look out her front picture window. A rusted old freighter slipped across the harbor, its running lights flashing red and white. Often, when a ship passed, Jane would scurry for her binoculars and stand on the cushion of the bay window, rocking unsteadily from one foot to the other. Peering through her binoculars, she would try to see where the ship was from, from what country, for no reason other than the adventure of it.

Tonight, however, as this ship crossed the sweep of her window, she didn't bother to find out where it was from. She didn't really have the energy, and for the first time since she had lived in this house, she didn't care.

The message light on her answering machine blinked twice. Two messages. She pressed the play button and the tape whirred backward, then played the first call. "Jane, it's Timmy. I know it's last minute, but Poppy's feeling better and he really wants to have a barbecue on Saturday. I tried to talk him out of it, but you know how he is. Hope you can make it."

Shaking her head, Jane made a deal with herself. If the other call was from David, she would call him back and ask him to her father's. And if he said yes, she promised herself, she would climb out of this depression and stop feeling so damned indulgent.

She pressed the play button again. "Hi, it's me," David's voice said.

"I called the station and they said you'd left. Hope you're okay. Uh . . . talk to you later. Bye."

Jane looked in the mirror above the Parsons table as the answering machine rewound. She remembered that it was into this mirror that she would stare after coming home from yet another disastrous blind date or yet another baby shower. And she would watch as her eyes filled with tears that would fall streaming down her cheeks. But on this night, even as her eyes brimmed, she knew the tears wouldn't fall, and she pursed her lips into a grateful smile.

"Thank you," she whispered.

58

――――

Dear Clarissa-

It's early Saturday morning and I couldn't sleep.

Your Mom got into a car accident. Some kids from school saw her at the market and she wasn't looking where she was going and she drove off the curb and into a parked car.

She didn't get hurt or anything, but the front of her car is all smashed up.

I heard Pilar talking to my Dad about you. She said that Carmen told her that your parents found some stuff in your diary about you and some older guy.

Were you really seeing an older guy? Was it one of your professors? How cool!

I wish we could have talked about it.

School's been okay and my Dad's still seeing that same lady. Kind of a lot. She's trying to get me to like her. So I'll let her keep trying.

Besides, my Dad is happier when she's around and I'm not so jealous anymore.

Later today we're going to a barbecue at her father's house. Might be fun. She's supposed to have this big crazy family. She's Italian.

I've been working really hard at my swimming. Coach Tanney says I've got ''the stuff'' to be really good if I keep at it.

Jobie (my best friend—remember her?) has a boyfriend on the boys' swim team and he showed us this door in the back of the pool building that has a broken lock. Sometimes me and Jobie sneak in and we fool around. Doing cannonballs and stuff.

Well, that's all for now. I wish I could just call you up and we
could talk.

I miss you.

Love,

Lily

P.S.: Pilar told me that your Mom and Dad put your house up for
sale. Weird, huh?

——

It was Ming Wei Wu's birthday, or at least she thought it was. The only
thing she was sure of was that it was a Saturday, because Barton Hubble
hadn't gone to work.

She lay on the bed, naked except for her necklace with the tiny diamond. Her flesh still pink from their furious lovemaking, she watched
Barton as he sat on the other side of the room and dialed the phone.
When he spoke, Ming was surprised at the change in his voice. Although she couldn't understand what he was saying, she noticed that his
voice was unusually high and thin.

"Yes, please," he said into the phone. "I need to speak to someone
about the murder of that wealthy lady who was found on Mount Tam."
He waited while the call was transferred. "Hello? Who's this?" he said,
his voice still higher than normal. "Oh, hello, Inspector Marks, working
a Saturday, huh?"

He listened. "Yes, I did say that I wanted to talk about that lady who
was killed. I forget her name, but . . . ah, right, Jenna Perry. Thank you."

Ming pulled the covers over her body and watched as Hubble stood
up and paced while he spoke.

"I'm a jogger, y'know? A pretty serious one? And this morning I was
doing a couple of miles up this trail on Mount Tam? And I took a little
break, just to catch my breath, y'know? And there was something in
the bushes, under some dead leaves and stuff? I mean, if I had stopped
anywhere else or been looking the other way, I never would have
seen it."

He looked out the window. "Yes, I picked it up. Maybe I shouldn't
have, but I did. Sorry." He smiled to himself, enjoying this. "Anyway,
once I saw what it was, I put two and two together and thought it might
be interesting to you guys. But, like, I didn't want to get too involved

199

with any police, if you know what I mean? So I put it back where I found it. Was that okay?"

Barton Hubble looked over to Ming Wei Wu and could tell she'd be asleep in a few minutes. "Yes, sir. It's on the east side of the trail just before the turnout. My name? Oh, I don't think . . ."

He hung up.

Ming gave a shallow sigh as her breathing steadied and she fell asleep. Hubble crossed the room and stood over her, thinking it was a shame, but he would have to kill her if the police ever got too close.

— —

David Perry lay on the dew-moistened grass with a stainless-steel colander on his head.

"Close your eyes," Jane whispered as she clipped a pair of jumper cables to the little curved feet of the colander and told all the children to stand back. Then she touched the other end of the cables to an iron sprinkler head and made exaggerated high-voltage sounds as if she were being horribly electrocuted.

David's eyes popped open and his body began to twitch uncontrollably. The kids, knowing what was coming next, prepared to run for their lives. Frankenstein-stiff, David rose to a sitting position, his arms extended in front of him, and surveyed the scene as if to pick out which child he would eat. The twins squealed and fled to the safety of Poppy's back porch. Then David creaked to his feet and set off in straight-legged pursuit of those children brave enough to tarry.

Laughing, Jane crossed over to the hammock where Lily swung lazily between the two oaks. She had noticed earlier that her little cousin Tony, just turning fourteen this Christmas, had separated himself from the younger kids, and that he and Lily had spent the entire day ignoring each other without ever taking their eyes off each other.

"How you doin'?" Jane asked as she gave the hammock a gentle nudge. "Not too bored?"

"I'm okay," Lily said, shielding her eyes with her arm. "It's good to see my dad acting stupid again."

"Yeah," Jane agreed as she looked to David, who was about to devour Danny, her second cousin Claudia's son. Then she looked to Poppy, who, still subdued in his recovery, sat on the aluminum glider going through his repertoire of grotesque faces to the endless delight of one of the babies. "Mine too."

Aunt Lucy sprayed the grill with the water bottle and poked at the chicken, sausage, and corn. Smiling, she caught Jane's eye and, gesturing toward David, gave her niece a nod of approval. Jane wiped the back of her hand across her brow, pantomiming her great sense of relief at having, at last, found this terrific man. She didn't really care if Lily saw her or not.

In fact, she hoped she did.

Tim came out of the house with his camera. "Hey, you guys! It's scrapbook time!" Pretending to reel from the chorus of mock protest, he waggled a finger toward Aunt Lucy at the grill. "No picture, no barbecue!"

With that, everyone scurried to surround Poppy's glider, some of the teenagers flopping on the grass at his feet. Aunt Lucy grabbed Jane by the arm and led her into the family circle while Timmy lined up the shot. Taking the colander off his head and raking his fingers through his hair, David stood with his arm draped over Lily's shoulder, watching from a deferential distance as Timmy called out, "One! Two! . . ."

"Wait!" Jane shrieked as she broke away and raced to David and Lily. "There is no way in the world I'm going to be in this picture without you guys in it." She grasped each of their hands and, walking backward, dragged them toward the glider. Hating it and loving it, Lily glanced at Tony and, to her delight, caught him staring at her again.

As everyone settled, Aunt Lucy leaned in and spoke softly into Jane's ear. "You sure you know what you're doing, honey? Maybe you should be careful."

Jane looked over to David just as he brushed Lily's hair back with his fingers and kissed his daughter on the forehead. "I've been careful all my life, Auntie," Jane whispered. "This is what I want."

With everybody posed and ready, Timmy reset the timer and resumed the countdown. "One! Two! Three!" He leaped in front of the camera, landing between two of the teenage boys, as the family yelled "Spaghetti!" just in time for the click of the camera.

Grinning broadly, David leaned down and gave Jane a kiss on her forehead. She put both her arms around him and said, "Thank you."

"For what?"

"For how I feel right now."

— —

Jane and Lily were deep in a conversation about competitive swimming as David crested the final hill before his house. "And at workout, we

201

wear these drag suits that slow us down with all this extra resistance," Lily said, still excited by her flirtation at the barbecue. "Coach Tanney says it could make the difference between . . ." She paused when she noticed both Jane and her father staring at the black Explorer in the driveway.

"What's he doing here?" David asked.

"I don't know," Jane said evenly. "Just give me a minute to speak to him by myself." She turned around to Lily. "Sorry, Lily. This is someone from my work I have to talk to. But remember where you were, 'cause I want to hear the rest, okay?"

"Uh, sure," Lily said, her eyes meeting her father's in the rearview mirror as he pulled into the other end of the crescent driveway.

Before the BMW came to a complete stop, Jane was out of the car and striding across the lawn toward Kenny.

"What the hell are you doing here?" she demanded. This tone wasn't really her nature, but as far as she was concerned, Kenny had drawn the line and she was simply honoring it.

Scratching the heel of his boot across one of the flagstone pavers, Kenny said evenly, "Believe me, this is the last place I want to be. But I need to talk to you."

"You already have," Jane replied, "and I heard you loud and clear." She started toward the house. "We're all a little beat from my dad's barbecue, so if you'll excuse us . . ."

"It's about Jenna Perry."

Jane stopped abruptly and turned around. Having started toward them as soon as he parked the car, David arrived just in time to hear the mention of his wife.

Kenny shot him a look and continued, "Something turned up on Mount Tam. Could be evidence." Jane glanced over to David, a flicker of worry creasing her face. "We need to check it out."

Jane hated how she felt just then. She was feeling diminished because she was no longer on the case, feeling guilty about having such a great time while Kenny was out there doing work that was originally hers, and feeling, once again, the frustrating sensation that she didn't deserve to be happy. Touching the back of David's hand with the back of hers, she saw Lily watching from the front door. "What'd you find?"

Kenny turned from Jane to make eye contact with David as he said, "This." He opened his hand and revealed a glassine plastic bag. Inside it was a man's Rolex watch.

Jane looked at the watch, then to David. He raised his eyebrows and said, "Why don't we go inside?"

——

Pilar brought a tray of tapas to the breakfast nook and set them before Carmen. It was a Saturday afternoon and their respective employers were gone for the day. As was their custom, the two women got together in either the Perry or the Gethers house for a meal and some gossip about the neighborhood. Since Clarissa's suicide, though, Carmen had been subdued, her ready laugh all but gone, her eyes often tearing up in the middle of talking about some unrelated topic.

Pouring lemonade for her friend, Pilar noticed the *Chronicle* magazine with its "The Golden Girl and the Golden Gate" cover atop the pile of papers on the banquette. She placed her tray on top of it, then, reaching beneath it and grabbing the magazine with her fingertips, lifted the tray and brought it into the kitchen. As she set it on the counter she was surprised to see the front door open and David, Jane, Kenny, and Lily come in.

Carmen rose quickly, blushing as if she and Pilar were doing something other than merely enjoying a little time off. David, noticing this, smiled at her. "Please sit, Carmen. We won't be here very long."

Her hand went to her mouth to conceal her chipped front teeth. "Thank you, Mr. Perry," she said, sitting down on the edge of the cushion, and David knew that when it was time for Kenny to leave, she would be gone.

He put his hand on his daughter's shoulder. "Lily, sweetie, would you please go upstairs?"

Lily hesitated long enough to show David that she didn't want to, but she could tell this was important. "Okay," she said and reluctantly climbed the stairs.

"Thank you," David called after her. He turned to Kenny. "Why don't we talk in my study?"

David slid apart the pocket doors and motioned for Jane and Kenny to follow him into the study. He crossed the room and opened the shutters, the late afternoon light streaming in to illuminate the beautiful oak-paneled room. "Sorry," David said as he switched on his desk lamp. "It gets a little dark in here."

Jane watched Kenny as he looked about the study. Ever the trained detective, his head never moving, his eyes darting about, he quickly absorbed the opulence, the view, the photos of Jane and David on the credenza behind the desk.

"So, Inspector Marks," David said as he turned on the floor lamp next to the reading chair, "you think that watch is somehow connected to my wife's murder?"

Jane knew the drill: if no one else in the room is sitting, you never sit down. If you do, you give up both physical and psychological advantages. She had taught Kenny this and was amused when Kenny leaned against the wall and answered, "Could be. Someone found it up on Mount Tamalpais and . . ."

"Who was it?" Jane interrupted. "Did you get a statement?"

Kenny shot her a look. "Some jogger who . . ." He made quotation marks with his index fingers. ". . . didn't want to get involved. So he left it there and called us." He hefted the watch in his hand. "I thought it might be worth talking to Mr. Perry about."

"Can I see it?" David asked.

"You bet," Kenny said, handing it over.

As soon as David received the watch, he could tell something was wrong with it. "Can I take it out of the bag?"

"Sure," Kenny nodded. "We've already dusted it."

"And?" Jane asked.

"Nothing traceable."

David turned the watch over in his hands. Then he held it under the desk lamp and examined it closely. "Can I assume, Inspector, that you're hoping to somehow tie me to Jenna's murder because an expensive Rolex turned up near where her body was found and you figured, 'Hell, this Perry guy's loaded, so this all fits together'?"

Kenny shrugged. "Crossed my mind."

"Sorry to disappoint you, but there's one thing wrong with your theory."

"And that would be?"

"This watch." David tossed it to Kenny. "It's a fake. Thirty dollars on any street corner in North Beach."

"How can you tell?" Jane asked.

"Couple of ways," David said as he came from his desk and stood next to her. "First, it's too heavy. Those scam guys think that if a watch weighs enough, some sucker will think it's expensive. Plus the logo has one extra point on its crown, and if you look closely at . . ."

"I get the message," Kenny said as he dropped the watch into his coat pocket, his face flushing red. Jane couldn't tell if it was embarrassment or anger. He turned to go. "Sorry if I've messed up your day."

David smiled. "Call me crazy, but with you standing in my study in the middle of a Saturday afternoon exploring theories about expensive watches, I gotta think you still consider me a suspect in my wife's murder."

Kenny turned and looked past David to Jane. "You tell him."

Holding out her hands in apology, Jane said, "Until we have the bad guy, everyone's a suspect in a murder investigation."

"Especially?" Kenny prompted Jane.

"Especially . . ." Jane shot Kenny an exasperated look. "Especially the husband in cases like this."

" 'Cases like this'?" David repeated, his eyebrows raised in curiosity.

Jane's body language made it clear to Kenny that this was his question to field. "Cases where there is a large inheritance," he said.

"You know, Inspector, I could take this two ways. I could get all pissed off and indignant and call my lawyer and tell him you're harassing me."

"Or?" Kenny asked, stiffening a bit at what he perceived to be a challenge.

"Or . . . I could appreciate the fact that you're as good a cop as Jane told me you were and thank you for being so concerned and so thorough," David said, defusing any confrontation. "I really don't have the stomach or the strength to be the angry, aggrieved guy, so I'm going with number two."

He opened the study doors and stepped out. As Jane and Kenny followed, David noticed that as he'd expected, Carmen was gone. Pilar, having walked her friend out, was just coming in the front door with a stack of mail. Dropping the mail on the kitchen counter, she took up the tray and started clearing away the dishes from the breakfast nook.

"I wish Carmen had stayed," David said to Pilar as he crossed to her.

"I know. But she gets too sad sometimes," Pilar said, her own sorrow sketching her face.

As David helped Pilar clean up, Jane slipped over to Kenny. "Did you have to do this? And on today of all days?"

"I don't give a shit what day it is," Kenny said, leading her toward the far corner where Lily's telescope stood pointed at the Golden Gate Bridge. "And neither should you, damn it. That watch was a strong lead and I wasn't going to sit on it just because you had a fucking barbecue!"

Jane deflated, her indignation evaporating. "You're right," she admitted, nodding her head slowly. "It's just so complicated right now."

Looking past her to ensure David was out of earshot, Kenny said, "Then simplify it."

"How?"

"Look. I can't pretend I don't have feelings for you. You know it. I know it. Hell, the whole goddam precinct knows it," Kenny began. "But this isn't the broken-hearted schoolboy talking here. Just cool your jets with this guy until we crack this case. Then, if you want, marry him and I'll throw you a shower."

Kenny glimpsed David coming toward them, the *Chronicle* magazine under his arm, and he understood that there was no way Jane could respond. Changing the subject, he nodded to the telescope and asked, "Use this much?"

"All the time," David said.

"May I?"

Dropping the magazine on the coffee table, David removed the lens covers. "Be my guest."

As Kenny bent to the eyepiece, he saw Jane's reflection in the window as she retreated to the kitchen. "If I had one of these and a view like this, I'd never leave the house," he said as he adjusted the focus. "God, the bridge is beautiful."

"Yeah," David agreed, his eyes drawn to the magazine's eerie cover.

Turning away from the view and following David's eyes to the magazine lying on the coffee table, Kenny said, "Is that the rich girl who jumped?"

David nodded.

"Those are the worst," Kenny said. "When I was a rookie, I had to clean up after a couple of those. Not too pretty." His eyes flicked to Jane returning with a blueberry yogurt, and the implied intimacy of that got the better of him. He reached out and offered his hand to David. "Sorry for the inconvenience, Mr. Perry. I'd better be on my way. I've got a city to protect."

As David led them to the front door, Kenny said to Jane, "Think about what I said. It doesn't have to be complicated."

After he had gone, David took Jane in his arms and asked, "You all right with all this?"

"It's a little confusing," Jane admitted. "But I've never been so happy in my life." She kissed him on the chest. "I'm gonna get back to my swimming lecture with Lily."

As she went up the stairs, David sifted through the mail Pilar had left on the kitchen counter. It seemed Saturday was junk-mail day as he dropped envelope after envelope into the trash. Then, after putting Lily's new issue of *Swimmers' World* aside, he noticed a plain brown envelope with his name and address written by hand. David ripped it open and took out a piece of paper. On it was a photocopy of a Rolex watch and his business card.

Beneath it was scrawled, "Where's my money, Dave?"

59

This particular courtroom had always been Jane's favorite.

The sheriff's deputy guarding the door to Alameda County Superior Courtroom Five-B recognized her and pulled open the double oak doors.

From her seat near the front of the nearly empty courtroom, Jane listened intently as David Perry questioned a frightened young girl who seemed as small as a doll in the witness stand. This was the final day of the Shepherd-Ramsey trial, and Jane was pleased that David had invited her to observe.

Kimberlee Sparks was fifteen, with wispy white-blond hair and tracks of braces on both her top and bottom teeth. When David had called her to testify, he had stood back and watched the jury as her mother helped her into her crutches. Holding Kimberlee's little broken body as upright as possible, Mrs. Sparks had escorted her daughter to the stand. With great difficulty, Kimberlee had lowered herself into the chair, her face red with exertion. Then she looked to David for her first question. David had paused a moment longer to give Mrs. Sparks time to return to her place at the front of the courtroom and arrange the crutches on the floor beneath her seat.

Satisfied that the jury had absorbed all this, David had Kimberlee recount her story of the crash of the yellow school bus. Pictures of the devastated hulk rested on an easel next to the jury box. Having struggled through her memories of that terrifying day, David's witness was wavering beneath the reality of what had happened to her and her friends.

"It's okay, Kimberlee," he said, his voice barely above a whisper. "Go on."

Taking a sip of water from the blue plastic cup at her side, Kimberlee looked toward the jury, her eyes filling with tears. ". . . and Talya and

Miss Cohen were all the way in the back . . . until we went over the side of the mountain and the emergency door popped open and then they fell out . . ." She hesitated and began to cry, her frail shoulders heaving with sobs.

David looked at the jury as he brought her a box of tissues. "Take your time, Kimberlee. Do you want to rest?"

The little girl shook her head and, after blowing her nose, said, "No. I want to finish."

"Tell me something, Kimberlee," David said, glancing over to Jane. "Did you learn in school to always wear your seat belt?"

"Yeah," Kimberlee nodded. "And from my parents."

"Good," David said, resting his elbow on the railing of the witness stand. "Were you or Talya or Miss Cohen or any of your friends wearing a seat belt when the bus, the school bus, went through the guardrail and over the side of that mountain?"

Kimberlee lowered her eyes. "No."

"Why not?" David asked, scanning the jury as if preparing each of them for her answer.

"Because . . ." Kimberlee said, ". . . because there weren't any."

"No seat belts on the whole bus?"

Kimberlee started to shake her head, then she paused. "Well, there was one."

"Ah, there was a seat belt," David repeated. "And tell me please, Kimberlee, who was wearing that one seat belt?"

"Mrs. Kennedy."

"And who is Mrs. Kennedy?"

"The bus driver."

"The bus driver," David said. "And what happened to your friend Talya and Miss Cohen?"

Her lips quivering, Kimberlee took a deep breath and said, "Miss Cohen got paralyzed and Talya . . . she . . . she died."

As she dissolved into tears, David looked once again at the jury to drive his point home, but it was apparent that wasn't necessary. Turning toward Jane, he noticed that she too was crying.

The judge swiveled in his chair, his eyes asking the defense attorney what she wanted to do.

"No questions, Your Honor," the lawyer said, shuffling her papers.

David retrieved Kimberlee's crutches from her mother and helped the girl down from the witness stand.

Once she was seated in the gallery, David turned to the judge and announced, "Your Honor, we call Mr. Daniel Ramsey, Jr."

Dan Ramsey, a puffy, pink-faced man in his mid-thirties, took the stand and was sworn in. David paced in front of him, never getting too close to his witness. It was an old trial lawyer's trick: if you keep your distance from the witness, the jury will be inclined to do the same.

"Mr. Ramsey," David said without looking at him, "where are you employed?"

Dan Ramsey glanced at the defense table and said, "At Shepherd-Ramsey."

"The school bus company?"

"Yes sir."

"Is it a coincidence, Mr. Ramsey," David continued, "that your name is the same as the name on the sides of the buses your employer manufactures?"

"No, sir. It's not." He paused. "My father owns the company."

"And what do you do at your father's company, Mr. Ramsey?"

"I'm vice-president in charge of sales."

"Good for you, Mr. Ramsey." David went to his table, checked his notes, and put an envelope into his jacket pocket. "Was it you then, who sold the San Francisco School Board one hundred and seventy-nine Shepherd-Ramsey Class A school buses in 1990?"

"Yes, it was." Dan Ramsey poured himself some water.

"Was the school board at the time considering buying its buses from its usual supplier, Magnus & Company?"

"Yes, it was."

"But you won the contract with various incentives and some creative salesmanship, isn't that right, Mr. Ramsey?"

"It was a big decision for the city and a big sale for us. I was happy to help them figure out a way to make it work." He looked toward the jury. "It's how the job works."

David crossed to the jury, putting his body between them and Dan Ramsey. He gestured to the photo blowups on the easel. "Mr. Ramsey, may I direct your attention to these pictures. This is one of the buses you sold to the City of San Francisco, is it not?"

"Yes, it's a Shepherd-Ramsey Class A."

"Do you see a seat belt at the driver's seat in this picture?"

"Yes."

"Look closely now," David said without turning to him. "Do you see any seat belts on any of the passenger seats—any of the child passenger seats—in any of these photographs?"

The defense attorney rose quickly. "Objection!" she shouted. "Mr. Perry has been implying all trial that by not providing seat belts for its passengers, Shepherd-Ramsey was somehow derelict in its responsibility." She moved in front of the table. "Your Honor, as we discussed pretrial, the California Vehicle Code does not require school buses to be equipped with seat belts for passengers. It does, however, require a seat belt for the driver." She threw an exasperated look at the judge. "It would seem that Mr. Perry's beef should be with the State of California, not with my client." She returned to her seat. "Can we please move off this line of questioning?"

The judge removed his eyeglasses and wiped them clean. "Mr. Perry?"

David stole a glance toward Jane, then turned to face the judge. "Point well taken, Your Honor. I only have a few more questions. May I proceed?"

The judge nodded.

"Thank you, Your Honor." David looked quickly at Dan Ramsey, catching him off-guard. "Mr. Ramsey, you've testified that you came up with some, uh . . . creative incentives to close the sale of your father's company's buses with the City of San Francisco."

Dan Ramsey shrugged. "Yes, sir, I did."

David pulled the envelope from his pocket and took out a piece of paper. Without completely closing the distance between himself and the witness, he held it up. "Does this stationery look familiar to you?"

"Yes, that's the Shepherd-Ramsey logo."

David handed the letter to Dan Ramsey. "Would you please read the letter aloud?"

Dan Ramsey quickly scanned the letter, and his hands began to tremble. David stepped forward. "Aloud, Mr. Ramsey."

Looking toward his attorney, his eyes pleading for intervention, Dan Ramsey hesitated for a moment, then began to read. " 'To the San Francisco City School Board, Purchasing Department. Confidential side-letter to deal memo dated October twentieth, 1990. In order to facilitate the sale of one hundred and seventy-nine Class A school buses, the following considerations will be made. One, if this confidential side-letter is signed within two weeks of the above date, a deduction of ten percent off the total sale price will be in effect.' "

One of the young defense attorneys hurried out of the room as Dan Ramsey continued. " 'Two, if this confidential side-letter is signed within two weeks of the above date, the service warranty will be extended from three years to five years. Three, if this confidential side-letter is signed within two weeks of the above date, replacement tires, brakes, gaskets, hoses, and all other expendables in Schedule D will be sold for twenty percent below the listed price.' "

Dan Ramsey felt the sweat streaming down to his eyebrows, and he whisked at them with the back of his hand. " 'Four, if this confidential side-letter is signed within two weeks of the above date . . .' " He took a long drink from the water cup. " '. . . passenger seat belts will be provided at no extra cost to the City of San Francisco on all of the Shepherd-Ramsey Class A school buses purchased under the terms of this contract.' "

David turned his back on Dan Ramsey and faced the jury. "Signed?" he said softly.

Fidgeting in the stand, Dan Ramsey looked to his lawyer.

She looked away.

David spun on his heel and pointed his finger at Dan Ramsey. "Signed?" he demanded, his voice rising to such volume that several of the jurors were startled.

"Signed . . . 'Daniel Ramsey, Jr., Vice-President, Sales.' "

David was about to return to his table when he looked toward Jane and suddenly stopped.

Dalton Hubble was sitting directly behind her, slouched back in his seat, a toothpick in his smirking mouth.

Instinctively, David started toward him. But before he could get there, Hubble rose and, staring at David, leaned forward to sniff Jane's hair. Then he walked up the center aisle, where a deputy opened a door for him. With an ominous grin, he passed through the door, turned right, and was gone.

"Mr. Perry," the judge said, "do you care to proceed?"

With a glance at Jane, David addressed the judge. "No further questions, Your Honor."

The judge turned to the defense table.

"Your Honor," the attorney began without rising, "this side-letter was not introduced during discovery, and . . ."

"Your Honor," David interrupted forcefully, "if this side-letter were to be introduced at all during discovery, then it was the responsibility of the defense to come forward with it. In that they didn't, we can only assume that either they were unaware of its existence, or they never wanted it to be read aloud in your courtroom . . . for obvious reasons."

"Your Honor," the defense attorney said, "we need time to research, authenticate, and respond to this side-letter."

"Good idea," the judge said as he banged his gavel. "Court will stand in recess until three this afternoon."

Gathering his papers, David nodded to the defense table, shook hands with Kimberlee Sparks and her mother, and worked his way up the aisle. Jane came up to him and he put his arm around her. "How'd I do?"

Jane smiled broadly. "Wow," she whispered.

60

Lily stood over the water, remembering her dream.

She thought about falling. Through space and through time.

She listened to the water, listened to it talk to her, and she wondered what had gone through Clarissa Gethers's mind that night. Had she been frightened? Or, more likely, Lily believed, had she been calm? Sure and resolute and accepting of the inevitable.

Lily leaned forward, her upper body poised, feeling with her toes the positive and negative balance points. She knew that if she were to allow her body just the slightest degree more of a downward angle, she would be unable to avoid the fall. Pulling in a deep, expansive breath, she relaxed the muscles in her back, dipped her head and shoulders, and finally yielded to gravity's magnet. Her body flexed and she was airborne.

But just for an instant.

Knifing into the warm water of the indoor practice pool at the Peabody Middle School, Lily cut to the surface and swam steadily. Her goggles were pinching behind her right ear, her rubber cap was pulling at some hairs on the back of her head, and her sleek black Speedo swimsuit was riding up a bit between her legs. But Lily didn't care. She was in the water. Her arms churning and her legs kicking, she moved gracefully and powerfully toward the far end, flipped into a turn, and stroked her way down the center lane.

This privacy, swimming by herself in an empty poolhouse with no sounds other than the slapping of the water and her own breathing, was the ultimate comfort for her.

She and Jobie had stayed late after evening workouts, practicing relay touch-ups with an assistant coach. But then Jobie's shoulder had popped out again and she had called her mother to come pick her up. Lily had lied to the young coach and told him that she would catch a ride with

Jobie's mom. After everyone had left, she sneaked back into the pool building through the unlocked door that the boys' swim team used on the weekends.

Lily had been alone for almost half an hour, and she could not remember any other time in her life when she had felt as free.

Or as happy.

—

David sat on the floor, his back against the love seat, reading the *Chronicle* magazine's cover story on Clarissa Gethers.

Pushing open the swinging kitchen door with her back, Jane padded across the oriental rug and laid a tray of homemade pizza and Caesar salad on the coffee table. "I'm still not sure about your oven, so this one's kind of an experiment," she said as she slid a slice onto a dinner plate. "Here you go, Counselor—turkey sausage, red peppers, and goat cheese."

Seemingly distracted by his magazine, David didn't respond. Shrugging it off, Jane asked, "You want wine or a near-beer with dinner?"

Turning pages, clearly no longer reading, David still did not answer. Jane squatted down next to him. "David, what do you want to drink?" she persisted, an edge of worry creeping into her voice.

Without acknowledging her, David flipped another page. Exasperated, Jane grabbed the magazine out of his hands and threw it onto the couch.

David looked up at her. "I was reading that."

"Yes," Jane responded, hating what she was feeling as a clutch of dread bubbled its way into her awareness. "And ignoring me."

Stretching his arms over his head and twisting his neck until he felt a satisfying crack, David explained, "I've got the biggest case of my life sitting in a jury room right now. I just need a little time to unwind."

Jane wanted desperately to let it go at that, but something in his behavior all evening had been just a little off, indifferent even, and she feared that she might be recognizing symptoms of a relationship racing along too fast and finally catching up with itself. "I appreciate that," she said. "But I get a little frustrated after the tenth unanswered question or so."

Looking at her with such force that Jane reflexively stood up, David said coolly, "Maybe the thing to do is not ask so many questions." His tone was remote, without intimacy.

"You don't give an inch, do you?" she observed, sitting on the arm of the love seat, swallowing the unmistakable sense of foreboding that had worked its way up into her throat. She had been here before, that place where it all changes, where, suddenly, the peak is crested and everything from then on feels like a downward slide. But she had trusted her instincts this time and wasn't yet ready to believe that David was like the others. She reached over to him and touched the back of his neck. He turned to look at her, and in that moment something in him softened.

"I'm sorry," he said as he picked up a slice of pizza. "I have to go get Lily soon, so let's just eat, okay?"

But this behavior, this inconsistency, had Jane alarmed. Willing for now to let it pass, she poured herself a glass of Chianti and left David to get his own drink.

"Fine," she said.

— —

Illuminated from below, the pool sent green luminescent clouds dancing across the ceiling of the poolhouse. Plowing through the water, Lily swam herself into what athletes called the zone. Her stroke, more a product of muscle memory than of exertion, sliced the surface with the precision and ease of a machine. Her breathing came naturally, unlabored, in perfect cadence with the pull of her progress.

And her mind, floating as effortlessly and as freely as her body, drifted on the tide of something simple, something primitive, that had nothing to do anymore with swimming. It was as if, somewhere in the far-off reaches of her soul, she were dreaming of swimming rather than actually cutting through the water.

So lost was she in her regime that she failed to notice the ripple at the side of the pool as someone slipped into the water.

Coming to the end of another lap, Lily flipped and kicked herself into a turn, luxuriating in her gliding underwater flight until she broke the surface and resumed her stroke.

"Excuse me?" came a voice, a man's voice; so strange in this cavernous poolhouse.

Startled, Lily stopped abruptly and, treading water, peeled her goggles onto the top of her head. Looking around, she spotted a man chest-deep in the water only a few feet away from her.

"Nobody's supposed to be in here," she said.

Dipping his head back into the water, Barton Hubble smiled at her. "But isn't this a public pool?" He kept his carefully measured distance, his powerful shoulders glistening in the bouncing light.

Lily's forehead furrowed in uncertainty. "No, this is part of my school."

The current created by the water he was displacing nudged Barton Hubble imperceptibly closer to her. "But wouldn't it be okay if I just swam a little, too?" he asked. "I'll stay out of your way. I promise."

Lily took a mouthful of water and squirted it out, her legs kicking in place, anxious to get back to her workout. "I don't think so. Nobody's supposed to be here but me. I'm on the swim team."

Hubble lifted his feet from the bottom and allowed himself to be carried nearer to Lily. "I could tell. You've got a great stroke for such a young girl," he said, bobbing his chin on the water like an alligator preparing to take its prey. "How old are you? Fifteen, sixteen?"

"I'm thirteen," Lily said, cocking her head.

"Really?" Hubble said, feigning surprise. "You swim much better than that. No kidding."

"Thanks, but Coach thinks I need to shave two seconds off my time this year," Lily said, her initial sense of unease ebbing away.

"I hate to say it, but you could pick up a little time in your turns," Hubble suggested. He was standing on the tips of his toes now, treading backward to keep his feet on the bottom.

Lily brightened. "That's what Coach said! Are you a swimmer?"

"Used to be."

Knowing that her father would be there soon to pick her up and eager to be swimming again, Lily asked, "Could you maybe watch my turns and tell me if I'm too early or what?"

"You bet," Hubble said. "Go ahead."

Pulling her goggles down and thrusting forward, Lily quickly regained her stroke and made for the far wall of the pool. Not wanting to break her concentration, she never looked in Barton Hubble's direction as she twisted into her turn. Because she didn't, she never saw that he was completely naked, his erect penis curving into his hand as he pumped it with his fist.

— —

Sitting next to David on the floor in front of the love seat, Jane watched as he silently ate his pizza. Then, feeling a need to have some sort of

communication, anything other than an evening passed in numbing silence, she asked, "How is it? Not too out there?"

Dropping the unfinished slice back onto his plate, David took a sip
from his wineglass. "I'm sorry. I guess I'm not a red peppers kind of
guy."

A mineral sensation bubbled beneath her tongue, and Jane immediately recognized the unwelcome signpost of an emotion she had been
trying all night to suppress. To her, fear tasted like metal, and she took
a heavy swallow of her wine to wash it away. Then she reached over
and started picking the peppers off David's pizza.

"It's okay," he protested. "I'll eat them."

"You're the lawyer here," she began, searching for a joke to lighten
the mood. "You should be the first to know there's no law that says
you have to eat something you don't like." She scraped the last of the
peppers onto her plate with her fork.

"Please!" David snapped. "I said I'll eat them."

Jane dropped the fork onto his plate and sat back against the love seat.
She looked at David for a long time, her chin quivering with sadness
and indecision. "We're not having such a great night, are we?" she
finally asked.

"Guess not."

Reaching behind, she placed her palms on the love seat and lifted
herself up. "Anything I should know?"

David shook his head and, tucking his foot beneath him, rose to his
feet. "Just a lot of stuff catching up to me."

Standing up to meet him, Jane said, "And you don't want to talk
about it, right?"

Touching her arms so lightly Jane wasn't sure if there was actual contact, David answered softly, "Right."

Jane filled her lungs with a long head-clearing breath. She had decided
earlier in the evening that she would not let this man see her crying
again. He had asked for her trust and she had carefully doled it out to
him, bit by bit, as he earned it with his warmth and his caring. But now
she felt it all evaporating, and she hoped she could at least make it to
her car before the tears came.

"I think I should go," she said. She grabbed up her coat and purse
and made for the door. Feeling David hesitate and then follow her, she
slowed her pace to let him catch up. She couldn't help herself; she still
needed him to touch her before she went out the door. Just as she put

her hand out to undo the deadbolt, David closed the gap between them and turned her to him. Peering into his distant eyes, Jane asked, "Are we okay?"

David nodded. "We're fine. Honest. I'm just a little fried tonight. I'm sorry."

Jane studied him, taking his features apart one by one, needing to know. "You sure?"

"Sure I'm sure," he said as he kissed her on the tip of her nose. "I'm gonna go pick up Lily, take a long hot shower, and crash."

"When will we talk?"

"Tomorrow," David promised as he brushed his lips across her forehead. "I'll call."

Shuddering at the last words she ever wanted to hear again, Jane kissed him lightly on the cheek and said, "Then I'll wait to hear from you."

Opening the door to the night air, she didn't bother to pull on her coat as she ran across the lawn to her car.

— —

Swimming with total confidence, feeling her body jump through the water, Lily flipped into a flawless kick-turn and, her arms stretched into a perfect point, speared through the water until she rose and broke the surface with a wide grin.

"How was that?" she asked, excited at how right it had felt as she swam toward Barton Hubble.

"Excellent!" he called. "Your timing was perfect."

"That one felt great," she smiled as she tried to catch her breath. "You were right about that extra half-stroke."

The water between them was like a bridge, an undulating connective tissue that made Barton Hubble feel closer to this young girl than he actually was. Needing that contact to make himself feel complete, he leaned forward slightly, and his body drifted toward Lily just as she kicked herself around and said, "This is so fun! I'm going to try it again." As she turned to get back into the center racing lane, Barton Hubble thrust his head in close, as if to kiss the back of her head.

Unaware, Lily swam away.

— —

The combination of the cold air outside and David's warm breath inside brought a thin moist fog to the windows of the BMW as he waited for

219

Lily in the parking lot of the Peabody Middle School poolhouse. It wasn't like her to be late, he thought, but maybe this was just part of her fast-approaching adolescence.

He could see the glow of the pool's lighting system in the high windows of the swimming structure. Suddenly the windows turned black as the lights were extinguished inside the building. Tensing, David started to get out of the car, but, not wanting to impose himself on whatever private ritual his daughter had in saying goodbye to her friends, he decided to wait another minute or two. Leaning back against the headrest, he tried to relax, closing his eyes. Then, with a start, he opened his eyes and scanned the parking lot.

His was the only car there.

He ripped open his door, his fear mounting, and got out of the car. He was about to tear across the blacktop when Lily emerged from the darkened building. She seemed, he thought, so small in her huge parka, her wet hair sending off a thin halo of steam.

When she got closer, she looked up to him with her pool-reddened eyes and said, "Hey, Daddy."

"Hey, Lilliput," David smiled. They got into the car and he started the engine.

Lily tugged the door closed and tilted her head against her window. David looked over to her. "Where is everybody?"

Without looking at her father, Lily said, "Jobie popped her shoulder and had to go home and I kinda lied and said I was going with her. Then I went around and snuck back in."

David pulled out of the lot and into the street. "Why, sweetie? Why'd you lie?"

" 'Cause I wanted to be alone for a little while," she said, her voice trailing off.

They rode a few miles in silence. David understood that something was on his daughter's mind, and knew that when she was ready, she would tell him.

After a while, Lily stirred in her seat. "Dad . . ."

"Yeah, honey."

She stared straight ahead, not looking at her father. "I don't want you to get all mad or anything, but I think you should know something."

"Oh God," David said, his mind racing through a catalogue of horrors.

"There was this guy tonight in the pool," Lily said. "A grown-up?"

Growing rigid with apprehension, David pulled over to the curb. "What guy? What did he look like?"

Lily looked at him, her eyes struggling to understand something new and troubling. "I don't know. Bigger than you. With really short hair . . ."

David pulled in a sharp breath; then, not wanting to alarm his daughter, he asked in a quiet voice, "Did he touch you?"

"No." She shook her head. "He kind of coached me with my turns. But . . . there was something else."

David reached over to smooth her wet hair. "What, sweetie? What else?"

Involuntarily withdrawing from her father's touch, Lily looked away. "I think he was naked."

61

Jane sat shivering in her car in front of her house, looking at her toppled trash cans through a thin veil of tears that would not fall. She had driven home like that, her eyes behind water, her heart clutching with sorrow. She didn't want to be confused anymore. She only wanted to be sure. Drained of all energy, she could have sat there all night, both hands still on the steering wheel. Crying and not crying.

The distant plea of a ringing telephone penetrated her consciousness. Her telephone. The thought occurred to her before she could raise her defenses to ward it off: David. Then she realized that her answering machine wasn't on. Not wanting to, hating herself even as she did it, Jane flew out of the car and raced up her walkway to the front door, the ring of the telephone growing louder, more urgent, as she went.

Hurling open her door, she ran across the living room, but even as she grabbed for the receiver, she knew she was too late. There was a finality, an echoing completeness, to the last ring of a telephone. Knowing it was futile, Jane picked up the phone and, holding her breath, she listened. The dial tone droned, unwavering, standing between her and whoever had tried to reach her.

Had it been David? Did she dare call him? And say what? "My phone was ringing when I got home and I thought it might have been you"? Replacing the receiver in its cradle, Jane caught herself in the mirror above the Parsons table. Here she was, at this stage of her life, having believed that these kinds of nights were finally over, unable to call her lover—her boyfriend, whatever the hell he was—because she wasn't sure about who he was, who they were . . . who she was.

And the tears fell.

As soon as David had hung up his phone, it jumped to life with a startling ring. He snatched it up. "Hello?"

Barton Hubble stood in the yellow glow of his open refrigerator, swigging orange juice from a carton. "We need to meet, Dave," he said. He tossed the empty carton into the sink. Ming picked it up and threw it into the trash can.

David's jaw set with purpose. "Don't worry, Hubble. I'll meet you."

"Market Street overpass," Hubble instructed as he slammed his icebox closed, the dim light from his window becoming the only illumination in his squalid apartment. "Thirty minutes." He hung up.

Pulling his key ring from his pocket, David unlocked the bottom right-hand drawer of his desk. He took out a small locked metal case, inserted another key, and popped the lid. His 9mm Beretta lay, loaded and waiting, on a white cloth.

As David picked up the pistol and chambered a round, the smooth sound of metal sliding on metal filling the room, he realized that the white cloth was one of Lily's old diapers.

62

A soft rain misted the air as Barton Hubble hunkered in his greatcoat on the Market Street overpass watching the traffic whip by
below. His short hair glistened like a dark helmet as he spit onto
the lower street and turned to face David.

Thinking he had approached in silence, David was surprised that
Hubble had known precisely when to turn around. His hands were
stuffed deep into the pockets of his parka. The reassuring solidity of the
Beretta was enclosed firmly in his right palm, the safety off, his finger
on the trigger.

"Cold's a bitch, ain't it, Dave?" Barton Hubble said, his eyes squinting against the drifting rain. "Something tells me you didn't bring my
money." He shook his head. "I'm so disappointed in you."

David strode forward, his teeth clenched in anger. "I'm telling you
for the last time, Hubble. Leave me and my family alone!"

The corner of Barton Hubble's mouth twitched in amusement. He
leaned into David, unintimidated. "Or?" he asked.

"Or this," David said, pulling out the pistol and aiming it at Hubble's heart.

Barton Hubble raised his eyebrows and looked around. "Smart,
Counselor. Very smart. No witnesses. A lonely street in the middle of
the city. Just another killing in the big city." He nodded in approval.
"Finally the big-shot attorney shows some balls. But once again, there's
a problem."

"What's that?" David demanded, jamming the gun into Hubble's
coat.

"You won't shoot," Hubble sneered. "I can just see you loading your
fancy new gun, putting it into your fancy new jacket, and getting into
your fancy new car." He threw his head back and laughed, puffs of

steam rising. "And here you are sneakin' up on me and telling yourself how you're going to blow me away like Dirty fuckin' Harry."

David's finger played against the trigger.

"But you know what?" Barton Hubble taunted. "Here you are and here I am. And you can't do it!" He reached out and put his hand on top of the pistol, forcing it down and around until it was pointed at David's stomach. "So don't waste my time pretending to be the big papa bear protecting his family. You don't have the . . ."

David rushed at Hubble, catching him off-guard. Driving him backward, David dug in against him like a charging fullback until Hubble's back was against the railing of the overpass. His work boots skidded on the rain-slick roadway and he began to lose his balance. David redoubled his effort and sent Hubble tumbling over the side. Desperately reaching out with his right hand, he managed to catch on to an iron support strut at the last possible instant. Dangling over the heavy traffic tearing by twenty feet below, Barton Hubble strained to tighten his grip around the slippery pipe.

David leaned over the rail to look at Hubble, his body twisting like a hanged man, and there was a long silent connected moment of pure hatred. Then, reaching over the barrier, David flipped the Beretta in his hand and pounded Hubble's fingers with the pistol butt, forcing him to let go. Finally he fell, his greatcoat mushrooming with the rushing air, into the swiftly moving traffic of the lower street.

Hubble thudded to the pavement and fell to his knees. The speeding vehicles braked frantically on the wet asphalt to avoid hitting him. Scrambling to regain his feet, Barton Hubble dodged a motorcycle, then another car, but a flower delivery van, its driver never seeing him, clipped him in the side and sent him reeling into a station wagon. A gasoline tanker truck jack-knifed in a long screeching skid, blue smoke bursting from its brakes, forcing car after car to slide to skidding stops from the center divider to the muddy shoulder until the entire boulevard was blocked.

David frantically scanned the roadway, trying to find Hubble beneath the blanket of tire smoke. But Barton Hubble was no longer there. David was about to turn away and head for home when something caught his attention on the far embankment, off to the side and out of harm's way. There, limping slightly, but otherwise unhurt, Hubble wiped a trickle of blood from his mouth and seized David with his eyes.

"You've changed the rules now, Dave!" he bellowed, his voice booming in hoarse angry bursts. "I'll be coming to visit real soon. Maybe we can all go swimming!"

He slid down the muddy slope and limped away, disappearing into the grove of trees that lined the highway.

63

—-—

Lily sat in the passenger seat, her leg bouncing nervously as she stared at her reflection in the muted orange glow of the BMW's interior.

"It shouldn't be for too long, sweetie," David said softly. "Besides, Grandma has a computer and a modem and you'll be able to e-mail Jobie all you want." Glancing in the rearview mirror, he caught Pilar's eye. She quickly turned away, a cluck of disapproval deep in her throat.

"But I don't want to go," Lily said, her tired little voice lapsing into a childish whine.

"I know you don't. And I wish you didn't have to," David said as he took the off-ramp for San Francisco International Airport and merged with the sparse midnight traffic. "But it's just till the police find this man and put him away. Then I'll fly to Miami and come get you guys myself." He put his hand on top of her head. "And when we get back, I'll take you to the top of the South Tower. Just you and me. Okay?"

Lily pressed her head into her father's hand. "Okay," she said, her eyes never leaving her reflection in the inner curve of the windshield.

—-—

Jane lay on the threshold of sleep thinking that someone should answer the door. She had dug around in her traveling kit late last night searching for that half of a Valium she thought was still at the bottom of the aspirin bottle. That pill and two glasses of wine were the only reasons she was finally able to get any rest at all. And now someone was knocking on a door somewhere out there.

Half-opening her eyes, she could tell by the greying of the light that morning was coming into her house like a fog drifting in off the bay. As her head cleared and the effects of the previous evening's indulgences waned, she remembered with crushing sadness her night with David. It all came rushing back to her like the memory of a death in the family momentarily forgotten.

The knocking persisted, insinuating into the house until, with a start, she realized it was someone at her front door. "Oh God," she moaned as she sat up in bed and forced her eyes open. The clock radio read ten minutes after five. No way this was good news, she thought as she pulled on a Giants sweatshirt and trudged out of the bedroom.

Just about to the front door, Jane braved a look in the hallway mirror, and the memory of watching herself cry in this same mirror only hours before flooded back to her. Taking a deep breath, she put her hand on the door and peered through the peephole. Gasping in surprise, she unfastened the security chain and ripped the door open.

David stood in the amber keystone of her porch light, looking haggard and hurt. He tightened his lips against themselves, his eyes red and unfocused, and after what seemed like an eternity of effort, finally said, "I need you."

Even as she helped David to the couch, Jane was aware of the collision of emotions going on inside. She was frightened about whatever would bring him to her at this hour, in this condition. And she was grateful that, whatever was going on, he had chosen to turn to her.

"My God, David," she said as they sat down. "What happened? Are you all right? Is Lily all right?"

"Everyone's fine," David said, shivering. Jane pulled an old patchwork quilt that Aunt Lucy had made for her years ago off the back of the couch and covered David's lap with it. "But there's something I need to talk to you about." He looked at his hands, unable to continue for a moment. Then he turned to her, his eyes pleading for understanding. "Something terrible."

Jane took his hands in hers and massaged the cold from them. "Anything. Please, just tell me."

Dropping his head back on the cushion, David stared at the ceiling. Somewhere outside a car started; somebody beginning the day. "It's about Jenna, about her murder."

And with that, all of Jane's ricocheting thoughts crystallized. Her presence expanded from lover to that of lover and cop, and the residual pain of the night before evaporated. "What? What about it?"

"I . . ." David hesitated. "I know who did it." He pulled his hands from within hers and thrust them under his armpits as he rocked back and forth on the couch. "I know who did it," he repeated.

"Jesus!" Jane jumped. "Who?"

"Some guy named Hubble," David explained. "This guy I met on BART when I was getting my ass whipped by Jenna's divorce lawyer." Unable to sit still, David rose and paced in front of Jane as he continued. "We got to talking, the way guys do. And then I bumped into him again at this Terry's SportsWall place, and things were even shittier with me and Jenna by then, and . . . I guess I probably said some things that he misinterpreted or something."

"What kind of things?"

David stopped and shook his head. "I don't know. I might have said something stupid like 'I'd give anything if . . .' or something like that. But it was just talk, just pain and embarrassment and beer talking." Using the heel of his palm, he pushed the hair out of his eyes. "I'm not exactly sure what I said. But he killed her." He sat on the edge of the coffee table and put his hands on Jane's knees. "He took her from our house and . . ." His eyes filled with tears. ". . . and he strangled her."

Jane's mind raced, ratcheting through questions. "But why? Why would he kill her?"

"For the money," David answered. "He's been all over me for a piece of what Lily and I are going to inherit from Jenna's estate."

Jane shot upright. "Then he's contacted you!"

"Many times," David acknowledged.

"But why didn't you go to the police?" Jane asked. "Why didn't you come to me? I could have helped you."

"I know. I should have. It's all so complicated. I guess I made a lot of mistakes in this." He crossed to the kitchen and opened the refrigerator. "I need something to drink."

"After last night," Jane said as she joined him, "all I have left is ice water."

"That's exactly what I need," he said as he leaned into her. "Speaking of last night—I'm sorry. This has been sitting on my shoulders like a ton of misery, and I guess I just started to crack."

Jane kissed him on the cheek as she lifted the pitcher from the icebox. "Thanks. I just wish you could have talked to me. You know I'd do anything to help you."

David closed the refrigerator and pulled two glasses from the dish drainer. "I wanted to. I started to tell you a hundred times. It's why I came to see you that first time when we ended up eating oysters that night. But . . ."

"But what?" Jane urged as she poured the ice water and put the pitcher in the sink.

"But Hubble kept threatening to implicate me, and I felt trapped."

"Implicate you? How?"

"Somehow he lifted my watch . . ."

"Your watch?" Jane interrupted. "Then it was Hubble who called Kenny about that fake Rolex!"

"Yeah, and he's still got the real one," David said. "This business with the fake was his way of jabbing at me. Reminding me that he wasn't going away. He said he would make sure my watch was found near the shallow grave. When I told him to go fuck himself, he told me he had this plan to just confess to the murder and say that I hired him to do it. He said that he had no motive to kill Jenna . . . and that I did." David lowered his eyes. "It's the money. It's always about the money."

Jane touched his face. "That kind of story from a loser like him wouldn't have held up very long," she said soothingly. "First of all, we know you didn't do it, because you were working that night. Kenny checked your story and . . ."

"That's my point." David rubbed the glass against his forehead. "Every time Kenny looks at me, you can see the suspicion in his eyes. The hatred. And the way he treats Patrick Colomby? You'd think the guy was Jeffrey Dahmer or something." He took a long drink. "But that stuff doesn't matter to Kenny. We're the rich guys on the hill, and he's, well . . ."

He set the glass on the counter and put his hands on Jane's shoulders, making certain his words hit home. "Look, my marriage had deteriorated to such a point, Jenna had been so awful to me, that anyone who doesn't know me would have the right to assume that I wanted her dead . . . and that possibly I could have had something to do with her murder." And now the tears that had been welling in his eyes fell. "To tell the truth, I don't even think I loved her anymore. But to hurt her? To kill her? I could never . . . She was Lily's mother, for God's sake! And I did love her once." Depleted, he pressed his forehead into Jane's.

Slipping her arms around his waist, Jane asked softly, "Why are you finally telling me? I mean, why now?"

David leaned back so he could see her. "He . . . he came after Lily. Went to the pool while you and I were having dinner last night."

"Jesus!" Jane said. "Is she okay?"

"Just scared," David said. "I sent her and Pilar to my mother's in

Florida." He explored Jane's eyes as he prepared to make another confession. "But before that, I met with Hubble again." He pulled away from Jane. "I went there to kill him."

"And?" she asked tightly.

"I couldn't do it."

"Thank God for that," Jane said, sagging with relief.

"I'm not so sure. I've been tortured all night that I just didn't blow that fucker away after what he's done to us."

"That's not your job, David," Jane said. Then she added solemnly, "It's mine."

"I don't know. I didn't want to drag you into this." David paused to listen to the calls of the seagulls as they chased the fishing boats across the bay. "Will you help me, then?"

"You and Lily mean the world to me," Jane said. "Of course I'll help you."

"But this whole thing could blow up in my face if Hubble feels us getting too close." David sat heavily on one of the kitchen chairs. "Shit! I'm already having second thoughts about all this. I don't know, maybe we shouldn't tell anyone just yet," he said. "I'm so afraid for Lily. Who knows what this guy will do?"

Jane crossed to him and brought his head gently to her breast. "We can do it any way you want," she said as she stroked his hair.

```
ITEM: Suspect Search
Enter.
NAME OF SUSPECT: Hubble, Barton (n.m.i.)
Enter.
ALIAS(ES): n/a
Enter.
GENDER: m
Enter.
LAST KNOWN ADDRESS: n/a
Enter.
OCCUPATION: Automobile mechanic
Enter.
SOCIAL SECURITY #: n/a
Enter.
HEIGHT: 6'0''-6'3'' (approx.)
Enter.
WEIGHT: 180-200 lbs. (approx.)
Enter.
RACE: Cauc.
Enter.
SCARS/TATTOOS: n/a
Enter.
BEGIN SEARCH (Press Enter)
```

Jane tapped the enter key one last time and waited as the ancient police computer whirred and clicked its way through the data banks of the various Bay Area law enforcement agencies.

David had showered at her house, and as the computer creaked along, she remembered the sounds of him in the bathroom—the faucets squeaking off, the shower curtain rattling open, the linen closet slapping shut, her hair dryer. Then he had come into the bedroom and, still naked, folded himself into her beneath the covers. She remembered too his smells as they made love while the sun rose to warm the day—the faint apricot aroma of her shampoo in his hair, the mint of her toothpaste on his tongue.

Afterward, Jane had made a pot of coffee and defrosted some bagels. But David had fallen back to sleep. Leaving him a note, Jane had taken her last yogurt from the refrigerator, refilled the water pitcher, and quietly slipped out the door. Although she too was exhausted, she had summoned her reserve of stamina, eager to dive back into the Jenna Perry murder case.

The faint beep of the computer, its sound almost inaudible against the clatter of telephones and typewriters in the squad room, brought her attention back to the monitor.

NO MATCHES FOUND

Clearing the screen with a frustrated sigh, Jane looked up as Kenny hurried across the bullpen. Pointedly avoiding her eyes, he crossed to Officer Finney's cubicle and was about to speak when an odor wafted up and assaulted him.

"Christ, Moby," he said, stepping back. "What the hell's that smell?"

"Nachos."

"How can you eat shit that smells like that?" Kenny asked, cupping his hand over his mouth.

"It only smells so bad, Inspector, 'cause it's from yesterday," Finney responded innocently. "Cleaning people musta missed it."

"You just can't get good help these days."

"Tell me about it," Finney agreed as he returned to his paperwork.

"Oh, Moby." Kenny put his hand on the leviathan's shoulder. "Please tell me something good. Like you got some answers for me."

"Y'know, I had just gotten the fax machine fixed and was gonna send off your stuff when Inspector Candiotti gave me another assignment," Finney replied. Then he puffed with purpose and added, "She said it was really important and I should forget whatever else I was doing. And so I did."

Exasperated, Kenny shot Jane a look and hurried for the stairs.

Watching him go, Jane turned to Finney and called out, "What did you learn, Mobe?"

Swiveling his huge body in his tiny chair, Finney rose and crossed to Jane's desk. "Well, first I called maybe ten or twelve garages . . . actually, first I got their phone numbers and then I . . ."

"Just tell me, Mike," Jane interrupted, not in the mood to indulge his meanderings. "Did you find my guy?"

"In a word, Inspector Candiotti?"

"In a word, Officer Finney."

"Uh, nope."

"Thank you. You've been your usual resourceful self," Jane said as she pulled on her coat and hurried toward the stairs.

"Anytime, Inspector," Finney called after her. "All you gotta do is ask."

But she was already gone.

In the stairwell, Jane passed Sally Banks and an older cop sharing a cigarette, and the thought of yet another blossoming office romance flitted through her mind. Then she heard the familiar sound of Kenny's Explorer starting up. Yanking open the heavy door, she ran into the garage, across Lieutenant Spielman's empty parking space, and, slipping between two cars, was able to intercept Kenny just as he was backing out. She raced around to the passenger side, opened the door, and climbed in.

"Aren't we forgetting something?" Kenny asked dryly.

"Like what?" Jane asked as she pulled the door closed.

"Like we are no longer partners. Hence, you'll have to get your yogurt somewhere else."

Jane closed her eyes, laid her head back against the headrest, and put her feet up on the dash. Wrapping her arms around her knees, she sat there, her jaw working against itself as she rocked in silence.

"That yogurt thing?" Kenny said. "It was a joke." Opening her eyes, Jane turned to him and was about to speak when he continued, "But, whatever you want from me, the answer is no."

"Look," Jane began, tiptoeing through the minefield of their injured feelings, "I know we're at war, and I've known you long enough to accept the fact that you take no prisoners . . ."

"As long as we know each other so well," Kenny interrupted, "get out of my car."

"Just shut the fuck up and listen to me!" Jane snapped, weary of the game and desperate to be heard.

Kenny flinched as if he'd been slapped.

"I know I've hurt you," Jane went on, pulling her soaring temper under control. "And I admit I probably screwed up when I got involved with David. But it happened." Jane took a deep breath, trying to find her rhythm. "But no matter what has happened, you're still the best cop I know, and . . ." She looked away, then back again, her eyes pleading. ". . . and I need your help."

Kenny eyed her skeptically. "With?"

Taking pains not to adorn the situation with anything that might reignite Kenny's temper, Jane said simply, "David's in trouble."

Furiously jamming the Explorer into park, Kenny wheeled in his seat. "You've got a lot of fucking nerve, Jane!" Kenny shouted, his voice booming in the car. "You come to me to help your boyfriend 'cause he got himself in some little mess?" He pressed into her, his wrath pushing her against the door like a physical, thrusting presence. "What is it? He forget to pay his dues at the country club and they're gonna take away his tee time?"

Jane pushed him away and said evenly, "He's being blackmailed by the man who killed his wife. And now the guy's threatened his daughter."

The wind knocked out of him, all Kenny could manage was, "Motherfuck."

"Well put," Jane said.

Kenny whacked the steering wheel with his fist. "Then he knows who did it!"

"Yes," Jane acknowledged. "But not how to find him."

A car honked, its horn reverberating through the parking structure. Kenny dropped the Explorer into gear and, tires squealing on the slick surface, pulled over to the side. Jane looked out her window to see a beige Toyota Camry pass by, the older cop driving, Sally Banks in the passenger seat. She wondered if they were secretly holding hands the way she and Kenny used to.

"And that's where I come in," Kenny realized. " 'Cause I'm such a good cop."

"Something like that," Jane said. "You've been insane over this case, and now we have the chance to break it and break it big-time."

Kenny squinched his lips and sat there, rocking his head as he filtered the intangibles through his mind. "Who knows about this?"

Jane shook her head. "Just us."

"We gotta tell the lieutenant."

"I know," Jane agreed. "But I promised David I wouldn't just yet. He doesn't even know I'm coming to you."

"Jane," Kenny said, rolling down his window to let in a thin slip of cool air, "this is a murder case. A big murder case. We can't keep something like this off the books."

"Only for a little while," Jane said. "This guy came after David's daughter, and he's terrified about what he might do next." Then, her eyes urging Kenny to understand, she continued, "We're cops, Kenny. We see this shit all the time. A bad guy comes into our lives . . . wham-bam, we deal with it. But think what it's like for a civilian. You're cruising along, living your life and minding your own business, and suddenly some lunatic falls from the sky and destroys everything you thought you knew about how to live." She reached over and put her hand on his arm. "Please help us," she implored. "You're the only one I can trust."

Kenny looked at her hand on his arm, then raised his eyes to hers, and for the first time in a long time, his abiding affection for her returned. "Put on your seat belt, Inspector, and let's go talk to this boy-friend of yours."

Before Jane could smile her thanks, Kenny gunned the Explorer and screeched down the exit ramp. As they shot across the street, police and civilian cars slamming on their brakes and skidding to a stop, Lieutenant Spielman, just arriving for another day of commanding the men and women of the Nineteenth Precinct, thought he saw Inspectors Candiotti and Marks racing away from the station in the same car.

Shaking off the impossibility of such an unlikely occurrence, he turned right, climbed the ramp, and parked in his space next to the stairs.

65

A s Kenny sped up David's hill, Jane sat looking at the Golden Gate Bridge between the houses with bayside views. They passed the grand home where Clarissa Gethers had lived, and her thoughts went to Lily and the turmoil she must be going through. Jane pledged to herself to get Barton Hubble behind bars so that David and Lily, and maybe even she, could get back to the glorious monotony of just living their lives in peace. The trip to the wine country she had planned with David floated on the horizon of her quiet fantasy like a dream she dared not hope for.

Kenny bumped up into David's driveway, parked half in and half out of the street, switched off the Explorer, and got out. Jane took a moment to rummage in her bag for her keys, trying to imagine what this encounter held in store for them: Kenny, so deeply distrusting of people like David and so profoundly hurt by Jane's relationship with him; David, his world destroyed by a madman, about to learn that, against his wishes, she had brought Kenny into their confidence.

Climbing out of the car, she joined Kenny on the front walkway. "This really is some fucking house," he said as he scanned the expansive roofline.

"Be it ever so humble," Jane replied as she turned her key in the lock. "It's me!" she called as she entered. She stopped with a tug of regret at having used the key David had recently given her in front of Kenny. It was thoughtless of her. She glanced back to where he stood, still in the doorway, and he just shrugged, letting her know that he was thinking the same thing.

David came out of his study and pulled Jane into a warm embrace. Then he noticed Kenny and separated from her to offer his hand. "Come in, Inspector."

Shaking his hand, Kenny said, "Mr. Perry." He wandered in, drawn, as before, to the telescope. Understanding the awkwardness of the situation, he let Jane and David have a moment alone.

"What's going on?" David asked as Kenny tinkered with the telescope. "I thought we weren't going to tell anyone about this until we knew what we were doing."

"I know. I'm sorry," Jane said. "But, David, your life is being threatened by the man who murdered your wife, and we have no idea when he's going to show up again. We need help, and Kenny's the best." She put her forehead against his chest. "Besides, it took me a lifetime to find you, and . . ."

Tucking his hand under her chin, he brought her face up to his. "I'm not going anywhere without you."

David took her hand and crossed to Kenny. "Jane told me that you've agreed to help. I'm very grateful that you understand how delicate this all is."

Jane held her breath, uncertain how Kenny would react. But he just said, "Any friend of Jane's . . ." and laughed that laugh of his, and she knew that they could do this.

"So," David offered, "what can I tell you?"

"For starters, Mr. Perry . . ." Kenny began.

"Please, it's David."

"Thanks. How in the world, David," Kenny asked as he took out his notebook, "did you ever get involved with someone like this Barton Hubble?"

David looked to Jane as if to ask how candid he should be.

"The only way we'll ever stop this guy," Jane said, "is if you tell us the truth. No matter how ugly it may seem to you, believe me, we've heard worse."

"It's not all that ugly really, just embarrassing," David said. "As you know, I was separated from my wife at the time of her . . . murder. One day I was doing some research on a case I was working on and I had to interview an injured child at her home in Daly City. As luck would have it, my car wouldn't start. Construction near my building had traffic backed up forever, and I couldn't get a cab. So I decided to take BART. I mean, there's a station right across the street from my office, and I'd never even been down there. And that's what happened, I met Barton Hubble on the subway. We got to talking. I told him about my car, and he said he was a mechanic and insisted he come by to fix it and . . ."

"Did he?" Kenny held out his hands to stop David. "Did he fix your car?"

David lifted his shoulders. "Yes, but . . ."

Before he could finish, Jane and Kenny were running for the front door. "I'll get the crime kit," Jane called as they raced outside.

——

While David recounted the rest of his story, Jane and Kenny lifted dozens of fingerprints from the engine compartment of David's BMW. After carefully numbering and cataloguing each one, Kenny slipped the evidence into his jacket pocket.

"It's a forensics smorgasbord under there," Kenny said as he lowered the hood. "I got some great possibles."

They looked up as Noble and Patricia Gethers drove slowly by in their Lincoln Town Car. The right front fender was still dented, the headlight cracked, from Mrs. Gethers's accident at the supermarket.

Noble drove, both hands on the wheel, his eyes always on the road. As they passed David's house, Patricia looked over to them, her face empty and sad. David gave a little wave. Mrs. Gethers turned away as their car continued down the hill and out of sight.

Jane and Kenny looked at David. "Mr. and Mrs. Gethers," he explained. "Clarissa's parents."

Kenny wiped off his hands. "Jesus." He pulled on his coat and started for the Explorer. "I'm gonna take this stuff downtown," he said, turning back to Jane. "You coming?"

"I think I'm gonna hang here a while," Jane answered, leaning into David.

"Okay then. Talk to you later," Kenny said and opened the driver's door.

Jane hurried up to him. "And Kenny . . ."

"Don't worry," he assured her as he patted his jacket. "I'll hand-carry these puppies all the way through the lab. Nobody needs to know a thing."

David stepped up and shook Kenny's hand. "Thanks for everything."

Kenny smiled and turned to get into the Explorer when Jane leaned in and kissed him on the cheek. "Now I remember why I like you so much. You're a lifesaver."

Climbing into his car, Kenny answered, "Let's just get this guy before that becomes an issue."

Starting the Explorer, he backed out of the driveway, swooped through a squealing U-turn, and sped away.

— —

Jane sat up in David's bed flipping through a magazine while David talked on the phone with Lily. It was uncanny to think that it had been only last night that they had had their first fight. Only last night that Barton Hubble had been in the pool with Lily. And only this morning that David had come to her, defeated and despairing, for help.

Listening to him speak to his daughter in the reassuring cadence of two people who knew each other so thoroughly, Jane wondered if she would ever enjoy that ease of spirit with anyone. Could she ever get there with David, pushing all this confusion behind them over the years to come? Just the prospect of thinking in terms of years brought a warmth to her face. As David got off the phone, she reached out and touched his back. Without looking, he returned the gesture, spreading his hand above her breasts on the flat part of her chest in a motion so natural and intimate that Jane took his hand to her lips and kissed it.

David turned and smiled at her. Then, his smile fading, he parted his lips as if to speak. Looking away, he drew in a short breath and remained silent.

"What?" Jane said. "David, what is it?"

"I need to tell you something," he began. "And I need you to understand."

"Of course I will," Jane assured him,

Swinging his body around so that he faced her on the bed, David took her hand in his. "Remember when I told you about Clarissa being obsessed with an older man and how it may have contributed to her suicide?"

"Yes?"

"I think that older man was me."

Jane sat forward, unfolding her legs. "My God, David. Why do you think that?"

Rising from the bed, David paced as he spoke. "She'd always had this thing for me. But I just thought it was a typical adolescent crush. I even mentioned it to Jenna, and she dismissed it as kid stuff. But Clarissa was always over here baby-sitting for Lily. So she was aware of our separate bedrooms. She was even here when Jenna and I had a couple of pretty nasty fights. Who knows what she thought?"

He stopped and turned to Jane. "Then she started sending me notes. There was one pretty serious one inviting me to her birthday party. Her folks had already invited me, and to tell you the truth, I would like to have gone to get out of the house and be with my neighbors. But the last thing I wanted, considering how unstable she seemed, was for her to make a scene over there."

He crossed back to the bed. Jane stood up and put her arms around him as he continued, "Besides, I was still trying to deal with Jenna's murder and to take care of Lily. Plus I had the trial coming . . . and I was falling in love with you."

"Oh, David," Jane said, putting her head on his shoulder.

"But I still blame myself. She killed herself that night, and I can't help thinking I could have done or said something to prevent it."

Jane gently pulled him down until they were both sitting on the edge of the bed. "Listen to me, David," she said. "You are a wonderful and caring man. You have a terrific understanding of your daughter, and I've never met anyone as considerate as you." She stroked the back of his head. "Clarissa had perfected the act of concealing how she felt to an art form. Her parents didn't see it coming. Neither did her friends at school . . . or even her shrink. There was no way for you to anticipate just how messed up she really was."

David turned to her, his eyes moist.

"It breaks my heart to see you put yourself through this," Jane went on. "You already have so much on your mind. Please let it go."

Nodding slowly, David pressed his lips to the top of her head and kissed her. "Thank you," he whispered. "I knew you'd help me make sense of this." He rose. "I'm going to wash my face."

As he went into the bathroom, Jane got up from the bed and crossed to the bay window. She leaned into the coolness of the glass and looked below to the Golden Gate Bridge, its pearls of lights glowing dimly in the fog.

Barton Hubble stood in the middle of the gardens, just beyond the pool, watching her. He reveled in the fact that she was looking directly at him, and that she had no idea he was there.

His heavy work boots sank into the mud of the flowerbed. But he didn't care. Let them find the prints. Let them know he had come. Let them understand he would be back.

66

Kenny had always hated it when his job required him to call on Castro Street. Parking the Explorer in a taxi zone, he walked up the block past Inches, past Drill, past Hole-in-the-Wall, weaving his way through what was probably the most famous gay district in the country.

Not that anyone cared about a cop's presence here anymore, the days of drugs and promiscuity having long since given way to the life-and-death necessity of monogamous relationships. But there remained the specter, the buzzing memory, of when Kenny was a young patrol officer and this was his beat. He had hated putting on his uniform, as if dressing for a costume party, and working these streets.

Now, all these years later, Castro Street was, on the surface, essentially the same. Only someone who had been there in its heyday could tell the difference. The music still throbbed, but with less urgency. Those men who had survived were a bit more conservative in style and politics and sexual proclivities. And many of the storefronts that had once been home to paraphernalia shops or body-piercing parlors or bathhouses were now occupied by health clinics, coffee bars, and the occasional one-room church.

Passing the Gay Men's Health Crisis, still open this night long after midnight, Kenny entered a coffee bar called Insanity. The double storefront was smoky and loud with same-sex couples lounging either on old overstuffed couches or at small tables along the walls, reading, smoking, drinking, yelling to be heard. The steam whoosh of the cappuccino machine cut through the racket of shouted voices and bass-grinding music as Kenny waded deeper into the room.

"Yo, Kenny!" Sean Temple waved from his corner table.

Kenny squeezed through the crush of patrons at the bar and arrived at the oasis of Sean's table. "Couldn't you find a noisier place?" he joked as he shook Sean's hand and sat down.

"Sorry, Inspector," Sean laughed, "but Denny's don't do Castro."

A slender Korean man, scarcely over a hundred pounds, arrived with two foamy coffee drinks and sat next to Sean. "You remember my Kim, don't you?" Sean said as he took his drink and kissed his lover lightly on the lips.

"How's it goin'?" Kenny asked, shaking his hand. He had busted Kim a couple of years ago for possession of three dozen poppers. It was then that he had learned that Sean, the former altar boy, the shortstop on the precinct softball team, the young cop going through a divorce, was gay. And that Kim was his lover. Sean, who now worked forensics at SFPD headquarters, had approached Kenny and asked for a favor: to, just that once, let the poppers thing slide, because Kim was in the United States illegally, and if he got his nose caught in the criminal justice system, he would be deported. Sean went on to explain that if Kim couldn't avail himself of the city's Free Clinic, he would die within the year.

Kenny had agreed to let Kim's file fall victim to a clerical error and thus float in the ether of the police computer for all eternity, and Sean had gratefully, and tearfully, promised to someday repay the kindness.

"Stayin' clean?" Kenny asked Kim with a wink.

"Stayin' Mr. Clean, Inspector," Kim shouted over the music.

Kenny turned to Sean, an unspoken message passing between them that it was time to get down to business. Sean nodded and reached down to the floor to retrieve a small, brightly wrapped package. "Happy birthday."

"Thanks," Kenny smiled. "Any problems?"

"Nah." Sean waved him off. "Those were some fine prints. Hope you get your man."

Kenny rose, put the package into his pocket, and, looking from Kim to Sean, was about to make a joke when Sean held up his hand. "Don't even say it," he laughed.

67

B arton Hubble lay on his four-wheel creeper beneath an older BMW 320i, its undercarriage as familiar to his experienced eye as sheet music to a pianist. Clearly, he thought, this car was being driven by a kid, probably a rich kid. No adult responsible for the upkeep of his own car would have treated it so carelessly. Racheting off the oilpan drain bolt and turning his head away from the initial splash of the viscous steel-blue fluid, he noticed a pair of hi-top Reeboks through the door of the waiting room and knew instinctively that they belonged to the owner of this car. What he hadn't expected was that the driver was a girl. From his vantage point, all he could see was a slender curve of tanned calf, but he knew already she was a blonde. Tanned this late in the year, he thought to himself. Definitely a rich kid.

Scooting his creeper along with his boots in order to get a better look at her legs, Barton Hubble saw two pair of men's dress shoes step up to the service counter. He tensed, his antennae focusing as he strained to listen over the clatter of the other mechanics working in the garage.

"You got a Barton Hubble here?" a voice asked.

When the two pair of shoes turned his way, obviously following the instruction of Otto from behind the desk, Hubble grabbed the underside of the BMW and pulled himself clear to the far side of the car. Scrambling to his feet, he crossed to his tool chest on the back wall. He wiped his hands on a greasy orange rag, unlocked the middle drawer of the chest, and tugged it open. An old Smith & Wesson revolver, dull grey bullet tips poking out of the cylinder like eggs in a nest, slid into view.

"You Barton Hubble?" came a low voice from only a few feet behind him.

Dropping the dirty rag on top of the gun, Hubble turned slightly, the weapon within easy reach. "Yeah."

The men wore inexpensive conservative suits. The older one stepped forward. "We're from Allstate Insurance," he announced. "You the one did the repairs on a dark blue '85 Mercedes coupe?"

His muscles uncoiling, Hubble nodded. "Engine fire?"

"Right, engine fire," the younger man said, as if, having spoken, he had somehow justified his showing up for work that day.

Hubble shrugged. "Fuel line was corroded so bad it leaked gasoline onto the manifold." He leaned back into his open drawer and nudged it closed. "Lucky the driver wasn't killed."

The younger man started to speak again, but was silenced by a curt glance from his partner. "You think," the older man asked, "this incident could have been avoided?"

"Maybe the owner could have taken better care of his car," Hubble offered, already bored with these two and looking past them at the girl smoking a cigarette in the waiting room. "But the fire was definitely caused by a parts failure."

"Okay, then," the senior insurance adjuster said, making a note on the back of a piece of paper. "Thanks for your time." He turned to leave as his partner caught Hubble assessing the girl's tanned legs through the door.

"Nice," the younger man said.

"Yeah, nice," Barton Hubble agreed as he dropped down to his creeper and rolled himself back under her car.

68

—-—

Kenny kept looking out through the interrogation room window, anxious for Jane to arrive. He had called her at David's at six-thirty that morning, excited both about what he had learned from Sean Temple and, using that information, about what he had been able to uncover on his own. After three and a half years of being her partner, he knew Jane wasn't exactly a morning person, but he hadn't counted on her being late either. He heard the stairwell door bang closed, and he flattened out against the wall to gain the angle to see who had come in.

Officer Finney, his arms around two large bags of bagels, lumbered to the coffee setup. He dropped the bags on the counter and, snatching a couple for himself, crossed to his desk. The door slammed again, and Kenny could see the reflection of Jane in the far windows as she hurried along the bullpen toward the interrogation room. Opening the door before she could get there, Kenny pulled her inside.

"I'm so sorry I'm late," she said breathlessly. "Sacramento Street's completely torn up, and I just sat there for half an hour."

Drawing the curtain closed across the interior window, Kenny turned to her and, with a satisfied smile, said, "Found him."

Jane's eyes widened. "Barton Hubble?"

"Yup," Kenny said as he crossed to the table and slid a sheet of paper out of a manila folder. "Real name's Simon Berke."

"Doesn't ring a bell," Jane confessed, shaking her head.

"Shouldn't," Kenny said. "He only moved to the city a couple of years ago, and, far as I can tell, he's kept his dick clean."

"Well put," Jane said.

"Wait, there's more," Kenny went on, his enthusiasm building. "He's done this before."

"No shit," Jane whispered.

"Back in 1984. There was this guy in L.A. who owned a huge carpet company with his brother-in-law. That's the good news. Bad news is his brother-in-law was a fuck-up. Hubble, uh, Berke . . ." Kenny riffled through the other pages. ". . . did some work on carpet man's Mercedes and they got to talking. Carpet man complained about his wife's idiot brother, and the next thing you know . . ."

"The idiot brother's dead," Jane said.

"The broken neck, the shallow grave, the whole megillah," Kenny finished the thought for her. "Same M.O. as Jenna Perry."

"Jesus," Jane said as she pulled a chair back to sit at the table. She was dying to rip the folder open, but she knew that Kenny was enjoying his little show-and-tell.

"It gets better," Kenny went on. "Our buddy Simon Berke goes to carpet man and says, 'I took care of your little problem for you'—a problem that, mind you, carpet man had merely complained about. He never said anything about killing the idiot brother-in-law. You with me?"

"Yeah, yeah. Go on."

"Anyway," Kenny continued, "Simon Berke says to carpet man, 'I made you a rich man. Time for you to return the favor.' Needless to say, carpet man's scared shitless and he goes to the police."

"Way to go, carpet man."

"Yup," Kenny agreed. "So Simon Berke is arrested. But the evidence is a little dicey and he's allowed to post bail. Before the case goes to trial, carpet man's feet get cold and he refuses to testify. The good guys don't have enough on Berke to hold him, and he walks."

Jane slapped her palms on the tabletop. "Berke got to carpet man's family!"

"The asshole showed up at carpet man's son's—let's call him carpet boy—at his Little League game. Scared the poor guy so much he coughed up fifty thousand dollars just to live in peace again." Kenny pulled the mug shots out of the folder and flipped them toward Jane. "This guy is one stone-cold motherfucker."

Turning the photographs right side up, Jane studied them for a moment, then caught her breath.

"What?" Kenny asked.

"I . . . I know this guy," Jane said, as she stared at the picture.

"How?"

"He showed up one day when I went to watch David argue a case over in Superior Court," Jane remembered.

"Not surprising," Kenny offered. "You told me yourself he's been harassing the guy."

"That's not all," Jane continued, her throat tightening. "The courtroom was empty. It was Five-B, you know how big that is. Anyway, there was hardly anyone else there and this guy sat right behind me!"

"I'd take that as a sign," Kenny said as the door opened and Finney entered. Without looking at Kenny, he crossed the room and handed Jane a slip of paper. Reading it as Finney left, Jane rose quickly and said, "Come on."

"Where to?" Kenny asked as he grabbed his coat.

"David said Hubble got off BART at Glen Park," she answered, handing him the paper. "Says here there are two German car repair specialists within walking distance of that station."

Kenny looked at the piece of paper in amazement. "Moby got this for you?"

"Sure," Jane said as she opened the door.

"And all this time," Kenny said, "I thought he was just a life-support system for a stomach."

Filled with purpose, they hustled out of the interrogation room and ran past Cheryl at the dispatch desk. "We'll call in our location from the road," Jane yelled to her as she rammed open the stairwell door, Kenny close behind.

— —

"I don't know," Otto Kohler said. "He was here this morning." The burly owner of Otto's Autos had a body roughly the shape and density of a refrigerator. Turning sideways to maneuver his bulk from behind the service desk, he gestured for Jane and Kenny to come with him. "You from the insurance?" he asked as he led them into the garage and over toward Barton Hubble's tool chest.

Jane yelled over the bracking pulse of a pneumatic drill, "No, sir. We're with SFPD Homicide. We wanted to ask Mr. Hubble a couple of questions about a case we're working on."

Quickly flashing his badge, Kenny added, "Routine questions."

An older mechanic, a burning cigarette stuck to his lower lip, peered out from beneath the hood of an Audi. When he saw Kenny show his badge to Otto, he quietly backed away from his work and slipped out the back door.

Kenny exchanged a knowing look with Jane and started to give chase when Otto said, "Let him go, Inspector. It's just old Karan. Poor bastard escaped from Serbia six months ago, and I am sponsoring him here in the States." They crossed to the door and saw Karan standing across the street, every muscle tensed in preparation for flight. "He was one of six men from his village to escape the killing squads. Six out of two thousand."

"I guess I'd be a little jumpy too," Kenny admitted.

"Come," Otto said. "I show you Hubble's things."

When Jane and Kenny arrived at Barton Hubble's tool chest, they immediately noticed something wrong. All of the drawers were partly open. Using her pen, Jane pulled several of them to her. All empty, except for one with a greasy orange rag. Hooking the rag with her pen, Jane lifted it and looked underneath. Nothing. "Looks like Barton Hubble has opted for early retirement, Mr. Kohler," she said as she dropped the rag back into the drawer.

Otto Kohler held out his hands and shrugged. "My boys leaving me used to make me crazy." He lit a cigarette, blue smoke curling from his nostrils. "But what can you do? Come back tomorrow and maybe Karan's nephew will be working right here." He patted Hubble's tool chest. "Maybe even tonight."

"I don't think," Kenny said, "I would take this as well as you, Mr. Kohler."

"We all have disappointments in our work, yes, Inspector?" Kohler observed as he made his way back to the office.

"Yes, we do," Kenny nodded without looking over to Jane.

"Is there any chance," Jane asked as they followed him, "that you have an address for Mr. Hubble?"

"Last address I have for him is Chinatown. If that still good, you can ask him your routine questions in person," Otto Kohler said. "Come. I give you."

"What about Karan?" Kenny asked. "Will he come back?"

Otto Kohler paused to look out the door. "He come back soon as you leave, Inspector."

Kenny shook his head. "Poor fucker."

"No. Not poor fucker," Otto Kohler corrected him. "Remember, he the lucky one."

69

—•—

"Just promise me one thing," Jane hissed at Kenny as they climbed the rickety stairs in Barton Hubble's building.

"What's that?" Kenny asked, pulling his weapon from his shoulder holster.

"When we get there, no macho shit."

"Tell you what," Kenny whispered when they reached the third-floor landing. "I won't shoot him for no reason if you don't try to have him get in touch with his feminine side."

"Deal," Jane said as they bracketed the door to apartment 3-F, their pistols tight against their chests. It had been a while since the two of them had been faced with a situation like this, and her heart was racing with the adrenaline-charged expectation of what might be in store for them.

She and Kenny had been in many tough scrapes together, and each time the thought had crossed her mind that this could be it. The one where it all ends. Who knew what lay in wait for them behind that door? Chaos, heroics, death? Or even worse: a mistake. A weapon fired in haste. Or not fired at all.

The difference between a partner saved and a partner lost.

Jane had started to signal to Kenny, wanting to make certain they were on the same page, when a door directly across the hall creaked open and a gnomic little man of indeterminate age and heritage started into the hallway. Kenny and Jane both whipped their pistols toward him, motioning for him to go back inside and close the door. Pausing to look at each of them, as if to see if he knew them from somewhere, the tiny hunchbacked man spit on the floor and, ignoring their warnings altogether, slowly poked his way down the stairs, his cane rattling loudly off the spindles of the banister.

250

After he was safely below the second-floor landing, Jane nodded to Kenny. "Ready? On my count. One . . . two . . ."

Before she could get to "three," Kenny wheeled around and kicked in the door, sending it shattering off the top hinge and falling partway into the room. "SFPD!" he shouted and bulled his way into Barton Hubble's apartment. Dropping to one knee, he did a quick left-right scan and called, "Clear!"

Jane raced into the room, her gun sweeping before her in careful regimented arcs. "Shit!" she exclaimed as she surveyed the tiny apartment.

The drawers of Barton Hubble's dresser were heaped in the middle of the floor and the door to the small closet next to the bathroom was open, naked hangers tangled together on the short wooden rod.

"This asshole's gone underground," Jane said, kicking at the broken front door.

"What?" Kenny asked, pulling open his jacket to reholster his pistol. "And leave all this behind?"

——

Jane was silent as Kenny pushed his way through the afternoon traffic, urging the Explorer to go just a little faster than everyone else up the series of hills leading to Pacific Heights. Pulling in a deep breath, she let it escape through her lips in a long audible sigh.

"What?" Kenny asked as he cranked right and floored it, passing a slow-moving cable car.

"I'm pissed," Jane answered.

"Don't worry," Kenny said with a confident smile. "We'll get this guy."

Jane shook her head. "Not about Hubble. About you."

Kenny tapped the brake and slipped into the flow of traffic. "Hey, I'll slow down, okay?"

"It's not your driving, Kenny," Jane replied. "It's you. The way you went into that apartment today, the way you barged into the back room of that grocery store last month . . . it's like you think you're gonna live forever." She turned in her seat, twisting against the seat belt. "Don't you get it? You won't slow down."

The light ahead changed to yellow, and Kenny, not realizing the irony of what he was doing, sped through the intersection. "It's just my way, Jane. It all came out okay, didn't it? The fucker wasn't even there."

"But what if he had been?" Jane shouted, thoroughly exasperated. "What if Barton Hubble had been sitting in a chair with a shotgun leveled at the keyhole? And you kick that door in before I'm ready to back you up and boom! One dead macho partner. Is that how you want to die? On the floor of some shithole apartment in the middle of goddam Chinatown?"

Kenny turned his head toward Jane and saw that her eyes were as fiery with anger as her voice. "Won't happen again," he said. "Besides," he went on, "didn't know you cared."

"Well, I do," Jane said softly.

After waiting for a bus from the Peabody Middle School to drop off three teenage girls at the corner, Kenny turned up the final hill toward David Perry's house, the Golden Gate Bridge spreading before them, defining the left side of the bay below.

"I never told you this." Jane nodded toward the bridge. "That's where David and I went on our first real date."

"The Golden Gate Bridge?" Kenny shook his head. "What are you guys, high school kids?"

"It was pretty intense. He has a key from when he was a kid," she went on. "Got us up to the top of the South Tower in this little elevator. Something like seventy-five stories over the water. It was absolutely amazing!"

"Seventy-five stories over the water," Kenny laughed as he pulled onto the sidewalk in front of David's house. "And you call me macho."

"The whole time I was up there," Jane said as they got out of the car, "I kept thinking about how much you'd love it. It's a completely different reality that high up."

"There's only about four things wrong with that scenario," Kenny said as they moved up the walkway. "One: I hate heights, and you know it. Two: I can't fly or swim, and you know that too. Three: I can't dance. I don't think you knew that."

"What's dancing have to do with anything?" Jane asked as she rang the doorbell, having decided not to use her key again in front of Kenny.

"Nothing really. Just thought I'd throw it in as long as I'm confessing stuff."

"So what's number four?"

"Number four is," Kenny began, "you're on a date with Mr. Wonderful seven hundred and fifty feet over San Francisco Bay and you're thinking about me. What's wrong with this picture?"

"Like it or not, Kenny," Jane said, a tender grin crinkling the corners of her mouth, "you're a part of my life. A big part of my life."

——

"We were this close," Kenny said to David, his arm resting on the telescope.

"I don't know," Jane added, flopping into the love seat. "Something spooked him."

David looked out the window toward Pilar's empty apartment. "Then he's out of my life?"

"That's the good news," Kenny offered.

David crossed away from the patio and sat on the arm of the love seat next to Jane. "What's the bad news?"

Jane looked up to him. "He'll be back."

"With what you stand to inherit?" Kenny said. "No way he stays gone."

David fell silent. Resting her hand on his leg, Jane said, "He's going to try to get to you again, David. And I gotta tell you, the next time? He's going to be pretty pissed off."

Kenny approached them. "Let's hope he makes phone contact first so you can notify us."

"But what if it's in person?" David asked.

Jane and Kenny exchanged a quick glance, then Kenny said, "We'll cross that bridge."

"Chances are he'll call," Jane offered. "And when he does, we want you to sound very frightened."

"Heh," David laughed nervously, "no problem there."

"Here's the deal," Kenny explained. "Soon as he calls, you tell him you'll give him whatever he wants if he'll just leave your daughter alone. Let him think you're totally surrendering and that he won. Set up a meeting with him. In the daytime. Someplace very public."

David rested his chin on his hand, listening intently.

Jane picked up the instructions. "Then you call one of us and we'll set you up with a wire. We'll get this bastard to incriminate himself, then we'll bust his ass so it stays busted."

"But," David asked, "why do we need the wire? Can't you just grab him?"

"This has to be airtight. He slipped away before and he could do it again," Kenny said. "We get him on tape, no amount of his threats

253

against you or Lily can keep him out of prison, maybe even the gas chamber."

"Last thing we want," Jane added, "is for Barton Hubble to walk out of jail again and show up a couple of years down the line in some other city ready to do this to someone else."

David slid down the armrest and into the soft cushion of the love seat. Kenny squatted before him. "I know this is a lot, David, and that you've already been through more than anyone should ever have to go through in a lifetime. But do you think you can do this?"

David nodded his head several times, his shoulders rocking with the motion. "Yeah . . . I can do this. No way we let this monster hurt anyone else."

The phone rang, its insistent trill freezing the three of them in place. Then Kenny raced into the kitchen and motioned for David to answer.

"Hello?" David said after the second ring, seeing that Kenny had picked up the cordless receiver over the sink.

Jane sat forward on the love seat, inhaling in shallow breaths as she willed herself to stay calm. Then she saw Kenny's face broaden into a smile, and she turned to David.

"Yes," he said. "I'm happy with my long-distance carrier."

As he hung up the phone, Kenny returned to the living room. "Those jerk-offs usually only call when I'm in the bathroom."

—\—

Jane dreamed that night of a different sea. Shimmering waves of silver heat billowed off an expanse of white-hot sand as boundless as an ocean. Floating on the crest of a dune, Jane saw Poppy in the valley of a sand wave, beckoning to her with his hand. But this time, she stayed where she was, not hurrying to rescue her father. Silently, he summoned her with his outstretched arms. Finally, but reluctantly, she allowed herself to lean forward, disengaging her hold on her wave and sliding down its face until she was only a few feet from her father.

Poppy opened his mouth over and over again, like a fish dying in the sun. He reached across the short distance between them, a drowning man hoping, at the last minute, to be saved. But Jane saw herself just watching him, letting the sand swallow him until he was immersed up to his neck. Then, with a final beatific smile to his daughter, he said, "Thank you," and slipped from sight, the sand quickly filling itself over as if he had never been there.

And then the desert was water and Jane sat in the riffles of its edge, her body cooling as she watched her now-pregnant belly grow, watched her breasts swell. And soon she gave painless and exquisite birth, there in the shallows, to a baby girl, a perfect diminutive version of herself.

And, somewhere in the half-light between the sweet lost world of sleep and the blooming of consciousness, Jane knew that she was free.

— —

It had been a late night at Wang Lu's Grill. The heavy tourist traffic in the mainstream Chinatown restaurants had kept the platoons of Chinese waiters and busboys working until well past midnight.

Wanting to unwind and to get away from their demeaning other selves, they had found their way to Wang Lu's, an oasis of light in the gloomy back alleys of their neighborhood.

After hours of beer and cigarettes, poker and mah-jongg, complaints and dreams, they had drifted away, alone and in pairs, to their tiny rooms off the fire escapes behind Chinatown.

Wang Lu dragged two heavy trash bags to the faded blue Dumpster in back of his grill. Heaving open the huge steel lid, sending it clanging against the brick wall behind it, he glanced inside. Something caught his eye. Something white in the darkness.

Reaching in, he brushed away the scraps of lettuce and Styrofoam. Then he understood what it was, and, curious, he raised his eyebrow.

A young Chinese girl lay on bundles of trash bags and restaurant refuse, her neck broken and bulging. Discarded with yesterday's garbage.

Wang Lu thought she looked like the girl he had seen with that white guy who drove the big tow truck, but he couldn't be sure.

He stood up on his toes and leaned over the side of the Dumpster until, straining, he could reach her. Then he looped his fingers into the diamond necklace around her neck and tugged. It broke free, and, dropping back to the pavement, Wang Lu slipped it into his pocket.

He flung the two trash bags into the Dumpster with a grunt and slammed the lid closed. Looking at his watch, he knew the garbage truck would be there in an hour or so, and this girl, insignificant in life and invisible in death, would soon disappear forever.

70

—•—

The foamy clouds of Jane's bubble bath crackled like burning paper as she slipped into the tub. Finishing a yogurt, she let the *Chronicle* magazine drop to the floor and watched David shave.

"You know," she said, "I've read this article on Clarissa Gethers twice now, and I still find it hard to completely understand her pain. That poor girl."

"That's because," David responded, rinsing his face, "only Clarissa knew the answers to her secrets." He smoothed moisture cream over his face and sat on the edge of the tub. "Now we know we should have been more observant, more careful with her. But when she was younger and acting kind of spacey, we thought it was just regular teenage stuff."

"Maybe it was," Jane agreed. "Maybe if she had been any other girl, she could have passed through it and nobody would ever have known about it."

David looked down to the magazine on the bathmat. "And now everyone knows."

Sitting up in the tub, Jane said, "I'm gonna clean up a little around here. Don't want Pilar resenting me any more than she already does. Want me to recycle that magazine with the other newspapers?"

"You do and Lily will have a fit," David laughed. "She specifically asked me to save it for her."

They sat there for a moment, each drifting on the current of an unspoken thought. Then David smiled and dipped his hand into the bathwater. With a sigh, Jane opened her thighs, welcoming David as he slipped his middle finger inside her.

"Oh God," Jane moaned, her pelvis pushing against the steady thrust of his hand as he slid a second finger home. Rolling onto her side, David's fingers still working within her, Jane took his swelling penis in her wet hand and massaged it until it was fully erect. Then, with a coy glance up to his face, she licked the tip of it. He responded by pumping his fingers inside her with even greater urgency.

Parting her lips, Jane turned her head and took him into her mouth, her hand sliding up and down along the loose sheath of his erection. David shuddered in an ecstatic reflex and bent his knees against the tub in order to give Jane a better angle. Using the tips of his fingers to pull along the upper ridge of her vagina, David pressed his thumb against her groin and, closing his hand, lifted her partway out of the tub. Jane felt the electricity of her coming orgasm building deep within her, when, suddenly, the telephone rang.

Pushing on, trying to ignore the intrusion, each of them intensified their giving and their taking, but they already knew that it was over. Such was the power any unknown caller held over their lives at this time.

Jane sat back into the tub as David removed his hand from the water. "If that's fucking MCI," she said, catching her breath, "I'm signing a lifetime contract with AT and T."

"Let's just look at this as an opportunity to move into the bedroom," David smiled as he reached for a towel and hurried to the bedside phone.

Jane sat up, poised to pick up the bathroom extension, as David answered on the third ring. "Hello," he said, his face already constricting with worry. He listened for a moment, then his body relaxed in relief. "Hi, sweetie!" Signaling Jane that it was Lily on the line, he sat on the bed, the towel across his lap, and talked with his daughter as Jane got out of the bath.

"No kidding? I'm really proud of you," he said. "Isn't there some kind of swimming school near you guys? Ask Grandma to take you, and if you like it, tell her to sign you up and I'll pay for it."

Lily was just about to tell her father that she didn't want to go to swimming school, she only wanted to come home, when David's call-waiting clicked in. "Hang on, honey. I'm getting a call."

He pressed the button. "Hello."

"How's the family, Dave?" Barton Hubble's voice cut through like a spike to the heart.

"Uh," David hesitated. "Let me get rid of a call."

Clicking again, David covered his nervousness with a half-hearted lilt. "Lilliput? I gotta go. I'll call you tonight. Love you." He turned and gestured frantically to Jane as she tied up her robe and arrived at the doorway. "It's him!" David mouthed.

Jane scurried back to the bathroom phone and nodded her head toward David. The instant he pressed the call-waiting button, she snapped up the extension.

"Hubble?" David said cautiously.

"Thought you forgot about me."

"I was talking to my . . ." David began. Jane, waving her hand furiously, warned him away from finishing the sentence truthfully. ". . . office."

"How nice for you," Hubble spit. "I really need to see you, Dave. Please don't make me come to your house . . . again."

David looked to Jane. Putting her hand over the mouthpiece, she hissed, "Set it up! We'll get this fucker!"

Sighing in resignation, David said to Hubble, "Okay. You win. When do we meet?"

"Today," Barton Hubble said. "There's an abandoned dock next to Pier 31. I'll meet you in the alley next to it at noon."

Jane shook her head violently. She dabbed toothpaste onto her finger and scribbled on the bathroom mirror: 'Public!' Grabbing up the *Chronicle* magazine, she dug into her makeup bag for a pencil stub. Flipping the magazine over, she made notes on the back cover as David spoke with Hubble.

David sat on the bed, trying to think. "Uh," he said into the phone. "No way I can get there by then." His foot bouncing in agitation, it came to him. "Tell you what. I'll meet you at the Powell Street BART station at twelve. Okay with you?"

"Just bring me my money, Dave," Hubble warned. "And leave your pretty little gun at home. Because if you do bring your pretty little rich-fuck gun, I will take it away from you and I will kill you with it."

David glanced at Jane, and she nodded. "Fine," he said.

He heard the line go dead and sat there on the edge of the bed as Jane rushed in. "You were great!" She took the phone from him and replaced it in its cradle. "We're gonna get this guy and get on with our lives, David."

David stood up and headed into the bathroom. "I think I'm going to throw up."

71

Kenny had been on hold for fifteen minutes.

During that time, Ozzie Castillo had changed in the locker room and gone out on patrol. Sally Banks had called in that she was going to be away from her car for a few minutes while she picked up clean uniforms at the dry cleaners. And Cheryl Lomax had chattered away at her dispatch console, efficiently keeping track of her charges. Lieutenant Spielman had come in from one meeting, gathered up some paperwork, and left for another. And Officer Finney had been in the bathroom.

Kenny was just about to hang up and start over when a voice on the other end of the line finally said, "Sorry to have you hold so long, Inspector Parks. But it's been kinda busy down here, with the rains and all."

"Two days of rain can be hell on a city," Kenny replied, the point of the joke whistling by unnoticed over the young Los Angeles police clerk's head. "And it's Marks. With an M," he corrected her for the second time. "Anyway, did you find the Information Request Form from our Officer Finney?"

"Uh, nope. Sure didn't," she chirped as if it were in her job description not to find things.

Just then Officer Finney emerged from his daily half-hour bathroom excursion, his habitually unfinished crossword puzzle under his arm. Kenny was about to hang up, annoyed at having to deal with the incompetence of someone else's city hall, when he had an inspiration.

"Tell me just one more thing," he said. "How are you spelling 'Finney'?"

"Usual way," the clerk answered. "P-H-I-N-N-E-Y."

Rolling his eyes, Kenny forced himself not to bite her head off over the phone. "Do me a favor," he asked. "Try looking it up using an F."

He heard the click-clack of a computer keyboard, and in about five seconds the clerk exclaimed, "Found it!"

"What's it say?"

"Says we faxed our responding letter to you guys three days ago."

Staring laser bullets of loathing across the bullpen toward Finney's massive back, Kenny clenched his teeth. "Thanks, L.A. 'Preciate it." He slammed the receiver down and was preparing to push his chair back when the phone rang.

Kenny snapped up the receiver. "Homicide. Marks."

"It's me." Jane's voice came to him like a soothing breeze. "He called."

"Hubble?"

"Yep," Jane said, her excitement mounting. "We set up a meet at noon at the Powell Street BART station."

"Fucker didn't waste any time," Kenny observed, patting his shoulder holster in the superstitious ritual cops always indulged in before they went into action.

"Fucker knows he got to David when he took that swim with Lily. He smells a payday," Jane said. "How soon can you be there?"

Kenny glanced at his watch. Eleven-fifteen. "Gimme twenty minutes."

"We'll be in the West Parking Structure. You got my portable number?"

"In my head," Kenny answered, his blood heating in anticipation. He hung up, pushed his chair back and, pocketing his car keys, strode over to Officer Finney. Just as he arrived at his cubicle, Finney swiveled around, his chair as small as a milking stool beneath his girth. Gulping down the remnants of some unrecognizable snack, he said, "Hey, Inspector. Got that fax on that Mr. Perry and his boss you wanted." Unable to suppress his pride at a job well done, he presented Kenny with a brown departmental envelope.

Ripping it open, Kenny tore out the thin sheaf of papers and quickly scanned them. Then, stunned at what he had just read, he shot Finney a withering look and demanded angrily, "When did you get this?"

"I dunno," Finney shrugged. "It was sittin' in the fax machine only maybe a day or two."

"Did it ever occur to you, Moby," Kenny went on, ready to pummel him to death with his own chair, "that, because I've been all over you about this, it just might be important?"

"How would I know?" Finney objected. "I didn't read it."

"Shit!" Kenny yelled as he wheeled around and raced for the stairwell door. "You better hope," he called, holding up the pages, "that this stuff is wrong!" Brushing by the sandwich lady who was making her way toward her favorite customer, he slammed through the door and hurtled down the stairs.

"If you want it to be wrong," Finney mumbled, "then why's it so damn important?"

72

D avid's jaw pulsed nervously, his cheek flexing and tightening, as he drove through the light midday traffic. Jane looked at the dashboard clock: eleven-thirty. She put her hand on David's arm. "Anything, but anything, goes wrong," she said, "and you bail. This is no place for heroics."

"Don't worry. I'm not the hero type."

Jane watched him intently as she played out the possible scenarios in her mind. It could go well; most times things like this, with proper planning, came off perfectly. It was completely conceivable that Barton Hubble would say something incriminating into David's wire and she and Kenny could swiftly move in, taking Hubble into custody, and David out of harm's way.

Or Hubble might not show. It was common for suspects to get cold feet this close to the endgame. She could remember countless times over the years when she and Kenny had waited all night, or even all week, for a criminal to appear at a predetermined location only to learn that the bad guy was already in jail on some other charge, or was too frightened to make the rendezvous, or, in one case of hers, was dead—killed the night before by his own wife. And every hour of those lengthy surveillances was spent numbingly on the edge.

Or something, anything, could go wrong. It had never happened on one of her stakeouts, but the very nature of the unruly beast was such that any one of a number of things could lead to the chaos of a police procedure gone bad. Hubble would be armed; she knew that. It was agreed that David should leave his pistol at home. He had no training; had, he'd admitted, never even fired it. The last thing anyone wanted was for the situation to deteriorate so badly that David—or anyone else, for that matter—would have to be involved in a shooting incident.

Jane began to have second thoughts. Should she have acquiesced to doing this without going through channels? Would Lieutenant Spielman have allowed her to stay on the case—be in for the kill, as it were?

She and Kenny could take care of themselves and each other. But what about David having to confront a wild card like Hubble in the middle of a crowded BART station? She looked at the clock again—eleven thirty-eight—and, a disquieting doubt welling in her chest, pulled her cellular phone from her bag. Pressing the speed dial, she called Kenny's desk at the station. No answer. He's already left to meet them, she thought. Ringing off, she turned to see David looking at her.

"I hope Kenny's as good a cop as advertised," he said as he pulled into the West Parking Structure of the Powell Street BART station.

"He is," Jane replied, knowing now that these things had a momentum of their own, and that they were going to go through with it.

— —

In the far reaches of the police station's basement, beyond the old bicycles left over from a community policing program, down past the stacks of dusty filing cabinets, were the precinct archives. Antique microfiche files from before the department's upgrading of its computer system sat undisturbed in the musty confines of the tiny, windowless room.

Kenny sat hunched over the only machine that still worked, its fan grinding noisily, and frantically pored over the film passing before the illuminated screen. Finally, he found what he was looking for.

"Son of a bitch!" he said to himself. Without bothering to turn off the machine, he grabbed up his papers and, seeing from his watch that it was eleven-forty, scrambled out the door.

73

It was only because the mail truck was moving so slowly that it didn't sideswipe the black Explorer that erupted from the driveway of the Nineteenth Precinct. Standing on his brakes, the postal driver skidded his unwieldy vehicle to a smoky, screeching stop as Kenny blasted across two lanes of traffic, turned hard to the east, and rocketed away.

Keeping the Explorer in second gear, coaxing every bit of power from its engine, Kenny whipped past a UPS truck and flew into a right turn down the steep incline of Mission Street. Steering with his left hand, he dug his cell phone out of the glove box and, pressing with his thumb, dialed Jane's cell number. But all he could get was a "no service" sequence of annoying beeps. Dropping the phone onto the passenger seat, he gunned the accelerator and, at the ledge of the intersection of Mission and Sixteenth, sent the Explorer airborne through the crosswalk.

Landing awkwardly on his back wheels and thudding forward, Kenny threw the car into a groaning, leaning left turn onto Ninth Street and screamed through a red light, barely avoiding a municipal bus and two teenage boys on skateboards.

— —

"It's time," David said.

Jane sat in the passenger seat of the BMW and looked at David as he squatted in the car's open doorway. "We should wait for Kenny," she said as she got out.

Rising with her, David took her in his arms and pressed his lips to her forehead. "I'm just going to talk to the guy and come right back to you."

Jane pulled back, leaning against his arms, to study his face. "You're sure about this?"

"I can't live like this anymore," David said, touching his hand to her cheek. "I want my life back."

Turning to kiss the palm of his hand, Jane pulled him into a long clinging embrace. "Remember, no leading questions," she reminded him. "Don't force his hand." She drew his face to hers. "And please . . . don't do anything stupid."

David kissed her. "Wouldn't think of it," he smiled. Unwinding himself from her arms, he turned and entered the station.

Jane took an involuntary step forward as David waved and passed from sight. Then she switched on the tape recorder and, with one last glance down the ramp for any sign of Kenny, sat back in the car.

— —

The clock over the southbound tracks read eleven fifty-eight as David entered Powell Street Station. Glancing around, he walked to the edge of the platform to make himself more visible to Barton Hubble.

He felt the wind first. A gust of warm, faintly oily air was pushed into the station, followed closely by the sloped prow of the first car of the seven-coach southbound train. As its brakes seized the tracks and it squealed to a stop, David sensed an abrupt flash of movement behind him and spun around. A young woman was dragging a reluctant toddler toward the train. The little boy, his heels scraping along in donkeylike stubbornness, squirmed to free his hand from the woman's grasp. Exasperated, she slapped him on the bottom and slung her arm around his waist, hoisting his writhing body onto her hip. When the doors of the train whooshed apart, she stumbled forward, pausing as she passed to say to David, "Fuckin' nephew."

As the doors closed behind her, David turned to survey the platform. Other than the retreating backsides of a few detraining passengers riding up the escalators, he was alone.

Then he noticed the tip of a heavy black shoe protruding from behind one of the broad cement pillars between him and the turnstiles. He tucked his chin forward and whispered into his tiny microphone, "I think I see something."

As he approached the pillar, the shoe was pulled back out of sight, and David, unsure now, stopped. He was just about to press on when the shoe reappeared, followed by another, then by a pair of black slacks. It was a young transit cop. Munching on a Milky Way, he saw that David was staring at him.

"Help you?" he asked.

"Uh, no. I'm okay," David said as he turned and made for the elevator. "False alarm. No sign of him here," he said into the mike. "I'm going to take the elevator down to the lower platform."

The steel doors of the empty elevator rattled open, and David entered, catching his breath against the foul smell. Pushing the button for the northbound platform, David stepped back as the doors began to close. Just as they were about to meet in the middle, a hand shot in and pushed hard against the black rubber bumper, causing them to split open once again.

Barton Hubble stood in the doorway. "Right on time, Dave. I like that."

Jane, hearing this, jumped out of the car. "Get out of the elevator!" she yelled as she grabbed her bag and started into the station. "David, get out of there!" This was exactly what she had feared. Kenny was inexplicably missing. David was alone in an elevator with Barton Hubble.

And she was on her own.

David stood against the back wall as the elevator doors pressed closed and the car shuddered its way downward. Hubble remained at the control panel. "Stinks in here," he said. His lip was swollen and he was still limping slightly from his encounter with David on the Market Street overpass. "Have something for me, Dave?"

"You just called this morning," David started. "I couldn't get it all. But I . . ."

Jane skidded to a stop outside the elevator and repeatedly poked at the call button. Pressing the earpiece in even tighter, she closed her eyes and tried to concentrate, pushing herself to be able to hear David in the impenetrable confines of the descending elevator. She realized that it was futile to wait for the elevator to return, and that she wouldn't be able to hear David until he arrived at the lower platform. She was about to run toward the stairway when her cellular phone rang.

The young transit cop, riding up the escalator toward the street level, turned at the trill of Jane's phone. Seeing that it was just some woman by the elevator whose phone had rung, he finished his candy bar and stepped into the sunlight.

Jane grabbed the phone from her bag and yelled, "Hello!" But all she could hear was the grating static of a cellular phone call thwarted by too many downtown skyscrapers and too much BART station granite. "Kenny!" she shouted into the phone, knowing it was useless.

"Shit!" she cried and dropped the phone back into her bag.

— —

"Jane!" Kenny screamed into his car phone, the same impenetrable static hissing back at him. "Motherfuck!" he yelled in frustration as he flung the phone onto the passenger seat. It bounced off the cushion and dropped to the floor near the center console. Up ahead, a cable car was in the middle lane, unloading nearly a dozen passengers. Kenny swerved to the far right lane. A produce delivery truck, its tailgate down like a scythe, was parked at the curb.

Slaloming back to the left, Kenny accelerated into a gap in the oncoming traffic and blasted past the cable car. Pounding on his horn, he sent the passengers scrambling like pigeons as he flew into the next intersection, where a pickup truck, it too speeding to make the light, slammed into the Explorer, crumpling the driver's-side door and sending it hurtling sideways into a utility stanchion. The passenger side caved in as it wrapped around the pole and the Explorer whiplashed to a crunching stop.

The driver of the pickup jumped out of his truck and ran to the Explorer. Kenny was slumped, unconscious, over the broken steering wheel. As people gathered, the driver thrust his hand through the shattered window and touched Kenny on the shoulder. Breathing shallowly, he fell over to one side, blood trickling from his mouth. The cable car conductor came rushing up and shouted, "Somebody call nine-one-one!"

Tugging in vain at the collapsed driver's door, the man from the pickup truck called out, "And hurry! This guy's all fucked up!" He and the cable car conductor scrambled around to the other side of Kenny's car. But the telephone pole was rammed halfway into the Explorer, abutting the center console, the cellular phone shattered into hundreds of pieces.

There was no way in to Kenny. And no way out.

74

T he elevator doors opened and David and Barton Hubble stepped into the relatively fresher air of the lower northbound platform. David, unaware of where Jane was and unsure whether or not Kenny had gotten there, moved closer to Hubble than he would have preferred. "I can get you your money, the whole five million, in a couple of days," he offered, speaking loudly over the squeal of an approaching train. "Or maybe a quarter of it by tonight."

Jane stopped at the top of the stairs and tried to calm her breathing as David's voice came through to her, clear and distinct. She paused for a moment to listen, then hurried down the three flights of steps.

The northbound train was about to emerge from the darkness of its underground cave, expectant passengers edging forward on the platform, when Barton Hubble grabbed David and pulled him out of earshot of the others. "This is not a negotiation!" he seethed. Shouting now to be heard over the clamor of the incoming train, Hubble roared, his eyes bulging in rage, "I didn't kill your wife to get fucked out of my money!"

Midway down the last flight of stairs, Jane slowed to listen to the wire. But the shrieking of the train's brakes had obliterated what she knew was Barton Hubble's confession. "Damn it!" she swore as she flew down the last few steps and rammed the door open. There, far across the platform, were David and Hubble, standing together like two old friends enjoying the subway as they chatted.

David, sensing that the train's brakes had drowned out the last transmission, turned to Hubble and said, "One thing I don't understand. Couldn't you have just blackmailed me, threatened me and my family, without killing my wife?"

Quickening her step toward them as David's words filtered into her earpiece, Jane cried under her breath, "No, David . . . don't!"

Barton Hubble snickered. "It's conceivable, Dave," he answered as the warning bongs sounded the imminent closing of the train's doors. "But how would I ever be able to convince you that I meant it when I said . . ."

He stopped abruptly, his eyes narrowing.

Before David could react, Hubble's hand flashed out and ripped open his shirt, exposing the wire. David took a step back and was about to turn away when Hubble moved in on him, tore the transmitter from his waist, and jabbed the sharp barrel of a pistol into his ribs.

His eyes swept the platform. "Let's take a ride." Poking David hard under the armpit, he forced him onto the train just as the doors slid closed.

Jane, her worst-case scenario now a reality, tore across the vast expanse of the platform, already knowing that the distance between her and the train was farther than she could possibly cover in time. The train churned forward and she skidded to a stop, desperately trying to spot David before he was swallowed by the tunnel at the end of the station.

There, on the far side of the third car, next to the doors, she saw David sitting with Barton Hubble. Although the train was gathering considerable speed, she felt that David had seen her too. Her heart exploding with fear, she wheeled and raced up the escalator, shoving and pushing her way past the recently arrived passengers, the keys to the BMW already in her hand.

— —

Rushing through the darkness, driving the air before it into a cylinder of wind, the northbound BART train surged out of the tunnel into the brilliant contrast of a sun-drenched day.

Jane rammed David's BMW through the West Parking Structure's security arm, splintering it and sending the tollgate attendant sprawling to the floor of her booth. Shielding her eyes as she shot out of the grey interior of the garage into the blinding daylight, she cranked the car into a sliding right turn and was just able to catch a glimpse of the northbound train as it sped away on its elevated rails. Having already pressed the speed dial on her cellular phone, she waited impatiently as she wove in and out of traffic, trying to keep the train in sight.

"Come on! Come on!" she urged, until finally someone picked up on the other end. "Finney, gimme Kenny!"

She listened to Finney tell her that Kenny had hurried out of there over half an hour ago and hadn't told him where he was going. "Shit!" she yelled as she tore through an alley, sending up walls of water from the puddles of last night's rain. "Okay, have Cheryl patch me through to BART Transit Police. Yes, this is a fucking emergency!"

Coming to the end of the alley, she was forced to slow down before blasting into the cross street. Honking the horn to warn the pedestrians ahead, she whipped into another sideslipping right turn and searched between the buildings for the train. Realizing it had traveled farther than she had anticipated, she looked off into the distance and spotted it, pulling away on its unobstructed path.

"Hello!" Jane screamed into the phone when the Transit Police operator finally answered. "This is Inspector Jane Candiotti of the SFPD. 3H58. I'm following the northbound train out of Powell. I need to know the next station!"

Braking the BMW to a stop in the middle of an intersection, traffic whizzing by in both directions, Jane watched as the train banked into a graceful arc and disappeared underground. "The next station!" she shrieked into the phone. "What is it?"

Behind her, a car honked in annoyance, followed soon by others as they stacked up in back of David's car, frozen in the heart of a busy intersection in the middle of San Francisco. "Montgomery?" Jane repeated as the operator answered her question. "Thank you!"

She ripped the car into a vicious left turn and cut across town.

— —

The bystanders mingling around the demolished Explorer didn't realize that Kenny, unconscious and badly banged up, had actually been lucky. The corner where he had crashed into the utility pole was only a block and a half from Fire Station 80. The crew had just been returning from a call, so they had been up and running when the 911 dispatch reached them.

One of the firemen stood on the hood of the Explorer and peeled away the collapsed windshield. Then a paramedic crawled inside to stabilize Kenny's neck and start an IV to ward off the onset of shock. Working swiftly to prevent a fire, one of the team cut the battery cables while another shot neutralizing foam into the gas tank. Uniformed police officers quickly set up a perimeter to keep the bystanders back.

Once the paramedic gave the sign that Kenny was sufficiently immobilized, the huge hydraulic tanks of the Jaws of Life were wheeled in. A yellow protective tarp was draped over Kenny as a burly firefighter lifted the enormous pincers into place and nodded, signaling one of his team to start the compressed-oil tanks to humming. Using the pike end of his Halligan tool, another team member jabbed a large ragged hole in the center of the driver's door so that the Jaws of Life could gain purchase in the metal.

"Green!" the team leader called, and the jaws gaped open, tearing the steel flesh of the door like paper. "Red!" came the command, and the hydraulic pressure shifted, causing the pincers to close again. Repeating this red-green sequence several more times, the rescuers removed the door and flung it aside.

Ozzie Castillo pulled up and was briefed by one of the young officers. As senior officer on-scene, he stepped inside the police line and approached the wreck. Then he recognized Kenny's Explorer and, dread welling inside, he raced forward.

The paramedic was just slicing through Kenny's seat belt while another fitted him with a backboard when Ozzie ran up. He stood back while Kenny was lowered onto a stretcher. Once he was strapped in and being hurried to the ambulance, Ozzie stepped in. "I know this guy!" he called out. "He's a cop! Ken Marks out of the Nineteenth."

Kenny's eyes flickered open, and Ozzie, running alongside the stretcher, put his hand on his friend's chest. Kenny's lips quivered as he tried to speak.

"Jane . . ." was all he could manage.

"Don't worry, Kenny," Ozzie said. "I'll let her know."

As Kenny's eyes slipped closed again, the paramedics hoisted the stretcher into the ambulance. "Hang in there, brother," one of them said. "The nuns will take care of you."

Securing the doors, he slapped the back of the vehicle with his open palm. Its siren whooping, the ambulance raced away, carrying Inspector Kenneth Marks to the emergency room of St. John's Memorial Hospital.

— —

Crammed next to Barton Hubble in the small seat, David shifted his weight away from the pistol under Hubble's coat.

He looked across the aisle at a well-dressed black boy, maybe ten or eleven years old, who rose and offered his seat to an elderly white woman who was having difficulty maintaining her balance as the train chased itself into a tunnel. Momentarily disoriented by the sudden light change, the old woman hesitated. But the boy persisted, gently taking her arm and guiding her to his seat. Once she was at ease, he stood by the door, his arm looped around a steel upright, looking for all the world like a miniature version of an adult.

Blue-white lights flicked by on the black tunnel walls as Barton Hubble allowed the yawing of the train to rock his body back and forth against his seat. Without moving his head, David scanned the car, looking for anything or anyone that he might use as a diversion. Just as his eyes came to rest on the glass-enclosed emergency stop handle, the train burst back into the sunlight, seeming to stir Hubble to speak.

"You've done two very bad things, Dave," he began. "You've disappointed me and you've made me angry."

"I'm a little peeved myself," David shot back. "What's to keep me from just yelling out for help right now?"

Barton Hubble raised his eyebrows in a mocking gesture. "Tell you what: you pick out any passenger in this car and I'll shoot him first. Who's it going to be?" He pointed with his chin. "That old lady? The bum down there? That Korean guy? That little black kid? Up to you, Dave."

The between-cars door slid open and a female transit cop stepped into their car. Closing his eyes, David calculated the chance and the risk involved. When he opened his eyes again, Hubble was staring at him. "I'll shoot that fuckin' cop in the back of the head, you so much as swallow in a way I don't like," he warned. "So, do the world a favor and just forget about it."

The recorded voice announced, "Montgomery, next. Mont-gom-er-y," and David felt the train begin its gradual deceleration as it slipped into another tunnel. Passengers stirred in preparation, gathering up their packages and books; a couple of the younger ones were already standing, eager to get off. Jabbing David with the gun, Hubble motioned for him to stand. "Time to switch trains," he said. "Get us really lost."

Rising quickly, David noticed the transit cop passing into the next car. "What are you going to do with me?"

An incredulous laugh shot out of Hubble's mouth. "Why, I'm going to kill you, Dave," he answered, his voice as calm as if he were ordering a meal. He nudged David forward as the train squealed into the Montgomery Street Station. "But don't worry. Somebody will find you. Somebody always does, don't they, Dave?"

The doors parted, and Hubble pushed David past the little black boy and onto the platform. Prodding his captive across the broad walkway to the westbound escalator, Barton Hubble took a brief moment to study the station. Confident that no one there posed any threat to him or his plans, he said, "Upsy-daisy," and leaned into David until they were riding the long escalator to the upper track.

At the next level, David began to drift to his right, merging with the flow of the other passengers. But Hubble quickly intercepted him and shouldered him to the left, where the westbound train sat waiting, its doors open.

"Our lucky day," Hubble quipped. He pushed David into the second car just as the bongs began to chime their warning.

Hubble had started to maneuver David to the seat across from the door when he heard someone call from the platform, "Hold the door, please!" Ever the gentleman, he held the door open with his forearm for a woman in a windbreaker. Laden with groceries, a weathered Oakland A's baseball cap pulled down over her forehead, she scrambled aboard. "Thanks," she said, out of breath.

"Pleasure," Barton Hubble nodded and motioned for David to sit down.

When Hubble sat next to him, crowding in close, David looked across the aisle as the woman arranged the groceries on her lap. Rooting around in one of the bags, she came up with an apple. David's eyes followed her hand as she raised it to her mouth and took a healthy bite. David's lips parted, as if to speak, but he caught himself in time as Jane munched on the apple, refusing to make eye contact with him.

When the train finally started out of the station, she scrunched around in her seat and stared out the window at the passing tunnel lights.

75

T he night-black view out the window had Jane thinking that this all must be a dream.

Was she really holding three bags of groceries she had taken from that woman outside the Montgomery Street Station, hurriedly showing her badge and cramming a fistful of twenties into her hand while mumbling something about official police business? Could it be that David was actually three feet away from her, that his wife's murderer had a gun aimed at his heart, and that she was unable to do anything about it other than wait? Was it possible that Barton Hubble was in this dream and that she, usually so able and confident, was so helpless?

She felt David's eyes on her body, felt them warming her ear as she turned her back on Hubble. Knowing she couldn't make a move until he played his hand, she made herself remember that, in choosing to yield control to him, she in turn retained control of the situation. Then, for a fleeting moment, she saw David's reflection in the window, and their eyes touched. Her heart tearing, she looked away as the recorded voice declared, "Embarcadero next. Em-bar-ca-de-ro." Out of the corner of her eye she saw Barton Hubble turn to David.

"We'll get off here," Hubble said, getting ready to stand. "Then we double back to Powell and pick up my car."

Drawing his eyes away from Jane, David looked at Hubble. "You're a criminal genius."

"I like to think so," Hubble said, enjoying himself.

David rose quickly to signal Jane that they were getting off at the next stop. Still looking out the window, she gathered her grocery bags together and nonchalantly uncrossed her legs. Barton Hubble stood and leaned into David. "I promise that when I kill you, Dave," he snarled, "the whole time you're dying, you'll know you're dying." He let out a little laugh. "There's a kind of poetry in that, don't you think?"

A quiver of dread shot through David's body, and the taste in the back of his mouth changed to an alkaline tingling of fear. He swallowed it as the train pulled into the Embarcadero Station.

The doors slid apart and Barton Hubble pressed into David, prodding him out of the car. Jane fumbled with her bags just long enough to give them a head start, wanting to keep them in front of her. Then she exited the train and, seeming as if she hadn't a care in the world, followed them toward the eastbound escalator.

Jane was dismayed to see Barton Hubble nudge David onto the down escalator. This meant they were heading away from the street, toward yet another subway ride. She figured he was making his way back to wherever he had left his car. But what would he do with David? Let him go and try to extort money from him at a later date? Not likely. Hubble had discovered David wearing a wire. In the twisted logic of a criminal's mind, that was a betrayal of trust, and now he would be compelled to do something about it. And with someone like Hubble there was only one option.

He was going to kill David.

Quickening her step, Jane was grateful that this BART station was relatively empty. When she started her descent on the eastbound escalator, she thought she saw Hubble turn around and look at her, but she had made herself so busy with the charade of looking for something in one of the grocery bags that she couldn't be certain. Glancing up from beneath the bill of her cap, she saw Hubble elbow David in the side, prompting him to turn to the left and out of sight.

Hurrying down the last few steps of the escalator and turning to the left, Jane felt the warm wind of an approaching train as she reached the platform and stopped. Something was wrong. The platform was empty, its square stone pillars lined up like sentries.

Jane scanned the area.

There were no doors, no exits for Hubble to have taken. He, and David, had to be somewhere in front of her. For a second, as she heard the distant rush of the incoming train, a hot dog wrapper fluttering in the nearing breeze, she considered that maybe they had dropped down to the tracks and were escaping through the tunnel. But Hubble didn't have to do that. He didn't know she was following him.

Or did he?

Her heart tightening with apprehension, every nerve ending on fire, she started forward, the tracks to her right, the pillars to her left. Her right hand still deep in one of the grocery bags, she passed the first pillar and glanced behind it. Nothing. She was just about to the next one when David lurched out from behind a pillar near the end of the row and fell to one knee.

Jane halted, trying to read the situation, and was about to start forward again when Barton Hubble strode in one long step from behind that same pillar and jammed his pistol against the back of David's head.

"Oh my God!" Jane cried out, purposely sending her voice into a higher register. "Is that a real gun?"

"Shut up!" Hubble shouted at her, his body clenched with rage. "Way I see it, there's two possible reasons why you're going back the way you came. One, you're lost. Or two, you're following us." He cocked the hammer of his pistol and poked it into David's hair. "I say it's two."

"Look, Mister. I don't know what . . ." Jane began, trying to buy a little time to think. The eastbound train would arrive at any second, and that would provide some distraction for her.

"I told you to shut up!" Hubble roared. "You know what? I think that under that jacket and hat there's a pretty little lady cop. So do us all a favor and put down those bags and open up your coat."

Shaking her head in resignation, Jane started to lower her bags. But then she stopped and straightened up again. "No," she said defiantly, trying to anger Hubble into turning the gun away from David and pointing it at her.

"Do what I said!" Hubble yelled. "Now!"

"No!" Jane screamed back at him. "Fuck you!"

Furious, Barton Hubble swept his pistol toward Jane and fired, the round taking a large dusty piece out of the pillar next to her. In that instant, David howled and thrust himself to his feet. He rammed into Hubble's side and propelled him back into the pillar they had been hiding behind. His hands flailing, he tried to grab Hubble's wrist and prevent him from firing again. But Barton Hubble, taller and stronger, stomped the heel of his work boot viciously into the top of David's foot and threw him to the ground. He strode forward, preparing to shoot David in the face, when his stomach exploded in a mist of red.

David spun around to see Jane, her hand still in the grocery bag, march toward them and fire two more shots—the first she had ever fired at another human being. The paper bag shredded into flaming bits as she squeezed the trigger again and again.

Hubble took another slug in the stomach and one in the shoulder.

With a look of stunned indignation, Hubble lurched to his right and fired his gun at David. Rolling onto his side, David was just able to avoid being hit as Jane ripped her weapon from the bag and blasted three more rounds into Hubble, the explosive echoes mixing with the screeching of the approaching train.

Barton Hubble staggered sideways, teetering at the lip of the platform. Jane, her gun empty, frantically started to reload even as she ran at him. But Hubble, his arm badly damaged, raised his pistol and took wobbly aim at her as she drew closer. Jerking the trigger, he sent a bullet caroming off the cement platform, the ricochet missing her thigh by inches. Before he could control his trembling arm and take aim again, David scrambled to his feet and lunged at Hubble, driving his shoulder into the wounded man's knees and sending him toppling over the edge to the tracks below, his gun skittering away.

His breath coming in wet, desperate rasps, Hubble lay on his back between the rails, thin trails of blue cordite smoke wafting down to him. His right leg, the work boot twitching uncontrollably, was crossed over the near track, and the side of his head was wedged against the far track. "Help me!" he begged weakly as Jane ran up to David and looked down at him. Her instinct was to jump down and rescue him before the train whipped into the station. David felt her body flex, and he grabbed her, holding her back as the train leaped out of the blackness of the tunnel, like an eel erupting from a sea cave, and ripped into Barton Hubble, devastating his body in a swift moment of savage death; his final agonizing screams swallowed by the shriek of the five-hundred-ton train grinding to a stop.

Jane stared at the train, at the spot where Hubble lay beneath its wheels. "Jesus," she whispered.

David wrapped his arms around her. "The whole time the train was coming at him," he said, "Hubble knew he was dying."

"It's over, David," Jane said. "It's finally over."

Burying his face into her hair, David said, "Thanks for coming after me."

Jane pulled back to look at him. "No way I'm letting you die, David. No way."

76

Jane spent the rest of the afternoon filing her report and being debriefed by an SFPD shooting-incident team. By the time Lieutenant Spielman released her, most of the officers from her shift had already gone home.

Wearily fighting off the image off Barton Hubble's last moments, Jane emerged from the police station and crossed the sidewalk to David's car. "How'd it go?" he asked as she got in.

"Basically it was awful," Jane said, fastening her seat belt. "But it's over now, and I want to see Kenny."

"We're on our way," David said gently as he pulled away from the curb.

— —

The first thing Jane noticed when she got there was that the nuns had put fresh lilies in Kenny's room. Where did they get lilies this time of year? she wondered. She stood over her unconscious friend, her hand flat on his chest, feeling the sturdy beat of his brave heart against her palm. Looking out the fourth-story window of this old building, Jane saw the reflection of the setting sun bouncing orange and magenta off the hospital's new wing, completed just the year before. In the courtyard below, two nuns helped a very old patient into a van and sent him on his way home.

Feeling her face warm at the sight, Jane promised herself that the next time she went to visit Poppy, she would stop off at her old church and make a donation. She had a lot to be thankful for.

As she bent over to kiss Kenny on the cheek, she closed her eyes and said a silent prayer of gratitude that he had escaped with only two cracked ribs and a mild concussion. After brushing his hair off his forehead, she turned to smile at David, who was just returning from using the phone at the nurses' station.

"I can't wait till he wakes up so I can tell him about what happened today," she said as she hooked her arm through his and led him from the room.

"Something else happened today," David said as they walked down the corridor.

"What?"

"Shepherd-Ramsey settled." He grinned. "Eighteen million. Plus, they'll install seat belts on all their school buses in San Francisco."

"Oh, David, that's wonderful!"

They stopped at the elevators. David pushed the button and leaned against the wall. Jane folded herself into him. "Are you as tired as I am?" she asked.

"It's like all the energy's been sucked out of me."

The elevator arrived. "Still want to take that vacation with me?"

David put his arm around her. "I think we've earned it," he said as they entered the elevator.

— —

"If it's all the same to you," Jane said as David pulled his car out of the hospital parking lot, "I think I need to sleep in my own bed tonight."

David turned to look at her as she sank deeper into her seat, completely exhausted. "Alone?" he asked. "Because if that's what you . . ."

Jane interrupted him by reaching across and squeezing his arm. "I need my own bed for all sorts of reasons I can't even begin to explain," she began, stroking the fine hairs above his wrist. "But I would love for you to stay with me."

"Okay. I'll go home first thing in the morning and pack," David replied. "And I'll be back in your bed before you even wake up."

"That's great. Thanks." She pressed her forehead against the cold smooth surface of her window. "I shot a man today," she whispered at her reflection.

"Hmm?" David asked absently as he changed lanes and headed for the Marina.

"Nothing," Jane said softly. "Just talking to myself."

— —

Jane wasn't sure how she got inside or how she got undressed, but she was sure that she slept soundly that night, as if under the spell of a benevolent drug. She remembered stirring occasionally, waking up almost on purpose so that she could revel in the ease with which she fell back asleep, her butt snuggled into David's stomach, her hand holding his next to her face.

Hours later, Jane felt the first soft light of day touch her face and heard the front door click as David left to pack for their trip to the wine country. She rolled over to his side of the bed and, like a cat, drank in the residual heat from his body as she dozed.

A while later, the sun climbing its morning ladder and imbuing her bedroom with a pale ivory light, she heard the front door open and close again as David returned. Still luxuriating in her slumber, as if etherized by the backside of adrenaline, Jane listened as he walked down the hallway, the floorboards creaking as they always did, and went into the guest bathroom. She smiled somewhere deep inside as the sound of his urinating drifted her way and she remembered how cozy, how complete, that sound made her feel.

Her door opened, with a slight scrape that Jane reminded herself to one day repair, and he came in. Crossing the room in what seemed like too few strides, he stood over the bed for a moment and watched her in her half-sleep. Jane felt him looking down at her and tried to imagine what, if she were to open her eyes, his face would tell her. She heard a faint crack in his ankle as he took the last step closer and was aware of the blanket being pulled slowly down her body to her waist, as if she were being undressed.

Her breathing became more rapid even as she heard his quicken, and, rolling onto her back, she opened her eyes and looked into the face of Barton Hubble.

Bloodied and torn, he was on her before she could take in the breath to scream. Holding her down, his stench assaulting her as he grabbed and clawed at her wrists, Barton Hubble ripped off his pants and tried to mount her.

Yanking the blanket from the lower half of her body and exposing her turgid cock, Hubble recoiled in horror. But Jane, understanding deep within the fathomless web of her unconscious that this was a dream, pulled him onto the bed and, in a display of inhuman strength, forced him over onto his stomach and entered him from behind.

His screams sent her into a frenzied thrusting, her hair flying, her sweat falling and mingling with his blood. She continued to pump furiously, urged to even greater ferocity by his pitiful cries, until, in a convergence of ecstasy and revenge, she closed her eyes and came, tremors of relief and freedom rippling through her body.

When she opened her eyes again, her breath coming in steady and soothing whispers, she looked down to see Barton Hubble, on his back now, looking up at her, his face etched in shame. Jane smiled down at him, certain and unafraid, as he faded away. Paling into a diaphanous shadow of himself, he finally and forever passed from this world, silently, into the next.

Later, when Jane heard David's key in the lock, she lay in bed for a moment, trying to pull from the distant clouds of her dream-rocked mind a memory of her journey to that place where demons are purged. She felt her face warm in the flesh somewhere beneath her cheeks, and she smiled.

77

The day had dawned cool and clear; even the usual morning mist
seemed to have lifted in tribute to Jane and David's finally getting away from the city. Jane grunted as she shoved one of David's large leather suitcases to the side of the BMW's trunk to make
room for her little valise. Someday, she told herself, I'll teach this guy
how to pack.

The nuns had said Kenny should be coming around sometime today,
and she patted her back pocket to make sure she had the number of St.
John's with her. She was just reminding herself to send both Kenny and
Lieutenant Spielman postcards when she heard her telephone ringing in
the house. Popping the CD changer out of its carriage in the underdeck,
she decided to let the answering machine pick up while she loaded some
music for the drive.

The machine answered on the fourth ring, and after her outgoing
message played, Kenny's voice came through, a panicked urgency fuel-
ing his words.

"Jane! Are you there? Jane? Shit!" He paused to catch his breath.
"Okay, listen to me. Remember that guy from the ice rink? Warren
Fincher? That guy with the foot? Turns out he and Barton Hubble
are connected!"

The nun had sent an orderly to fetch the doctor, because Kenny, as
soon as he had come to, had insisted on leaving. She stood in the doorway of his hospital room, her arms folded across her chest, making
clucking sounds as Kenny spoke into the phone while he struggled to
get dressed. "And what's the connection?" he continued, grimacing as
he wriggled into his shirt. "Hold on to your jockstrap. Because the
common denominator between Fincher and Hubble is your boyfriend,
Mr. BMW, oh-so-wonderful, long-suffering widower . . . David

fucking Perry!" He winced an apology to the nun for his language as he crossed to the tiny closet and searched for his shoes.

"Here's another one for you. Guess where Fincher worked? Monterey Airport. Guess where the flight originated that killed Perry's richer-than-God father-in-law? Monterey fucking Airport!" He sat painfully on the edge of the bed and pulled on his shoes. "Fincher and Hubble each had a rap sheet a mile long," he continued. "Guess who was a young prosecutor working for the DA down in Los Angeles when their cases came through? The aforementioned David fucking Perry!" He finished tying his shoes and stood up as the doctor came rushing into the room.

Back at Jane's house, the answering machine kept on recording as Kenny finished his message. "His notes are all over their case files. This guy arranged to have the old man killed. Which left only one thing standing between him and a zillion dollars. Jenna Perry didn't have a chance. Jane, I'm coming to get you, then we're gonna pick up this asshole!" He hung up, and the tape stopped with a clicking sound.

Jane was walking up the path to her front door when a finger reached in and pressed the erase button on her machine. The tape rewound, erasing itself with a high-pitched squeaking noise. A moment later, Jane came in the door and smiled. "Any messages?"

"No," David replied as he moved away from the answering machine. "Must have been a hang-up."

"Just as well. I don't want to talk to anybody," she said, brushing a kiss on his cheek as she headed for the bedroom. "I just want to get going." She stopped in the doorway. "By the way, think you have enough bags for three days?"

"I never was a very good packer," David said as he followed her into the bedroom.

"Just let me have you for five minutes and you'll be a packing god," Jane laughed as she crammed the new Anne Tyler into her shoulder bag. Reaching inside the bag, she pulled out her pistol and turned to David. Had she been looking for it, she would have noticed his shoulders straighten as he tensed almost imperceptibly.

"Won't be needing this in the wine country," she said, dropping it into her top dresser drawer and shoving it closed with her hip. "Okay, big boy, let's go. Got some fresh film and the car's all packed."

David watched her as she folded her ironing board and slid it under the bed. Then, stretching his arms over his head, he said, "You know, I don't think I slept ten minutes last night." He kissed her on the forehead. "Would you mind driving?"

"That piece of shit?" Jane joked. She kissed him on the ear. "I'd be happy to. Just sit back and let me take care of you."

Walking down the path to the sidewalk, Jane stopped and took the keys to the BMW from David's hand. David continued on a few steps, then, realizing Jane hadn't joined him, turned back to her.

"What?" he asked, anxious to be underway.

"Oh, David. Look at the bay," Jane said. "And the bridge. It's so beautiful."

David came back up the walkway and, taking Jane in his arms, gently tugged her along. "It is beautiful. And the sooner we're across it, the sooner we're on vacation."

Putting both her arms around his neck, Jane pulled him into a long, loving kiss. "Thank you for making me so happy."

A siren wailed in the distance, its pulsing cry growing closer. "C'mon," David urged, stealing a glance up the street. "We've got massages waiting."

"Yum," Jane purred as she used the remote to unlock the car. Noticing her ever-present trash cans still in the gutter, she made a mental note to turn over a new leaf and actually pull them back onto the sidewalk, maybe even return them to the shed next to the kitchen. The keening of the siren caught her attention and she looked up just as an ambulance raced through the cross-street two blocks away. "Somebody's having a bad day," she observed as they got into the car.

— —

"But, Mr. Marks," the doctor protested as Kenny strapped on his shoulder holster, "you have a couple of cracked ribs and a possible concussion."

"They can wait," Kenny said, checking the clip of his service pistol and slipping it into the leather sheath under his arm. He grabbed his coat from the closet and headed for the door. "But I can't," he said as he hurried into the corridor.

Kenny stood at the elevator bank, grimacing as he pulled on his coat. The stairwell door opened and Officer Finney, carrying a small and incomplete gift basket of muffins, stepped out. "Inspector Marks!" he exclaimed, his tongue sliding over to wipe a tiny fleck of powdered sugar from the side of his mouth. "They release you already?"

"Moby!" Kenny said, happy for the first time in his life to see him. "You got a car?"

"Got the wife's new van. Parked right out front." Then, enjoying this new amiable connection with Kenny, he offered, "Need a ride?"

Kenny thrust out his hand. "Gimme the keys."

Finney hesitated, immobilized by confusion. "But . . ." was all he could manage. He pulled the key ring from his pocket just as an elevator arrived at their floor.

Snatching the keys away before Finney could formulate a second syllable, Kenny ran into the elevator and punched the button for the lobby. "Call Spielman and tell him Jane's in trouble! Have him send some people to her house!" Kenny shouted as the doors slid closed.

Finney stood there staring at his empty hand. Unable to comprehend why he was standing alone in the middle of a hospital hallway with a half-eaten basket of muffins and without his wife's car keys, he looked around and said to a passing nun, "Uh . . ."

78

Jane drove along Marina Boulevard and noticed the wind whipping up whitecaps in the bay. She thought about the seasons changing, about the coming of another San Francisco winter. In the past, the cooling of the days had been the harbinger of the loneliness of the coming holidays. The approach each year of Thanksgiving was always the signpost of the melancholy times to come.

She found herself thinking of Christmas Eves alone. Of Christmas mornings with Poppy and Timmy and Aunt Lucy. Of exchanging useful but unimaginative gifts and watching the clock until she could gracefully escape back to her house.

And, around the corner, New Year's Eve and the lies that it brought out in her. Showing up at the station after the holidays, making up stories about traveling, or about some fantastic party, or about suddenly getting too sick to go out.

Jane looked over to David as he reclined the passenger seat and laid his forearm over his eyes. Smiling to herself, she found that she was looking forward, for the first time in years, to the holidays. This time she would have someone to share them with her. Someone to help her feel whole again, a part of the world.

"Want some music?" she asked. "We've got your Miles Davis, your Beethoven's Sixth, your Joan Osborne, your Lyle Lovett."

"I don't know," David said, his face still beneath his arm.

"There's some other stuff back there," Jane offered. "*West Side Story,* I think, and maybe an old Peter Gabriel. Up to you."

Turning his head away from her to glance surreptitiously in the outside rearview mirror, David settled back into his seat and didn't respond.

"Hey," Jane said gently, putting her hand on his shoulder. "Where are you?"

"Thinking about Lily," he answered. "About going to get her and getting back to living our lives again."

Jane waited for him to include her in those plans, and when he didn't, she felt stung. Her own thoughts about involving David in her holiday fantasies, in light of his exclusion of her, plucked a primal chord of dread in her heart.

But then, as she rounded the point of the San Francisco Peninsula and the Golden Gate Bridge revealed itself a couple of miles ahead like a motherly angel, her wings spread in welcome to all who passed, it occurred to her that David was entitled to ponder his own life on his own terms. She was just setting herself up for, perhaps even creating, her own disappointment if she expected him to be thinking of her rather than his daughter at a time like this. She realized she had a choice. And she chose to relax; to be patient and generous.

"God," she said, leaning forward and looking up to the top of the South Tower. "Look at that."

Lowering his arm and sitting up a bit, David also ducked his head to look up at the bridge. "Yeah," he said. "Beautiful."

Steering with her left hand, Jane reached to the floor behind her seat and brought her bag forward onto her lap. "I want to get a picture," she said as she dug through her books and cosmetics. Then it dawned on her and she whapped the steering wheel. "Shit!"

"What?" David asked as he lay back again and buzzed his seat to recline even farther.

"I forgot my camera," Jane moaned, furious with herself.

"Don't worry," David sighed. "We can pick up another one at the hotel."

"But . . ." Jane started to protest, but everything about David's posture indicated to her that he wasn't in the mood to talk.

——

Not noticing the trash cans in front of Jane's house until it was too late, Kenny smashed Finney's wife's brand-new van into them, denting the right front fender and scoring a long scratch in the passenger door. Throwing open his own door, he ignored the pain in his ribs and ran up the path to her porch. Lifting the geranium in the frog-shaped pot, he snatched up the spare key, and, pulling his weapon from his shoulder holster, unlocked the door and cautiously entered.

The house was still, as if no one were there; or, the thought invading his mind, as if someone, Jane, were there, but too hurt to call out.

"Jane!" he shouted, figuring that if David Perry were there, he would already be aware of Kenny's presence. "Jane!" he yelled again as he quickly scanned the living room. Moving deftly down the hall, following the barrel of his pistol as he went, he checked the guest bathroom before passing into Jane's bedroom.

Shaking off the vision of Jane lying injured, or worse, on the floor next to the bed, he searched her closet and master bathroom. Confident he was alone in the house, he reholstered his gun. He was about to leave, was almost to the hallway again, when something occurred to him and he crossed back through the bedroom to Jane's dresser. Pulling open the top right drawer, he saw Jane's service revolver lying like a forgotten toy among her rolled-up socks.

"Damn it!" he cursed and raced back outside.

Looking up the road in the direction from which his backup should be coming and seeing nothing yet, Kenny made the quick decision to keep moving. He climbed into the van and tore away from there, all the while cursing Finney for not having a car phone.

— —

As the BMW passed beneath the sign announcing "Last Exit Before Golden Gate Bridge," Jane glanced over to David, wanting to say something. As if sensing her need to talk, he shifted his weight into the passenger-side door, effectively turning his back on her. Slowing a bit and signaling to get over to the right, Jane considered her options and came to the decision that, after all she had been through, with David and before David, she wasn't about to get into a relationship in which she couldn't speak her mind when she wanted to.

"I know this is a pain, and I know you really want to get over the bridge and into our vacation," she began, "but that camera means a lot to me." She slid the car over one lane to the right. "I'm going to turn off here and go back for it. Fifteen minutes tops," she assured him. "I promise."

When she reached up to adjust the rearview mirror, she felt David stir and heard the hum of his seat rising back to a normal position.

"I said *no!*" he shouted, his words bouncing around like missiles in the confines of the car. "Why the fuck couldn't you just leave it at that?"

Jane whipped her head around, not so much to confront him as to see if he were all right, and she was stunned to be looking not at David's face, but into the tiny black eye of his 9mm Beretta.

"David?" she choked. "Why, what . . . ?"

"Just stay on this road," he demanded. "Nobody's going home right now."

Jane switched off the turn signal and eased up on the accelerator, slowing slightly, trying to cadge a little more time to think. "David," she said, "what are you doing? What's the matter?"

David turned in his seat, leaning his back against the passenger door so that he could face her. He felt a surprising rush of relief now that his charade was finally over. Taking care to keep his gun below the window line and out of sight of any passing cars, he said, "If only your Kenny weren't such a good cop."

"What are you talking about?" Jane asked, driving now only by instinct, her attention focused entirely on the gun aimed at her chest and the man holding it.

"Your partner, through diligent police work no doubt, discovered that certain coincidences in my life may not have been . . . so coincidental."

Tearing her eyes away from the Beretta, Jane stole a glance at the road ahead, the Golden Gate Bridge drawing closer, as if it were coming to them. "Hubble!" she said as the first piece of the awful puzzle fell into place.

"For one," David acknowledged.

Then it hit her, hit her so hard it was as if she had been punched in the stomach. She seized David's eyes with her own and asked, "Me?"

David's wry smile told her she was right. "My father-in-law's plane goes down?" he began. "Let's say it wasn't entirely an accident. You remember Warren Fincher, don't you? From the ice rink? He worked at the airport where the old man's plane took off from."

"And?"

"And when I was in the DA's office in L.A., I did him a favor. A big one. The get-out-of-jail-free kind of favor. So he owed me." He paused. "Who better than a former flight mechanic to make sure poor Graham's plane falls from the sky in a most undetectable manner?"

"My God," Jane said. "And then you killed him."

"Regrettably," David nodded. "He got greedy on me and I had to make sure he stayed quiet for a long time."

"And you killed all those poor people on Graham's plane, too?"

"Cost of doing business." He looked at the speedometer and waggled the gun at her. "Speed it up a little. I really don't want to get stopped by any of your cop friends."

Jane gripped the steering wheel tightly, her knuckles turning white. "So Graham Maxwell's plane crashes," she said, working out the rest of the puzzle. "Which makes Jenna, and by extension you, very wealthy?"

"That's my smart girl," David said. "But then Jenna goes and gets independent on me and wants a divorce, which would have screwed me out of any inheritance."

"So . . ." Jane concluded, looking into the pit of the awful truth, ". . . so you had your wife killed."

"I was always going to . . . someday . . . but not quite so soon," David admitted. "The divorce sort of forced my hand."

"What about Barton Hubble?"

"I knew of Hubble's involvement with that carpet-company guy from my days in the DA's office in L.A." He smiled, the pressure of the lie he had been living dissipating as he spoke. "I made some calls and learned that he had moved up here." He glanced in the mirror. "Laying the trap was easy. Finding him on his usual BART train, getting him to offer to fix my car, leaving my watch for him to steal, bumping into him at the sports bar and spilling my heart out . . ."

Jane shot him a look. "You baited the poor fucker."

"Yes," David acknowledged. "And he bit big-time."

Jane choked on the sudden awareness of all that had happened. "And so did I," she said almost inaudibly.

David shook his head in amusement. "You were like a gift from heaven. A lonely lady cop who could take Hubble out of the picture for me."

"Fuck you," Jane said, not caring about the consequences, in fact welcoming a confrontation. She wanted to tear him apart, to rip the gun from his hand and shoot him in the face with it, such was her rage and her humiliation.

Forcing herself to think clearly, Jane told herself that David must have a plan and that she had to disrupt it. "Where are we going?" she asked.

"Over the bridge. I'll tell you more when you need to know it."

The BMW curved onto the Golden Gate Bridge concourse, the sign for Vista Point coming up on the right. Abruptly, without signaling, Jane veered across three lanes of traffic, a semi-trailer just missing the back bumper, and headed for the Vista Point exit.

"What the hell are you doing?" David yelled. "I told you to go over the bridge!" He grabbed for her wrist, but she ripped it away.

"Tough shit," Jane said.

Leaning across the console, David pressed the gun into her side. "Take the bridge," he said evenly.

Jane checked the mirror and swerved over another lane to the right. "What are you going to do?" she challenged. "Shoot me when I'm driving on the freeway at sixty miles an hour?"

She took the off-ramp and swung into the Vista Point parking lot.

The tour buses hadn't yet arrived and the lot was almost completely empty. Jane cruised past the Golden Gate Bridge gift shop; a huge street sweeper parked in the carport beneath it. Then she drove past the hot-dog cart. The vendor, his boombox playing mariachi music, was just now lighting a fire under the steamer.

The car slipped along at twenty miles an hour as Jane pondered what to do next. She steered toward the hot-dog cart, and David sniffed a little laugh. "Let me tell you something I learned from the evil mind of Barton Hubble. If you approach anybody out here, I don't care if it's a cop or that hot-dog guy, I will shoot him dead." He paused, making sure Jane understood him. "So, if you want that kind of blood on your hands, make your move."

Nudging the BMW to the left, Jane moved away from the hot-dog stand. She spotted a Port Authority guard motoring down the path from the bridge in a white golf cart. Jane considered racing up to him and jumping out of the car. But she knew he'd be unarmed and she didn't want to be responsible for his death.

The guard waved to the vendor, stopped in front of the rest rooms, and went inside.

"When you're done sight-seeing," David said, "why don't we get back on the bridge and be on our way? It'll be so much easier for both of us."

Jane let out a long exasperated sigh. "Shit," she said as she steered toward the exit on the other side of the gift shop.

"That's better," David nodded, turning to check the traffic on the bridge. "It's starting to get crowded up there. Let's go."

He didn't notice Jane's right hand slide off the steering wheel and furtively unfasten her seat belt. Returning her right hand to the wheel, she slowly lowered her left hand and slipped her fingers into the door handle.

She was ready.

As the BMW approached the back of the gift shop building, Jane suddenly jammed the gas pedal to the floor. The car leaped forward, its tires screeching on the moist asphalt. Before David could react, Jane crashed head-on into the gigantic street sweeper, the front of the car folding in on itself.

"Hey!" David shouted as both airbags exploded.

Jane grabbed the keys and was out of the car before David could figure out what was going on. She looked around to see if anyone had seen the collision. The Port Authority guard was still in the rest room, and the hot-dog vendor, still listening to his stereo, was too far away to have heard anything.

She thought about attacking David and disarming him, but her instinct told her it was too risky. Clutching the keys in her fist, she started running up the path to the bridge, urging her legs to keep churning. When she was almost to the top, she chanced a look back over her shoulder. David was just then untangling himself from the air bag and opening the passenger door.

He rolled out onto the ground and, scanning the parking lot, saw her just as she was about to reach the roadway.

"Goddamn it!" he bellowed and chased after her.

Jane lowered her head and raced the last few yards up to the bridge. As she got her bearings, a squadron of Rollerbladers, a team of some sort, snaked their way past her, weaving as one body like a Chinese dragon.

She stood at the curb, the sidewalk thrumming with the vibration of the cars and trucks whipping by. She tried to cross to the other side, but couldn't find an opening. To her left was the toll plaza. She knew that if she headed that way and David followed her, she might be endangering the lives of innocent people.

There she stood on one of the busiest bridges in the world, hundreds of people speeding past, and she was utterly alone.

Looking back down the path, Jane strained to see David. But he was nowhere in sight. Troubled by not knowing where he was and desperate to put as much distance between herself and him as possible, Jane turned to her right and started running across the Golden Gate Bridge.

As she closed in on the South Tower, she willed herself to go even faster. Looking ahead at the gentle rise of the roadway, she saw that she would be running, her back exposed, for almost two miles before she could get off the bridge again.

Her lungs heaving for breath, she stopped at the base of the tower and tried to collect herself. Where the hell was David? Maybe he had an extra car key, she thought, and was able to drive away.

She hurried across the sidewalk to the bridge railing and peered back to the parking lot. David's car was still there. "Shit!" she screamed, pounding the rail with her fist. David's keys pinched into her palm, and as she opened her hand, she had an idea.

Wheeling around, Jane scurried to the tower elevator door and inserted David's key. She tugged the door open and threw herself inside. If she could just get the door closed and the elevator working, she would be safe.

She inserted the key into the panel and tried to turn it. It wouldn't rotate. The sound of running footsteps came to her from outside. At first she hoped it might be a jogger, but then she recognized the footfall of hard street shoes.

David was on the bridge.

Terrified, Jane twisted the key again. It still wouldn't budge. The sound of the footsteps was getting closer. Pulling out the key and reseating it in the panel lock, she finally got it to turn.

The elevator stayed in place.

Then she remembered that it would operate only if the door was closed. She reached for the handle, the footsteps outside almost upon her, and started to yank the door closed.

David burst into the doorway, huffing as he caught his breath, and violently pushed Jane back into the elevator. Reaching behind, he slammed the door closed. Then he shoved the pistol into Jane's throat as the elevator rumbled to life and began its ascent.

"Have it your way," he said.

Jane slumped against the back wall. "What are you going to do?"

David lowered his pistol, its muzzle pointed at her stomach. "Why, kill you, of course."

Incredulous, Jane shook her head. "Who are you, David?"

"Oh, I'm David Perry," he answered as the car neared the top. "I'm just not the David Perry you thought you knew."

"You son of a bitch," she spit as she contemplated throwing herself at David, perhaps catching him off-balance. But she decided against it. This tiny tomblike cubicle was not the place to make her play. As frustrating as it was, she knew she had to wait.

The elevator stuttered to a stop and David yanked open the diamond-grated security door. His pistol still trained on Jane, he leaned his shoulder into the thick steel outer door and forced it open. A pair of seagulls took off and cawed in startled irritation. Still squawking, they floated back to their nest tucked under the convergence of two guano-covered girders.

David unhasped the safety chain with his free hand and motioned for Jane to step up onto the platform. She climbed the two steps to the slick steel surface of the deck and turned to face him, the wind lashing at her. David fished in his pocket for a coin. "Wanna make a wish?" he shouted above the wind.

Jane squinted into the biting blast of sea air. "You bet I do," she yelled back.

— —

Peering in through the small inset window in David Perry's front door, Kenny could see the tiny green light on the security panel. Seeing that the house alarm hadn't been activated, he took the butt of his gun and, stealing a glance back out to the empty street, shattered a small side window. Reaching in, he unlocked the door and went inside. Even though the BMW hadn't been in the driveway, Kenny swept his pistol in cautious arcs as he raced through the downstairs rooms looking for Jane, looking for anything that might lead him to her.

David's study was dark, the oak shutters pulled closed, the only illumination coming from the screen saver of his laptop computer. Kenny riffled through the papers on the desk, looking for any sort of clue. After checking the answering machine and seeing that there were no messages, he pulled the drawers open, one by one, until he got to the bottom right drawer. There, still open, was an empty childproof gun box, and what appeared to be an oil-stained diaper lying next to it. Kenny reached in and examined a box of ammunition, a half-empty carton of hollow-point bullets, and whistled.

"Motherfuck," he said as he hurried out of the room.

Quickly moving through the kitchen and breakfast nook, through the swinging door and to the windows overlooking the gardens, Kenny stopped next to the telescope to catch his breath. There was no way for him to know that if he looked into the eyepiece, he would be able to see the tiny figures of Jane and David high atop the South Tower of the Golden Gate Bridge.

He tore across the living room and bounded up the stairs, punishing his aching ribs as he took the steps two at a time.

A quick survey of Lily's room and the guest rooms yielded nothing. Unwilling to give up, Kenny sprinted down the hallway and into the master bedroom.

Certain now that he was alone, he slipped his pistol into his shoulder holster and pulled out drawer after drawer of David's dresser and armoire. Finding nothing of use there, he dashed into the walk-in closet and saw the empty hangers and the wide gap in the row of Bottega Veneta luggage on the high shelf above the shoe racks. He started to bolt back downstairs, then remembered to check the master bathroom.

A crust of dried bubble bath coated the bottom of the tub. Turning to his right, Kenny noticed the ivory toothbrush he had given Jane a couple of birthdays ago lying across a tube of Colgate on the counter and an empty yogurt container in the waste basket. Next to the wastebasket was a wicker magazine rack, and on top of the piles of *Architectural Digests* and *National Geographics* was a magazine, lying facedown, with handwritten notes on the back cover.

Kenny picked it up and recognized Jane's writing. The words "Pier 31" were crossed out. Then the words "Powell St. BART, 12p." He recognized that as the time and place for yesterday's rendezvous with Hubble. Slipping the magazine into his coat pocket, he hustled back down the stairs.

79

The whipping wind at her back threw Jane's hair forward over her face. She cringed as David reached out to brush it away in a gesture that mocked the false intimacy he had once so easily displayed.

"What a pity," he said over the noise of the safety chain rattling against a girder.

"What?" Jane asked as she stepped back against the low railing of the bulkhead to avoid his touch. Her eyes searched the corners and surfaces of the deck, looking for something to use as a weapon.

"What a pity you chose to jump to your death from the Golden Gate Bridge. Like so many broken-hearted lovers before you."

Her arms wrapped tightly across her chest, her mind recoiling in revulsion, Jane slumped against the bulkhead and allowed her body to slide down to the cold iron floor of the deck.

There was only one way she was going over the side, she pledged to herself. David Perry would have to throw her over.

——

After searching David's study a second time, Kenny stood in the kitchen and pressed the redial button on the phone over the sink. He got Jobie's answering machine. Hanging up, he flipped through the pages of the notepad by the phone, looking for any sort of clue. Nothing.

Reaching into the cabinet under the counter, he pulled out the wastebasket and turned it upside down. Empty. He tossed it aside and pushed through the swinging door into the dining room.

His frustration mounting, but unwilling to give up, Kenny passed into the living room. There was a small writing desk in the corner. He hurried to it and pulled out all the drawers, spilling the contents onto the floor. Then he yanked open the two drawers on either end of the coffee table. Still nothing.

Looking out the window, he noticed Pilar's apartment on the other side of the pool. He started toward it, fiddling with the lock on the sliding glass door next to the telescope. He couldn't force it open and was just about to run out the front door when he remembered the folded magazine in his jacket pocket. He took it out and quickly flipped through the pages, looking for any other notes Jane might have written.

He turned it over and saw the image of Clarissa Gethers against the Golden Gate Bridge on the cover. Peering through the glass door, he spotted the bridge far off to his left and decided to get a closer look through the telescope.

Kicking the stool aside, he bent over and squinted into the eyepiece. The South Tower loomed strikingly close. But there was no one there. Kenny panned down to the Vista Point parking lot. A tour bus was just pulling in from the eucalyptus groves of the Presidio. It swung into the lot and stopped near a small souvenir stand. Nudging the scope to the right, Kenny saw a hot-dog vendor warming his hands in the clouds of steam wafting up from his cart. Still panning right, he came to the back of the gift shop. He tilted down to the building's lower level and saw a black BMW halfway into the carport, its rear end scratched and dented.

David Perry's car.

Kenny caught his breath. Panning quickly, he waved the telescope back and forth, intent on finding Jane. Back up the incline, back along the roadway to the midpoint of the Golden Gate Bridge. She wasn't there. He was about to tear out of there and race blindly to the bridge when he remembered Jane's telling him about her first date with David, about the key and the elevator. He brought the scope back to the South Tower and raised the lens along its extraordinary height until the wind deck came into view. Just at that instant David roughly lifted Jane from below the top of the bulkhead.

Staggered by the impact of seeing Jane, Kenny shot back across the living room toward the front door. He hesitated for a heartbeat, thinking about using the telephone over the sink. But, realizing he had no time to make a call, he tore out of the house and into the van.

As he cranked the engine, he pulled the magazine with Jane's writing on it from his jacket pocket and tossed it onto the passenger seat. He jammed the car into gear and fishtailed across the lawn, the rear tires gouging deep scars in the grass, and sped off down the hill.

80

"You know what's the saddest thing in all of this?" David asked as he jammed the pistol under Jane's chin and lifted her to her feet. "What?" Jane hissed through clenched teeth.

"People will understand about poor Jane, understand about your jumping," he sneered. "Understand about poor lonely ironing-board Jane the same way they understand about poor tormented Clarissa."

The truth came rushing at Jane and took her breath away. "You slept with her!" she shouted. "You took advantage of that needy little girl and then you destroyed her!"

David nodded. "She was living a lie, and so was I. We were perfect for each other." Tilting his head to the side, David added, "Not so unlike you and me, wouldn't you say?"

"Is there no end to your cruelty?" Jane demanded, her anger building into white rage. She sidled to her right along the bulkhead, creeping away from the bayside of the tower toward the relative safety of the elevator. "You know that Kenny's onto you," she shouted, hoping that her words would distract him from the tiny progress she was making. "How will you get away?"

"Maybe there's a private jet waiting for me right now at some out-of-the-way airstrip not so far from the wine country," he answered, his eyes following her as she moved.

Jane stopped. "But you don't have the money."

"Oh, but I do—a lot of it, anyway. In the car, right next to your things in the trunk," David said. "Remember? It wasn't even an hour ago that you teased me so lovingly about my heavy suitcases. How, next time, you were going to teach me how to pack."

Tilting her head back as if to deflect the shame of the insult, Jane asked, "How'd you get so much so fast?" She bent her knees slightly, ready to leap at him or away from him depending on what happened next.

"It's so interesting how much people want to help you when you've been visited by tragedy the way I have. First my unfortunate father-in-law, then my poor dear wife." He sidestepped slightly to the left in a silent gesture that told her he was aware of her movement.

"Dear old Patrick Colomby damn near broke the law pulling strings and calling in favors. But I'll say this for him, he managed to get me a good chunk of my money. Then it took me a couple of days, but I figured out how to wire most of it to a bank we do business with in Panama." David laughed derisively. "Of course, he thought he was doing it for me and Lily. I'll have to remember to send him a postcard."

— —

Scraping the entire right side of Finney's wife's new van along the high cement curb of the Golden Gate Bridge's roadway, Kenny jumped out of the passenger side. He abandoned the vehicle, blocking the right traffic lane beneath the South Tower. Vaulting over the berm, he raced across the sidewalk, pushing past the recently arrived tourists who were only now cresting the incline from the parking lot. A chaos of car horns and angry voices trailed after him as he scrambled around the tower to the bayside walkway and skidded to a stop at the elevator access door. Tugging at its immovable bulk, he quickly saw that it could be opened only with the special key. Spasms of pain tormenting his ribs, he went to the railing and bent his body back to see the top of the tower.

His eyes traveled to the right and followed the massive suspension cable, three feet thick, that swept down from the airway beacon at the South Tower's peak to the roadway at the center of the bridge, over a third of a mile away. A plan began to take shape in his mind as he surveyed the cable to his left and saw that it came down to street level only about a thousand feet from where he stood.

His hand reflexively going inside his coat to make sure his pistol was secure in its holster, Kenny dashed to his left, shouldering his way through the stream of elderly tourists. When he reached the nexus where the suspension cable touched the roadway, he looped his fingers into the chain-link fence that separated it from the sidewalk and hoisted himself onto the four-foot-high cement wall. Digging his toes into the fence and straining against the pain in his aching ribs, he clambered over the sturdy orange barrier and lowered himself down the other side to the cable.

Gripping the waist-high guy wires that were suspended three feet above the cable as safety lines for the bridge's ironworkers, Kenny, squinting into the stinging wind, began to climb.

"Hey!" someone shouted.

Without stopping, and fearing the worst, Kenny turned to look back down to the sidewalk, where an old man in a "First Baptist Church of Tyler, Texas" sweatshirt pointed a camera at him and snapped his picture. "We're prayin' for y'all," the old-timer called as he scurried to rejoin his group.

The Port Authority officer, having used the rest room, was returning to the roadway to investigate a minivan blocking traffic in the number one lane when he came across a clutch of elderly tourists joining hands and looking heavenward.

"Anyone here know anything about this van?" he asked, assuming it belonged to them. But the good Baptists, their eyes closed and their lips moving feverishly in silent prayer, were too intent on saving the soul of the poor man climbing up the South Tower suspension cable to answer.

Thinking they were praying for their van's salvation and choosing to stay in the real world for the time being, the Port Authority officer pulled out his walkie-talkie and called for a tow truck.

81

— —

Jane tensed as David came at her, her body coiled like a snake, on edge and aware. If the only way she was going over the side was for David Perry to throw her over, she vowed to herself that it would be after the most frenzied, clawing, insanely fierce battle either of them could imagine.

She held her hands out before her, ready for anything. "Why do I have to go over the side?" she asked, trying to make sense of it all. "Why don't you just shoot me and get the hell out of here?"

David brought the pistol up until it was pointed at her chest. "All of the evidence against me is pure conjecture. There are no surviving witnesses, partly thanks to you." He smiled. "And now I'm going to put a bullet from my own gun into you? I don't think so." He stepped across the narrow gap between them. "Time to see if you can fly."

Hunched now, her fingers trembling at the prospect of his attack, Jane stalled for time. "But if Kenny knows what you're doing," she began, each word perhaps prolonging her life by another second, "and if you're taking a plane to the South Pacific or wherever you're headed . . . then why do you have to kill me?"

"You're forgetting one thing!" David shouted. "You created this. You had to get off the highway before the bridge and crash the car." He inched forward. "You had to get in the elevator. You had to screw up my plan!"

"Like you weren't going to kill me anyway?"

"Actually, I wasn't," David said. "We were going to spend the night in the hotel tonight. And tomorrow morning I was going to make love to you and then slip out for *The New York Times* and by the time you realized . . ."

Jane brought her knee up hard into David's groin. But he was ready for it. Swinging broadly with his free hand, he cracked her across the

301

jaw and sent her sprawling to her left. She grasped at the railing to keep from falling.

That's when she saw Kenny.

Still over two hundred feet away, he was struggling to maintain his balance. The frayed guy wires sliced into his already bloodied hands as he fought the searing pain in his ribs with every step.

Moving back to her right, exposing her back to the bayside in order to divert David's attention from Kenny's approach, Jane wiped the trickle of blood from her split lip. "And Lily?" she demanded, no longer able to keep the fear from seeping into her voice. "What about your daughter?"

Jane saw David's eyes flicker with hesitation, and she pressed him further. "Or is your daughter just another disposable person in this grand plan of yours? Another trusting casualty like Jenna, like Clarissa . . . like me . . . you only pretended to love?"

David's shoulders sagged. "Make no mistake, my love for Lily is very real. That's what tortures me. This wasn't supposed to go like this," he lamented. "Jenna wasn't supposed to file for divorce. Hubble wasn't supposed to threaten my little girl. You weren't supposed to be so goddam smart and drive my car into that street sweeper."

"Yeah, well, all that happened," Jane challenged, "and your daughter, your sweet loyal daughter, is going to get fucked."

"Shut up!" David yelled, his finger tightening on the trigger. "Somehow, somewhere down the line, I'll find a way to bring her to wherever I am."

"Oh, that'll be a healthy relationship," Jane sneered.

David's eyes narrowed in irritation and he leveled his pistol at her face. "Enough with the questions. I've got a plane to catch," he barked. "Get up on the railing."

Jane spread her legs defiantly, planting her feet and lowering her center of gravity. She touched her tongue to the blood rising into the cut in her lip and narrowed her eyes in determination. "No! You'll have to throw me off!"

"That can be arranged!" David said. He rushed toward her, ready now to finish the endgame.

Kenny was far enough up the suspension cable to see David close in on Jane. Turning his feet sideways and digging in with the inner edges of his shoes, he forced himself to quicken his pace, using his torn hands to pull himself upward with each step.

Jane, not about to let David trap her against the bayside railing, dove to her right and tried for the elevator. But David grabbed her by the wrist just as she passed and stopped her flight in midair. Reaching out, her other hand snagged the safety chain, and she whipped it, screaming through the wind, at David's face.

At the last moment, David let go of Jane's wrist and was able to raise his arm to deflect the worst of the chain's impact.

Out of his mind with rage, David bent down and seized Jane by the hair, his pistol jammed into her throat, and dragged her back to the railing. Her arms and legs flailing, Jane fought back desperately as she stole a glance at the suspension cable connection, praying that Kenny could get to her in time.

Only a few feet below the wind deck, Kenny let go of the guy wires and grasped the railing with his tattered hands. Straining with all he had left and fighting off the nausea of his pain, he pulled himself up and saw that David was just about to force Jane over the side. As her eyes swept around and touched his, he scrambled his feet on the wet steel of the deck, trying to gain a foothold. When he did, he inadvertently disturbed the nesting pair of seagulls again and sent them screeching into the sky.

David, alerted by the sudden flight of the birds, spun around and spotted Kenny just as he came over the railing. Without hesitation, David raised his Beretta and fired, shooting Kenny in the chest. His breath catching in his throat, Kenny lurched forward and fell onto the deck.

"Kenny!" Jane shrieked.

As she tried to shoulder past David to get to Kenny, David viciously kneed her in the stomach, knocking the wind out of her. Seizing the advantage, David clenched his arms around her thighs and heaved her onto the top of the railing.

Panicked by the rush of emptiness below, Jane summoned the last of her strength to kick and scratch at David's face. But he pressed forward relentlessly until she could feel the final pull of gravity at her back. In a last anguished attempt to save herself, Jane relaxed for a moment, causing David's face to come close to hers. Then she bit him on the forehead, clamping her teeth over his eyebrow and ripping out a chunk of flesh.

David wailed in pain and, incensed, thrust at her with the full brute force of his body, sending her toppling backward over the rail.

Bleeding heavily and gasping to catch his breath, David looked over to the still body of Kenny. Then, straightening wearily, he staggered to the railing and peered over to watch Jane's death fall.

Just as he did, Jane erupted with a primal roar, shooting upward from the far side of the wall and smashing the top of her skull into David's face, crushing his nose and throwing him backward. His gun clattering away, David tripped over Kenny's legs and fell heavily on his side.

Pulling herself off the painter's scaffold she had landed on, Jane hoisted herself back onto the wind deck as David recovered his senses and attacked.

He came in low, trying to tie up her thighs again, but Jane brought her knee up into his fractured nose and sent him reeling to the deck. Scrambling back to his feet, David charged and, throwing a sweeping roundhouse right, caught Jane in the temple and sent her sprawling next to Kenny's body.

Scurrying to retrieve his gun, David advanced on Jane and, blood streaming down his face, pulled the hammer back with his thumb. "It didn't have to be like this!" he shouted, his blood misting into the air before him as he aimed the Beretta at her head.

He used his free hand to swipe at the blood flowing into his eyes from the deep bite wound in his forehead. When he did, Jane, thinking quickly, rolled over and reached into Kenny's bloody jacket. She yanked his service pistol from his shoulder holster and came up firing, pulling the trigger over and over again.

David's face twisted into a rictus of surprise as four, then five bullets slammed into his chest, their momentum sending him backward and finally pitching him over the railing, his body hurtling through the air toward the bay far below.

Still alive for the moment, David plunged at over a hundred miles an hour. His final breath was squeezed from his lungs by the accelerating thrust of air pressure, and somewhere in his descent, the realization coursed through his oxygen-starved brain that he was dying.

Kenny's gun hanging limply in her hand, Jane crumpled to the deck, shaking and exhausted. She crawled to Kenny and took him in her arms and, weeping, rocked him back and forth.

As she did, David's body continued to fall, gathering speed until it hit the unyielding water like a clay brick hitting pavement. His skull and spine splintered on impact, his clothes abraded from his rupturing skin, and his brain pan flattened like an eggshell. His body lay there for a moment, not in the water but on it. Then, in a motion as timeless as the sea itself, the waters of San Francisco Bay took him, swallowing the devastated body of David Perry for all time.

Jane sat up, her back against the bulkhead, and, still swaying on her knees, held Kenny's head in the crook of her elbow and sobbed.

"He dead?" came Kenny's voice, a soft painful whisper.

Startled, Jane pulled back to look into his eyes. "You're alive!"

"I seem to be." He grinned weakly. "So, you shoot him?"

"Yeah." Jane nodded tightly. "I shot him."

"Shit, I came all this way. I really wanted to shoot him."

"Sorry," Jane said. "How'd you find me?"

"Combination of good police work and an assist from Clarissa Gethers."

Before Jane could ask him what he meant, he was seized with a racking cough. "Any chance you can call for some help? I have, after all, been shot in the chest."

Jane started to rise, but hesitated. "I . . ." she began haltingly. "I don't want to leave you."

"Then we have a problem," Kenny said, laying his head back. "Because, basically, I'm bleeding to death."

Breathing in sharply, Jane felt herself clutch with fear.

"Look," Kenny said when he had recovered his breath again. "Aren't I the one who's always here whenever you come crawling back?"

"Yeah," Jane said, her eyes creasing into a grateful smile. "Yeah, you are."

"Then go," Kenny urged. "I promise I won't go anywhere."

Taking off her jacket and folding it into a pillow, Jane rested Kenny's head on the floor of the wind deck. She started to rise, but stopped to kiss him softly on the lips. Then, standing shakily on her battered legs, she limped to the elevator.

"Don't you die," she cautioned as she turned David's key in the control panel.

"Never crossed my mind," Kenny called, raising his hand in a little wave as the elevator door slid shut.

82

———

Jane slumped in the corner as the elevator rattled its way downward. She tried to collect her thoughts, scattered before her like the aftermath of an explosion.

Kenny was alive, thank God, and now her entire being was focused on getting him off this bridge.

David was dead, and with him, she promised herself, a part of her had died too. That part of her that acted out of longing and loneliness. It was time for her to bury that needy little girl forever and move on.

The elevator ground to a stop at street level, and Jane stepped out into the world; out from the darkness of who she had been and into the cold fresh rush of the coming wind.

Turning to her right, she spotted the Port Authority officer signing a clipboard as a dented minivan was hoisted on the hook of a tow truck. Seeing that he had a walkie-talkie, Jane started running toward him.

She tore across the sidewalk and, without a word, snatched the walkie-talkie from his belt and pressed the talk button.

"This is Inspector Jane Candiotti, SFPD, 3H58," she called. "Officer down! I need an ambulance at the South Tower right away!"

Looking up to where Kenny was, high on the tower's summit, Jane closed her eyes and whispered into the wind, "Hang on, Kenny . . ."

Letting the walkie-talkie slip from her fingers and drop to the pavement, she raced back to the elevator.

The truck towing Finney's van pulled away from the curb, and as it did, the van's passenger door popped open. As the tow truck slipped into the next lane, the magazine with the picture of Clarissa Gethers on the cover fell out and landed on the roadway.

It fluttered in the wind created by the speeding vehicles until a cement truck ran over it, shredding the paper. The truck moved on as a steady stream of traffic ground the remnants of the magazine into the corrugated surface of the Golden Gate Bridge.

83

—▪—

J ane and Lieutenant Spielman stepped aside as an orderly wheeled
Kenny into the same hospital room he'd been in before. Jane was
about to step into the room when Kenny's surgeon approached, a
nun following close behind.

The doctor nodded to Lieutenant Spielman and turned to Jane. "He
was lucky, Inspector. The bullet was deflected by his sternum and shattered two of his ribs." He shook his head. "Combined with the ribs he
broke in his car accident, he's going to be pretty sore for a long time."

Jane blinked back tears of gratitude. "Any other damage?"

"His hands are pretty torn up from the bridge cables, but nothing
that won't heal." He glanced over to the nun. "Someone was watching
over your friend today." The nun smiled tightly and went into the
room.

As the doctor made his way down the corridor, Jane turned to Lieutenant Spielman. "Ben, I . . ."

"Jane, listen to me," he interrupted, putting his hand on her shoulder.
"Kenny's gonna be okay. You didn't get yourself killed, and we got the
bad guy." He smiled. "Maybe next time we'll handle it a little different, huh?"

Jane pulled him into a deep hug. "Thank you," she whispered into
his ear.

"You're the best I've got," he said as she released him. "Now go
take care of your partner."

As Lieutenant Spielman headed for the elevators, Jane stepped into
the doorway. The nun adjusted Kenny's bed and turned toward her.
"I tried to keep him here, y'know," she said. "But he needed to get
to you."

Jane started to respond, but Kenny stirred, and she hurried to his bedside. She had promised herself that when Kenny opened his eyes, she would be the first person he'd see.

Kenny's eyelids parted, then closed. Jane took his bandaged hand and leaned in. "Kenny," she said in a hush. "Kenny, it's me."

Turning his head to the sound of her voice, he opened his eyes, and his lips lifted in a weak smile. "Hey . . ." he rasped.

"Hey . . ." Jane said as she sat down.

Kenny looked around the room.

"Am I waking up from a car wreck," he asked, "or did that stuff on the bridge really happen?"

"The stuff on the bridge really happened," Jane said. "You saved my life."

"He still dead?"

"Yup."

Kenny looked down to see his hand in Jane's, then he looked at her. He started to say something else, but the pain in his chest held him back.

Jane reached behind him and adjusted his pillows. "How you doin'?"

"Thirsty," Kenny whispered. "Any chance a hero cop . . . can get a little water around here?"

Before Jane could move, the nun scurried across the room and gave her a cup of ice water. Jane smiled her thanks and brought the straw to Kenny's lips. He took a long sip and, exhausted, fell back. His gaze drifted to the window, and he lay quiet for a moment, the waning sunlight falling across his face. Then he looked to Jane. "I'm glad you're here," he said.

"Me too," Jane said as she bent over and kissed him on the cheek.

Kenny's lips relaxed and his eyelids fluttered closed as he fell back to sleep.

The nun stepped in and checked his heart monitor. "He's going to be asleep for quite a while, Miss," she said to Jane. "Maybe you should go home and get yourself some rest."

Jane reached over and brushed the hair off Kenny's forehead. "Thank you," she said, "but I want to stay with him."

"I understand," the nun replied and shuffled out of the room.

As the door clicked closed, Jane noticed the soft muted light of the coming sunset warming the window. She pushed back in her chair and rose. Still looking at Kenny, she crossed to the window and felt the twilight glow on her cheek.

She closed her eyes and stood there. Unwinding. Letting the tension drip from her body.

Then she opened her eyes and glanced outside. There, at the bottom of the hill, shimmering in the slanted light of day's end, was the Golden Gate Bridge.

Silently, she reached up and drew the curtains closed.